To Ri[...]

Great working with yo[u]

Enjoy!

V/R

R.L Galbraith

The Caretaker's Bible

The Caretaker's Bible

R. L. Galbraith

iUniverse, Inc.
New York Bloomington

The Caretaker's Bible

Copyright © 2007, 2008, 2009 Richard L. Galbraith

All rights reserved. No part of this book may be used or reproduced by any means, graphic, electronic, or mechanical, including photocopying, recording, taping or by any information storage retrieval system without the written permission of the publisher except in the case of brief quotations embodied in critical articles and reviews.

This is a work of fiction. All of the characters, names, incidents, organizations, and dialogue in this novel are either the products of the author's imagination or are used fictitiously.

It must be noted that 80 St. Martin Strasse, and 501 Marlybone Drive, are not in any way associated with Adolf Hitler or the Third Reich; they merely enhance the story line. Other than historically recognizable names, all other characters are the product of the author?s imagination.

iUniverse books may be ordered through booksellers or by contacting:

iUniverse
1663 Liberty Drive
Bloomington, IN 47403
www.iuniverse.com
1-800-Authors (1-800-288-4677)

Because of the dynamic nature of the Internet, any Web addresses or links contained in this book may have changed since publication and may no longer be valid. The views expressed in this work are solely those of the author and do not necessarily reflect the views of the publisher, and the publisher hereby disclaims any responsibility for them.

ISBN: 978-0-595-45923-0 (pbk)
ISBN: 978-0-595-70028-8 (cloth)
ISBN: 978-0-595-90223-1 (ebk)

Printed in the United States of America

iUniverse rev. date: 3/30/2009

Dedicated to Lynne, my wonderful wife,
who endured endless hours alone while I wrote this book.

Many thanks to my editors, Kurt Florman, Proof-It Professional Proofreading Services, and Daria Bessom, for their invaluable insight and professional editing. Also, many thanks to Stephanie Pieper who designed my cover. It's truly awesome.

Captive souls are still the masters of their own thoughts.
— *Heinrich Glossen*

Suffering by nature or chance never seems so painful as suffering inflicted on us by the arbitrary will of another.
— *Arthur Schopenhauer*

The more unintelligent a man is, the less mysterious existence seems to him.
— *Arthur Schopenhauer*

If you are compelled to know the truth ... then let nothing stand in your way.
— *Brian Allen Bennett*

chapter 1

Hagenmünster Monastery, Austria—1939

THE BITTER COLD WEATHER was accompanied by freezing rain, making the narrow roads difficult to travel. Heinrich Glossen sat in the rear of the second car of a small motorcade that slowly made its way to the entrance of a large monastery.

Recoiling in his seat, Glossen fidgeted out of anticipation. His mouth was dry and he asked to sit in the car for a few minutes longer when they arrived. He had waited for this moment for far too long.

When the pretentious delegation finally entered the front of the abbey, a representative of the Abbot greeted them. They were immediately escorted by the older monk to a reception room and asked to take a seat. Not used to being told what to do by anyone other than a Nazi, Glossen held his temper—trying to smile.

The meeting with the Abbot would be simple. Glossen had asked to have an audience by himself and had decided not to wear his uniform, which he thought would be less threatening. Handing a picture to the Abbot, he demanded to see the individual who had so meekly posed for it.

"You want to speak to Brother Matthias," the Abbot said. "May I ask why?"

"It is by decree of the Führer that we talk to this person. I must remind you we have come a long way."

"Yes. Of course." The Abbot instructed one of his papal secretaries to find Brother Matthias and take him to one of their prayer rooms.

Within several minutes, Glossen was taken to the room and the door was shut behind him. A monk dressed in a black robe was standing by the window. His hair was cropped short around the sides. When he turned toward Glossen, the Nazi's breath was practically taken away. The likeness between Brother Matthias and Adolf Hitler was incredible. The only thing missing was the signature mustache. "So you are Brother Matthias?"

"Yes. May I help you?" The smile was congenial and sincere.

"I am here at the behest of the Führer. I only want to talk to you."

Brother Matthias' smile disappeared. "We do not recognize such people. We are not affiliated with Nazis."

"Of course. I understand. But I am not here to hurt you. I only have questions I need answered."

"I have nothing to say." Brother Matthias started to walk toward the door when there was a knock. One of Glossen's associates handed him some papers, saying they had just found them and that they appeared important. Glossen read over them quickly. He asked Brother Matthias to sit down.

"Where were you born?" Glossen asked. "Are you Austrian?"

"Yes, I was born here in the area."

Glossen glanced at a birth certificate. "Were you born on April 20th, 1889?"

"Yes. I grew up in and around Linz."

"Who were your parents?" Glossen read over the note from a Brother Dimitrius.

Brother Matthias paused for a second. "My parents were farmers and lived a fair distance north of the monastery. They were good and decent people who raised me to be subservient to God."

"Are they still alive?" Glossen asked nonchalantly.

"Only my mother. Why?"

"I would like to talk to her."

Brother Matthias' eyes squinted a bit and his jaws tightened. "I will not let you do that. She is old and frail."

"When did you decide you wanted to become a monk?"

"When I was very young. I was drawn to it because I attended school at the monastery. When I was old enough, I took the required classes to be a monk and then I dedicated my life to serving God."

"Do you still believe you are acting in the interest of your God's will?"

Brother Matthias expected such a question from a Nazi and knew any answer he gave would not make sense to someone subservient to Adolf Hitler. "I am as faithful to my God as you are to your so-called Führer."

This comment stuck like a dagger into Glossen's heart. "There is no God above our leader. None. You and your righteous clergy—how dare you criticize us! We and we alone will cleanse the Germans and the others we rule from their sins."

"How can you deny God?" Brother Matthias defiantly asked.

"For a Nazi, it is not debatable. God does not exist. But the Führer does!"

"May I leave? I have nothing else to discuss."

Glossen reached into his coat pocket, brought out a small photo and handed it to the reluctant monk. "I think this might look familiar to you."

Staring at it, Brother Matthias didn't say a word.

"I imagine it is like looking into a mirror," Glossen said.

Brother Matthias raised his eyes to Glossen for a second, and then looked back at the picture. The silence was eerie. Glossen waited patiently for the monk to say something.

"Where did you get this?"

"I have had it for a long time. It is a picture of our Führer. But why is it that it looks exactly like you?"

Brother Matthias was at a loss to say anything. He knew it was a spitting image of him. He couldn't explain it—couldn't reconcile it to himself.

"Come, Brother Matthias. Surely you can see the resemblance." Glossen smiled as he waited for a response. He didn't get one. "Why is it that you look so much alike?" Glossen read the note from Brother Dimitrius. "What can you tell me about a baby left on the very doorstep of this monastery on the same day you were born? Please, I want to know everything."

"I do not know what you are talking about," Brother Matthias replied.

"Yes. Of course you do. I think you were that baby. Left to die, but spared by the loving arms of a monk."

"Why would you think that?"

Glossen studied his subject. "I think you are Adolf Hitler's twin brother. No one knows it and no one can prove it, but I believe it is true."

Brother Matthias' face dropped. "It is not possible."

"I understand why you would deny it. But you must face the facts."

"It cannot be possible." The monk started to tremble at the idea that he could be related to Adolf Hitler.

"It is not only possible," Glossen suggested, "it is the truth. I am convinced that you were the baby left on the doorstep. And more than that, I think it is extraordinary fate that led me here to find the twin brother of the Führer."

The monk stood up and went over to the window. He looked at the picture, and then gazed at the image of his face in the glass. It was not believable to him. How could it be? He was a man of God, and Hitler was a feared dictator.

Glossen went over and patted him on the shoulder. "You must resign yourself to it. I admit it has to be difficult for you to understand, but it cannot be denied."

Brother Matthias turned around abruptly. "What do you want from me?"

"Come sit. We want what is best for you. It is only fitting that you have the opportunity to meet your natural flesh and blood."

"I have no desire to leave Hagenmünster."

"Of course not. But the Third Reich awaits you. More importantly, your brother awaits you."

"I will not leave here. This is my home. I have lived here my entire life."

Glossen knocked on the door and two Nazi foot soldiers came in. He asked them to watch over Brother Matthias until he returned.

Moments later, Glossen was standing in the Abbot's office. "No one must know where we are taking him. Is that understood?"

"But he belongs here," the Abbot replied. "He is doing God's will."

"I warn you. If you ever divulge where we have taken him, you will feel the wrath of the Third Reich. We will destroy you and this entire monastery. Perhaps it is best you forget he was ever here. I trust you will comply with my wishes."

The Abbot was speechless. He knew he had no choice but to let Brother Matthias go, and could take no action other than to ask God to watch over the monk.

In the early evening when the dusk began to turn to darkness, they left. The motorcade departed much as it had arrived—except with the addition of a reluctant soul: a monk confused about who he had been, who he was, and who he was about to become.

chapter 2
Berlin—1939

HEINRICH GLOSSEN STOPPED DEAD in his tracks before entering the sanctuary of his office. It was two o'clock in the morning. He looked around, making sure no one was watching. He had purposely left the frightened monk in his car with several security guards because he knew he couldn't afford to make a mistake and show his hand before he was ready. Tired from a long day, he sat down for a moment before he called the guards to bring in Brother Matthias.

Glossen reveled in the fact that he actually pulled it off—finding and bringing the monk to the Reich Chancellery. He had had no idea—even though he had studied the photo—how much Brother Matthias really looked like Adolf Hitler. It was incredible. Now Glossen believed he was in a position to change the dynamics of the Third Reich.

Two guards brought the monk into the office. Brother Matthias reluctantly sat down while the guards departed the room and said they would be waiting outside. Glossen stared at the monk like he was some sort of deity. Brother Matthias looked down at the floor. He had barely said two words since he left the monastery.

"Are you comfortable?" Glossen asked.

"I have no reason to be here."

Glossen winced. "You will understand in due time."

"I cannot believe what you have done."

Glossen smiled even though he was angered by the monk's careless remarks. "It is important for you to listen to what I have to say. You have a destiny that must be fulfilled. That is why I brought you here to Berlin."

"My place is with my fellow monks at Hagenmünster. I demand you take me back."

There was a knock at the door. A young man, perhaps Brother Matthias' age, came in and sat down.

"I want to introduce your bodyguard. He will be with you at all times."

"My name is Peter Duckert. It is good to meet you." The guard, a lieutenant in the *Schutzstaffel,* the SS, explained that he had been chosen above all of his peers to protect the monk. He was a dedicated security guard that had pledged his life's support to the Third Reich.

"Peter has your best interests at heart," Glossen said. "He will take care of you."

Brother Matthias showed a sign of a smile. "I cannot believe for one moment that you think I am somehow related to your Führer."

"We believe it, or you would not be here in my office. I have wanted to bring you here for some time. I can assure you that I have taken the proper precautions to keep your identity a secret until we can arrange a meeting with the Führer."

"I cannot imagine that he would want to meet a monk regardless of what you tell him about me."

"You must allow us to make that determination," Glossen replied. "We have already taken much into consideration. When the time is right, you will meet him."

Peter patted the monk on the back. "You should not agonize over it. I am sure the meeting will go fine."

Glossen looked at his watch, then said to the guard, "We must take him to the hotel."

They traveled without fanfare along the streets in a small staff car. Arriving at the hotel, they ushered the monk in a side door while two security guards stood watch. They had placed a blanket over Brother Matthias' head so no one could possibly see his face. Once inside the suite they had set aside for the monk, they removed the blanket and told him to think of the hotel as a home away from home.

Glossen showed Brother Matthias around the suite. He explained that he would not be allowed to leave unless under maximum escort and in disguise. The truth was that he would not be allowed to leave until he had met with the Führer.

"The security guards are here to protect you," Peter said.

Brother Matthias sat down on the couch. "Protect me from what?"

Peter sat down next to the monk. "Surely you can see that because of your likeness to the Führer, you could be taken advantage of by people who do not have your well-being in mind."

Glossen stood over the monk like an eagle looking for prey. "Pay attention! This is important."

"Please take me back to the monastery. That is all I ask."

"It is not that simple," Glossen replied. "You are not going anywhere. This is where you belong." Frustrated, Glossen decided to leave. Peter and several of his men stayed behind.

*   *   *

Several days later, in the early frost-laden morning, the Propaganda Minister, Joseph Goebbels, and a former SS soldier, Manfred Wormser, briefly visited Glossen. He had already reported his success with Brother Matthias to Goebbels, and they had agreed that no one else in the hierarchy should know about the monk for the time being. Goebbels was now concerned over recent events

The Caretaker's Bible

that could have been damaging to the Führer, especially now that they had invaded Poland.

"There appears to be dissention in our ranks," Goebbels said.

"Certainly, none of us," Glossen replied.

"No. I mean the army. They are not to be trusted."

"Why is that?" Glossen asked.

Goebbels replied quickly. "It is no surprise that a number of general officers are at odds with the Führer. It could prove to be difficult."

Wormser, who had sat silently, decided to speak. "Our Führer wants to attack the West, so he must have the full attention and dedication of our military services. It will not be easy."

Glossen replied, "I wager to say that there are many besides the army who are against such a hasty endeavor."

"Perhaps," Wormser said. "But Hitler knows what he wants to do and that is the end of it."

Glossen looked over at Goebbels. "How should we proceed?"

The Propaganda Minister sat in thought for a moment or so. "We must ask for an audience with the Führer and convince him that we are ready to do what it takes to meet his goals."

"I am at your disposal," Glossen replied.

Immediately leaving the meeting, Glossen went to the hotel to see Brother Matthias. Peter met him at the door.

"How is our monk?"

"He is depressed," Peter replied. "Naturally. You can understand that."

"Of course, but he will change his mood when he realizes he is the twin brother of the Führer."

"Are you sure?"

"Yes, I am positive." Glossen asked to speak to Brother Matthias, who was now confining himself to his bedroom.

Peter brought him out and told him to sit down on the couch. "Herr Glossen would like to talk to you."

"What have I done?"

"He merely wants to see how you are doing."

Glossen walked into the room. "So, Brother Matthias, have you come to your senses?"

"About what?"

"Come now. You know what I am talking about. Have you now resigned yourself to the fact that you are the Führer's brother?"

"Of course not. How dare you insult me!"

Glossen's face became hot with rage; he looked like he would explode. "Never use that tone of voice with me! You will do as I say and that can never be negotiable." He walked over to the wall behind the couch and pounded his fist against it.

Peter leaned over and put his arm around Brother Matthias. "This can be easy or it can be excruciatingly painful. You must realize that you will never leave here. It is forbidden. You must accept your fate."

"But I know in my heart that it is not true."

"It is not up to you to judge," Glossen replied. "We know the truth and that is all that matters."

"All I have ever wanted to be is a priest. That is what I believe God wants me to become."

Glossen started to smile, then took it back. "I understand what you think your destiny is, but your life is now part of a much larger scheme, I can assure you."

"What can that possibly be?"

"You will know very soon now." Glossen grinned and shook his head.

"It will be all right," Peter told the monk as he briefly smiled.

*   *   *

A week later, Goebbels, Glossen, and Wormser sat in a large waiting room preparing to talk to the Führer. They all appeared nervous, even though Goebbels talked to Hitler almost every day. Goebbels had requested the audience and Hitler had agreed without much hesitation, seemingly amenable to such a meeting.

Once inside the elaborate office, they were asked to sit down in three small chairs strategically positioned in front of the Führer's desk.

Hitler stood by the side of his desk for a moment before he sat down. "What have you come to tell me? I simply want to know why the three of you had to see me on such short notice."

Goebbels replied, "Yes, mein Führer. I offer support in your quest to attack the Western powers. It is only a matter of time before we can declare victory, but we must consider certain consequences."

"And what would those be?" Hitler began to fidget somewhat.

"The Russians seem neutral now, but I believe they could become a great enemy in the future after all else is won."

"I understand that premise. Perhaps we will wage war in the future. But you must let me worry about Stalin. I must be truthful; I think for now we remain allies."

Goebbels glanced over at Glossen and Wormser and replied, "Of course, mein Führer. We should perhaps craft a story we can tell the German people."

"What do you have in mind?"

"It might be in our best interest to create a mandate. This would simply be that the threat of further war is placed on the shoulders of the West; that they would have to respect both Germany and Russia in the event of a larger conflict."

"What does this have to do with our goals?" Hitler yelled out.

"You simply can feel free to attack the West without fear that we will be attacked on our eastern borders because of our supposed respect for the Soviets."

"But will it work?" Hitler asked.

"I have every reason to believe it will," Goebbels said. "I am in charge of propaganda and know what I am doing."

"I suppose so," Hitler said, but he seemed a bit agitated.

"We must do what it takes to win the war," Glossen said.

Goebbels continued. "Yes, mein Führer. I believe we must be prepared to ensure victory to the German people."

Hitler sat and stared at him.

Glossen listened intently as he sat no more than ten feet away from Hitler. He knew he had to be in lock step with Goebbels, but his heart and mind were predisposed. *Perhaps I should just tell the Führer about Brother Matthias,* he thought. *I have a well thought-out plan; at least one that is believable and for the betterment of the Reich. But will Hitler listen? What will Goebbels say?*

He knew the real truth was that he needed more time, so he kept perhaps the greatest revelation of the twentieth century to himself.

chapter 3
Radda in Chianti, Italy—1972

VILLA PONTEVECHIO WAS NESTLED in a towering expanse of poplar and pine trees. The off-white stucco house had been constructed on a hill overlooking the small town of Radda in Chianti, approximately forty-five kilometers south of Florence, Italy. Brian Allen Bennett, an investigative reporter for *Time* magazine, slowly drove white-knuckled up a narrow gravel road in an old, beat-up car he had borrowed from a friend in Milan.

The uniqueness of colonial Tuscany was flourishing once again. The coffee houses and taverns in Florence and the surrounding areas that had once been frequented by Fascist propagandists and anti-government liberals during World War II were now filled with young poet laureates, avant-garde artists, and free spirits that believed in peace, free love, and anything other than war. The peaceful province had now become a haven for American professionals that wanted to get away from the monotony of the workweek.

Vacations didn't come easy for Brian. This was the first one he had taken in five years. It seemed that getting far away from New York and the hustle and bustle of twelve-hour workdays had long eluded him. His only regret was that his fiancée, Laura Prescott, couldn't come along. She was too busy being an associate editor for a publishing house. But he decided to make the best of it without her.

The narrow climb up the worn-out concrete steps to the front door was steep. Brian stopped short of going in, and walked around the villa instead. The grounds were immense—several large flower gardens and a marble fountain were in the back. The view from the side by the swimming pool was magnificent: rooftops, steeples, and beautiful vineyards as far as the eye could see.

He really wasn't sure how he had ended up planning to stay at the villa. A friend had rented it from a friend of a friend. The owner apparently lived somewhere else and a real estate firm based out of Siena managed the property. None of it really mattered, though. He was poised to enjoy the tranquility of his two-week retreat.

Once inside, he took his luggage to the master bedroom and nonchalantly threw both bags on the bed. Looking around, he realized how sparsely it was decorated—only a bed and one chest of drawers. He saw heavy dark oak shutters—no screens, no windows. He was glad he had brought repellent. He knew early June really wasn't that bad for flies and mosquitoes, but he also knew it only took one to drive a person crazy.

He made the normal inspection of the rooms: a large living area, a small kitchen, a smaller den, and a bathroom that had a toilet that you flushed by pulling a rope that hung over it. Then he noticed what he thought was a room at the far end of the villa. Slowly opening the door, he saw that it was cluttered, with clothes thrown on the bed—as if it was being lived in. Brian thought that perhaps they belonged to someone who was managing the estate. He shut the door and began to unpack.

Late in the day Brian watched the sun go in and out of the clouds as he lay in a hammock near the pool, methodically sketching out his schedule for day trips to San Gimignano, Pisa, Lucca, Montevarchi, Mont Savino, Florence, and Siena. Brian remembered his love of Italy had begun when he was in college. A good friend of the family had invited him to spend a summer in Verona to help him run his export business. The establishment was located on a side street just around the corner from the Roman Amphitheater, or Arena, as it was called. He must have seen at least five operas while he was there, never being overly impressed, but never letting on.

Brian had learned just enough Italian to be dangerous. He had met a girl that summer—a beautiful blond with shoulder-length hair, hazel eyes, and coconut-colored skin. Shamelessly, he spent the entire time from June to August trying to make love to her. Finally, on a hot night on the banks of the Adige River, he made his conquest. The next week, he went home—never to see her again.

Slowly turning around, he sensed something. It was like the villa had eyes. Feeling strange, Brian sank down in the hammock a bit—suspecting he was being watched. It was the feeling he sometimes had when being stared at in a room filled with people.

A large white cloud began to block the sun and shadows enveloped the lawn and gardens. He could hear the sounds of cars below, but they were faint. This was the quiet he was after. It would give him plenty of time to read the six or so novels he had brought along.

Suddenly, he thought he heard the back door of the villa shut. Almost out of nowhere, emerging from the shadows came a figure. Adjusting his eyes, Brian could see that it was an old man wearing dungarees and a faded orange plaid shirt. The man's hair was rather short and very gray. He had a full beard that was more black than gray. His skin was tough looking, like old leather, and very tan. He stopped and looked at Brian. His gaze seemed peculiar at first.

Getting out of the hammock, Brian went over to shake hands with the stranger. Still looking like he was just out of college but now 35—skinny, long black hair parted in the middle—he gave the old man his usual pretentious smile. "Brian Bennett. Nice to meet you."

The stranger hesitated. Finally, in broken English, he introduced himself as Horst the caretaker. "I am responsible for the well-being of the property and villa. Every summer I come here and help the owner while he is away."

"You're German," Brian said.

"Yes. From Munich," Horst replied. "I very much love the Italian summers and feel comfortable in Tuscany. I do not spend much time in Munich anymore, but rather split my time between Germany and northern Italy."

Brian asked him to have a seat by the pool so they could talk. His first impression was that Horst was a fascinating fellow with many years of stories to tell. He hated himself for even thinking of it. After all, he was on vacation. But the eternally inquisitive reporter in him surfaced, wanting to know everything about the old caretaker. "You said you know the owner. Does he live around here?"

"No. In Germany."

"Is he German?"

"Yes."

It was obvious to Brian that the old man was prone to giving short answers. "What is his name?"

Horst didn't answer but began his own interview. "Why have you come to Tuscany and how did you hear that the Villa Pontevechio was for rent? We do not get many patrons, even though the villa is probably the nicest one in the entire town of Radda in Chianti."

Brian explained rather quickly, then asked, "Have you always been a caretaker?"

"No. Only for twenty years. Maybe."

"What did you do before that?"

The caretaker laughed. "It is not so important. At some point I will tell you. You must excuse me. I have to go away for a few days but will return."

By the time Brian had collected his belongings and gone back into the villa, Horst had already departed. Tired, he wanted to go to bed early, so he got dressed and went to dinner.

The next morning, Brian stood in front of a very large bookcase he hadn't noticed the day before. It was amazing; there must have been several hundred books. Slowly, he began taking them out one by one to review—something he had liked to do ever since he was a kid. Many were in German, some in Italian, and a few in English. He keyed in on what appeared to be a German history book. The pictures clearly depicted World War II—many bloody battles fought by the German Army. There were numerous photos of the Führer and members of his staff as well as the Gestapo. Not being able to read the narrative, Brian concentrated on looking at the pictures.

Wanting to take a dip in the pool, he decided to come back later and continue where he left off. But he noticed a mid-sized book at the end of the bottom row of the bookcase. It was an old German Bible and it was in fairly good shape. The words *Heilig Bibel* were embossed in a slightly faded gold color on the spine. The typeset was very small and there were no pictures. If nothing else, Brian figured the Bible could be worth a little money. Putting it back, he went for a swim.

The next couple of days he spent being a tourist. He traveled to Pisa and Lucca and spent a wonderful afternoon in Siena—most of the time at an outside café drinking vintage Chianti. Unfortunately, he couldn't stop thinking about his next assignment—writing an editorial piece on the impact of folk music on American society, interviewing such artists as Bob Dylan, Joan Baez, Arlo Guthrie, and Dave Van Ronk. Not usually something an investigative reporter did, he was filling in for a music reporter who had taken a leave of absence. He was looking forward to it and figured by the time he got back from Italy, he would be ready to get to work.

*   *   *

It was a hot and dry Saturday morning. Brian was lying by the pool reading a book when the caretaker and sat down and asked how he was doing.

"Fine. It's good to see you again." He heard classical music playing faintly in the background.

"I trust my being away didn't inconvenience you."

"No. None whatsoever."

"I plan to water the flowerbeds and treat the pool, if you do not mind. I am a little bit behind in my work and have to make up for my time away."

"Where did you go?"

The caretaker just smiled. "What line of work are you in?"

"I'm a reporter."

"Wonderful. I am convinced that anything written down will eventually reveal important facts to those who read the historical accounts years later. When I was young and living in Germany, I wanted to be an artist—a painter—but it never really happened. At least I could not support myself doing just that. I spent a lot of time doing odd jobs, and eventually went into the military."

"World War I?" Brian asked.

"When I was a young lad in 1915, I was a corporal in the army assigned to the List Regiment and working at regimental headquarters in Flanders. I spent most of my time there during the war and did not see much action, except a bombshell exploding, which injured me enough to put me in the hospital for a fairly lengthy stay. I have always considered myself lucky since most of my comrades were killed by the blast."

"I can only try and imagine what World War I was like," Brian remarked.

"It was horrid. I was blessed to get through it all right. The nights I spent running through trenches delivering messages were terrifying. Even though I was young at the time, the stress of fighting took its toll on me. When I finally was relieved of duty, I vowed never to fight in another war."

"What did you do when you got out?"

"Nothing much at first. I was so shell-shocked from the fighting that I went back to Munich and took on small jobs until I could get back on my feet."

"Did you get involved in the next war?" Brian was rather excited that the old caretaker was more willing now to talk about who he was and about his past.

Horst was rather hesitant to answer at first. He mumbled a few words, and then said he wasn't sure he wanted to discuss it. Brian said he understood and asked if he wouldn't mind a late breakfast by the pool.

During the course of the wine, bread, and cheese brunch, Horst began to talk about World War II. "It was a war that Germany should have won, but I believe the Allied offenses were just too overwhelming. There were mistakes made; perhaps Sicily, or even the occupation of Italy itself, and maybe even the push into Russia. But I know the leadership of the Third Reich believed in what it was doing."

"You mean Hitler!"

Horst nodded. "The Führer and his noble ideas meant everything to the German people. They wanted the same thing he did: a purified and blue-blooded nation that was respected by the rest of the world. I can remember the speeches, the enthusiasm, and the excitement that were embodied in the Führer. They knew no bounds."

"Did you fight in the war?"

"There were terrible battles right here in Italy—in Tuscany. The Germans endured as the Gothic, Arno, and Albert lines swept across Italy from Genoa to the Adriatic. The Germans were proud of their infantry divisions. Many had engineering battalions made up of very skilled warriors that were adept at laying minefields, constructing booby traps, and breaching fortifications. Our Panzer and Waffen-SS divisions were revered. But, regrettably, the fighting had been fierce. Conditions were often worse than miserable with the fog, constant rain, and muddy fields."

"It must have been intolerable," Brian surmised.

Horst began to laugh, but stopped abruptly. "Allow me to tell you a story of the Allied bombing of a Benedictine Monastery at Mount Cassino near Naples in 1944. It presented a dilemma for the Allied Forces. It was in their way; they decided to bomb it. They apparently dropped leaflets telling the monks and refugees to vacate, but not everyone got the word. The old Abbot and many of the monks went to the cellars and were spared. Other monks were killed during the attack. The bombing was an act of barbarism;

the monastery was a place of worship and was considered sacred ground."

"There's a saying in the States," Brian said. "'War is hell!'"

Horst stared at Brian for a few seconds. "Yes, I suppose that is true. In Germany, we have a saying also: 'Only a storm of glowing passion can turn the destinies of nations, but this passion can only be aroused by a man who carries it within himself.'" Brian had a puzzled look on his face, so Horst explained. "What I really mean to say is that men must make sacrifices in war because of strong convictions shown by the example of others. Even if it is hell."

This reminded Brian of a story he had heard about German soldiers blindly walking into an ambush because they were following their leader, who had apparently lost his sense of direction. The result was total annihilation of the small battalion. When he told the caretaker, Horst appeared insulted by the comment. "Germany certainly does not send soldiers out blindly to fight a battle with incompetent leaders. Men must believe in what they are doing. The nation comes first."

Brian excused himself to go in and get the history book he had found. He wanted to ask some questions about some of the pictures he had seen. As Horst freely and completely answered his questions Brian began to realize how well informed the caretaker was—about not only the military but also about the Third Reich—putting everything Brian wanted to know in perspective.

The conversation continued for some time, but the sun began beating down—stinging the skin. Both men decided they would curtail their discussion until some later time. Horst went to attend to his duties and Brian went into the villa to take a nap.

*   *   *

On Wednesday of the next week, Brian was feeling that his vacation was coming to a close. He had spent two wonderful days in Florence—a city he believed was the most beautiful in the world. Now all that was left was to go to several of the smaller towns in and around the villa. He swam laps to get his exercise for the day.

The Caretaker's Bible

When he was done, he saw Horst sitting by the pool, smiling at him. Wiping himself off, Brian threw the towel on the chair and sat down.

"You look refreshed," Horst said.

"That's why I came to such a beautiful place. I had a good time in Florence. I managed to buy a leather jacket for myself and a leather purse for my fiancée, and eat at a few outdoor cafés. Just walking along the Arno River is peaceful in and of itself. I had a wonderful time at the Duomo as well. I think it's a religious experience just visiting Florence."

"I remember a time when Florence was not so nice. But it was wartime then, and the Germans had to destroy that which could be used against them. The High Command had decided not to stay and defend the city. They had made a conscious decision not to bomb the Ponte Vecchio Bridge, but they destroyed the houses that lined both sides of the Arno. I have always felt bad that much of medieval Florence was damaged beyond repair."

"If you don't mind me asking," Brian said, "what is the difference between the Allies bombing the monastery and the Germans destroying thousands of years of art and historical artifacts?"

The caretaker paused. "War never follows any prescribed formula. Often military commanders or government leaders act on gut reactions based on defensive or offensive postures. It is like a soccer game. The objective is to move forward and score a victory. How one does that depends on the type of resistance one encounters; it is just that simple. But sometimes it is not worth the effort."

"You sound like you regret the war," Brian suggested.

"I believe in what Germany was trying to achieve, but saddened at the number of Germans who died trying to legitimize the Führer's vision." He then paused for a second before continuing. "I do not regret our attempt at immortality."

This left Brian with the impression that if they had won it might not have mattered how many Germans died. Knowing he had hit a nerve, Brian wanted to further explore the caretaker's feelings. "Do you believe the Nazi cause was justified?"

"Of course. Would you expect me to say anything else? Being a Nazi was no different than being an American Democrat or Republican. It was a party with principles and a vision for the future. In my opinion, the Nazi Third Reich and the Führer have been completely misunderstood by the rest of the world. Hitler was not an evil man hell bent on destroying people's lives. He knew full well what he was doing."

"You believe he was steadfast in his beliefs."

"I am convinced that the Führer had a brilliant mind, and that not many people appreciated it. He had a remarkable memory—could recall mundane facts about military history and equipment like tanks and naval ships. He even had a wonderful appreciation of German philosophy. Hitler was not a madman as everyone said."

Brian had never talked to a German citizen about Hitler before, especially one who had been through the war. It was fascinating. "The Americans don't have the same fondness for your Führer as you do."

He laughed. "I am not surprised. Germany was America's enemy during the war and I know the American sentiments for the Führer are not favorable. Most Americans do not know that the Führer was actually a caring individual—loved children, respected the men who were loyal to him, and at banquets or military functions would usually not eat until all of his men had been fed."

This began to anger Brian because he had always believed Hitler was a psychotic tyrant who only thought of himself and didn't give a damn about the German people, especially the Jews. "I know this is a terrible question, but if he was so caring, why did the Holocaust happen?"

The caretaker didn't hesitate. "Another misunderstanding. The Führer wanted an Aryan race, but he never wanted to exterminate all of the Jews. He thought they had their place in German society, but the High Command misinterpreted his straightforward convictions and began murdering Jews. It got out of hand, and as hard as this is to comprehend, the Führer was powerless to stop it."

Brian knew that wasn't the truth and began to think that perhaps he had stepped over the line. He didn't want his anger to show and alienate the caretaker, so he changed the subject. "You said you fought in Italy. What was it like at the end of the war?"

"The Allies were pushing toward Vienna. Once they passed the Po River Valley, they fanned north through Verona, Venice, Milan, Trento, and Bolzano. Italy was completely taken over. Many Germans died at the end. It was terrible."

Brian could tell from the caretaker's tone and raspy voice that he was very bitter about the defeat. "What did you do after the war?"

"I went to live in southern Germany. I tried to forget about the horrors and devastation the German military suffered. Unfortunately, I never could completely get it out of my mind. The nightmares never seemed to stop."

"Do you have a family?" Brian asked.

"No. I was never married." He seemed melancholy when he answered. "I always wanted children, but I am convinced it was not to be. You're a young enough lad. Are you married?"

"No. Engaged though. We plan to get married next summer."

"Congratulations are in order. We should have a drink." Horst disappeared for a few minutes. When he came back he had a bottle of wine and two green crystal glasses. "To your future!"

Brian savored the moment. He had actually grown to like Horst very much, even though he had known him for less than two weeks and even in spite of his support of the Third Reich. There was something about him. Brian couldn't put his finger on it, but he was just glad he had been granted the opportunity to meet him.

When the caretaker took a short nap sitting in his chair, Brian went in to take a shower and shave. On his way out, the Bible caught his eye and he took it outside with him.

"I see you have been looking through the library," Horst said.

"This Bible's in pretty good shape considering it appears to be a hundred years old." Brian was looking at the Roman numerals.

"It is very old, yes."

"Does it belong to you?"

"It belongs to the owner, as do all the books in the study."

Brian was interested in how the religion of the German people contrasted with the principles of the Third Reich. His belief was that religion probably had no place in Nazi Germany. "What would happen if a Nazi found a German citizen with a Bible?"

The caretaker looked at him like he was insane. "Nothing. A good German Christian would never have been placed in that position. Their Bibles would be neatly tucked away—out of sight of any Nazi."

Brian skimmed quickly through the Bible, seeing faded pen entries every so often. "It must have been difficult to be a Christian under Hitler's reign."

"As long as they did not flaunt their religious beliefs, it was not a problem. The Führer himself had been born Catholic and never officially left the church, despite his outward views. Make no mistake; the Führer believed in a Nationalist State—one that he expected the German people to revere. That was his church."

"And did you believe that?"

The caretaker held the Bible in his hands and stared at it. "When I was a young boy, I was taught to be a good Catholic. As I grew older, I began to question the tenets and the very meaning of the church. It was far more logical to place one's faith in the State because it was tangible. Still, there were many lessons to be learned by reading the Bible."

"So you're a Christian," Brian said.

"No. Not in the traditional sense. I cannot really explain it because it is very complicated. Perhaps over the years, I have changed my mind. The war and the influence of the Third Reich are things of the past. I have had many years to reflect."

Brian stared at the caretaker and could see the pain and anguish in his worn and crinkled face. It was obvious that Horst had been through hell in his life and now wanted only to forget all about it and go on. "I see why you chose to be a caretaker. It is a simple and rewarding life."

"It allows me to enjoy what the heavens have given us." Horst smiled. Brian was pleased to hear the caretaker acknowledge a being higher than the Führer. It was at least encouraging.

Horst handed the Bible back to Brian. "Would you like to have it?"

"I'd love to take it, but I thought you said it belonged to the owner."

The caretaker sat back in his chair and thought for a moment. "I do not think he has much use for it. Besides, he gave it to me a while ago. You take it. I know you admire it. It is a wonderful historical document."

Brian didn't know what to say, but when Horst insisted, he agreed to take it, realizing he actually had a few other rare books and this would be a welcome addition to his collection.

The afternoon seemed to blend into the early evening. Brian was tired and he knew he had to get up early the next morning to go to Siena one last time. He asked if Horst would like to go to dinner, but he declined, saying only he had other things to do.

Brian departed in the early hours of the next morning and made the forty-five minute trip into Siena. There he spent a lazy day wandering from piazza to piazza—sitting at an outdoor café at every one. Before he went back to the villa, he rested his feet by dangling them in Siena's underground river, located in a beautiful spot under a large brick façade—something he had done in years past. When he finally got back to the villa, he went to ask Horst if he could take the German history book home with him as well. But the room was empty. All of the caretaker's belongings were gone. Perplexed, Brian stood in the middle of the room looking at the bare furniture. He couldn't believe that Horst would just leave without saying goodbye.

The following day he packed and prepared for his trip back to Milan. He still couldn't get over meeting Horst. He was probably one of the most interesting people Brian had ever met. Standing out by the pool, he glanced one final time at the surrounding area. He knew he would be home in New York City in just two day's time. Slowly turning around, he looked for the caretaker again—thinking he would show up as mysteriously as he had the first time. But the shadows never moved.

chapteR 4
New York City—1972

THE SMELL OF GASOLINE fumes and the sound of dozens of horns blaring simultaneously seemed all too familiar to Brian as he sat stuck in traffic heading to work on a Monday morning. Being away for two weeks hadn't changed his perspective—the daily routine still got on his nerves.

He had left his East 42nd Street apartment no more than five minutes earlier in his '69 Corvette Stingray. Nothing would ever change, he figured—trucks blocking lanes, cabs cutting in front of cars. His goal every morning was to get to his office at 1000 Avenue of the Americas where *Time* magazine was published, and on any day of the week it seemed to take forever.

When he finally walked into his office, he remembered how hastily he had left, not bothering to clean up. Papers and old magazines were stacked up on his desk and the bookcase. Both of his typewriters still had unfinished copy in them. He felt absolutely unorganized and went to get a cup of coffee.

An avid reader, Brian had picked up two newspapers at the reception desk on the way in. Looking at the *Washington Post*, he saw an article that immediately caught his eye. Five men, including a former CIA agent, had been arrested on 17 June in what authorities had described as an intricate plot to bug the offices of the Democratic National Committee in the Watergate Hotel.

According to a spokesman, nothing of a sensitive nature was housed there, only financial records and associated files. Two ceiling panels of the adjacent room of the secretary of the Democratic Party had been removed, and it appeared possible to slide a bugging device through the panels of the ceiling of the chairman's office. There was no immediate indication of why the suspects would want to break into and bug the office, and it wasn't established whether they were working for another individual or organization.

Brian laughed when he read that the suspects had actually rented rooms at the Watergate and had dined on lobster the night before. It sounded like a typically political charade—one that Brian wouldn't put past the Republican Party.

Binneker, Brian's boss, rounded the corner and sat down in a small chair—cramped in the corner. His utmost concern was that the two weeks away had put Brian significantly behind, and he needed some reassurance that Brian could meet all of his deadlines.

"Don't worry, I'll take care of it," Brian said.

Binneker smiled briefly and said he knew he could count on Brian. Then he raced out of the office. Brian realized how great it was to be in a profession where no one had the time to say more than two sentences to one another because time was always of the essence. It was the nature of the business. He began to wonder how a kid from Long Island, a kid whose father owned a small insurance business and a mother who was an interior decorator, ever decided to be a journalist. When he had attended New York University, he had thought he wanted to be a lawyer—only to realize he liked writing better.

Sitting back in his chair, Brian began to think about writing a story about the caretaker. Perhaps his approach would be to explore the former loyalties of the old German and contrast them to what he felt today. Brian had never really been interested in Nazi Germany, the Third Reich, or Hitler for that matter. But talking to Horst made him more inquisitive. It must have been difficult for the caretaker to admit that he had reservations about his former life—that he was possibly caught between being a Christian and following the tenets of the Führer.

The pretext of the article would be to combine the philosophical and psychological aspects of the caretaker's life. Of course Brian had to consider the problems he would have selling the story to his management. Not many magazines these days really wanted to run stories about Nazi Germany. It brought back too many bad memories.

He remembered he had a dinner date with Laura that night. It was a comforting thought since he hadn't seen her for a little over two weeks. He was grateful to have met her three years earlier at a writer's conference in Connecticut. When they had first sat down and talked, he knew she was special. She came from a wealthy banking family in Philadelphia. Her father had inherited a large estate in the fashionable section of Jenkintown.

Graduating from Temple University with honors in journalism, she had worked on a local newspaper before going to New York City to try her hand at editing. When Random House hired her, she could hardly believe it. Laura had been there ever since and had worked her way up to be one of the senior associate editors.

At the end of a very long day, Brian decided to take a cab over to the restaurant. Donnetello's, an Italian eatery, had become one of their favorites. In fact, they ate there at least three times a week. Walking in, he could see Laura's platinum blond hair all the way in the back. After the long embrace, they ordered wine to celebrate.

"So how was Tuscany?" Laura asked.

"How do I explain it? It's hard to put into words." Brian ignored the subtle tap on the arm. "I'm convinced it's really heaven. It's just a well kept secret. We should go there together as soon as both of us can break away."

"So what did you do?" Laura asked.

"I met a very interesting man at the villa."

"I thought you had the place to yourself."

"No. He was the caretaker." Brian explained everything that had gone on. "His name is Horst."

"So he fought in World War II under Hitler."

"He talked about it quite a bit. I honestly think he regrets not only the war, but pledging allegiance to Hitler, even though he seemed to defend the Führer whenever I said anything."

Laura was intrigued and wanted to know more about Horst. She spoke fluent German and could read and write it just as well.

"I'm not sure there's much more to tell. But I'm pleased I finally met someone who had lived under the shadow of the Third Reich." He studied her alabastrine face and dark red lips, and thought how much he had missed her—her beauty reflected in her dark blue eyes, petite dimpled cheeks, and her constant smile. "So, what have you been up to?"

"Nothing much. Except my workload has increased tremendously; it seems like I'm working fourteen-hour days lately. I'm working on at least five projects that sooner or later should get published. Oh, I met someone the other day who said she admired your work."

"Who?"

"Her name is Gerta Honiker. She had come into my office the other day to drop off a query letter and a sample of her work."

"I thought you didn't like that sort of thing."

"We don't, but she showed up nevertheless. She does have an interesting past. She too comes from Germany. Her story is about a young Jewish family that had escaped certain death by making their way into France, but the wife was pregnant—raped by a Nazi soldier. Gerta had been only a young girl herself during the war and managed to flee to Italy where she lived for many years."

"Does she live here in New York or is she just visiting? How does she know about me?"

"She said she reads *Time* magazine faithfully and likes your articles especially. What is really strange is that I never told her that we knew each other."

"Did you ask her how she knew?" Brian asked.

"Yes, but she really didn't answer the question. She just told me she would let me read the sample material and return sometime later, but I haven't seen her since."

"Is it good?"

"It's very well written. Unfortunately, our policy is to reject unsolicited work. I referred Gerta to several literary agents in town. That's all I could do."

"Sounds reasonable."

"Do you want to see *The Fantastics*?"

Amused, Brian replied, "I'd rather go see Led Zeppelin or The Who in concert, but if have to, I wouldn't mind going to the theater."

With a smirk on her face, Laura said, "I'll get tickets as soon as I can."

After their meal, they ordered dessert and had amaretto to toast the evening. Brian hinted at spending the night, but Laura was not feeling up to it. Living right off Park Avenue, she didn't have far to go. They kissed outside the restaurant and Brian hailed a cab.

Sitting in his living room, Brian began to study the German Bible Horst had given him. He skimmed over the first twenty-five or so pages. Tired, he wasn't sure he was giving it his full attention. Then the phone rang. Brian could tell right away that the deep, resonant voice belonged to Ronny Whitaker, an old friend he had met through his fiancée.

Dr. Whitaker was a history professor at New York University. They had a lot in common, including a penchant for knowing the truth and stopping at nothing to find it. Ronny was curious about Brian's vacation; he had always wanted to go to Italy. He figured if he could get a good recommendation, he would rent a villa the next summer. Brian had to admit he was tired and asked if they could meet for dinner on the weekend. It seemed to fit in well with Ronny's plans. He was looking forward to it.

*   *   *

Thursday morning, Brian's boss approached him and asked if he could have a few moments of his time. "I need one of my best writers to go with a small team of writers and photographers to cover the Summer Olympics in Munich in late August. I think you're the perfect choice."

"I'm not so sure. Can I give it some thought?"

"I need you to go."

Brian didn't respond.

Binneker also had ideas for two articles—one of which Brian could write, but it would be up to him. The first would be a well-thought-out piece concerning the modern day influence of Jesus on the young generation. The second would be the predominance of the Beat generation that made way for the advent of Hippies and how it was now manifesting itself in other countries, such as Great Britain and France.

Brian liked challenges. He sat and weighed his choices. Writers like Allen Ginsberg, Jack Kerouac, and William Burroughs dominated the years when Brian was in his early twenties. He was influenced by their writing styles and, more importantly, by their thinking. Philosophically speaking, Brian knew that thinkers such as Nietzsche, Hegel, Schopenhauer, and Sartre had influenced many of the Beat generation writers.

Many of the writers of the 1950s and the '60s believed in the virtues of existentialism. Regardless of the metaphysical and philosophical underpinnings, he knew that term really meant living in the moment and enjoying the essence of life. In a very strange way, that kind of living seemed to be part of who Brian Bennett had become.

Brian considered trying to combine the essence of both choices he had been given. It would perhaps be a complicated story to tell. In theory, the two groups appeared to be very diverse. But as he began to think more about it, he realized that it wasn't necessarily the case. Many of what some called a lost generation believed in Christ but were wandering around in total confusion about what they were supposed to be and what the meaning of life really was. Not sure of how to craft the piece, Brian decided to think about it later.

He was still on the hot seat to write the article on the influence of folk music. He had already scheduled an interview with Dave Van Ronk for the following week. Next he would meet with Bob Dylan and Woody Guthrie. He had actually spoken to Dylan a number of times over in a bar on 42nd street—just casual talk and never very exciting, but Brian believed he knew quite a bit about him. On the other hand, he had only seen Guthrie in concert once. He knew if he was smart enough, he could possibly tie the theme about the Beat generation into this music article and kill two birds with one stone. What he was really thinking about was how he was going to make it to the weekend. With all the work piling up, it was just a matter of time before he would have to work Saturdays, and even some Sundays, in order to catch up.

*   *   *

Brian got out of the cab at the corner and walked the half a block to Donnetello's Restaurant. It was a fairly humid Saturday night in the city and he had decided not to get too dressed up. Both his fiancée and Ronny had agreed to meet him there at eight. After a fifteen-minute wait, the maître d' seated him in a secluded corner just behind two tall ferns that were potted in very large Greek-looking basins. He knew the menu by heart, so placed it down on the table.

He patiently waited, and after ten minutes Laura and Ronny finally showed up—late because they had met across the street and talked for a little while. Brian knew that they had been friends since college. Ronny had dated Laura's best friend in their senior year. They were like brother and sister. When she first started dating Brian, Laura had gone to Ronny for his opinion. Ronny couldn't think of a reason to tell Laura to forget about him, so they had continued to date—now glad that she had.

They ordered quickly. Ronny was overweight for his small frame and hated to sit in cramped spaces. Brian was never surprised and would always tell Laura how Ronny reminded him of a tiny Jackie Gleason. He even had the gruff voice. After a few minutes,

Ronny asked how the infamous vacation had gone. Brian told him, not trying to bore Laura with the details again.

"Sounds like Horst had quite a life," Ronny said.

"I'll say. Not sure how old he is, but he looked somewhat frail. Being out in the hot sun certainly doesn't help the old man's complexion much. The fact that he had spent a good number of his formidable years fighting in wars doesn't help either."

Laura suddenly grabbed Brian's arm and shook it. "I know you've already thought about this, but your friend would make a good story."

"Of course."

"Perhaps I can help," Ronny suggested. "The subject of my Ph.D. thesis was the German Third Reich, with an emphasis on the influence of the High Command on Hitler from day to day as World War II progressed. I'm now teaching a course about Nazi Germany."

"It would have been great for you to meet Horst. He would have had you mesmerized. Having him there at the villa was an unbelievable surprise. But I never had the chance to say goodbye."

"Why not?" Ronny asked.

"I don't know. The afternoon before I left to come home, I went to his room to talk to him and he was gone—his clothes, his belongings. He had vanished."

"That's very strange," Laura said. "Why would he do such a thing? I mean not even say goodbye?"

"He's a caretaker," Ronny said. "Perhaps he had somewhere else to go and simply packed his stuff and left. Germans can be impersonal sometimes."

Laura smiled at her friend and nodded. Brian wasn't convinced, but he ordered a round of drinks to celebrate meeting Horst anyway. He wanted to change the subject. Brian knew that he and Ronny had long argued over the Vietnam War. It was a harmless rivalry. Ronny believed in what the United States was doing and had always supported the war effort. Brian thought the U.S. was there for the wrong reasons and that the youth of America were dying with absolutely no justification.

Brian looked over at Ronny. "Do you remember three months ago, in March, when North Vietnam launched a three-pronged invasion of South Vietnam? A lot of American soldiers were killed."

Ronny smiled. "It's good the President suspended peace talks and ordered Operation Linebacker."

"I'm disappointed in the President," Brian remarked.

"You shouldn't be," Ronny said. "Thank God for President Nixon. He understands what has to be done to bring the war to a successful conclusion. It doesn't hurt to have Henry Kissinger on our side either. The idea is to live together in harmony in the world regardless of your ideology."

"That's political bullshit and you know it."

"Of course it's not," Ronny replied. "You just don't like Nixon."

"I don't like Kissinger. Nixon's okay. The President and his men are playing games that are getting a lot of young soldiers killed. I mean, we should have stayed out of Vietnam. We went there just to advise. What the hell happened?"

Ronny looked over at Laura and sipped his wine. "He says this every time. You know how we got into it, and by the way, it wasn't on Nixon's dime. He inherited the war. You can't change the past. You just have to live with it."

Laura, who had been quiet the entire conversation, said, "I believe it was an unfortunate set of circumstances that the United States got in the war in the first place, but I believe it has to be brought to an end in a diplomatic way."

"Military might beats diplomacy any day," Ronny said. "War is hell."

Brian broke out laughing. "That's what I told Horst when we were talking about the campaign in Italy."

"Really?" Ronny replied. "You didn't mean it. I trust you didn't talk about 'Nam. Did you?"

"Hell no." Brian could never get over how Ronny lost his temper so easily. Deep down inside, though, he loved it. No matter what, Brian could always piss his friend off without much effort. "I think war is a hell that all men have to go through once they get thrust in the middle of it. Not just the enemy. Don't you think?"

Ronny began to choke on his wine. "War is a necessary evil. Why can't you just admit that? Vietnam's just not going away. We have to deal with it."

Brian noticed a figure standing a few feet away out of the corner of his eye: a rather tall brunette with a large bosom, thin lips, and wide blue eyes beneath large tortoise-rimmed glasses. She was dressed in a dark blue suit, bright white blouse, and a light blue beret. She was stunningly beautiful. Ronny waited for Brian to respond to his remark, but noticed he was preoccupied.

Laura finally noticed the stranger. She introduced her as Gerta Honiker and asked the bystander to join them. Gerta said that it was fate that they would see each other again so soon. As it was her last night in New York, she wanted to splurge. Laura introduced her around the table and asked where she was going.

"I leave for Italy tomorrow afternoon," she replied.

"What part of Italy?" Brian asked.

"Rome and then Florence."

"Florence. I was just there. Well, in Tuscany. It's so beautiful there."

Gerta flashed a sexy smile. "You were? Yes, it is a wonderful place."

Laura interrupted. "I must tell you that we can't accept your manuscript at this time, but I can give you several leads on agents if you would like."

"Thank you for your help. But I will submit at another time."

"Why?" Laura asked.

"It's too difficult to worry about it now. I have other things on my mind. Perhaps I'll reconsider later."

"What is your book about?" Ronny asked.

Gerta tried not to elaborate while she summarized it, but found that she was getting into the minutest of details. Ronny was intrigued and wanted to know if it was a true story. She said she had heard it secondhand, but it supposedly really happened. Her guess was that this sort of thing probably occurred more than anyone knew.

Brian was trying to figure out how Gerta supported herself, given the fact she seemed to travel around the world and didn't appear to be employed. But he really didn't want to embarrass her in front of the others. "Are you visiting friends over there?"

"Relatives. My brother lives in Rome and my younger sister lives in Florence."

"Were you born in Germany?" Laura asked.

"I was born in Munich and lived there until I was twenty when I moved to Stuttgart with my older sister. Most of my family went to Italy later, where they live today."

"Do you prefer Italy to Germany?" Brian asked.

She shrugged her shoulders. "I like them both. Being European is something I admire. Life is so much different there. I would not trade it for anything."

Ronny rolled some spaghetti on his fork, stuffed it in his mouth, and washed it down with a swig of Chianti. "What do you think about Vietnam?"

Laura and Brian looked at each other and laughed. Gerta didn't know quite what to say.

"No, I mean what do the Italians think about the war? Justified? Waste of time? What?"

Brian could tell his friend had had a glass too many. Even his words were beginning to slur together.

Gerta gave Ronny a soul-piercing stare. "I think it is none of your business."

"When are you returning?" Laura asked.

"After the New Year, but I'm not exactly sure."

"I would like to read your manuscript sometime," Brian said.

Gerta seemed a little embarrassed, but was willing to oblige. "If you don't mind me saying, I think you're one of the best writers at *Time* magazine."

Flattery was something Brian relished. "I give one hundred percent on every story I do. I've even been thinking about writing a novel, but I'm so damn busy at work it will probably never happen."

The Caretaker's Bible

"Come on, Brian," Ronny said. "That's a bit much, don't you think?"

"What are you talking about?"

"A novel? You never said anything about writing a novel."

Laura tried to come to Brian's defense. "Yes, he's said that to me many times."

Ronny shook his head and didn't say anything more.

Gerta's seriousness showed. "It's difficult to write a book and I gave credit to anyone who even tries."

Laura smiled and looked over at Brian. "I agree. Unless a person has gone through the pain of writing a novel and trying to get it published, they should stay silent."

Ronny uncharacteristically apologized and said he was just giving them a rough time. Not sure whether he were serious, Brian thanked him—realizing at this point that his friend wasn't capable of knowing what he was saying.

Laura was feeling the pressure of a long day and hinted that they should finish their meal and leave. No one ordered dessert and they all passed on the after-dinner drinks. On the way out of the restaurant, Gerta said she enjoyed their conversation and would be obliged to see them all again sometime. She slipped into a cab and was gone.

Later that night, Brian sat down at his kitchen table, determined to spend more time looking at the Bible that fascinated him so. He had to admit his procrastination was directly related to his busy schedule at work. Most nights he was just too tired to do anything when he got home. Setting the Bible on the placemat before him, he studied the condition of the binding. The natural color of the leather had faded over the years. It was bruised in several areas, especially the back. The lettering on the spine was raised, but the yellow color was splotchy. Even so, the binding seemed to be rather strong—as if the Bible had been restored at one time.

Brian opened it to the first several pages. The parchment was somewhat stiff, but he attributed that to the fact that the Bible was over a hundred years old. He noticed that in the middle many of the pages were lightly stained, as if they had experienced water damage or something had been spilled on them. What was interesting to Brian was that on many of the pages there was writing, as if someone had been interpreting or remarking about individual verses. Of course, not being able to read German, he didn't have a clue what any of it meant.

Skimming to the back, he could see that the remarks became more prevalent. When he put the Bible down, he noticed that the back cover was thicker than the front. It had a soft feel to it like it had padding in it. He knew he shouldn't deface the Bible, especially if he were going to try to sell it, but instinct took over; he wanted to see what it was that made the back cover so thick.

He retrieved a small pocketknife from his bedroom. Slowly and methodically, Brian made an incision at the top of the inside of the back cover. When he was done, he saw what appeared to be two folded pieces of paper stuck inside. Carefully, he pulled them out; knowing they were probably very old, he didn't want to rip them. He put them on the table before he tried to unfold them. When he opened the first piece of paper, he wasn't sure what it was. It looked like some sort of birth certificate. There was a seal at the bottom right-hand side. His guess was that it was German, or possibly Austrian. Looking it over, the only thing he recognized was what appeared to be a date. It said *April 20, 1889*. Picking up the next piece of paper, he saw what looked like a one-page letter that was signed at the bottom by someone called Dimitrius. Even though he couldn't read the words, he stared at it for the longest time.

chapteR 5
New York City—1972

A WEEK AND A half later, on a Wednesday, Brian arrived early at the office, still incredibly inspired by his discovery. After having interviewed Dylan the day before, he had to correlate his notes to get ready to write his first copy. Arlo Guthrie had cancelled, which forced Brian to use material from other interviews the artist had consented to since he was under the gun to finish the article and submit it to editing.

At lunchtime, while Brian was eating a tuna submarine sandwich, his boss came in. Brian never liked these little invasions because they invariably meant more work. "The copy for the folk music article is just about finished," he said with his mouth full.

"You always seem to read my mind," Binneker replied. "But I'm more concerned about the Summer Olympics. I need you to go."

"I haven't decided yet." This was the kind of thing that really pissed Brian off. He continuously felt pressured by his boss to jump on every story that was out there. He had to admit that going to Germany wasn't too bad of a deal; however, he knew Binneker would want him to get there three weeks early and stay the entire two weeks the games were going on. That was just too long to be away from his other work and his fiancée.

Binneker pointed his finger at Brian, "You're one of my best reporters. I'm counting on you."

It was obvious to Brian he had no choice. "Okay. I'll go." Binneker smiled, got up, and departed.

Brian looked at his watch. He had made an appointment with Laura in her office to show her what he had found in the Bible and he was running late. He knew she could translate the letter and tell him more about what he thought was a birth certificate. Cramming the remains of his sandwich into his mouth, he ran down to get a cab.

Laura was sitting in her office reading a manuscript when Brian walked in.

"I'm going to the Olympics."

"What? When did you find that out?"

He told her what had just happened. "I believe I'm between a rock and a hard place. What was I going to say to Binneker? No?"

"I guess not. It's an important event. I know *Time* has a long tradition of covering sports events. It makes perfect sense that your boss wants you to go."

"Why don't you come along?" Brian asked.

She looked at her calendar. "I think the Olympics are in late August or early September. Maybe I can swing it."

"I'll have to go there sometime in the middle of August, which is only about a month away."

Laura smiled. "It's all part of the job. I would love to join you once the Olympics start."

Brian placed his briefcase on her desk and took out the Bible and documents he had found. Handing Laura the Bible, he asked her to look at some of the scribbling and tell him what it said.

She read several passages before she replied. "It appears that someone is questioning the validity of the particular verses in some cases while extolling others."

"What does it mean?" Brian asked.

"I'm not sure. It's hard to read a lot of the writing since it has faded over the years and most of the sentences are incomplete. I'd be curious to find out who this Bible belonged to. I'm willing to bet it was a Jew."

"Why do you say that?"

"I don't know. Just a hunch." She skimmed through the Bible while Brian quietly watched. When she was finished, he handed her the birth certificate. She looked at it for a few moments. "So this is what you found hidden in the Bible?"

"That's part of it. What does it say?"

"The best I can tell it's Austrian. There's no date of issue, only a date of birth. The baby is unnamed, but has a reference similar to the American identification of Baby Doe." Brian handed her the letter. She read it over carefully, at least twice.

"It was signed by someone named Dimitrius," Brian said.

"Brother Dimitrius. Apparently he was a monk from the Hagenmünster Monastery in Austria. He had found a baby on their doorstep. It was sick and he took it in. This is a letter of commitment he had written to his brethren—that they would take the child into their hearts."

"That's interesting, but probably doesn't have any literary value."

"I don't know what to think about it. The monk must have been touched by the incident. He probably considered it a sign from God. For him it was likely a very moving experience."

"So what to do you think? Did the baby grow up to be a monk?" Brian asked with a smirk on his face.

The expression on Laura's face was a bit more serious. "A very good possibility. He would be what—eighty-two now."

"If he's still alive." Brian was calculating the monetary value of the Bible in case he wanted to sell it. The documents really didn't add much to it, he thought, but he would keep them as a reminder of his Tuscany holiday.

Laura said, "There doesn't appear to be a story unless someone wants to verify the papers and find out what happened to the baby."

"I'll pass. It isn't worth my time, especially now, since I agreed to go to the Olympics."

"May I make a copy of the documents?" Laura asked.

Brian had an appointment with a representative of NASA about the pictures he needed for his article about the Apollo 16 mission that had landed on the moon just two months earlier. He waited patiently until she finished, then left in a hurry.

*   *   *

On the following Monday morning, Brian was immersed in a new project—one that had fallen in his lap because a fellow writer had come down with a slight case of pneumonia. The subject was terrorism in Europe. The impetus for the article was the recent capture, in June, of several of the Baader-Meinhof gang members in Germany. The local authorities were ecstatic that they had stopped a reign of terror that had gone on for several years. Admittedly, there were other groups in Germany and especially in Italy that were waging war against the establishment, but the capture of Baader-Meinhof was significant. Knowing that he would soon be in Germany, Brian figured it was imperative that he find out what was at stake.

Brian had collected a few articles from his magazine's library about the extent of the European terrorism. He read over them quickly.

He then threw the magazines on the desk, thinking about a way to tell the story that made sense. His first thought was that the article should not be published until after the Summer Olympics. It would only scare Americans who had planned to attend. The other thing that crossed his mind was that he should probably wait until he had a chance to interview some German citizens to see what their thoughts were concerning the subject.

Brian went to get a cup of coffee. He needed to mull over everything he had learned. It wouldn't be easy to write about this subject, and he wasn't looking forward to it. Perhaps he could stall Binneker long enough for his colleague to recover.

Before sitting back down, Brian pulled a history book off the shelf. Its focus was World War II and Brian wanted to look through it. Ever since he had met Horst, he had become more interested in finding out about the Führer and how he really became the leader of the Third Reich. After a few moments, Brian found a section dealing with Hitler and how he had come to power.

After the first paragraph, Brian put the book down and went immediately to his office to retrieve the documents he had found in the Bible. When he came back down, he compared the birth certificate to Adolf Hitler's birth date. It was the same: April 20, 1889. His birthplace was a small town called Braunau am Inn. According to a small map on the page, it was roughly eighty kilometers west of Linz.

Hitler's father, Alois, was a customs inspector in the town of Braunau. He had already been married twice, sired nine children, and had numerous affairs by the time he married his second cousin Klara Pötzl in 1885. He was stern and ruled with an iron fist. Adolf never liked him.

Young Adolf did well in primary school, but once he attended secondary school, everything somehow changed and he never excelled in any school after that. He was rejected from the Academy of Fine Arts, which he really wanted to attend because he sought a career as an artist. His mother, whom he had loved beyond human comprehension, died of cancer in December 1907 when he was just eighteen. Devastated, he went to Vienna to live until 1913, and then moved to Munich to begin a new life. The years in Austria's capital were not kind to Adolf. By the time he arrived in Munich, he was bitter about the world. After only two years, he joined the German Army and served well, according to many of his peers.

Following military service, he joined the German Worker's Party, and by 1923 he had become the leader of what was now called the National Socialist German Worker's Party. In only eleven years, his party became the one to be reckoned with. Because of his oratory skills and his mysterious charisma, he managed to become Chancellor of Germany.

Brian put the book down. He was confident he knew the rest of the story. What stuck in his mind though was the date Hitler was born—the fact that it was exactly the same as the one that appeared on the birth certificate. He went to his office and called Laura. He wanted to talk to her about it.

That night he left work and went directly to her posh apartment complex on 72nd Street, just around the corner from Rockefeller Center. Laura met him at the door. They went into the living room and sat down.

"Do you know when Hitler was born?" Brian asked.

Laura got a funny smile on her face. "No. Why?"

"The 20th of April, 1889."

"Is that supposed to mean something?"

Brian reached into his briefcase and brought out the birth certificate. "Look."

Laura took it, put on her glasses, and read it. "It's the same date. That's certainly suspicious."

"Hitler was born in Braunau am Inn, which is on the Austrian-German border and, according to a map I looked at, is very close to Hagenmünster, where the monastery is located."

"Probably a coincidence. I'm not sure we can deduce anything from it. The only thing you can do is to try to investigate it. But that means you will have to travel to Austria, and since you have to cover the Olympics that is probably out of the question."

Brian said, "I'm was beginning to think we should have the Bible analyzed by a book dealer. It's at least worth a try."

"Did you bring the Bible with you?" Laura asked.

He cautiously took it out of his briefcase and handed it to her.

Looking at it again and taking her time, she read over some of the scrawl. She said something that made Brian pause for a second. "It's entirely possible the Bible could have belonged to a German, possibly a Nazi."

"I thought you said a Jew wrote these notes."

"I did, but it could also have been a soldier, a sympathizer, or someone in government."

"Why do you think that?"

"The sentiments are often crude and contradictory to the verses. Some of the rambling sounds almost sacrilegious."

"Like a Nazi trying to deny the Gospel."

Laura nodded her head. "Yes. Something like that." Laura studied a few more of the entries. "We probably should have a handwriting expert look at it."

"Okay," Brian said. "But do you think it's really necessary?"

"Yes. Of course. And I know of one of the best. His name is Dr. Myron Lewis. He's completely conversant in German. I'm sure he can at least tell the personality of the individual who wrote the remarks."

"How long will that take him?" Brian was uneasy about letting the Bible out of his possession. Years ago he had had a bad experience loosing a family heirloom to a swindler. He had never forgotten it.

"It will take a few days or so if Dr. Lewis is not otherwise engaged. He's pretty busy most of the time."

"Does he work for the government?"

"No. He's the curator of the Guggenheim Museum. He did extensive work translating documents of the Third Reich memorabilia when he was younger. Of course, it has been awhile."

"It sounds like a good idea. I'm curious to see what he comes up with."

Laura closed the Bible and put it on her coffee table. "You can leave it with me. I'll take it to Myron—if you don't mind."

Brian's heart thumped a bit. He could feel his blood pressure going up. "I can take it to him. I really don't mind. What's his address?"

Laura stared at her fiancé for the longest time. "Trusting me is a virtue, and in this case a necessity."

Brian knew he was on thin ice and figured it was better to change his mind than live in hell for the next few weeks. "Have you thought any more about going to Munich? It won't be a vacation by any stretch of the imagination, but it'll allow us to get away from New York. I still feel refreshed after spending two weeks in Italy."

"I can tell. I'll have to talk it over with my boss; see what he says."

Brian was getting ready to leave, but kept looking at the Bible, which was driving Laura crazy. She blurted out, "I'm not going to lose it. I promise." He didn't say a word. The kiss was patronizing and he quietly walked out the door.

*   *   *

The next several days were hectic and Brian was working at backbreaking pace. By Thursday afternoon, he had finally stopped to take a breath. He went down to the library to do some research at a rate he could handle. Looking around, he found a book on the Third Reich. After his conversation with Laura, he had started to become more anxious to find out more about the Führer than he could discover in an ordinary history book. Thumbing through, he realized the book made many references to Hitler. Sitting down, he turned to the table of contents.

Apart from high school and a course on World War II in college, he had never taken a real interest in understanding the causes of the war or anything about the Germans. Talking to Horst had made him think about how devastating the war was for both sides. As far as he could tell, it would have been hell living under the dictatorship of Adolf Hitler.

According to the first passage he read, after Hitler had led the National Socialist German Worker's Party into the hearts and minds of the German people, he became the Chancellor of Germany in 1933. He spent the next two years formulating his ideals for national socialism and slowly taking his country's fate solely into his own hands.

To effectively consolidate his power, he had formed an army to protect the Third Reich called the *Sturmabteilung,* or SA. It would fight for Germany's independence and eventually be used as the aggressor in Hitler's grandiose plan to extend Germany's borders. The Führer's obsession with total and uncompromising security was the impetus for a second group to be formed—the *Schutzstaffel*, or SS. Taken over by Heinrich Himmler in 1936, it became the most notorious secret police force in the world.

Long before Himmler took over, the Führer had decided that a National Socialist state could not tolerate wealthy groups that could threaten the Third Reich. Unfortunately, the prime victims of that decision were the Jews. Ideological and political enemies such as communists and socialists were also targeted. Either out of boredom or a willingness to impress the Führer, the SS looked for other enemies to persecute—common criminals and antisocial types.

Brian turned to a chapter that had to do with the war in Italy. But, looking at his watch, he realized he needed to get back to work. He wanted to take the book home and read the rest of it. He took a pink card, filled it out, and put it up on the shelf.

When he got back up to his office, Binneker was sitting there smoking a cigarette, which completely freaked Brian out. It would take forever to get the smell out. His boss said he had something to discuss and asked Brian to shut the door. Brian had to draw the line—not unless Binneker put out the cigarette. It appeared that there was a story in the making. Some prominent New York lawyer had been arrested and charged with the savage beating and consequent death of his best friend's wife. Binneker's first inclination was that they were having an affair, but a story had just surfaced that the lawyer was employed by the Mob.

"Maybe the husband of the deceased wasn't really a friend," Brian suggested.

"It's too early to tell. But I can tell you one thing. Stories like this tend to grow into major news items." Binneker took out another cigarette and held it in his hand.

Brian cringed. "What do you want me to do?"

Binneker shrugged his shoulders. "I'm really not sure how to proceed. First, it must be investigated and then I will decide if we can write an intelligent article about the Mafia without going over the top."

"When do you think I'm going to have time to do this?" Brian asked, looking at his calendar. "You asked me to go to the Olympics, not to mention the fact that I have three other articles to finish. I'll be leaving in only a few weeks."

With that, Binneker got up and started to walk out. "By the way, a young lady was here to see you yesterday."

"Who?"

"She didn't give her name."

"What did she look like?"

"A rather tall good-looking brunette with a slight accent. She was neatly dressed and was very polite."

"She didn't leave a message?"

"No. I'm afraid not. When I told her you weren't here, she just smiled and left."

Brian watched his boss walk down the hall. Who in the hell was it, he thought? By the description, it sounded like it could have been Gerta, but that was impossible since she was in Italy. The phone rang. It was Laura. She wanted to talk to him as soon as she could break away. She thought it best if they meet in Central Park on Saturday morning. Brian agreed, sat down, and began thinking a bit more about his mysterious visitor.

* * *

The sunlight reflected off the lake as Brian made his way to their usual meeting spot. He was just glad to be out of his office or his living room for a while. It gave him time to relax. Sitting on a park bench, he read the *New York Times* and waited for his fiancée to arrive.

"Hi, Honey. I hope you didn't have to wait too long," Laura said.

Brian gave her room to sit down, folded his newspaper, and put it in his lap. Laura opened her briefcase and handed him the Bible.

"What did your friend say about the writing? Did he come up with anything?"

"It's a good thing you're sitting down."

Brian laughed. "Why?"

"Myron has extensively reviewed the entries made in the Bible. He recalled seeing writing very similar to it years ago. He decided to match the writing with samples he could find of prominent Nazis. His conclusion was not believable at first, so he decided to get a second opinion from another well-known handwriting expert. After he concurred, Myron had to make it official."

"What did they say?"

"Brian, the writing in this Bible belongs to Adolf Hitler."

"What? There's no mistake?"

"Myron Lewis doesn't make mistakes. It's Hitler's handwriting."

A myriad of thoughts raced through Brian's mind. *Who was the owner of the villa and why did he have this Bible? Did he even know what he had? Why did Horst give it away?* This was an extraordinary find. It had to be worth thousands of dollars. Any museum would want to have it. "Is he really certain?"

"Myron couldn't believe it at first either—not because he didn't trust himself, but because he didn't think Hitler would keep a private Bible. According to Myron's analysis of the ink, some of it dated back to the late 1930s."

Brian held it in his hand. "So this could have actually been Hitler's Bible."

"Believe it or not, it could have been."

Brian started to wonder why the birth certificate and letter had been hidden in the back cover. Who could have put them there? "Do you think there's a story here?"

"I don't know. Could be worth looking into."

"What is the connection between Hitler and Brother Dimitrius? Or the baby, for that matter? I can't imagine there is one."

"The only way to satisfy your thirst for the truth is to go to Austria, do your homework, find out the exact location of the monastery, and go talk to the Abbot."

"I'm not sure it's possible. I'm already inundated with work, not to mention the Olympics. How in the hell can I do it all?"

"Tell your boss you're onto a fascinating story and maybe he'll let you off the hook for the Olympics," Laura replied.

"Not Binneker. He's way too demanding to tell him that. He'll want me to do both."

"Austria does border Germany. You could go there first. Then go off to Munich."

Brian began to think perhaps that's what he would do. He would leave a week early and visit the monastery. "I want you to come along."

"Oh, I don't know. It's going to be hard enough to get off to go to the Olympics."

"No. You have to."

Laura started to think about it. She knew this was a once in a lifetime deal, even if nothing panned out. It was almost like being a detective trying to solve a mystery about the Third Reich. Even if they came up empty, they could just travel on to Munich and enjoy the summer games.

Brian looked at his watch. They would have to make plans and be on their way in about a week. He would go to the library and find out more about the monastery and pinpoint the location. He would then have Laura make the air and hotel reservations. The anticipation was starting to excite him. He looked at the Bible—opened it and stared at the handwriting. It didn't seem possible that it could have belonged to Adolf Hitler. *What could this all mean? What possible value could this have to the world?* The only thing he did know was that if they didn't go to Austria, no one would ever find out.

It was early afternoon and they sat on the bench with their arms around one another watching the ducks skim across the water. Brian clenched the Bible in his right hand—assured that, if nothing else, he possessed a very interesting and possibly very important artifact of history.

Chapter 6
Berlin—1939

He met with Goebbels in the early morning. The Minister of Propaganda was in a ghastly mood and abruptly told Glossen to be seated while he collected his thoughts. Glossen glanced around the office while his mentor fumbled with a rather large dossier.

"We are at a crossroads here," Goebbels said with a cold stare.

"What do you mean?"

"The document I hold in my hands is the memorandum that Hitler released sanctioning war against the West. It is in fact a decree. The idea is for the German Army to swiftly move across Holland, Belgium, and Luxemburg and destroy the opposition before they can react."

"Did we not anticipate this? We just recently discussed this very item with the Führer."

"That might be so, but he wants to accelerate the schedule. He wants to attack now."

Glossen looked at his watch. "Today?"

"No. Of course not today. But he wants to begin initial operations within the week."

"Remember the propaganda strategy we proposed to Hitler the last time we met? The German people will be no wiser to the actual rationale behind the attack."

"It is not the German people I am concerned with," Goebbels replied.

"Then who?"

"We must be concerned with our military commanders. The Army Chief of Staff does not want to attack so soon. Other commanders are supporting his decision."

"It would seem we are caught in the middle. I presume that is what you are talking about."

Goebbels slammed the dossier down on his desk. "Yes! We are not in a position to tell commanders what to do."

Glossen stuttered a bit, knowing he was saying the obvious. "I would say, ah, we have quite a dilemma."

"We must act appropriately. There is no reason why we cannot attack before the end of the year. I do not understand the reluctance on the part of the head of the Army General Staff, General Halder. The army has been ready to attack for some time. We cannot wait."

"May I see the memorandum?"

Goebbels put it on the corner of his desk. "We should decide what course of action we must take."

Glossen glanced through the document. "It will not be easy."

"I am well aware of that." Goebbels sat back in his chair. "I want you to consider approaches we might take and meet again with me in a day or so."

*   *   *

Glossen walked slowly from the Reich Chancellery to the hotel where they had sequestered Brother Matthias, or Horst, as he was now calling him; it was only fitting that the monk have a different name to codify his new identity. Glossen began to realize the enormity and magnitude of his job. Trying to appease Hitler was very difficult at best. The Führer's hatred of the West dominated everyone's caseload day in and day out. He could only hope that he could make a name for himself and survive Hitler's relentless attacks against subordinates that did not always agree with him.

Glossen walked up to the third floor. An army officer met him before he had a chance to get to Brother Matthias' room.

"What is the matter?"

"You do not want to go in there."

"Get out of my way." Glossen stormed past the guard, practically breaking down the door to get in. When he did, a visibly shaken Peter Duckert greeted him.

"What has happened?"

"He has escaped!"

"What?"

Peter frantically tried to explain. "I took the monk for a short walk because he was getting restless. When I turned my back for a moment, the monk slipped away."

"You idiot! We must find him immediately. Do you know what will happen if someone else finds him?" Glossen ordered the guards to dispatch and not come back until they had captured the wayward monk.

"What were you thinking? You knew he was not to leave these premises."

"He somehow convinced me to allow him to get some fresh air."

Glossen stood right in front of Peter and pointed his finger at him. "You are on report. If my plans are foiled, I will have you executed."

No more that a kilometer away, a dozen guards with police dogs combed the area. They crossed paths several times in order to effectively search the park.

One of the dogs began barking and started pulling toward park benches surrounded by a small group of trees. As the guards approached, a man jumped up and started running toward a building in front of them. They yelled for the man to stop. He did so just before the guards prepared to release their dogs.

Brother Matthias was brought into the hotel room in shackles. Glossen ordered them removed. He dismissed everyone but Peter. He took Brother Matthias in the living area and sat him down.

"You have disobeyed my orders. What have you to say?"

The monk didn't respond at first. He looked at the floor. Finally, he responded. "I do not want to be here."

"That is apparent. But you have no alternative." Glossen turned toward Peter. "I suppose I should fire you for incompetence. Can you think of a reason why I should not do so?"

"Please, it will never happen again. Please forgive me."

Glossen was torn. He liked Peter very much and believed he was only acting out of concern for the monk who had been cooped up in the apartment for some time. "I will ignore your inattention to detail this time, but if it happens again, I will ensure that your life becomes a miserable hell."

Brother Matthias sheepishly said, "It is not Peter's fault. I convinced him to take me outside for a short while. It was my idea to escape. I must take the blame."

"It is of no consequence now," Glossen replied. "These walls are the only scenery you will see until it is time to meet the Führer."

Glossen was hesitant to leave them alone, but had personal matters to attend to and departed with regret.

*   *   *

The Army Commander-in-Chief, General Brauchitsch, and his immediate staff sat in a small anteroom waiting to be escorted into Hitler's grand office.

The Führer was perched behind his massive oak desk reading when his personal secretary, Martin Bormann's assistant, Klara Petrun, walked in to address him. He asked her to sit down for a few minutes.

This was not the first time he had asked Klara, who was in her late thirties, to join him. He seemed to treat her like a relative—a sister of sorts. He would share his intimate thoughts with her. On numerous occasions, he would discuss religious philosophy with Klara.

"Sir, General Brauchitsch is waiting to see you."

"He can wait."

"Yes, mein Führer."

Hitler cradled his Bible and turned several pages to a passage he wanted to discuss with Klara. His hand was steady as he began to transcribe a few entries as he talked.

Klara listened.

"I would say that God created the heaven and earth for a reason. But I believe God wants man to be in charge of his own destiny, to exercise a certain free will."

"Yes, mein Führer."

"God and all that surrounds him cannot be seen or felt. Man cannot be guided by this kind of entity."

Klara stared at Hitler.

"Man must rise up and take control of what he can feel and understand, not rely on the unknown. Do you not agree?"

"Yes, mein Führer."

"I and only I am the savior of the German people. I do it with God's blessings. Nevertheless the history in this book gives me sustenance."

Hitler had always believed the Bible was like a forum in which to debate. He never subscribed to faith, but rather looked for logical conclusions that could be readily verified, at least in his own mind.

After thirty minutes of rant, Hitler decided he wanted to meet with Brauchitsch. He put the Bible on the side of his desk.

The general and his staff were ushered in and immediately sat down in chairs placed directly in front of Hitler.

"Mein Führer, it is of utmost importance we talk to you today," the general said.

"I trust you have good news for me."

"We believe that it would be in our best interest to postpone our attack against the West to allow us more time to be totally prepared."

"Why are you saying these things? We are ready to defeat the enemy. The time to attack is now, today!" Hitler sat up straight and adjusted his collar—a nervous habit that meant he was becoming angry.

"It simply is not possible. We believe that the will of the German infantry in Poland is dismal and not reliable. The weather is not cooperating as well."

"Why have you kept these facts from me? Do you somehow think I am a clairvoyant? I want you to listen to me. The attack will occur and you will ensure that it is orchestrated in such a manner that we are victorious. Is that understood? I want nothing less for the German people."

"Yes, mein Führer."

Hitler started pounding his desk. He picked up the Bible and shook it. "You see this! It is a philosophy book. It makes you think. It gives you reason to believe in yourself. We are Germans. We are destined to be the leaders of Europe. But we will never inspire that if we sit back and scratch our behinds. I want action! I want you to attack. Now get out."

The general and his staff filed out of the office. They had gotten the reaction they knew they would get before they first entered.

*   *   *

Glossen left his office early to meet with Goebbels. He had thought quite a bit about what the Propaganda Minister had said the last time they met. He was learning that there were many dimensions to Hitler's Third Reich and he was desperately trying to develop creative solutions to the countless difficult problems they faced.

Goebbels was pacing the floor when Glossen arrived.

"What is the matter?"

"I just met with the Führer. He is very angry because General Brauchitsch does not want to attack. He wants to wait for a while."

"I can only guess he was the recipient of Hitler's wrath."

"The Führer will have no part of it. He wants to attack on 12 November. Without fail."

The Caretaker's Bible

"What can we do?"

Goebbels smiled. "Only a few days ago, the German Army attempted a possible insurrection with help from members of the High Command. Their objective was to remove Hitler from power in order to reach a settlement with the Western powers that the Führer wanted to attack, thus saving Germany from a possibly embarrassing situation. In a communiqué, I can say I am furious and want to expose every single soldier and their commanders for their indiscretions. But I think it would be better to tell the German public that any rumor that something like that had occurred is completely false; it never happened."

"You mean the explosion at the Bürgerbräukeller in Munich?"

"What about it?" Goebbels replied.

"I am concerned about the audacity of the army trying to assassinate Hitler after he had just given a speech on the anniversary of the 1923 putsch. Hitler escaped by only minutes."

"Yes. He was very lucky." Goebbels smiled.

"Is there something I should know?"

Goebbels was unapologetic. "The Gestapo orchestrated the bombing to try and raise the fervor in the country for the Führer. My position is that it is often necessary to scare the populace into rallying around the High Command of the Third Reich. In this case, it is imperative that the country as a whole look at Hitler as an inspired leader who thwarted death."

"I cannot imagine that rational citizens will not question it," Glossen said.

"You will be surprised," Goebbels replied. "It is propaganda at its best."

"That still does address our current dilemma."

"Perhaps there is nothing we can do directly to entice the army to go to war. But I think we can release documentation that suggests incompetence within the ranks of our military—an unwillingness to allow Germany to fulfill its greatness."

Glossen smiled. He knew his boss and mentor was certainly on to something.

Chapter 7
Austria—1972

THE AUTOBAHN TWISTED ITS way through valleys and small mountain passes. Large multi-colored castles in the distance seemed to dominate the infinite scenery. The travelers had departed Vienna in the morning and headed for Linz. Brian had learned that the monastery at Hagenmünster was located about 25 kilometers to the south of Linz, where they had decided to stay.

Brian had done as much research as he could before he left.

The monastery dated back to AD 780. The initial colony of monks was from lower Bavaria. The Hungarians destroyed the monastery in the 10th century and all of the remaining possessions were divided among the Duke of Bavaria and other bishops and nobles. After finally being restored, it became one of the most flourishing places of worship in Bavaria. Over many years, eminent scholars came to Hagenmünster to study in the monastic library, which was considered by many to be the best in all of Europe.

The Order of the Benedictines had a long and humble history.

It dated back to Saint Benedict, who had been born in the waning years of the Roman Empire. When he was old enough to make a life for himself, he had dedicated his soul to God and turned his back on the idea of living in the real world. Upon his death, religious men began to flock to his ideals and way of life. Believers at Hagenmünster were no different. Many came over the years to dedicate their lives to Saint Benedict. Today there were well over a hundred monks at the monastery. They attended to religious matters, taught, and prayed daily that their humble souls would be of some value in extolling the passion of God to the masses.

Crossing over the Danube, Brian knew they would be at their destination in roughly one hour. They had decided to stay at a small Gästhaus in the Hauptplatz, Linz's main square. If the weather cooperated and it didn't rain, they would travel to the monastery in the morning.

Later, as they drove over a hill, Linz spread out in front of them. Brian could easily see the castle on the Pöstlingberg to the north of the city. As they got closer, Laura, who had not been in Austria before, commented how beautiful the countryside surrounding the city appeared and how it took her breath away.

When they arrived at the Hauptplatz, they parked their car and walked the short distance to the Gästhaus. The lobby was very small, with bright white marble tile. It was narrow, and was furnished with only two wing-backed chairs and an oval oak table with a vase of daffodils in the middle. The receptionist spoke English and said they had managed to reserve the last accommodation available for at least a week. Their room was actually fairly large by European standards. It wasn't what Laura was used to, but she had to admit it was acceptable. They unpacked and took a walk around the square—stopping to eat at a quaint little café. Brian was convinced they had done the right thing by coming to Linz.

"Time will tell," Laura replied. "I'm not totally sure our questions will be satisfactorily answered."

"Why? They should have a record of it." Brian had read earlier that the Benedictines had a penchant for history and that they preserved documents, most of which were in their library.

"What do you think they're going to say?" Laura asked.

"I don't know. I simply want to find out if a baby had been left at the monastery and, if so, what had happened to the infant—did he live, did he become a monk, and most importantly, where was he now?"

Laura had a smile on her face. "How do you know the child was a he?"

Brian burst out laughing. "What? If it were a she, it wouldn't have been left at a monastery full of monks."

"I'm just kidding."

Brian didn't know whether to believe her or not, but played along. "Okay. We'll go there in the morning. If we come up empty handed, we'll leave."

The Hauptplatz was especially crowded. August was a big holiday month for the Europeans. Laura noticed there seemed to be a large number of tourists; almost everywhere Italian was being spoken. When they finished their meal, they slowly wandered back to the Gästhaus. Brian began to get that feeling again—like he was being watched. What was reassuring to Brian about it was that Laura felt the same way.

*   *   *

A thin ray of light woke them both up the next morning. Brian knew that it had rained overnight since he had awakened a number of times and could hear the downpour. Knowing their accommodation didn't offer breakfast, they dressed and went down the street to a bakery where they ate freshly baked strudel and had some Viennese coffee.

The fog was rather heavy, but they decided to drive down to Hagenmünster anyway. Brian had a map he had brought with him from the States. After several wrong turns, they entered the small town adjacent to the River Krems. The monastery was prominently perched on a small plateau.

After parking, the fog now subsiding, they climbed up a narrow set of granite steps that were surrounded by trees and heavy foliage.

The Caretaker's Bible

As they got closer to the monastery they could see the spirals of the chapel glistening in the faint sunlight. Once they entered the courtyard, they could see dozens of monks dressed in black robes walking between the chapel and other areas of the large monastery.

Brian had phoned the afternoon before and asked to see the Abbot. Brother Dominique, the Abbot's personal secretary, told Brian that the Abbot would see them when he had a chance and that they should be patient. The inside of the chapel was ornate, and to Brian it looked like it probably had centuries ago. Brother Dominique escorted them down a long hall to a room that looked like a small museum. The monk informed them that he would ensure the Abbot knew they were there.

Curious, they began to look around. The walls of the museum were stone and the room was cold and musty with a slight sewer smell. In the middle were several glass exhibition cases that displayed religious artifacts from the history of the monastery and the Benedictine Order. Brian especially noticed what appeared to be a small notebook. Laura told him that according to the inscription, it belonged to Saint Benedict and had been found by Allied soldiers in Italy after World War II.

Close to the walls on both sides were placards with historical information about the Benedictine Order. Laura translated one for Brian. It was from the prologue of the Rule of Saint Benedict and began by asking each and every monk to listen carefully to the master's instructions and attend to them with the ears of their hearts.

According to a brief biography that hung on the wall at the end of the room, Saint Benedict was born in the Umbian town of Nursia in AD 480. When he was older he had traveled to Rome to study law, but he was somehow transformed from a man of worldly academics to a man of God. He had joined a small community of like-minded souls on the foothills of Mount Affile.

A miracle had befallen Saint Benedict there. As the story goes, Benedict's nurse had borrowed an earthenware sieve and, after having used it, left it on the table. It was knocked off and broken in two. The nurse was devastated and Benedict began to pray for her. He picked up the remains of the sieve and asked God for forgiveness. When he stood up, the sieve was whole again. He was so admired after this incident that it changed his whole life.

Later, after experiencing time of love and solitude at Subiaco, where he prospered attending to the needs of twelve monasteries in the valley, he founded Mount Cassino, where it is said he composed his rules of obedience to God. He died at his beloved Mount Cassino in AD 547.

Brother Dominique quietly came in and asked them to follow him. He took them down a very narrow hallway to a small waiting room where a young man was sitting at a small table. He looked scared. Brother Dominique informed them that he was Postulate, a candidate to be a monk, and had been summoned by the Abbot for consultation. He said the Abbot would see them momentarily.

They watched as the young man was marched into the Abbot's office, much like he was going to see a prison warden. Brian thought to himself that it was very strange. They waited almost half an hour before the boy departed, then at least another half-hour until they were escorted into the chambers.

Brian noticed how sparsely decorated the office looked. It contained a rather small dark wooden desk, several straight-back wooden chairs, and two religious paintings, which were hung haphazardly on the faded concrete walls. The only impressive thing he saw was a large bookcase behind where the Abbot sat. It was filled with hundreds of antique-looking books. The Abbot was tall and lanky, and appeared to be very old. He looked plain in his black robe—not any different than the other monks. He introduced himself as Brother Thomas Burnier. He asked them to sit down and offered them some tea. Brian declined but Laura loved tea and thought it was a nice gesture.

"It is not often we have Americans come for a visit," the Abbot said. "I am enthused that your interest allowed you to make the journey down to this wonderful sanctuary."

Brian reached into his small briefcase and brought out the

documents. "Father, I have brought some papers I found. I would like you to look at them and tell me what you think."

The Abbot motioned for Brian to give him the papers. He looked at the birth certificate first. "1889. This is very interesting. The child was born in this province somewhere."

Brian asked him to read the letter. Brother Bernier took his time—actually reading it twice.

"Does it make sense to you?" Brian asked. "Who was Brother Dimitrius?"

The Abbot paused for a second. "There have been three with the name Dimitrius. One is with us now. One died almost ten years ago. The only other candidate that I can think of died in 1940."

"Could he be the one?" Laura asked.

"I do not know. Where did you find this letter?" Brother Bernier seemed perplexed.

Brian told him the entire story and handed him the Bible. "I really can't explain how the documents got into this Bible, but they were there."

The Abbot's manner became somewhat abrupt. "What makes you think this Bible belonged to Adolf Hitler?" He skimmed through the pages.

"The handwriting has been analyzed. It belongs to him," Laura replied.

"The Lord God never intended for such a man to exist. He was misguided and lost his way. But I suppose God has forgiven his sins."

Brian could tell they had stepped on a land mine by bringing up Hitler. "Father, do you know anything about this child that was found on your doorstep?"

"No. We have no record of it."

"Are you sure?" Brian looked at the letter. "This appears to be a genuine document."

"Yes, I am sure."

"We should have had the writing analyzed to insure it isn't a hoax," Brian said, "but I believe it's accurate, given that it was found with the birth certificate."

"Being the Abbot of this monastery and a historian of the order I would know if such an incident occurred. I have to tell you that this letter is a fake."

Laura was convinced of the validity of the letter. "He would be 82 now, if he were still alive. Is there no way we can look through your archives? It's possible that apart from the actual letter itself, the event may have never been recorded. Could we perhaps look for birth dates of the monks that had lived here over the years?"

"I believe such an effort is not going to satisfy your wishes," the Abbot said. "Not all the dates of birth have been recorded. It would be impossible to tell. You must believe me. This is a terrible hoax. Please accept my apologies. I am at God's mercy to turn you away. I have nothing against your willingness to find the truth; I simply cannot help you."

Brian was distressed. He honestly believed he had a possible story in the making. Not knowing how to respond, he told the Abbot he respected his feelings and would take his word that it was all a hoax.

Brother Dominique led them out past a small courtyard where they could see young men huddled in prayer. Walking down the steps to their car, Brian wondered if they had left too easily. Perhaps they should have stood their ground. If they could have only researched the records, maybe they could have found something to corroborate the story.

*   *   *

In the morning they went to breakfast to discuss what they would do next.

Laura said, "We have no choice but to forget about this and go on with our lives."

"I'm not so sure. I have this feeling that the Abbot was dismissing us for a reason."

"Why would he do that?"

"It was like we were bringing up something from the past he didn't want to talk about."

The Caretaker's Bible

"It appeared that way," Laura said. "But I can't really put my finger on it, although he did seem agitated when you mentioned Hitler."

"Yeah, I know. But I can understand how he feels about Hitler. We probably shouldn't read too much into that. It's the Abbot's demeanor I think is suspect—the fact that he acted a little nervous and did not want us to do any research. I think he was afraid we would find something."

As usual, Brian had convinced Laura to accompany him even though she had some reservations. "I think we have to admit defeat. I feel a bit foolish for coming along."

"What are you saying? You want to go home?"

"I don't know. But I really need to get some work done. I can come back in a few weeks and meet you in Munich."

"We should go back to the monastery and snoop around."

"That's not a good idea. What if we get caught?"

"I didn't think you would go for it. But I hate the thought of coming all the way over here and not getting what we want." Brian was desperate. He wanted to get to the truth. For as long as he could remember he had wanted to know what made things tick. He had been so curious as a child that he drove his teachers nuts at school from the endless questions he had had about anything he didn't know about.

"Did you ever stop to think that just maybe the Abbot was telling the truth?" Laura asked. "That it could be some kind of hoax?"

"Anything's possible, but I have a gut reaction these documents are real." He pulled them out and looked at each one again. "Damn it, we should have had them analyzed as well. At least we would know approximately when they were written."

"I have an idea. I'll take them home with me and get Myron to look at them. I'll bring them back when I meet you in Munich."

Brian didn't say much at first. He hated having them out of his possession again. "I guess if Myron can prove they are authentic, the two of us can go back to the monastery with the evidence."

They decided to take a walk to a nearby park with a small pond. It was two kilometers east of the city. As they slowly made their way to the Walkplatz, they could see several men in the distance looking like they were following them. Brian told Laura they were probably just feeling paranoid, but he handed her the Bible and documents anyway and told her to keep them in her handbag.

"Why don't we leave this afternoon for Vienna? I can get a flight out and you can make your connection to Munich," Laura said.

"I don't mind, except I'm a bit tired. Let's wait until tomorrow morning. That way we can get a good night's rest."

Looking around, she agreed it was so beautiful there that she couldn't justify her own argument.

They finally reached the park, then sat down. *And people think Central Park is so wonderful*, he thought to himself. He couldn't get enough of Europe. It would be an understatement to say that he should have been born there. Every time he came, he was reluctant to leave. He wasn't sure Laura felt the same way, but he was confident she would give in once they were married.

In the distance they could see someone coming toward them—a rather tall person, dressed in black, and walking slowly. As the figure got closer, they realized it was a monk. Brian immediately thought that was very odd considering that the closest monastery to Linz that he knew of was Hagenmünster, which was some distance away.

The monk walked up to them and asked to sit down. "I am but one of the faithful from the monastery near the River Krems and I must talk with you."

Brian looked at the man. He had a very thin face with a thin beard and appeared to be middle-aged. He also looked a bit nervous.

"What is your name?" Laura asked.

"I am here at the behest of God's will and must tell you something that is of utmost importance."

Brian looked over at Laura. They had no idea what the monk could be talking about. "What do you mean?" Brian asked.

"I must ask you to forget everything you know about the letter you have found."

"But why?" Brian asked.

"It is important that you listen to me. It can never be proven that

The Caretaker's Bible

a sick baby was left on the doorstep of our monastery or that the child grew up to be a monk. Do you understand?"

Brian was about to lose his temper, and it showed in his voice. "Did the Abbot send you here?"

Laura tried to be somewhat more congenial. "Why is this so important that you had to travel all the way to Linz just to tell us?"

"Please believe me. You must stop looking into this matter. Go home, pretend you never found the documents, and go on with your lives. You have God's blessings."

"What the hell is going on here?" Brian asked.

Laura began to feel like she and Brian had stumbled onto something that was forbidden—verboten. She was starting to get scared, thinking the monks of Hagenmünster were hiding a terrible secret. "Why don't you want us to know the truth?"

"The Holy Father looks after his flock. I am only but a mouthpiece. Truth is in the eye of the beholder. What you have found is not only unimportant, but it cannot be verified."

Brian was having a hard time dealing with any of the conversation. He believed it was obvious that if the monastery had nothing to hide, they wouldn't have sent a lowly monk to try to persuade them to go home. "Can we have another audience with the Abbot?"

"I am afraid that is simply not possible. You must leave and never return."

Brian became enraged. "I'll tell you what I think. I believe this has something to do with Adolf Hitler. I don't know what, but I'm going to find out!"

The monk's voice raised a decibel. "Please! It is none of your business. You will be in great peril if you pursue this nonsense."

"What kind of peril?" Laura asked. Brian looked like he was going to explode.

The monk reached into his pocket and brought out a small piece of paper. "May God be with you." He handed the folded note to Brian, got up, and began walking away. Brian called for him to come back, but he walked steadfastly into a crowd of tourists and then was gone.

Laura opened the note. There was a name and a partial address—*Heinrich Glossen, Chiemsee near Munich.*

Brian just stared at the piece of paper. "He's trying to warn us."

"About what?"

"It's blatantly obvious that we are on to something that certain people don't want others to know."

"What do we do now?" Laura was a bit afraid.

"I guess we have two choices. Either put the documents away and forget this ever happened, or try to get to the truth."

"If we ignore what the monk told us, we're putting ourselves in danger," Laura said. "It's clear to me the monk meant what he said. We're only asking for trouble if—"

"If what? This could be the story of a lifetime. I won't stop 'til I find out what the hell is going on. I want to talk to Herr Glossen." Brian quickly said. "I know it isn't going to be easy; this story has to be built piece by piece. You must go to Munich with me. The name on this paper could be the key to everything."

"I want to talk to Glossen too." Laura knew he was right. The helpful monk had already provided them with the first clue. Placing her hand in his, they made their way back to the Gästhaus.

Chapter 8
Munich, Germany—
1972

WHEN THEY ARRIVED IN Munich, they made a decision to stay at the Hotel Kempinski. Brian had been there many times before and loved the location and surrounding area because it was close to the Isar River and a block below the *Englischer Garten*, where he could get his favorite Pilsner. After talking to the receptionist, Brian felt lucky that they managed to get a room earlier than planned. Most of the hotels in the city were full with tourists getting ready for the Olympics.

Even though Laura had decided to come along, she was somewhat reluctant to pursue the story. Getting cold feet wasn't her style, but she knew they were venturing into unknown territory. She had learned a long time ago that it was often better to be distrusting of a situation than to ignore the warning signs, and this had all the trappings of a dangerous endeavor. After all, they had no idea what they were getting into, let alone who else could possibly know about the hidden documents.

Brian wanted to visit the Olympic Stadium and Village. In the mid afternoon, they took a cab to the site, north of the city. They decided to walk around and get a bite to eat later. The competition was only several weeks away. Many of the athletes had already come to prepare for their events. Workers were busy making last minute preparations and putting finishing touches on many of the buildings. The entire afternoon they spent watching time trials and practices out on the track. Brian had brought a small notebook with him so he could take notes. He knew Binneker expected one hell of an article when he got back. He wasn't going to disappoint him.

*   *   *

Brian rose early the next morning and took a walk down the Maximillian Strasse to the river. Not sure of himself, he worried they wouldn't be able to find Heinrich Glossen, and that even if they did, they wouldn't be able to get anything out of him. He figured the first thing he had to do was to take Laura to the city library and find as many articles about the Third Reich as he could—pore through them and try and find out who this Glossen was. It still didn't make sense to him why they would be in grave danger simply because they knew about the documents. Sitting on the grass, he let the morning sun envelop his face and thought about how much he loved it there.

When he got back to the hotel room, Laura said she had just gotten ready to go to the library. Standing in the hallway, Brian began to laugh, saying he thought it was crazy—they really thought too much alike. They agreed to spend as much time as they needed to find what they wanted to know. It took only ten minutes to get there.

The central library in Munich was enormous. One could spend several days exploring it. They concentrated their efforts on finding historical documents that gave accounts of the war. Laura made sure Brian realized that the historical perspective would probably be from a German's point of view. Once they collected as many books as they could carry, they went to a large table and sat down to sort out the information. Laura translated as they began reading the first article they came across.

In 1933, shortly after Hitler became Chancellor, the Reichstag building was set on fire. A young Dutch communist was caught and arrested. Many of the Nazi leaders believed it was the beginning of a communist uprising aimed at destroying the Third Reich. Hitler was advised that the fire was the work of a madman with no ties to any known organization. Hitler dismissed that thinking and said the arson was a communist plot bent on his destruction.

Much later, after the war, some followers believed Hitler had given a secret order to Joseph Goebbels, chief of propaganda for the Third Reich, to destroy the headquarters, thus proactively engaging the communists. The day after the fire, Hitler had persuaded President Hindenberg to sign an emergency decree that allowed Hitler to completely suspend all civil rights and also to arrest and execute any person he believed to be suspicious—all for the good of the Reich.

Laura shook her head and whispered to Brian, "Once Hitler had the authority, the fate of anyone he didn't like was sealed."

"I'm getting angry just thinking about it," Brian replied. "How in the hell could the Germans have elected someone like Adolf Hitler to be their leader?"

Several months after Hitler was seated as Chancellor, he began what can only be described as a reign of terror against elements in his society that he thought posed a threat, such as communists and labor union leaders. Considering them the enemy, he arrested and put them in prison without affording them the fairness and due process of a legal system, which was never part of Hitler's grand scheme.

In the summer of 1933, the first Nazi concentration camp was opened at the old Royal Bavarian Gun Powder factory in Dachau, outside the city limits of Munich. Hitler confined many of what he considered to be political prisoners there, fearing they could have some influence on the common German citizen. While official confirmation came that the Nazis were sending Jews to concentration camps for petty grievances, Hitler, who had grown up Catholic, had already made a pact with the Vatican that he would guarantee the liberties of the Catholic Church if they stayed out of German politics. Hitler then began his vengeance against the Jews by simply boycotting their businesses.

Brian wanted to take a break, but he thought they should resume where they left off when they returned. Laura asked the librarian if they could leave the books on the table while they took a walk. She promptly smiled and said that would be fine.

They walked around the corner onto Karl Strasse. The sun was rather intense and hurt Laura's eyes. Worse, she realized she had forgotten her sunglasses.

"Going through all that data gives me a headache," Brian said. "What about you?"

"You know, I'm not sure we will ever find out about Heinrich Glossen. Frankly, I've never heard of him. Have you?"

"No. I can't remember every reading about him, but it isn't like I'm a history buff or anything—at least not of German history. The American Civil War is my style."

"Good. But I'm sure you won't find Glossen in a confederate uniform." They walked over to a small outside café with a couple of tables haphazardly placed out front. Laura wanted to get a cup of coffee.

Brian was beginning to feel the strain of trying to run down a story while at the same time preparing to cover the upcoming Olympics. The problem was that he worked for an over-achiever and he always had to measure up so he could keep a sense of status in the office. The workload never seemed to stabilize, and over time most of the writers on the staff had become overwhelmed. It was a fast-paced business, much like advertising. One always had to be one step in front of the competitors. That's just the way it was. Looking over at Laura, he asked, "Would you rather spend the day reading a lengthy manuscript in your office or being with me on a sunny street in Munich, Germany?"

"Let me think about that one," she replied.

The Caretaker's Bible

Brian frowned at her and she burst out laughing. "Finish your coffee. We need to get back and get to work," he said.

They walked slowly back to the library—figuratively dragging their feet. Once they sat back down at the table, Laura took a deep breath and continued reading on.

By January 1934, Hitler's power was beginning to seed. In July he appointed Heinrich Himmler, chief of the SS, to be the supreme commandant of the Nazi concentration camps. This gave Himmler the power to sort out citizens not loyal to the Third Reich and deport them to the camps at will. After President von Hindenberg died in August, Hitler was in complete control of Germany's destiny. He declared himself both President and Chancellor of the Third Reich, as well as Commander-in-Chief of the military. This, in effect, set the stage for the terrible oppression of a race.

By the summer of 1935, the subjugation of the Jewish people had greatly intensified. It knew no bounds. Hitler had begun to consolidate his power by segregating his advisors and very seldom being in the receive-mode when listening to his staff. He stepped up the arrests of Jews for nefarious reasons, and by then the Nazi Congress had adopted the swastika as the national flag.

It was well known that many historians questioned whether Hitler knew in 1935 how the Jewish purge would play out. There were two schools of thought. Many believed Hitler simply reacted day to day, wanting to place the Jews on the lowest strata of society, thus allowing him to cultivate and exalt the Aryan race—not considering annihilation. The realization of extermination came later, but he ignored it. Others believe that he had a well-thought plan of pogrom etched in his mind from the time when he was young and had been rejected by Jews.

By January 1938, the Führer was very close to dominating 70 million people. The German High Command focused their hate on the Jews, who were now forbidden to attend concerts, plays, or movies. Their children could not attend German schools. They were now completely relegated to bondage.

Brian paused and looked over at his fiancée. Her eyes were moist. He apologized for putting her through what could only be described as agony. But he had to find out the identity of Glossen and this was the only way he knew to do it. Laura put the book down and rested her head on the table. She was spent from reading about the oppression of innocent people. Brian put his arm around her and tried to comfort her. He thought they had had enough, but then he noticed a small book entitled *Leadership of the Third Reich*. It was by an American author and, oddly enough, it was in English. Picking it up, he started looking through it.

He found a section about Nazi propaganda and how it codified and solidified the philosophy of the Führer's leadership. The premise was that Joseph Goebbels was the mastermind of the Third Reich. He was a genius at making the German people believe in the dreams and vision that Adolf Hitler had for Germany. Some believed he was like a good public relations man—creating an image of the Führer that was indeed larger than life.

By early 1939, Goebbels who had a Ph.D. in 18th century romantic drama and had been a journalist realized that his propaganda machine had to branch out. Even though he had several key staff members, he needed to solicit the help of the intelligentsia. He went to a selected set of universities and scoured them for members of academia who could assist him in further defining the Third Reich. Because of his scrutinizing personality, Goebbels found it difficult to find the types of people that suited his purpose. However, he did find one individual who he was convinced would bring the new blood that he needed to further the cause of the Führer. He was a young professor of economics at Freiburg University. His name was Heinrich Glossen.

Brian smiled and showed Laura the reference. The few hours they had spent in the library had paid dividends. They now knew Glossen's identity. Laura was grateful, but she was beginning to get sick to her stomach.

According to the author, Glossen was in his thirties when a representative of Goebbels approached him in January of 1939. He didn't belong to the Nazi Party, but he wasn't averse to it. He had been teaching at Frieburg for ten years. Considered by some to be one of the top intellectuals in the country at the time, he had actually received his Ph.D. when he was only 22. He had studied under Martin Heidigger and was grounded in philosophy. Goebbels believed he needed someone that could sanitize and better convey the principles of the Third Reich. He was sure that Glossen would do exactly that.

The negotiations took at least six months, but after persuasion he couldn't deny, Glossen became an assistant secretary to Goebbels. For the first month he worked on the propaganda staff, and he impressed the Führer himself with ideas about how the Third Reich could go down in history as a nation to be envied and about how Hitler would be remembered as a leader as great as Napoleon.

At the end of the war, after Hitler had committed suicide and other high-ranking commanders had been caught and taken to Nuremberg, Glossen was nowhere to be found. According to the author, to that day his whereabouts were unknown. A report had surfaced in 1960 that he had been spotted in Italy somewhere, but most scholars believed he had been killed or had committed suicide himself.

Brian looked over at Laura. "That bastard could still be alive."

She shook her head. "It's certainly possible."

Neither one talked on the way back to the hotel. Brian knew it would be difficult to locate Glossen, especially since they had no address. Chiemsee was a huge lake area and they would be foolish to go out there unless they had some clue of where he might be living.

Sitting down on the bed, Laura said, "Isn't there some kind of registry we could go to and get his address?"

"I don't know. I don't think so. He probably doesn't want to be found. Why would he want people to know where he lives?"

She looked a bit embarrassed. "Let's get some rest and discuss it over dinner." Laura watched as he winked. She knew better.

They took a cab to the west of Munich to go to a restaurant they had been told was magnificent. Located right off the Bayer Strasse, it was considered to be a five-star establishment by many. They were escorted to the back to a quaint little table. They looked the menus over closely and ordered the specialty of the house.

"You know," said Brian, "I'm frustrated as hell about Glossen. I mean this guy probably has the answers to all our questions. He has to know what these documents are all about."

"I agree with you. But will he tell us?"

Brian smiled. "That could be a problem. If he doesn't want to be found, he sure as hell isn't going to answer questions about the monastery. But I still want to find him."

Laura wasn't going to kid herself. Brian was an investigative reporter and his interest in this story was boiling over. "I'm concerned that even if we locate Glossen, it won't matter. How can we prove we talked to him?"

"Perhaps we could trick him. Maybe we can track him down and interview him, letting the Polizei come get him after we're finished."

"I'm sure he's not that stupid," Laura said. "Besides, the police aren't going to stand by while you interview the guy. Not only that, you won't get any credit for finding him."

"You're probably right."

"I'll tell you what I think. If there is a story here, it's never going to be told."

"What makes you think that?"

"There's no way to figure out something so obscure. We were turned away from the monastery. We have no idea where Glossen lives; at least we don't have his actual address. And we really don't have a reasonable guess about the connection between the birth certificate, the letter, and Hitler's Bible. None of it makes any sense, and now we are at a dead end."

"So you're just giving up."

"I don't know what else to say."

"Perhaps we should go back to Hagenmünster. We can find the monk that gave us Glossen's name. He has to know something. Why else would he tell us we could be in danger?"

"I'm not so sure. The monk probably won't want to be approached about it, and he probably will deny it."

"You know I'm not one to accept defeat. There's always a way for a reporter to get what he wants."

The Caretaker's Bible

"Maybe we should call Ronny. He may be able to help," Laura suggested.

Brian didn't think it was a good idea, at least not yet. He had purposely not informed Ronny about the contents found in the Bible or the fact that it belonged to Adolf Hitler. Looking askance at Laura, he said, "You never told him about this, did you?"

"No. I never got the chance."

Brian felt better. Even though he liked Ronny, he had a hard time dealing with his know-it-all personality. It was probably best if they tried to investigate the situation themselves instead of letting Ronny essentially take over.

Brian watched as a man walked into the front of the restaurant. He was tall, slender, and wearing a black cape and fedora—he caught Brian's eye only because he looked ominous. He noticed that the man stopped and surveyed the crowd. Suddenly, the man started to walk to the back of the restaurant, right to where they were sitting. He stood in front of them. Laura grabbed Brian's arm. The man asked if he could sit down. Brian reluctantly agreed.

"My name is Manfred Wormser and I only wish to talk to you." He undraped his cape and put it over his chair, then took his hat off and placed it on the table to the side before finally sitting down.

Still clutching Brian's arm, Laura squeezed harder. "What can we do for you, Herr Wormser?" Brian asked. He couldn't help but notice that Wormser was wearing a gold plated onyx ring on his right hand—engraved with what looked like the letter F raised in gold, which seemed peculiar to Brian.

"I know who you are, Herr Bennett. It is good to finally meet you." Wormser's accent was rather heavy, but he spoke very good English.

"How do you know who I am?"

Wormser laughed. "I read American periodicals. I know you write for *Time* magazine. I even saw your picture in one of the issues. I admire your work, Herr Bennett."

"Thank you." Brian felt a sense of déjà vu. He had heard the same thing from Gerta in New York. It seemed strange, but Brian wasn't sure what to make out of it.

"You must be on holiday here in Munich. It is such a wonderful place to visit, is that not so?" He gave Brian a cold stare and ordered a Weizen Beer. "Given the choice, I would not live any place else."

Brian had been sizing up Wormser. He appeared to be in his mid-fifties. He had a gaunt narrow face with a scar on his left cheek, and was wearing small, round, black-rimmed glasses. His black suit and tie accented his bright white shirt. What was disconcerting was that his jet-black hair was shaved around his ears similar to Hitler's style.

Laura, beginning to get even more concerned, asked Wormser, "How did you know we would be in this restaurant eating?"

"Do not be alarmed. It was just a suspicion, I assure you." He sipped his beer and put the glass down, looking around. "Will you be in Munich long?"

Laura shook her head. "We are just here for a few days."

"We're on vacation," Brian added.

"That is very interesting," Wormser replied. "I thought you were here to cover the Summer Olympics. Is this not true?"

Brian paused and looked over at Laura. He wasn't sure what to say. "How would you know such a thing?"

"I have my sources, Herr Bennett. I told you, I am interested in your work. It is not unusual for me to know these kinds of things. So I ask you again: Are you here long?"

"Yes. I am covering the Olympics. But of course you already knew that."

Slowly, Wormser took a cigarette case out of his pocket and put it on the table. "Do you like sports, Herr Bennett?"

Brian's eyes shifted down to a small swastika, barely noticeable, on the silver case. Wormser took out a long thin cigarette and lit up. The smoke had a putrid smell.

Wormser's attitude was starting to wear thin on Brian. It was as if he were interrogating them. And it was obvious by his display of the Nazi symbol of power that he was still living in the past. Brian replied, "I enjoy sports. I've written about them for years and seem to have a knack for it."

Wormser smiled. "I am a great admirer of physical competition myself. I played soccer when I was young and love the idea of winning. Of course that is what sports are supposed to be about. Would you not agree?"

"Yes," Brian replied, beginning to feel uneasy.

"I thought so. But that is not why you are here, is it, Herr Bennett?"

Brian could see Laura out of the corner of his eye straighten in her chair. He knew she was nervous and wanted to be careful about what he said. "What do you mean?"

Wormser puffed on his cigarette. "I simply mean you are not just here to write a story about the Olympics. You have other business here."

"I'm not sure I know what you're talking about."

"Come now, Herr Bennett. Surely you must realize I know why you have come to Munich." He put out his cigarette and lit another one. "We can talk about it, can we not?"

"If we must."

"I did not join you at your table just to be cordial," Wormser said. "I represent a time-honored and clandestine organization that is called the *Freundenreich.* Our objective is to protect the integrity of the greatness of the Reich under the leadership of Adolf Hitler."

Brian was beginning to get annoyed.

"We must preserve what was once grand. Do you think Nazi Germany is dead?"

"Yes, of course. But what does this have to do with us?" Brian asked.

"It has everything to do with you," Wormser replied. "You recently came into possession of some documents. Where are they?"

Brian glanced over at Laura. "I think you're mistaken."

Wormser frowned. "I do not make mistakes. What have you done with them?"

"Nothing! Now I want you to leave and let us finish our meal."

Wormser looked deeply into Laura's eyes and said, "Perhaps *you* will tell me the truth."

Brian put his arm around her. She was scared and replied, "I have no idea what you are talking about."

Wormser sneered as he talked. "Let me tell you a story. After the war ended, the Russians confiscated many of Hitler's private and personal artifacts. It is conceivable that the Americans managed to salvage a few themselves. Ever since then, the *Freundenreich* has made every effort to get them back. We will stop at nothing to get what rightfully belongs to the Third Reich."

"What do you want?" Brian angrily asked.

"I want the Bible. Where is it?" The piercing look in Wormser's eyes was almost evil.

"It doesn't belong to you or the Third Reich," Brian replied.

Wormser pounded the table, practically knocking everything off. "You obviously have not been listening to what I have said. I want the Bible, and you will give it to me."

Laura looked around, realizing all eyes were on them. It was embarrassing. She asked Brian if they could leave. He agreed, but he wanted to end the conversation.

"What about the other documents?" Brian asked.

"The letter and birth certificate? They are not important. They mean nothing."

"I don't know how you found out about the Bible, but I don't have it with me. And even if I did, I wouldn't give it to you."

"You must stop your meddling into our affairs and stick to what you do best—writing." Wormser drank down much of his beer and stared at Brian.

"Where is Heinrich Glossen?" Brian asked. "I want to talk to him."

"It will not do any good."

"Why?"

"Because he is dead."

"Why should I believe you?" Brian asked.

"Glossen died only days ago and we have already buried him with full Third Reich honors."

The Caretaker's Bible

"I believe the documents do mean something and I'm going to find out what the hell that is. Let me tell you, Herr Wormser, you don't scare me one bit. There's a story here, and once I find out what it is, I'm going to tell the world."

Wormser finished his beer and casually collected his things. "I warn you, Herr Bennett. I will have that Bible. You are interfering with something you know nothing about. If you persist in this madness, you will be in serious danger." He stood up and put his cape back on. "I hope I have made myself clear."

They both watched as Wormser started to weave his way through the tables, finally walking out the door. Laura was shaking and Brian tried to calm her down, but they were both in shock, experiencing total disbelief over what they had just gone through.

Laura said, "I think that whole conversation was like something out of a movie. I can't believe that a group still exists in 1972 that promotes Nazi thinking and values. It's scary—and you and I are in the thick of it. We apparently have walked into the wolf's lair. I'm starting to think we should forget about the whole thing."

Back in the hotel room, Brian immediately asked to see the Bible and both documents. Laura pulled them out of her handbag. Seeing that they were intact, he sat down on the bed.

Laura said she was terrified. "What if they know where we are staying? I mean, he knew where we were having dinner. How are we going to hide these things?"

Brian thought for a second. "We need to get out of here. I was thinking on the way back to the hotel, why don't we go to Radda in Chianti and track down the caretaker? He has to know something about the origin of the Bible. Besides, that will get us away from here."

"How are we going to get there?" Laura asked, frustrated.

"We'll go to the airport and take our chances." He pointed to the suitcases and told Laura to start packing.

"What about the Olympics?"

"We'll worry about that later. Besides, they don't start for two weeks." Brian now knew that time was of the essence. And because of the unfortunate meeting with Wormser, he would be forced to stay one step in front of him.

Within the hour they were standing at a ticket counter, booking a flight to Milan. Every so often, Brian would have Laura check her handbag just to ensure the Bible and documents were still there.

chapter 9
Berlin—1940

THE SOUNDS MADE BY the cleats on the officers' boots as they walked down the high polished floor of the Reich Chancellery echoed throughout the building. The high ceilings created a sense of power. The first floor was highly decorated with Nazi flags, replicas of swastikas, and several pictures of the Führer in different attire. It was all a tribute to the man who had single-handedly transformed Germany into an elitist nation.

The culture in the Chancellery was such that every issue discussed and every paper signed was in direct support of the Führer. It would have been an understatement to say that Hitler was a man busy waging war. However, most of what he dealt with was self-imposed. He had never really learned to delegate authority; he had to be informed on a continuous basis about everything that was occurring, mainly because he didn't trust anyone. His aim was total domination of the Third Reich.

After several failed attempts to energize the army in late

1939, Hitler had decided again to attack the West in January 1940. Unfortunately, a German staff officer who had made a forced landing resulting in a crash en route from Münster to Cologne on 10 January had inad vertently compromised some of the operation because paperwork had ended up in Belgian hands. This event tried Hitler's minimal patience as he decided what to do next.

Even though he didn't show it, at times like this, the Führer appreciated the views of his staff. He listened to men he believed were gifted. Heinrich Glossen's insight into Hitler's personal thoughts was always astounding. He seemed to be attuned to what the Führer was thinking before he said it. Other leaders under Hitler, such as Manfred Wormser, ultimately benefited from Glossen's sense of clairvoyance. Glossen's insight also created a fertile ground for jealous behavior by individuals who thought they had the respect of the Führer.

* * *

Glossen sat in his spacious office waiting for his secretary to join him. He was still infatuated with his position within the ranks of the Third Reich. It was hard to believe he had such influence. He realized, however, that working with Goebbels could be either a blessing or a curse, and that was foremost in his mind.

"Excuse me, sir, is this a good time?" Eva Dofmünster asked as she stood in front of his desk.

"Please, sit down. Be comfortable."

Eva sat down in a chair positioned on the right side of Glossen's desk. "You wanted to talk to me?"

"Yes," Glossen replied. "In a recent meeting with the Propaganda Minister, he decreed that it is time to allow a small group of trustees to learn about Horst and to help make a decision how to proceed in regards to telling the Führer."

"I understand. I can set up such a meeting."

"Splendid. I also have been asked to write a report concerning German military prowess and the respect the High Command members have for their leader."

"Propaganda. Of course." Eva showed a slight smile.

"It could be nothing, but our generals are tired of the Führer's misguided leadership. They are not sure that it is in our best interest now to attack the West. There are far-reaching consequences."

"The Führer is adamant. What can we do?"

"It is somewhat of an enigma. But we must be cognizant of the feelings of most citizens. I have talked to many Germans about Hitler's plans to wage war and they are not well received. It is our job as the propaganda directorate to turn that perception around."

"We can only do what is humanly possible. We cannot be expected to perform miracles."

"Indeed, we cannot. I will draft a memorandum and let you edit it. Expect it on your desk within the week. Meanwhile, we must contemplate what must be done to prepare Horst for the inevitable."

Eva departed with the straight face she usually wore when confronted with a challenge.

*   *   *

The meeting had been set for two days. Eva sat in the corner with a notepad. Glossen had called together a select group of his staff to listen to the plan he would present to Goebbels concerning the introduction of Hitler to his brother. It was a delicate operation. To date, no one had even discussed the issue with the Führer. Glossen knew that had to change. Hitler most assuredly would not be receptive to such a thing unless he had been briefed and made aware of the reality that they could be related. Even then, he might not accept it. After all, there was only one Adolf Hitler.

The tiny conference room was full. Glossen cleared his throat. "I want to be clear. Horst is on the top of my agenda. He will be ready to meet the Führer in only days now. Is that understood?"

Wormser, who had arrived at the meeting late, said, "Certainly, Herr Glossen. But to what end do we take the chance the Führer will accept the notion of a twin?" His stare was typical.

"Horst is now ready to meet with the leader of the Third Reich.

The meeting shall go off as planned. I want to introduce him with only Herr Goebbels present."

"I fail to see the importance of that," Wormser replied, standing up abruptly. "I want to be there. I must be there."

Glossen's awkward smile signaled to Wormser that he wasn't welcome.

"Have you thought what will happen if the Führer dismisses Horst as a fraud? And will you take all the credit then?" Wormser sat back in his chair and snickered under his breath.

"Of course, Herr Wormser. But I believe it will be undeniable. If not, you may take the credit." The attendees tried not to laugh, but it was blatantly obvious they all thought the exchange was funny. Glossen smiled. "My plans are to meet with the Führer within two day's time to broach the subject with him. I am not sure of the words I will use, but I believe they must be awe-inspiring. If not, the grandiose plan will fail. I must focus Hitler's attention enough to discuss his family—something that is not out of the question if the subject is approached properly. Hitler often reflects on his mother and his siblings. That is a start. I will tell the Führer how much research I have done to find Horst in a small town outside of Linz. The problem is whether to tell him that Horst is his twin brother or just introduce the two of them and let Hitler make the inference."

Wormser leaned forward on the table. "You must be careful, Herr Glossen. The Führer is a busy man. I would not want you to anger him in spite of your seemingly good intensions."

"Your concerns are baseless," Glossen replied. "That I am sure of."

The attendees at the meeting looked around at each other—not one wanting to agitate either of them.

Wormser stared straight ahead for several seconds. "I am convinced the Führer will not believe Horst is his twin any more than he believes that the long-suffering Russian Army can defeat Germany. Remember several years earlier when someone in the cabinet had the idea to create a double for Hitler so he could be better protected? Do you recall what happened, Herr Glossen?"

"Yes, of course." Glossen didn't want to talk about it. Hitler had gone into a tirade when he found out what they were doing and had lectured Goebbels for over an hour at the top of his lungs, saying there was only one Führer. "I understand it was a terrible occasion for the Minister of Propaganda."

"We must learn from our mistakes. Always," Wormser said rather tersely. "I am rather surprised that Goebbels has even agreed to this nonsense."

Glossen pounded his fist on the table. "It was his idea to go to the monastery and find him. He considers this an ideal situation and thinks it is time for the Führer to at last have some rest."

"So Goebbels believes the Führer's reaction will somehow be much different now?"

"Yes." Glossen wanted desperately not to get pulled into the mind games Wormser was known to so eloquently perpetrate. Glossen knew what he had been told to do and was comfortable with the way he was executing the plan. Both Glossen and Goebbels had to prepare the way for Horst. They believed that even though Hitler was consumed with war, he could be persuaded to listen to what they had to say. Certainly the birth certificate and letter from Brother Dimitrius would be of great value. It would give the Führer a base of reference from which to begin to believe the truth about his brother.

*   *   *

Several weeks after their meeting, Glossen and Eva went to see Horst. Light snow was falling and Glossen decided to walk from the Chancellery to the hotel to relax. He confessed to her that he was still not sure Brother Matthias had really become Horst. He was leery to let Hitler see and talk to him for fear that the lifelong monk would say the wrong thing and upset the Führer. Undoubtedly, it was one of the most difficult things Glossen had ever tried to accomplish.

Once inside the room, Glossen asked Horst to take a seat so they could talk. After taking off his snow-covered coat, he hung it up on a hook by the door. Eva kept her fur coat on. Horst appeared to be angry about something. Glossen wasted no time in engaging him in conversation. "I know what is wrong. You miss Hagenmünster."

Horst shook his head while he looked at the floor. "The monastery is the only home I have known for many years. Berlin is not the same."

"You must understand the importance of being here." Glossen didn't want to give a lecture, but he knew he had to make it clear to the monk why he was sitting there instead of someone else. "You are the identical twin of the leader of the Third Reich. You must take your rightful place next to him. You will have to remain in the shadows, but just your presence could give the Führer the incentive he needs to reach his goals."

"I have asked God for forgiveness," Horst said.

"Why?" Glossen asked.

"I have a hard time explaining it. I know I have to come to grips with being the brother of a dictator, but it is still hard for me to understand. Part of me believes it and another part of me doubts deeply whether it could be true. But in a strange way, I am honored that I might somehow make the Führer's life a bit better by being here for him. I have been taught ever since I first became a monk that God's will is embodied in doing good deeds such as taking care of people. I have somehow been chosen to look after my brother—at least that is how I look at it."

"Are you prepared to meet the Führer?" Glossen asked.

"No. I do not feel worthy. I do not think Hitler will accept me as his brother. Even if he believes I am related to him, what will my role be? What do you want me to do?"

Glossen thought he was making headway at last. It appeared that Horst was serious about his new identity. He wasn't taking it lightly and wasn't rebelling. "Assuming that the Führer accepts you as who you are, I believe we will have to make further decisions as to what to do. I am convinced that over time I can possibly persuade Goebbels to allow you to stand in for some events—cordials, parties, and perhaps some meetings with dignitaries, especially if Hitler is feeling under the weather."

The Caretaker's Bible

Horst asked, as he had done numerous times, "Will I ever be allowed to return to the monastery?"

"It could be possible, but it is too early to make promises. We must spend our time rehearsing for your meeting with Hitler. I have an idea. Perhaps you should be dressed in similar garb as the Führer. It would give him the impression that he is looking in the mirror." Then he remembered what Wormser had said about the attempt to introduce Hitler to his double. As Glossen recalled from what he had been told, the double looked nothing like Hitler. It was a farce from the beginning. In fact, Hitler never even saw him.

"What if he meets me and he thinks I am an impostor? What will happen to me?"

"That is a fair question," Glossen replied. "I certainly will protect you against retribution. If nothing else, if things do not go well, I will take you back to Hagenmünster. But I really believe in my heart that Hitler will accept you as his brother. We just have to take a little more care in the preparation phase."

While walking back to the Chancellery, Glossen told Eva he realized that it was now only a matter of time until he could formally introduce the Führer to Horst. He couldn't wait to solidify his plans.

* * *

After sleepless nights, Glossen, who was now practically hallucinating, decided he would simply go to see the Führer and tell him about Horst without any consultation with his colleagues. As he was walking out the door, Wormser asked for a minute of his time.

"What do you want?" Glossen asked.

"I want to know if you have come to your senses."

"What does that mean?"

"You are committing suicide if you think the Führer will believe your ridiculous story. You must abandon your grandiose ambitions."

"I think you are out of line."

Wormser walked into Glossen's office and sat down. "Come now. Do you really even believe it yourself? You are certainly not that naive."

"I know it to be true."

"Perhaps you want to make a name for yourself? Is that it?"

Glossen walked in front of Wormser. "You know what I think? I think you are jealous. I think you would like nothing better than to announce Horst as your own, making you a hero—at least in your own eyes."

"There is no truth to that and you know it. Conversely, you will make a fool of us all. You must take the monk back to where he belongs and forget about falsely impressing the Führer."

"You have made your point. Now I have other important things to do."

After Wormser left, Glossen agonized over what to do, but within several minutes thought better about telling Hitler about Horst prematurely. He would wait until he was more likely to get the response he so feverishly sought. Though he would never tell him, he had Wormser to thank for saving him a tremendous embarrassment.

chapter 10
Italy, Austria—1972

The four-hour drive from Milan to Tuscany was extremely hot because their rental car had no air conditioning. As they detoured through San Gimignano, they passed fields of tall sunflowers still worshiping the sun in the mid afternoon. Many of the vineyards were still ripe with grapes. The narrow, two-lane roads didn't have much traffic, but they were hard to navigate simply because of the way the early Romans had designed them: twisting up and down hills.

Laura seemed impressed with what she had missed two months earlier. She gazed around her and said the scenery in all directions appeared like an Italian master had painted it with bold strokes of dark, rich colors. It couldn't have been any more beautiful. They traveled east closer to Radda in Chianti. Brian realized that Horst often times went away so the chance of him being there was not good.

"Do you think the caretaker will be honest with us?" Laura asked.

"I have no idea what Horst knows about the Bible. It's entirely possible he doesn't even know the Bible belonged to Hitler. If he had known, he would have probably never given it away."

They slowly drove up the gravel road to Villa Pontevechio, where they parked and looked around. Brian noticed that there were no other cars parked in the driveway and that the villa looked empty.

"I would think this place would be rented all the time," Laura said.

"You would think so."

"How'd you find this place? Wasn't it your friend in Milan?"

"Yeah. According to the caretaker, the man who owns this villa is from Germany and lives there most of the time. I think it's rented through an agency in Siena."

They walked up to the villa. Brian went around to the back. The pool had been drained. It looked like no one had been there for a while. He peeked through a window behind the villa; there were no signs of life.

"Maybe they rent it only a few months a year," Laura said.

Brian wanted to get inside, but the doors were locked.

Laura said, "Don't do something stupid. We don't know the laws in Italy. If we get caught breaking and entering, we could end up in a local jail not knowing the language."

"Damn it. I knew he wouldn't be here." Brian stood near the pool and looked around. He noticed a smaller villa off a dirt road down the back slope. It looked like they could drive the car there. "Got an idea. Let's go ask if anyone there knows anything about this villa."

Laura laughed. "Okay. They may not speak English or German. How are we going to communicate?"

"Hand signals. How the hell do I know?" He was convinced they could get their point across.

When they got there a young man was in front of the villa watering the flowers.

Brian approached him and asked slowly if he spoke English. The man smiled and said he spoke some. Brian asked if he was the caretaker.

"No. My name is Otto Brandt. I am the owner. Can I help you?"

Brian said, "I just spent two weeks at the Villa Pontevechio and met the caretaker. I need to contact him. It's important."

Otto seemed confused. "As far as I know that villa has not been rented for at least a year. I have no idea who the caretaker could be."

"You don't understand. I was just there in June. The caretaker's name is Horst. Do you know who I'm talking about?"

"I am sorry. I do not know a Horst. The owner of the villa was making repairs over a year ago and said he would not be renting it out for a long time."

"Who is the owner?" Brian asked.

"He is German. I do not know his name."

"But you've met him," Brian said.

Otto chuckled a bit. "Yes. I did say that."

"What does the owner look like and does he ever stay at the villa for periods of time?"

"The owner is older, and it is hard to describe him. He only visits every once in a while."

Laura said she was beginning to realize the problem. If the villa had been closed down for repairs, then how did her fiancé stay there for two weeks? And who was the caretaker? "Are you saying that no one has rented that villa for the entire summer?"

"Not that I know of. But I was away in June, so I suppose it is possible."

Brian was at a loss, but he knew he wasn't insane. He had stayed at the villa and talked to Horst on numerous occasions. "Why would they just rent it for two weeks?"

"Perhaps you should try to contact the real estate agents in Siena. They would know. It had to be rented through them."

Brian looked through some of the papers in his briefcase. He found the address. He thanked the owner and they departed.

"What's going on here?" Laura asked. "Something's not right."

"I agree. If the owner is being truthful—and there isn't any reason to believe he is not—then how did I get to rent the villa? What bothers me more is the identity of the caretaker. Who in the hell is he?"

It took about forty-five minutes to get to Siena. Then they drove around for at least another twenty minutes until they found the rental agents.

A young lady greeted them in Italian, realized they were Americans, and then asked them in English to have a seat. "What can I do for you? Would you like to rent a villa?"

Brian immediately explained their confusion over Villa Pontevechio and asked if the lady could verify that the villa had been rented in June. She said she would have to check the rental agreements in the back. Brian said they would wait.

A half-hour later, a much older woman, stern looking and not as pleasant, sat down at the table. "What do want to know about Villa Pontevechio?"

Laura tried to explain. The older woman stopped her in mid sentence. "This villa has not been rented for a year. At least! I am sorry, but it is impossible that you were there in June."

Brian said rather loudly, "No. I was there. I was just there in June."

"You are mistaken. Perhaps you were at a villa close by. If you had been at our villa, we would have known about it. Besides, it was closed."

Laura leaned over and whispered in Brian's ear. "We're not going to get anywhere. Are you sure your friend rented the villa from this agency?"

"Yes. He gave me the address. It has to be this one."

The woman apologized and said she had other matters to tend to and promptly got up and excused herself.

Not knowing how to respond, Laura convinced Brian that they should just get out of there and go think things over. They decided to spend the night at a small hotel in the old part of Siena, a beautiful area surrounded by an ancient Roman wall.

Sitting at an outdoor café, drinking a blush wine from the region, Laura said, "I can't help but feel the old lady was hiding something."

"Why do you say that?"

"I'm not sure, but she seemed to be on the defensive to me. Maybe there is something they don't want you to know."

Brian was frustrated. "I'm starting to think they didn't want us to know the identity of the caretaker. But that makes absolutely no sense. Why the hell would that be?"

"I haven't any idea. But why would they claim they never rented the place when you actually stayed there?"

Brian didn't have an answer. He looked around him. He was beginning to look at everyone as a threat. He wouldn't put it past the *Freundenreich* to follow them trying to get their hands on Hitler's Bible. "We've got to go back to Hagenmünster."

"I don't know. I don't think so," Laura replied.

"No. We must. I'm convinced someone there knows the truth."

Laura didn't understand the connection. "Not about the villa."

"No, but once we find out what they're trying to hide, it may shed some light on what's going on here."

None of this sat well with Laura. "I'm exhausted. I think it would be less stressful reading manuscripts in my office."

"Just indulge me here. I'll tell you what. If we come up empty handed at the monastery, you can go home. I'll go cover the Olympics."

Laura didn't respond. She just gave Brian a contrived smile.

*   *   *

By the middle of the next day, they were making their way across Austria again, headed for Linz, hoping to stay at the same Gästhaus. Laura had agreed to go, but informed Brian she would not accompany him to the monastery. She knew what he would be up to: sneaking around the grounds and inside the sanctity of the monastery itself, which she considered to be God's house. He tried to persuade her that it was the only way he could get what he wanted, because the Abbot certainly wouldn't welcome him there. Laura wasn't buying it.

His plan was well organized. He would drive down to the monastery in the early morning hours. He would wait until the monks were in Morning Prayer in the chapel. Then he would go in and see what he could find. His real hope was that he would find the monk that gave him Glossen's address. It was at least worth a try.

In the morning, Brian got up slowly. He had tossed and turned all night—not getting much sleep. He hated leaving Laura by herself, but she had insisted. He left the Bible neatly tucked in Laura's handbag, but took the two documents just in case he found the monk he was looking for.

* * *

Parking the car at the monastery, he could see no sign of life anywhere. He cautiously climbed the granite steps and hid behind an oak tree, looking to see if there was anyone out in the courtyard. It was still dark, and the poor lighting within the courtyard complex made it hard to see. He needed to try to get inside before the bell sounded, waking the monks. He would have to find a suitable place to hide and wait for Morning Prayer. His mother had always been told that the front door of a monastery was always open in case a lost soul had to find his way. He didn't feel like one, but he had a mission to carry out.

He stepped as lightly as he could down a corridor. The church bell sounded, startling him. He ran down to a vacant room and hid in a corner and waited. He had researched the monks' routine. They rose, attended to personal hygiene, said silent prayers in their cells, and then went to Morning Prayer. Breakfast would be served after the service.

Once they were all gathered in Morning Prayer, Brian figured he had about an hour and a half to look around, given they all attended

The Caretaker's Bible

breakfast. He wasn't as calm as he thought he would be. He knew it was wrong to sneak around behind the monks' backs, but as far as he was concerned, he had no other choice. It was entirely possible the key to this mystery was right there at Hagenmünster.

He found the offices. There were a number of them—probably for counselors and secretaries of the Abbot. He entered a small but cluttered room adjacent to the Abbot's study. There were several pictures on the wall. Brian could tell at least two were older—possibly 1930s or '40s. Looking closely, he noticed that in every picture a congregation of monks was standing in front of the monastery. The pictures almost looked like college yearbook photographs.

He really wasn't sure what he was looking for. He glanced around and found nothing of interest. During the next half-hour, he crept from one room to another and was beginning to get discouraged. Finally he sat down and picked up what appeared to be a registry with names and dates. Thumbing through it, he noticed that some of the dates were in the early 1900s. He assumed the dates had something to do with when postulates finally became worthy of becoming monks. Still, he had no idea if the abandoned baby was among them. At best, he would have to verify the data, and that meant he would have to ask someone.

Out in the hallway again he moved slowly around a corner and walked to a rather large office. The light shining in the window seemed to fade quickly. The shadow overcame him. When he turned around, he noticed an imposing figure staring at him.

The middle-aged monk with his potbelly, long straggly beard, and crew cut moved closer. "May I help you?"

Brian tried to walk away quickly, but the monk asked him to please stop and talk to him. He asked Brian to go to his chambers. When they got there, the monk closed the door and offered Brian a chair.

"I am Brother Flavius. You must not be afraid. I will not judge you."

"No. I was just leaving. I didn't mean to alarm you," Brian said.

"Why have you come here to Hagenmünster?" the monk asked. He sat quietly and gazed at Brian like he knew who he was.

"I need to get some information. I don't know if you can help me."

"You must only ask, my son. I cannot help you if you do not tell me what it is you want."

Brian reached into inside pocket of his sports coat and retrieved the two documents. "Here. Look at these."

The monk put them on the table and reached into the desk, pulling out his glasses. He read both thoroughly and sat back for a minute. "Why do you want to know about these? Why do they matter to you?"

Brian tried to think how to express his feelings. Even if he discovered the truth, he didn't know if it would mean anything. He was reluctant at first, but finally said, "A slender monk approached me in Linz and warned me that I would be in danger if I pursued the story about Brother Matthias."

"I see. Did he tell you his name?"

"No. He never did."

Brother Flavius stood up and went over to an old bookcase, bent down, and grabbed a large book. It was a photo album that appeared to be very old. He blew the dust off and came back to his desk and placed the book in front of Brian. He opened it to a page a quarter of the way through and moved it closer to Brian. The monk pointed to a picture of a man, a monk, standing in front of the monastery. "His name is Brother Matthias."

Brian stared at the picture. The monk looked very young. "This must have been taken a long time ago."

"It was probably taken in the early 1920s."

"Who is it?"

The monk sat back in his chair and smiled. "It is the man you are after." Brian appeared confused. "He is the baby that Brother Dimitrius found on the doorstep of our monastery."

"So he does exist!" Brian blurted out, then apologizing for his over exuberance.

Brother Flavius began to tell the story. "In the late evening hours

The Caretaker's Bible

of the 20th of April, 1889, close to midnight, Brother Dimitrius, while taking a walk, discovered a baby abandoned on the steps leading up to the rectory. Upon retrieving the baby and taking him to the Abbot, the monks made a decision to contact the local physician who took care of the health concerns of the monastery. The baby was very sick and the doctor recommended that they prepare for a funeral mass and subsequent burial. Determined not to give up, Brother Dimitrius took the baby to his sister, who lived in a small town outside of Linz. Miraculously, over the course of several months, the baby's health improved and the monks of the monastery believed it was a blessing from God.

"After nursing the baby back to health and bonding with the child, the sister of Brother Dimitrius decided to raise the baby as her own. When he was old enough to go to school, he attended classes at the small Catholic school in the monastery. In his late teens, he decided to join the order of Benedictine monks. Brother Matthias had grown very close to the man he knew as his uncle, Brother Dimitrius, who had always believed the baby he had found was a sign from God—making him responsible for a special soul that had been wrongly deserted."

Fascinated by the story, Brian didn't want to interrupt, but he couldn't contain himself. "So Brother Dimitrius never found out who left the baby at the monastery?"

"No. He really did not want to know."

"Why?"

After a pause, Brother Flavius said, "There was no reason for him to know. Things happen for a reason in this life. This is but one example. Once Brother Matthias was ordained as a monk, he quickly showed himself to be a loving and caring representative of the Benedictine order. He was well respected by his brethren and exalted by the Abbot as an exemplary servant of God."

"Is he still here?" Brian asked.

"I am afraid not. He left many years ago. I cannot remember the exact date, but I think Brother Matthias departed Hagenmünster sometime around 1939 or 1940."

"Where did he go?"

"I do not think anyone ever knew," Brother Flavius replied. "I have always thought it was strange that such an exalted member of the order would just disappear into thin air."

"Did you know him personally?"

"Yes, but I was a young monk and had only been at Hagenmünster for two years when he left. I never knew him that well."

"What was he like?"

"He was gentle and kind."

After sitting and listening to Brother Flavius talk about Brother Matthias' life at the monastery, he still didn't see what it had to do with Hitler's Bible. He explained to Brother Flavius how he had come to find the written documents in the Bible that supposedly belonged to the Führer. Brian wasn't sure he should even bring up his meeting with Manfred Wormser, but he did. The monk denied knowing the former Nazi. Brian moved his chair closer to Brother Flavius. "If you don't mind me asking, why would the *Freundenreich* be interested in the Bible where I found these papers?"

The monk seemed at a loss. "I have no idea. I have no knowledge of the *Freundenreich*, and furthermore, how could I possibly know why they are interested in the Bible?"

"Why would one of your own warn me that I would be in danger if I pursued this story?" Brian asked.

"I said I don't know."

Brian described the monk.

"That description is indicative of roughly half the brethren at the monastery."

"He gave me a note with the name Heinrich Glossen on it. Have you ever heard that name?"

"No. I have not."

Brian explained that Glossen was a Nazi working for Joseph Goebbels. Brother Flavius seemed neither surprised nor shocked but repeated he had no idea of the man's identity. Brian was trying to hold back his anger and was now more frustrated after listening to Brother Flavius' story. The pieces were not coming together. He had heard a lot of interesting facts, but none of them seemed to bridge a logical connection between Brother Matthias, Hitler's Bible, or the intense interest of the *Freundenreich*.

Brother Flavius sat with a docile smile on his face.

"Why are you telling me all this?" Brian asked. "I mean, the Abbot told me only a few weeks ago he knew nothing about a baby being left here at the monastery."

Brother Flavius replied, "Many at Hagenmünster simply dismissed the fact that Brother Matthias had been an integral part of the monastery, perhaps because he had left so suddenly. I cannot really explain it. It has never made sense to me."

Brian was staring at the picture. "May I have this?"

"Is it necessary?"

"Yes!" Brian really didn't know what he was going to do with it, but he figured if the monk were telling the truth, the picture would be at least some kind of proof that the abandoned baby had actually existed.

"I certainly have others. I will not deny you what you so passionately want." Brother Flavius slowly took the picture out of the album and handed it to Brian. "You must leave now. I will show you the way out." With that, the monk stood up and motioned for Brian to follow him. Minutes later, Brian was making his way to his car.

On the way back to the hotel, Brian had mixed feelings. While he had finally confirmed that the documents he found were valid, he still hadn't gotten enough conclusive evidence for a story. It was annoying—all that time spent trying to unravel a mystery and he still didn't have much to go on. When he got back to the hotel, Laura was lying on the bed reading the notes in the Bible. Brian sat down on the bed and threw the photo in front of her.

"What's this?"

"It's a monk."

"I can see that. Who is it?"

"Brother Matthias." Brian explained.

Laura was more than enthusiastic. She picked up the picture and studied it.

"What's the matter?" Brian asked.

"Have you really looked at this photo?"

"Yes. Why?" Brian looked over her shoulder. She didn't say anything at first. It was driving Brian crazy. "What are you talking about?"

"Look at his face. Look closely."

Brian took the picture and stared at the facial features.

"Do you see what I see?" Laura pointed at the face. "He looks like a spitting image of Adolf Hitler when he was a young man."

Brian thought he saw a resemblance, but he hadn't seen very many photos of Hitler when he was young. "How do you know that?"

"When we were in the library in Munich, while you were reading the book on Nazi leadership, I was looking through a book with several pictures of Hitler as a youth. I'm telling you, this is identical to what I saw."

"All right. But it has to be a coincidence."

"Does it?" Laura pointed out very adroitly that the birth certificate Brian had found was dated the same day Hitler was born.

"So what are you saying?" Brian's adrenaline increased—his heart beat a little faster. "You're not suggesting Adolf Hitler had a twin brother. Are you?" He thought of the consequences of what he had just said. "What if it's true? It would be an extraordinary story to break to the world. What do you think?"

Laura looked over at Brian and shrugged her shoulders. "I'm not sure it makes any sense."

"Why?" Brian asked.

"Why would parents abandon a baby like that? Why would they take it to a monastery? Besides, history books don't mention anything about a twin."

"It was probably sick. Maybe the parents wanted to give it to God by taking it to a monastery." Brian laughed about the reference to the history books. "If the parents took the child away, if they only recorded Adolf's birth, who would have known? Perhaps the doctor or midwife who delivered them could have been sworn to secrecy."

Laura got up and paced the floor. "You know, there may be something to this. Why is this Nazi group so interested in what we are doing? They have to be protecting something. What the heck is it? How are we going to prove Hitler had a twin? No one is going to believe us unless we have real proof. No one. I find it extremely hard to believe myself."

"Brother Matthias left the monastery sometime between 1939 and 1940."

"Where to?"

"No one knows; at least the monk I talked to didn't have any idea."

Laura grabbed the picture and looked at it again. "This looks exactly like him."

Brian tried to put the facts into some kind of reasonable order. They had a birth certificate of a baby that was born the same day as Hitler. They now had a picture of the abandoned child as a monk, and he closely resembled Hitler as a young man. Both the birth certificate and the letter from Brother Dimitrius were hidden in a Bible that once belonged to Hitler.

Laura grabbed the Bible and stared at it.

"Maybe the twin is still alive," Brian said, "and, for some reason, they don't want anyone else to know."

"But that would assume the Nazis had found out about the twin. Wouldn't it?"

"You're right. That's a logical conclusion. I think they must know. Why else would they be interested in us?"

"What are we going to do now? Laura asked. "It might be smart for me to just go home and think about things for a while."

"I don't agree. We need to pursue this. I want to get to the bottom of the story one way or another. I think we need to go to Branau am Inn. Try and find someone who knew the Hitler family."

"What for?"

"I'm not sure, but it's the right thing to do."

"But you have to go cover the Olympics. Do you really think anyone in Branau would discuss Hitler and his family now?"

"I don't know, but we have to try." Brian sat down and looked at his map. It looked like Hitler's birthplace was only 80 kilometers away. He figured they could find a cheap Gästhaus in the town and stay for as long as it took to get some information. Then they would go on to Munich.

"I'm getting tired," Laura said. "This isn't my idea of a vacation. I'm also getting scared. Who knows what Herr Wormser and his colleagues will do to get what they want. It's like witnessing a murder. The killer never gives the witnesses the opportunity to tell what they know. They're usually eliminated."

Brian realized his charm was evaporating. Laura was becoming disenchanted with his constant promises that they would figure it all out. "We now have a very importance piece of evidence—a picture of Brother Matthias. I guess it doesn't prove anything, but it's better than nothing."

Laura looked out their window. "What have we gotten ourselves into?"

"If any of this is true, this could be a hell of a story."

Laura spun around abruptly. "If we live to tell it!"

"I'm reasonably sure we will find someone in Braunau who can remember Hitler's family history. Perhaps even a childhood friend."

"But will they tell us what we want to know?" Laura asked.

"That remains to be seen."

chapter 11
Austria—1972

As they drove into Braunau am Inn, Brian felt completely unprepared. Other than going house to house, he didn't have any idea how to find out what he wanted to know. Undoubtedly, Brian knew they wouldn't find anyone privy to the birth, which of course meant that he would not find out who had delivered Adolf—doctor or midwife. But perhaps they could locate descendents of friends of the Hitler family. They might have vital information that could help round out the story.

They stopped at a Gästhaus in the middle of town. Brian introduced himself to the beer meister and said he was writing a story about dominant personalities in history and wanted to know if anyone in the town could discuss Hitler's early years. The response was not exactly forthcoming, but he told them of a woman who lived nearby whose grandfather was a customs inspector and had known Hitler's father very well.

Armed with the address, they made their way down several

blocks to talk to the woman. The home looked bleak, as if it had been there for centuries—faded brown concrete row house, black shutters, and a small dismal garden of dead flowers in front.

A middle-aged woman answered the door. Laura told her who they were and what they were doing. She said her name was Anna and that she would tell them what she knew but that she had to go to an appointment in several minutes. "My grandfather once told me that Adolf Hitler was born on Easter Saturday, 1889. It was not known who delivered the baby, but it was believed to be healthy and Alois Hitler was pleased he had a son."

Brian wanted to know more about Adolf as a young child. "Did he have many friends? Are there any still alive?"

Anna replied, "I personally know nothing about any friendships he had as a youngster. I must make it clear that the Hitler family moved away to a farm in the small town called Hatfield when Adolf was only six years old. They then moved to Lambach, roughly 37 kilometers south of Linz, two years later. One year after that the father bought a small plot of land in Leonding on the outskirts of Linz. Given that he moved around a lot, I believe it will be difficult to find anyone who knew the family, but I think I can help. There is a man who lives in Lambach who apparently had been a childhood friend of Adolf. He is a doctor and his name is Thomas Heisler. That is the best I can do."

Sitting in the car again, Brian looked at his map. They could make Lambach in probably less than an hour. There they would try to locate Dr. Heisler and ask him many of the same questions. Brian hoped he would be as cordial as Anna had been. He was frustrated that he hadn't gotten much information about Hitler's birth, but deep down inside he knew it was probably next to impossible to find out if there really had been a twin.

Locating Dr. Heisler was not as easy as they had hoped it would be. The doctor was retired and living right outside of Lambach. After an hour or so, they found the small farmhouse where Dr. Heisler now lived. He seemed reticent to let them in at first, but he agreed to talk to them for a short while. He escorted them into a large, rustic living room with a mammoth stone fireplace.

"We understand you were a childhood friend of Adolf Hitler," Laura said.

The doctor chuckled a bit. "That was many years ago but I did attend school with Adolf and at the time only lived down the street from him."

"What was he like?" Laura asked.

"Quiet. He did not have many friends."

"Did you spend a lot of time with Adolf?"

"We had an occasional relationship. We did things young boys do. Nothing unusual or special. He moved away after two years."

"Do you know anything about where or how Adolf was born?" Laura asked.

"I know nothing. I suggest you be careful; not many people want to discuss Hitler. It is understandably a touchy subject. I cannot be sure, but I believe there has to be someone in Leonding who would remember Adolf. It would be worth a try. But I do know of an individual living near Linz that had been close friends with Adolf after Hitler had left the *Realschule* at Steyr in 1905 and moved to Linz."

"Adolf would have been sixteen then," Laura said. "We should go and talk to this individual. He could possibly have more to offer."

"I really think we need to talk to someone who would have known Hitler in his early twenties," Brian replied.

Dr. Heisler said, "You will have to travel to Vienna for that since that was where Adolf lived from 1908 to 1913.

Laura turned to her fiancé. "We should make a decision what to do as soon as possible."

"I must ask what your interest is in Adolf Hitler," Dr. Heisler said as stood up, and then offered them a drink.

Brian asked Laura to show the doctor the Bible and tried to explain. While listening, Dr. Heisler thumbed through the pages, nodding as he went. Laura pointed out several of the passages she thought were most intriguing. "So you are convinced this Bible once belonged to Adolf?" Dr. Heisler asked.

"Yes," Laura replied. "There's no mistake."

Dr. Heisler put the Bible down on an end table. "This is a valuable document. I trust you know that. You must protect it. There are people who will do almost anything to get their hands on it. I would even go as far as to say there are a few wealthy individuals who would pay as much as a million *deutschmarks* to have it."

Brian wasn't sure he should bring up their meeting with Manfred Wormser. Instead, he asked Laura to show the doctor the picture of Brother Matthias.

Laura pulled it out and handed it to the doctor. "What do you make of this?"

After a few seconds studying it, Dr. Heisler handed it back to Laura and said it obviously was a picture of a young monk.

"Did you notice anything about the monk's facial features?" Laura asked.

"No. Not especially. Why?"

Laura showed the doctor the picture again. "Look at his face. It's Hitler's face."

He took the photo and squinted a bit. He admitted it did have a resemblance. "Where did you get this?"

Brian explained. The doctor seemed a little uneasy. Laura thought perhaps they had said something wrong because of the way he acted.

"I do not understand the meaning of this photograph. This is not Adolf Hitler—only a very good resemblance."

"Do you think it is possible that Hitler had a twin?" Brian asked.

"Absolutely not. That is utter nonsense. Why would you say such a thing? It is inconceivable that anyone would believe that Hitler had a twin brother. History is very clear: four siblings had died in childhood, a younger sister died twelve years ago, but he never had a twin."

Brian could tell the conversation was not welcome and apologized for upsetting him. "Who should we contact in Vienna?"

Dr. Heisler excused himself and went to his library. When he came back he had a registry filled with names. Sitting there for a few moments, he fixated on a name. He took a piece of paper out of a small notebook and wrote down the name and address of Joseph Schäffer and handed it to Brian.

"Do you think it's worth our while to go to Vienna?" Brian asked.

"Yes. Of course. He knew Adolf very well. A close friend, as I understand it. You must talk to him. But he will tell you the same thing: Hitler did not have a twin, if that is what you are after."

Laura looked at her watch. "We must be going."

Driving down the street, Brian had to confess he felt embarrassed about telling Dr. Heisler his suspicions. It was insane to think it could be true. Except every time he looked at the photo and remembered the birth date, he had no choice but to believe it.

Laura stared at the picture as they maneuvered out of town. It seemed to mesmerize her.

Heading east, Brian had a plan. They would drive to Vienna, probably getting there very late in the evening. The next morning they would track Schäffer down and see what he knew—at least get an understanding of what Hitler was like when he was living in the Austrian capital.

*   *   *

A gusty wind added a terrible dimension to the downpour that deluged Vienna in the late morning hours. Brian and Laura stood in their room and looked out the window. The weather forecast called for rain all day. Brian thought they should wait for the winds to at least die down before they ventured out to find Schäffer. He sat on the bed and put his head in his hands, resting his elbows on his knees. He was tired. Mentally collapsed. He was beginning to think they were chasing a phantom idea. But no matter how Brian looked at it, the Friends of the Third Reich had an intense interest in what they were doing, and it wasn't just the Bible—and that bothered him. What in the hell did they really want? It was disconcerting, but he knew he had to continue his investigation.

Laura wanted to head out and locate Schäffer regardless of the rain, so they agreed to go. The address they had been given was in the south of the city. Finding the street was fairly uncomplicated since they had a map. Once they pinpointed the address, they parallel-parked the car.

Joseph Schäffer appeared to be older than he must have been. He was hunched over, very thin and emaciated, and his face looked a hundred years old. He was reluctant to let Brian and Laura in, but when Brian said it was imperative they talk to him, he reconsidered.

He took them into a small living room. Brian glanced around. It was very plainly decorated with an uncomfortable-looking couch, several straight-backed chairs, and a coffee table. What caught Brian's eye were the paintings hanging on the walls—city squares, castles, and magnificent, mountainous countrysides. They were exquisite.

Schäffer slowly sat down and asked, "What can I do for you? You seem like such a nice couple."

Brian didn't want to alarm the old man. "We are doing a documentary about Austria during World War II."

That apparently excited Schäffer. "I will certainly take the time to answer your questions."

"Would you tell a bit about yourself?" Brian asked.

"I was born in Vienna in 1887. My father was a banker and my mother an opera teacher. I attended school in Vienna from grade school to university. After graduating, I became a banker."

"What did you do during the war?" Brian asked.

"I remained a banker. I must say I never fought in the war."

"What do you know about Adolf Hitler?" Brian carefully watched for Schäffer's reaction.

"I know a little. Why?"

"I understand you knew him personally," Laura said.

Schäffer's demeanor suddenly became sullen and his face whiter. "Is this why you have come here?"

Laura replied, "We are trying to find individuals who knew Hitler before he ever envisioned he would be the leader of the infamous Nazi regime."

The look Schäffer gave her made Laura believe he was about

to ask them to leave. But he spoke freely. "Yes, I knew him. We were young. Here in Vienna." He sat back and began to tell them his story. "Oddly enough, Adolf Hitler and I met in line waiting to attend *Lohengrin*, an opera by Wagner. It was in 1910. We seemed to get on well together right from the beginning. We both had a love of the opera, especially compositions written by Richard Wagner. At the time Adolf was living at the Men's Home and did not appear to have much money. His outward appearance was not the best—shabby clothes, dirty hair and fingers. By all indications, he was down and out. He admitted he had moved around quite a bit in the two years he had already been in Vienna."

"So the love of opera brought you two together," Brian said.

"I suppose. Nevertheless, there was something that attracted me to him. I am not sure what it could have been."

"What was he like?" Laura asked.

"Adolf had a complicated personality," Schäffer replied. "He was quiet much of the time, but when presented with a matter he felt strongly about, he would voice his opinion in no uncertain terms. Adolf believed he was destined for greatness somehow. He wanted to write an opera—one that would be revered as much as the operas written by his beloved Wagner. Or he wanted to be a renowned artist of oils and watercolors."

"What were your feelings about him at the time?" Brian asked.

"Obviously, he lived in a dream world. Did he seem to have delusions of grandeur to you?"

"I never thought of it that way. Adolf was a person who thought anything was possible. Even after being rejected as an artist, he still maintained a sense of inner survival."

"Did he ever say anything to you about his hatred of Jews?" Brian asked.

"We spoke of it often. Hitler had been exposed to many different views about the Jewish race since living in Linz. He believed he was poor for no apparent reason other than fate, and many Jews were rich and appeared to have a say in the government. He resented that, but he was an avid reader and developed much of his anti-Semitism from others he believed to be scholars. When Hitler lived on Felber

Strasse before residing at the Men's Home, he would go down to the kiosk on the corner and buy periodicals that ridiculed Jews. These magazines were clear in their message; the blue-eyed, blond-haired races of the world had to unite against what they considered to be the threat of domination by races such as the Jews. While the rhetoric was aimed at theory rather than practice, Hitler seemed to embrace it as everyday gospel."

"You knew him well. Did he ever talk about the consequences of being Jewish?" Laura asked.

"If you mean annihilation of the race, no. He was an enigma at the time. He actually had a few Jewish friends. At least acquaintances."

"What about the magazines?" Brian asked.

"I believe those periodicals influenced Adolf later in life. I remember that whenever Adolf passed what he knew to be a Jewish store such as a jeweler or a doctor, he would say that he resented Jews being in charge when the Aryan race was certainly destined to be the ruler of the world."

"Once he left Vienna and went to Munich, did you keep in touch?" Brian asked.

"Yes. For a number of years. We wrote letters to each other during World War I, but then we stopped. Once Adolf became involved in politics, he had little time to correspond with friends. I only saw him one time later. It was during the annexation of Austria when Hitler came to Vienna. He wanted me to join the Nazi Party and be his Finance Minister."

"You declined," Brian said.

"Yes. Adolf said he regretted my decision, but respected my reasons for not accepting. It was not what I wanted to do. I knew it would be a great honor, but I did not share the same philosophy as the Nazi Party. I thought I would be better placed as a banker in Vienna where I could do the most good."

"You never heard from him after that?" Laura asked.

"No. Never."

Brian took the Bible out and showed it to Schäffer. "Do you recognize this?"

The Caretaker's Bible

Schäffer gazed at it. "It looks like a well preserved Bible."

"It belonged to Hitler. That has been confirmed," Laura said.

Schäffer scrolled through it, stopping every so often to read the comments in dark pen. "This does look like his writing to me. Where did you find this?"

After Brian explained, Schäffer got up and went over to an old wooden bookcase. Sitting back down, he showed them a small notebook filled with flamboyant writing. "This belonged to Hitler also. He gave it to me before he left for Munich. In it he talks about his artistic expression and how he longed to be an artist."

Brian could see the similarity in the handwriting between the notebook and the Bible. He asked Laura to show Schäffer the picture of Brother Matthias.

"Is this some kind of joke?" Schäffer asked with a scowl on his face.

"No. It is a picture of a monk taken in the mid-to-late twenties. It was taken at Hagenmünster, a monastery near Linz."

"You could have fooled me. It looks like Adolf—thin, sunken cheeks and hair down on his forehead. This is how I knew him. This is incredible."

"Is there any possibility he could have had a twin?" Laura asked.

"That is impossible. He would have told me."

"What if he didn't know?" Brian asked.

"I am confident that even if he never knew, some historian by now would have figured it out. Just what are you suggesting? That the twin was separated at birth and taken away not knowing he was Hitler's brother?"

"Yes. It could be conceivable it happened that way," Brian said. "Don't you agree?"

Schäffer seemed taken aback and had a hard time responding as he stared at the photo. "May I have this?"

Brian looked over at Laura. He didn't want to part with it. In his mind, it was proof that a twin existed. "I'll tell you what. I'll leave it here tonight and be back tomorrow to pick it up. Can we take the notebook with us? I'll return it when we get the photo."

Schäffer agreed and asked if he could have the Bible as well.

Brian immediately declined, saying he was inclined not to let it out of his sight.

Disappointed, Schäffer asked them to come over in the early afternoon.

After they departed, Brian said he wanted to get a bite to eat and then go back to the Gästhaus and have Laura translate the notebook. That's how they would spend their evening.

*   *   *

Lying on the bed with light shining from the lamps on both end tables, Laura began reading some of Hitler's thoughts from the notebook while Brian laid back and listened. It was apparent from the start that Hitler tended to ramble and his thinking was not always coherent. But, of course, this was something of a diary. She remembered reading the long and wordy *Mein Kampf.* Yet this read much better.

Hitler talked a great deal about his love of art and that he found himself realizing early in life that he wanted to be an artist—a painter who could reveal beauty to the world. He was incensed that he had been rejected by the Academy of Fine Arts in Vienna. From what he had seen, he was as good if not better than most of the students who attended. His life's dream had ended with outright rejection from what he called an evil institution that was biased against strong Aryan blood, instead giving more credence to the Jewish population that seemed to have completely taken over the arts in Austria. It would not last. He knew Vienna was a hotbed of anti-Semitic thinking. The Jews would get what was coming to them. There was no doubt in Hitler's mind.

Brian shook his head. He figured any history buff would go nuts reading this kind of material. It was unbelievable. It was basically a prelude to *Mein Kampf.*

Periodically through the notebook, Hitler made reference to his life when he was very young. Events that occurred as a youngster had affected him greatly. The death of his father was welcomed, while the death of his mother was unequaled to anything else that ever happened to him. According to the notebook, he felt like the weight of the world had been lifted off his shoulders when his father died in 1903. Conversely, he felt the earth had ended the day his mother passed away from breast cancer in 1907. He saw no godliness in it and he believed she didn't deserve such a wretched, painful death. His tears would wash down his cheeks for months. Embittered, he carried on—day by day, month by month.

Somehow between the two incidents Adolf reconciled himself to be more than a common citizen, and his personality took on new dimensions. But he was restless and felt like he had lost direction by the time he had gotten to Vienna.

Laura skipped a few pages. She told Brian she was fascinated with Hitler's innermost thoughts. According to the text, Hitler seemed obsessed with music, art, and politics. He was passionate about all three. Music took him to places he had never been, art gave him an outlet for his soul, and politics gave him something to philosophize over. Sometimes his daydreams would blend together with the dreams he had at night. It was like he lived between two worlds.

Brian thought it was interesting that he tended to show extreme emotion every so often. Hitler hated the fact that he had been rejected a second time from the Academy of Fine Arts in October of 1908. His career as an artist was seemingly destroyed. He had no way of digesting the failure. His watercolors and oils were magnificent—at least in his own eyes. The rejection was more than he could take.

Hitler spent a great deal of time discussing Jews. It was obvious that it was something that obsessed him more than anything else. The more he saw them, the more he set them apart from humanity. He wasn't sure why. But everything he read castigated them. He could sense the bitter feeling right there in Vienna. If nothing else, Hitler believed that the Jews had a place in society, but he knew it wasn't in government. He saved that for the mighty Aryan race.

Toward the end of the notebook, Hitler rambled on about his future. It was 1913 and he had avoided the Austrian draft for three years by then. He was twenty-four and thought he needed to go to Munich to try to reconstitute his life. He was positive that the Austrian authorities would not pursue him there. Admittedly, he didn't have what it took to be a soldier—the sense of rigid discipline, the stamina to fight in terrible, rugged terrain, or the willingness to die for something he didn't believe in. There was more to life than floundering in the military. It just wasn't apparent what that was, but he figured he would soon find out. He planned to leave Vienna with no regrets, only a small suitcase and a dream for a better tomorrow.

Laura turned to Brian and put the notebook down. "I really wish we could keep this."

He smiled. "Well, so do I, but a deal is a deal. Maybe if we hint around, Herr Schäffer will offer it to us." Laura didn't think they should hold their breath.

*   *   *

The next morning, after a late breakfast, they headed over to see Herr Schäffer. When they arrived, they noticed a couple of police cars were parked out front. A young officer met them at the front door and immediately asked who they were and what they wanted. Brian explained and asked if he could go in. The young officer allowed them to pass and an older gentleman asked them for identification.

"What's going on?" Brian asked. "What happened here?" He noticed the paintings on the wall were missing.

"I am a detective with the Polizei. I am investigating the savage attack on Herr Schäffer last night."

"Is he all right?" Laura gasped.

"I am afraid he is in critical condition. How do you know him?"

"We just met him yesterday. We are researching a book and had talked to Schäffer in the early afternoon." He looked around the room for the picture of Brother Matthias.

The detective asked, "Where did you stay last night? Can it be verified? After Brian explained, the detective said, "I must warn you that he is fighting for his life. He was unmercifully beaten and many of his possessions were taken. The motive appears to be robbery."

Laura knew Brian was getting nervous over the photo. He kept glancing around the living room.

"Are you looking for something?" the detective asked.

"No. Not really," Brian replied. "Can we see him at the hospital?"

The detective asked the young officer to escort them there immediately.

They briskly walked down the wide corridor to the nurses' station. Brian thought if they could just talk to him, he might be able to tell them who did this to him and—equally as important—the location of the photo. The look on the nurse's face said it all. She sadly announced that Joseph Schäffer had passed away an hour earlier of complications from the attack. There was nothing they could do.

"Did he have any belongings with him?" Brian frantically asked.

The nurse nodded no and walked away.

"What the hell are we going to do? We need that picture!" Brian slammed his fist against the wall.

"Calm down. It isn't the end of the world. After all, we have the diary."

"Damn them. It had to be the *Freundenreich*! We need to go back to the house and search for the photo."

Laura put her hand on his shoulder. "No. I'm afraid it's gone. We'll have to live without it now."

Brian looked out the window. He knew the stakes had just gotten much higher.

chapter 12
Munich—1972

THEY ARRIVED BACK IN Munich on September 2nd, six days after the Olympics had begun. Brian knew he would now have a tremendous workload. He had missed the opening ceremony, the first few days of intense competition, and the opportunity to interview athletes before they started their quest for a medal. It wasn't good. If Binneker found out, Brian would probably be severely chastised—or worse. Fortunately for him, several *Time* staff writers and photographers had arrived on time and covered what he had missed. He would have to convince them not to tell Binneker about his tardiness if they hadn't already done so. His plan was to make up for the lost time by spending most of his days at the games.

Laura thought perhaps she should go home since Brian was going to be so tied up. She wasn't sure even he should stay. Setting the Bible on the nightstand, she said, "It's a good thing we didn't give Herr Schäffer the Bible. It would now be in the hands of Manfred Wormser. This is only going to get worse. Maybe we should cool it for a while." She opened up the diary and began reading again.

"I can't leave now. You know that. Let's just back off for a week or so. Then we'll figure out what to do next."

Laura looked at her watch, calculating the time difference between Munich and New York. "I'm going to call Ronny."

"Come on. Is that necessary?"

Laura grinned. "I believe in strength in numbers—three heads are better than one. My friend knows quite a bit about the Third Reich and he can possibly help us figure out what to do."

"I don't know. I think we're doing a pretty good job ourselves."

Laura smiled and dialed for the international operator. The phone rang several times before Ronny picked up. He was surprised to hear from her. She briefly explained that they needed his help and asked him to join them in Munich. After a short pause, he said he would. He could be there in a day or so. Laura thought that was wonderful and said she would try to get him a room since they were in short supply. If not, he could stay in their room. She told Ronny to call when his flight was booked. They would meet him at the airport.

"He can't stay in our room," Brian said. "What the hell are you talking about?"

"I know. I just didn't want to discourage him from coming. I assume there has to be a hotel in the area somewhere that has a room available, even if it's 20 kilometers away."

"What's he going to do? We could have just asked him questions on the phone. He wouldn't have had to leave New York City."

"I believe we need someone who has some knowledge of Nazis and how they think. We have been fingered by the *Freundenreich* because we have Hitler's Bible, and who knows what other reasons they might have." She paced the floor. "We can't solve this alone."

He was tired of talking about it, and he had a lot of catching up to do with the games. He got dressed and told Laura that if she wasn't coming with him to guard the Bible and documents with her life.

Placing the Bible in her handbag, she decided to join him. They grabbed a cab and within no time were at the Olympic venue. With Laura right behind him, he immediately headed for the Aquatic Center. He had wanted to see Mark Spitz swim again, since he had seen him four years earlier at the Olympics in Mexico City. He looked at the program. It was the first of September and there were ten heats scheduled that day.

Once he saw Spitz swim, he wanted to go over to see the weightlifters. He wanted to do a piece on soviet heavyweight Vasily Alexeyev—a man who apparently didn't know his own strength. Brian had prepared a small notebook with people he needed to interview as well as events he needed to cover. In all, it would be a long two weeks.

Laura remembered reading an article about the 1936 Olympics. Hitler had presided over it and at one point had a zeppelin, the Hindenburg, make a pass over the stadium to show German supremacy. But athletes such as Jesse Owens and his astounding victories made it difficult for Hitler to depict the Aryans as the dominant race. Laura knew that Germany had certainly come a long way since the Nazi regime was in power.

After a long afternoon of moving from event to event, they decided to go back to the hotel. Laura was suspicious and walked around the room looking to see if anything had been disturbed. Brian sat down and wrote a few observations in his notebook. He had briefly talked to Frank Shorter and several of the basketball players and had to translate his notes into something that looked like coherent interviews.

His objective for the next several days was to cover as many main events as possible and interview as many gold medal hopefuls as he could find. Under the gun, Brian had to make this article one of the best he had done in years. He had to be honest with himself about his investigation. Even though he knew that something was terribly wrong and that they had stumbled into a hornet's nest, he wasn't sure what to do about it. Finding out the truth would come at a price, but now the trail had gone cold. He was at a loss as to what to do next. If Laura had anything to say about it, Ronny would tell them.

*   *   *

On 3 September, Laura and Brian met Ronny Whitaker midmorning at Munich Airport. After waiting nearly an hour to get his luggage, they drove Ronny to his hotel, which was roughly 40 kilometers outside the city limits in a small town called Bad Tölz. Laura had tried to get him a room at their hotel, but they were booked for the entire Olympic Games. Ronny wanted to get some work done and said he would be available for dinner if they so desired. Laura thought it was a great idea and offered to pick him up at seven o'clock. She said she would call first in case he had given in to jet lag and wanted a rain check.

The two of them went off to spend the day watching wrestling, boxing, swimming and—if they could swing it—a basketball game. Brian also decided to call his boss to reassure him that everything was going as planned. He was shocked but relieved to find out that his colleagues had never called his boss about his absence at the opening ceremony. When he reached him, Binneker was pleased that *Time* magazine was covering an Olympics where an American swimmer was breaking records right and left—winning gold medals like they were nothing at all.

At the end of the day, Brian wasn't at all sure he wanted to go to dinner, but Laura sweet-talked him into it. They found a small Gästhaus down the street from Ronny's hotel that served full meals. Even though it was a bit smoky and smelled of cigars, they decided to eat there.

"You're looking fit," Ronny said, looking at Laura.

"And you. I'm glad you came."

"I came as soon as I could. What's so important? I could hear a sense of urgency in your voice, so I'm happy to oblige. Besides, I needed a break from lecturing for a while."

Brian didn't know where to start. He thought that perhaps

explaining how he came to possess the Bible and what they had uncovered about it would be a good place to begin.

Ronny listened as Brian described the situation in a low tone, almost whispering, and then asked if they had the Bible with them.

Laura looked around the room and then reached into her handbag and handed it to him. He sat and studied it for a few minutes. Reading some of the passages seemed to arouse emotion in Ronny that he normally wouldn't exhibit. "Much of what I'm reading is pure hatred of mankind and of the Holy Bible itself. It's obvious a nonbeliever who made these comments."

Laura leaned over the table. "According to Myron Lewis, this Bible belonged to Adolf Hitler."

"Hitler? Did he get a second opinion?" Ronny asked.

Brian didn't hesitate. "Of course he did." Brian sneered at his friend. "I also found two very interesting documents in the back cover of the Bible."

"Why do you really think the caretaker gave you this Bible?" Ronny asked.

Brian replied he didn't know and explained that when they went back to Radda in Chianti, the caretaker was nowhere to be found. Then he related the story about the rental agency.

"Let me look at these documents." Ronny adjusted his chair closer to Laura. She was unsure whether she should show them then or back at his hotel, but realized they were sitting in the rear of the establishment and no one was paying any attention to them.

Ronny reviewed both pieces of paper. "These are interesting, to say the least, but I don't know what you can make out of them."

Brian stared at Laura. He asked Ronny the significance of the birth date. Ronny said it was the same as Hitler's. Brian began to tell him what occurred when they visited the monastery in Hagenmünster the first time.

"Perhaps he was telling the truth," Ronny replied.

"The Abbot told us a baby was never left at the monastery and that he wasn't even sure about the identity of Brother Dimitrius. A monk from the monastery approached us in Linz. He said we would be in great peril if we pursued this any further. He told us to just forget about it and go home."

"He didn't tell you why?" Ronny asked.

"No. But he gave us a name and an address of someone to contact."

"What's the name?"

"Heinrich Glossen."

Ronny sat in pensive thought for a minute or so. "I seem to recall that Glossen had worked for Joseph Goebbels in the latter years before the end of the war. He was a professor recruited by Goebbels to help him enhance the propaganda directorate. Apparently he was a brilliant tactician and was especially liked by Hitler. Glossen was perhaps one of the catalysts for convincing the Third Reich to step up their program of segregation against the Jews, but I can't be certain. Glossen, I believe, was one of the instigators and a key architect of The Final Solution to the Jewish problem that unfolded in early 1942. Later that same year, Glossen apparently helped in successfully using the United States' War Relocation Authority, which interned over a hundred thousand Japanese within the borders of the U.S., as a propaganda tool to show the world that the German government was merely acting in the best interest of their people, as was the United States."

"You seem to know a hell of lot about him," Laura said.

Ronny shrugged his shoulders. "I studied Nazi Germany for years. I also know several other scholars that have a good solid understanding of both Hitler and his Third Reich."

Brian asked, "How did Glossen escape allied hands at the end of the war?"

"It's impossible to tell. There were actually many lieutenants that got away. It was impractical for the allies to hunt down all suspected Nazis. The concentration of effort was against the leaders. Have you tracked him down?"

"He's dead," Laura said.

"How do you know?" Ronny asked.

Laura began to tell Ronny about their encounter with Wormser. Brian cut her off and finished telling the story.

"Manfred Wormser. I've also heard that name before." Ronny scratched his head.

"He is involved in a group he calls the *Freundenreich*," Brian said.

"It's roughly translated as the Friends of the Reich—the Third Reich. That's where I heard his name. The *Freundenreich* has existed since the war ended. It essentially is a secret organization that was created to preserve the dogmas of the Third Reich as well as its patriots. They have managed to recruit a diverse membership—doctors, lawyers, police officers, housewives, and even a large contingent of military officers. It was essentially impossible to know who they were by just looking at them."

Laura explained her feelings about the encounter in the restaurant. "I'm afraid of Wormser. He has a sinister appearance and gave me the chills." She glanced around the smoky dining room and said she was afraid he could show up at any minute.

Ronny said, "I'm concerned about your coincidental meeting because the *Freundenreich* doesn't play games with people. They are serious about their cause. I recall an article I read about them that appeared as if it had come from a defector. In it, the author made it clear that the *Freundenreich* was destined to gain power again by simple subversion, thus giving the Third Reich a place in history once again. If they obtained enough members, they could establish a party just like Hitler had in the 1920s."

"Let me guess. If they succeeded, Heinrich Glossen could have been the new Führer," Laura said.

"Perhaps. But if he is dead as you say he is, then I would think Wormser is the best bet," Ronny replied.

They finished their meal and Brian suggested they go to Ronny's hotel room where they could talk more privately.

When they got there, Brian told Ronny what had happened the second time he went back to the monastery. "The picture of Brother Matthias has a striking resemblance to Hitler."

"May I see it?" Ronny asked.

"We don't have it. We gave someone the picture to look at and never saw it again," Laura replied. She explained how they came

The Caretaker's Bible

to find Joseph Schäffer, an old friend of Hitler, and how he had met with foul play.

"You think the *Freundenreich* did this?" Ronny asked.

"Yes. Of course they did," Brian replied.

Laura said, "We have determined from reading the letter from Brother Dimitrius and seeing the photo of Brother Matthias that it was possible Hitler could have had a twin. I believe that's why the Friends of the Third Reich are so interested in Brian and me."

Ronny started to laugh. "A twin! That's preposterous."

"Why?" Brian asked.

"There's no record of it. Someone by now would have uncovered it, if it were true. I don't believe it."

"You might if you saw the picture of Brother Matthias," Laura said.

"I don't think so. But I would be careful. This is still a serious situation. I'm convinced you're wrong. But it is possible, however, that the *Freundenreich* could be very interested in Hitler's Bible and possibly the documents simply because they are artifacts of the Third Reich."

Laura nodded her head. "I agree, but I now think more than ever that Hitler had a twin brother—one that had become a Benedictine monk and disappeared in 1939 or 1940. There was no record of what happened to Brother Matthias after he departed the monastery."

Ronny didn't say a word.

Brian asked Laura for the notebook Schäffer had given them. He handed it to Ronny. "This is a diary. It belonged to Hitler when he was in Vienna before he went to Munich."

Ronny seemed excited. He began reading from the beginning. "You don't know what you have here. This could be worth a lot of money if it is authentic."

"That's not important," Brian replied. "What if Hitler did have a twin and he's still alive? Maybe the *Freundenreich* doesn't want anyone to find out and is protecting him."

"Do you really believe that?" Ronny asked. "It doesn't make a lot of sense. Why would they care?"

"Perhaps the *Freundenreich* doesn't want Hitler's twin to be put under a spotlight," Laura said. "His life could be continuously in danger. If they have the power to protect the twin, why not?"

Ronny quickly replied, "You said yourself the monk you think is Hitler's twin disappeared from the monastery years ago. There's no record of him after that?"

"We couldn't find out," Laura replied. "The Abbot at the monastery didn't wish to tell us."

"It's entirely possible he didn't know. I think it's next to impossible to track him down now," Ronny said.

Brian's voice boomed. "Why in the hell would the *Freundenreich* take the photo? It was just a picture of a monk. A thief wouldn't care. They must have been following us and somehow knew we gave it to Schäffer."

"I agree," Laura replied. "The robbery and subsequent attack weren't by accident."

Ronny stood up and began walking around. "I don't believe for a moment that Adolf Hitler ever had a twin, but it's also true that what I'm being told doesn't add up. I know enough about the *Freundenreich* to realize that they are a devious organization hell-bent on resurrecting the Third Reich. I know something is wrong and I would like to help you figure it out."

"At least that's some consolation," Brian said.

"I can assure you, though, that it has nothing to do with Hitler having a twin." Ronny looked at the birth certificate and letter again. "If I'm not mistaken, the monastery where the baby was found is a good distance away from Braunau. In fact, there is a monastery closer in Lambach. Why wouldn't the father have gone there? At any rate, it doesn't seem possible that the baby could have survived the long trek."

"I understand. But that's just speculation," Brian countered.

Laura hugged her friend. At least he understood the potential danger they were in, and that made her feel better. Brian looked at his watch and suggested they leave. He had a long day staring him in the face.

Driving back to their hotel, Brian confided in his fiancée that he wasn't sure Ronny was really on their side—that he was being patronizing. Laura laughed and told Brian that he didn't know Ronny as she did. In her opinion, they had his full attention.

*   *   *

Several days later, at four-thirty in the morning on 5 September, all hell broke loose at the Olympic Village. Terrorists slipped into the compound dressed as athletes, carrying gym bags filled with guns and ammo instead of athletic equipment. They killed two Israelis and took nine as hostages. The initial word was that the terrorists were Palestinian and were targeting Jews. As the standoff began, many of the other athletes feared for their lives. American Jewish competitors were segregated and advised to leave the country.

Brian and Laura heard about the kidnappings when they went out to get a cup of coffee and some pastry. They immediately left for the Olympic Village so Brian could cover the events.

Later in the morning it was learned that the terrorist group claimed to be from Black September, a Palestinian guerrilla organization, and they were demanding the release of 200 Arab guerrillas that were jailed in Israel, and safe passage for themselves and the hostages. Escorted by West German police, terrorists and the captive Israelis made their way to the airport via helicopters. At the airport, the police attempted a rescue, but it unfortunately ended with one police officer dead, along with all the hostages and five of the captors. Three Arabs were captured.

The president of the International Olympic Committee decided to continue the games even in spite of the terrorist acts. But many of the athletes didn't want to compete.

Brian sat in a near-empty arena trying to make sense of what had transpired that morning. Innocent Olympians had been killed for no reason other than the fact that misguided Arabs wanted to make a statement to the world. He knew the Arab-Israeli sentiment had never been civil. The animosity could be cut with a knife. But this was totally uncalled for. Inspired, he sat and wrote a piece about terrorism and how it had no place in the world of sports. When he was finished, he took Laura by the hand and they walked around the

Olympic compound trying to come to grips with the heartache of the remaining Israeli athletes. It had to be devastating for them.

Later that afternoon, after Laura couldn't reach Ronny on the phone, they decided to go over to his hotel. When they knocked on the door, there was no reply. Laura started to get concerned. Brian decided to go down to the desk and ask if the receptionist could open the door. Finally, with the door open, they saw Ronny sitting in the corner of the room appearing to be in shock. Laura quickly ran over and asked what was wrong. He didn't say anything at first. He looked white as a sheet.

She held Ronny for a few seconds. He finally said a few words. "I'm terrified about the terrorist incident at the Olympics. I think it could be more widespread. In my opinion, all Jews are at risk."

"Why are you so concerned," Brian said, rather indignantly. "You're not Jewish."

"Yes, I am. My mother is a Jew. Her maiden name is Feinberg. She lives in California." He took a few breaths. "My mother's parents were killed at Auschwitz. In a twist of fate, their children had been taken by an uncle, a German soldier, and smuggled out of the country to Stras bourg, France, a week before they were arrested and deported to the camp."

"You never told me that," Laura said.

"It's not something I want people to know. But now I'm scared. I don't know who is worse, the Palestinians or the Neo-Nazis. One way or another, today Jews will have to bear the consequences of being Jewish."

"It's okay. It's an isolated incident. You'll be fine." Laura began to feel bad that she had invited Ronny to come to Munich. But of course she couldn't possibly have known that terrorists would infiltrate the Olympic Village.

"You're not in imminent danger," Brian said. "No one could possibly know you're part Jewish. You don't look it and you don't have a Jewish last name. We should all go out for a drink."

"Not tonight. I just need to rest."

Laura, wanting to respect his feelings, told Ronny they would see him the next evening.

*   *   *

The following morning, final preparations were being made for the memorial service that would take place in the main stadium. Competition had been suspended temporarily and the XX Olympiad was in jeopardy of being cancelled. Brian called his boss to tell him he was all right. As soon as Binneker found that out, he reminded Brian that he was expecting one hell of a story—especially now. All Brian could do was to appease him by reminding him he had never failed to produce a great story—even under pressure.

After the somber ceremony, Brian managed to interview a few athletes to get their feelings on the violent Palestinian attack. None of them were positive. But not one athlete he talked to wanted the games to end even though many of them had said previously they would go home. They all denounced the attack as cowardice and barbaric anarchy by a bunch of outlaws. Once the president of the International Olympic Committee announced he would resume the games, there was a feeling of resolve and solidarity among the international competitors. Brian spent the entire afternoon moving from event to event trying to get a sense of how the athletes were really affected by the tragedy. Laura finally pulled the plug and said they had to go back to their hotel and get ready to go over and see Ronny.

The *Englischer Garten* was crowded. They ordered their beers—sitting down at a long table. Laura put her handbag in front of her so she could keep it in her sight. The Bible and the documents, including the diary, were neatly tucked inside. Over time, she had become more nervous about having them in her possession. But what else could she do with them? Trying to hide them would only lead to disaster. Sooner or later Wormser was going to make his move and it would be all over. She was also perturbed because Brian had been so engaged in covering the Olympics that he had virtually let her worry about everything herself. It was getting on her nerves.

Brian offered a toast to their friendship. They slapped mugs, spilling beer all over the table—like an early Octoberfest. They stopped to look around, concerned they might appear like they were celebrating. The terrorist attack seemed to be sobering to most Germans.

"What are you going to do when the games end?" Ronny asked.

Brian replied, "I'm scheduled to go back and finalize my article for an early November release. But I don't know if I'm going. We're on to something here and I need to think it through."

"I believe you're at a dead end," Ronny said. "There's no way to corroborate your story. And no one in their right mind will believe it without definitive proof. Being a journalist, you should know what I'm talking about."

"I understand, but I just can't let it go. There are too many loose ends and certainly too many coincidences." Brian gulped down a few swigs of beer.

"Maybe we need to start from the beginning," Ronny said.

"The beginning?" Brian threw Ronny a funny look.

Ronny kept on talking. "The Bible was given to you by the caretaker in Tuscany. He either didn't know the significance of it or he gave it to you purposely. Probably the former. It isn't uncommon for Europeans to give away books to foreigners. I spent time in Frankfurt right out of college and remember the family I stayed with gave me several German history books before I went back to the States."

"So what about the documents?" Brian asked.

"They're probably valuable. Just like the Bible. But they don't amount to much."

"What about the Abbot's warning? What about the monk in Linz? What about Wormser?" Brian pointed his finger at Ronny. "If these documents don't mean anything, then why are these people so interested in telling us to forget about what we know?"

Ronny put his beer down. "You told me that Wormser was interested in the Bible, not the documents. Did you not?"

"Yes, but I think he's playing a game with us," Laura said.

Brian cleared his throat. "It's obvious to me they don't want anyone to know about this letter or the birth certificate. Because, for whatever reason, they don't want the world to know Hitler had a twin."

Ronny shook his head. "Say you're right. How in the hell are you going to prove it?"

"I don't know."

Ronny threw up his hands. "See, that's what I'm talking about. You have no way to corroborate the story."

Laura didn't want to give up hope. She quickly lectured Ronny on why they had asked him to come over—certainly not for his health or a vacation, but to help them figure out what to do. He wasn't being cooperative and she was losing her patience.

Ronny replied, "The *Freundenreich* is probably trying to hide an old secret to protect an individual or individuals, but nothing like you think. I'm sorry, I just don't believe your theory."

"Well, tell us yours," Laura said.

Suddenly, Brian caught a profile of a familiar face out of the corner of his eye. The person was far enough away that Brian couldn't be sure—probably 50 meters. He began to walk over to where she was standing to see if he was right. She was drinking a beer and smoking what looked to be a cigar. As he made his way over to her position, a group of drunken Italian tourists passed in front of him, blocking his view. After they finally moved to the other side, the woman was gone. He ran over to where she had been standing and looked around. It was like she had never been there—vanishing into thin air. He went over to an older man drinking a beer nearby and asked if he had just seen a beautiful young woman standing there. The man laughed and said no.

Brian still walked around for a few minutes before he went back to the table.

"Where'd you go?" Laura asked.

Brian pointed in the direction he had just come from. "I could have sworn I just saw Gerta Honiker right over there."

"Somebody who looked like her, I suppose," Laura said.

"I don't know. By the time I got over there, she was gone."

Laura, still angry with Ronny for his reply that he didn't have a theory either, told Brian, "You've had too many beers. I can't believe you would be able to see her face that clearly 50 meters away in a crowd."

"I'm sure it was her."

Laura didn't want to argue. "She was born in Munich, so I guess it could have been her."

Brian didn't respond. He was thinking. The idea of dealing with a group such as the *Freundenreich* bothered him even more now that he realized what he could be up against. And could Gerta somehow be involved? He stood silently, drinking his beer and looking around the immediate area for any sign of her.

chapter 13
Berlin—1940

EVA WAS SUMMONED TO Glossen's office on the tenth of March when the weather was still cold and snow from the last storm still clung to the corners of the buildings and the sides of the streets. Because February had come and gone and Hitler still had not met his brother, Glossen was now more determined than ever—setting his sights on mid-March, only a week away. In a continual series of rehearsals, Glossen had assured himself that all would go well.

"May I be of some assistance, Herr Glossen?" she asked, standing completely erect and in place as she had always done.

"Please sit down," he said. "I need to ask your opinion. I cannot make up my mind about what I should have Horst wear when he has his audience with the Führer. It is confusing. Should Horst present himself dressed as an average citizen, or should he be made to look like a spitting image of Hitler?"

"I think that perhaps he should not shock the Führer with his appearance. I am inclined to believe that Horst should be simply dressed, in a plain shirt and pants or, at the very most, a black suit and white shirt with a black tie."

Glossen asked, "Should we leave them alone to get acquainted?"

"I do not think that is such a good idea either." Eva was beginning to think Glossen had not thought his grandiose plan through. She was concerned Hitler would want to know what his brother's role would be in the Third Reich—if he even believed Horst was his brother. That was certainly where the conversation could break down. "Have you really considered what you want Horst to do?"

Glossen looked around the room for a minute as though he were collecting his thoughts. "I think he could stand in for the Führer when he is sick or otherwise indisposed."

Eva tried not to laugh. "Do you really think the Führer would let someone else speak for him? I cannot imagine."

"He would if there was no threat that his brother would want to take over. Considering what I know about Horst, that would never happen."

"I think you must be prepared for any outcome. The Führer might not have the same enthusiasm as you over this plan of action. I only trust you have warned Horst of this possible reaction by his brother." She was quiet for a moment. "What kinds of meetings would you have him attend in the Führer's absence?"

"I am not sure. It is all predicated on whether or not Horst is believable as the Führer. I guess the decision will be made by trial and error. The initial test will be whether he can fool some of the aides and workers in and around the Chancellery. If that is the case, I will begin to rely more and more on Horst."

"But what kind of life is that going to be for the Führer's brother?" Eva asked.

Glossen shrugged his shoulders. "It is all for the good of the Reich. I think it should be his honor to serve."

Eva looked at the clock on the wall behind Glossen's chair. She realized that Wormser was due any minute for a meeting with Glossen. She wanted to get out of there and go to the canteen for lunch.

When she returned, Wormser still hadn't arrived. Glossen sat in his chair, still waiting for him. She knew that Glossen hated dealing with Wormser. Wormser had gained prestige as a devout member of the Gestapo and had earned the title of Jew Killer because he would take the life of a Jew first in any situation. This bothered Glossen tremendously. In fact, he actually regretted letting Goebbels talk him into putting Wormser on his staff as his deputy. But as Goebbels would always say, he knew they both had the interest of the Third Reich at heart and had to learn to work together.

"So you are ready to go through with this charade," Wormser said when he finally arrived, tossing his hat on Glossen's table and sitting down.

"It is time. I will talk to the Führer tomorrow morning. If he is agreeable, I will introduce him to his brother."

Wormser smirked and said, "Well, you cannot say I did not warn you, Herr Glossen." He brushed his pants off and straightened his tie. "You must value your position here."

"My tenure here is not in jeopardy, if that is what you are talking about. Certainly there are no vacancies to be concerned with."

Wormser ran his fingers through his hair and then rested them behind his neck. "I understand you have some reservations concerning the Führer's war planning. Have you talked to him directly about this? I believe Hitler is well within his right to want to expand his empire beyond the physical borders of Germany. I am fully behind Hitler's determination to immortalize the Third Reich."

"Are you suggesting I do not support such an effort?" Glossen asked.

"Of course not. I only want to know your feelings on the subject. After all, you are apparently second in command to Goebbels, and I would think your opinions count around here."

Glossen shuffled some papers around on his desk and stood up. "Propaganda is not an easy profession. I recall when I had first taken the job working for Goebbels. It was extremely difficult for me as a former economics professor to thrust myself into the limelight of the Third Reich and to become a salesman for Hitler's flamboyant dream. There were many times at first when I simply made silly mistakes—somehow minimizing the Führer's well-meaning intentions. But in time, I managed to impress Hitler more than I thought I could. I made Goebbels look like he was a genius in the Führer's eyes. It was then I knew I had mastered the calculating game of propaganda."

Wormser seemed a bit agitated. He squirmed in his chair, he began sniffling as if he had a cold, and tapped his right foot on the floor. Glossen was convinced he had unleashed Wormser's psychotic side—something that was not very hard to do. Wormser actually sounded a lot like Hitler when he got mad. Sitting up straight, he ranted and raved about how he was going to be in the Führer's good graces by helping to eliminate every Jew on the face of the earth. It was because of him that the Third Reich was thriving, he said. Glossen laughed and told him to collect his hat and vacate the office, as he was ready to meet with one of his staff. Glossen could hear Wormser yelling all the way down the hallway. It was a common occurrence.

*   *   *

The next day, late in the morning, Glossen walked slowly to the Führer's executive office while silently practicing his speech. Eva dutifully carried his notes. He had made an appointment through the Propaganda Minister to ensure he would be seen. Goebbels elected not to be there, and Glossen knew he was protecting himself just in case Hitler didn't like what he heard. Glossen was sure that the timing would be right. The Führer was known for rising late, often not until the early afternoon. It would have been a bad tactical move to try to see Hitler after a long day of frustration.

Even with a supposed appointment, Glossen had to pass muster with several of Hitler's personal security guards, his personal executive officer, Martin Bormann and Klara Petrun, and Joachim Ribbentrop, who happened to be standing there demanding to see the Führer. It was well understood that Hitler was the most protected individual on the face of the earth while he was head of the Third

Reich. After a half hour of dropping Goebbels' name and insisting he had a valid reason to see the Führer, even though he refused to say what it was, he was permitted to enter the chamber that Hitler called his office.

In normal fashion, the Führer was dressed in the uniform of the Third Reich—immaculate, hair combed back, and standing by the side of his desk in a pose of dignity—when Glossen walked in. The persona was incredible. Glossen stopped well in front of his leader and saluted with the accompanying *Sig Heil*. Hitler asked Glossen to take a seat. He seemed especially cordial and it was obvious to Glossen that the Führer must have had a good night's sleep.

Glossen realized that Hitler had a short attention span and knew he had to get to the point almost immediately or he would be in jeopardy of being asked to leave. He told Hitler he had someone he wanted the Führer to meet—that he had located an individual he believed was a relative. Hitler seemed responsive. Privately, Hitler had a deep affection for family. It was a sentimental side not many people knew about. Glossen explained, using words he thought Hitler would want to hear, that he had located a monk near Linz Austria who was born the same day as the Führer. More than that, he looked identical to him.

The sound of the chair moving back echoed throughout the chamber. "What is the meaning of this?" Hitler was waving his fist around before he pounded the table. "There is no one who looks like the Führer. No one! I have built the Third Reich with sweat and determination. I have no one else to thank. How dare you tell me you have found this person! You have me believe that he is a relative?" The Führer's face began to contort. "Is it that you want me to believe? That I somehow have a twin brother? That is utter nonsense, and I will not have it." Hitler stood up at attention, which signified his disgust with what he was being told. "I never want to hear of this again. Is that understood?" He dismissed Glossen with a flick of his wrist.

*   *   *

The next morning, still unnerved from his embarrassment at angering the Führer, Glossen sat at his desk struggling with what had gone wrong. He fully realized that his grandiose plan could have now completely dissolved. In Goebbels' office, Goebbels accused Glossen of total incompetence and said that perhaps he should take Horst back to where he had found him. He was emphatic that he would not take any of the blame and that Glossen alone was responsible for angering the Führer. Glossen's ego was severely damaged.

Glossen had been given the untenable chore of developing a strategy of deceit concerning the Nazi's intentions for waging war. Postponed from the last few months of the previous year because of weather and technical problems, Hitler was adamant the Germans would begin their campaign in early April.

Glossen thumbed through a report written by one of his deputies concerning Italy's position on attacking the West. In it, the writer speculated that Mussolini, who had just met with Hitler at Brenner Pass and reaffirmed his willingness to go to war, would probably renege when the time came to act. Italy appeared to be less willing to risk sovereignty and soldiers to appease the whims of the Führer. Glossen disagreed in principle with the assessment in the report. He had long believed that Mussolini was afraid of Hitler's resolve and didn't want to be considered an enemy, and because of that, they would soon join the war.

Eva unexpectedly came into the office. "May we have a word?"

"Yes. Is there a problem?"

"I want to discuss an important issue relative to something Herr Wormser said to me. In a brief discussion a few hours ago, Wormser made a point to say that in only days now I would be working for him since you would be punished for your incredibly arrogant act of treachery."

"He is delirious if he thinks he can get away with this. Perhaps I was wrong. I suppose I should take the monk back to where he belongs."

"Do you really want to do that? You are not one to give up."

Glossen turned away for a moment. "I believe in my heart that Horst is the Führer's true brother. Making him accept it has been considered difficult from the very beginning. I do not know what to do."

"If you believe it, you must act. I have not seen Herr Goebbels in here with the SS portending an arrest. I think you have another chance."

"I cannot imagine Goebbels allowing me to meet with the Führer again. I have to believe it is over."

The door was opened abruptly. Wormser walked in and took a seat next to Eva.

"Do you have an appointment?" Glossen asked.

"Of course not. But we must talk."

"What about?"

Wormser replied, "I just finished reading an Army memorandum about secret weapons that are being affixed to parachutes that are designed to blow up when handled by the enemy."

"Yes. I know of such devices."

"We must ensure the enemy hears of this technology and that it is much more devastating than I believe the devices to be."

"That is our job," Glossen replied. "We will simply put out a communiqué that says so; that the bombs are designed to kill and maim without fail."

Wormser leaned over a bit and looked at the report on the desk. "What is this?"

Glossen explained. He asked Wormser for his opinion.

"I know nothing about Italy, but attacking the West is imperative. But I believe we must correct problems within our own country."

"We have been through this before. We are taking steps to eradicate the scourge. It will take a while."

"Jews must be purged like the enemy. That is the only real solution to Germany's problems."

"Is there anything else? We are having a private meeting."

"No. But I would not get comfortable in that chair. I know about your failed meeting with the Führer." With that, Wormser got up and walked toward the door.

"I would not pack up your office anytime soon. It is difficult conducting business standing in the hallway."

*   *   *

The morning of 18 April, Glossen received a phone call from Goebbels. The Minister of Propaganda was exuberant. He told Glossen that he had just had an emergency meeting with the Führer and that he said he had changed his mind—now desperately wanting to meet Horst.

Glossen left the office immediately and went directly to see the monk with the news, but the reception was not what Glossen expected. As they stood looking at each other, Horst said he now had reservations about whether he wanted to go through with it. Glossen couldn't believe what he was hearing. After all this time and effort, and especially after getting dressed down by the Führer himself, Glossen had no patience for such behavior. "You must understand. You have no choice now. You have been summoned."

"I have prayed about it. I think I should go home now." Horst was resolute. "I do not think I can ever allow myself to act and think like my brother. I cannot rectify the horrors of the Third Reich as a man of God."

This infuriated Glossen and strained his already short patience. He tried to contain himself. Asking Horst to sit down, he decided to take a philosophical approach to his problem. Apparently the mild administering of pacifying drugs and the endless sessions with doctors were not helping. He had to turn things around. "You have an opportunity no one else in the world can claim. You are the flesh and blood of our leader, the man who will change everything for the Fatherland."

He waited for some sort of response. When he didn't get one, he continued. "I believe you can make a contribution to Germany that will make you a hero in the eyes of the leadership. You will go down in history as a true patriot."

Horst stared at the floor. "I ask God every day why I have been chosen. I cannot deny that I look exactly like the Führer, but it is a fate I never asked for." He looked up at Glossen. "What shall I do?"

Glossen grasped Horst by the shoulder and said, "You must do what is right. Meet with him and tell him you know in your heart you are his brother. He will be grateful for it. There can be no other result."

*   *   *

The day of reckoning came without much flourish. Horst stood in Glossen's office after being moved from the hotel in the early morning hours under heavy guard while wearing a disguise. He was dressed in a plain black suit with a black tie. His hair was combed back and his mustache was much fuller than Hitler's small clump of hair under his nose. Glossen didn't want to startle his leader by making them completely identical at the first meeting. It was still obvious that Horst resembled Hitler. There was no mistake.

Eva sat in a chair directly across from Horst. She tried to counsel him in order to calm him down. He was so nervous he had a hard time talking without sounding like his voice was vibrating a mile a minute. The meeting was scheduled for eleven o'clock in the morning, and Eva had her work cut out for her, as it was only nine. She began asking him questions about his life at the monastery. When Glossen realized what they were talking about, he put an end to it. She decided to tell him all about herself instead.

At ten forty-five, Goebbels arrived at Glossen's office. Asking Horst to stand up, he examined him much like a military commander inspects a soldier. He asked a few relevant questions to ensure Horst would not say something that would send the Führer into a fury.

They escorted Horst to the executive offices under cover. Once they arrived, Goebbels went in first and set the stage for what Hitler would experience. When Glossen and Horst walked in, Goebbels and the Führer were sitting at his conference table.

Hitler immediately stood up and walked over to Horst, making him extremely nervous. Hitler stared at him for the longest time. His eyes seemed to bore a hole through the soul of the monk.

Suddenly, Hitler said, "I understand we share a birthday." He asked Horst to join them at the table.

For Glossen, this had broken the ice. It was a sign that things were going well—at least so far. He hoped that it would continue that way. He believed it all would go smoothly as long as Horst didn't offend the Führer.

Goebbels explained that Glossen had found Horst at a monastery in Austria after he had seen a picture of him. When he had gone there, he had discovered paperwork that led them to believe Horst could be related to the Führer.

"May I see the paperwork?" Hitler asked.

"Of course." Glossen removed the documents from a binder and handed them to Hitler. He read over them several times. Goebbels tried to explain what they meant, and Hitler put his hand up to signify that he wasn't interested in explanations.

Hitler ignored everyone but Horst. "You were abandoned. I cannot imagine such a fate. You never knew who your real parents were?"

"No, mein Führer. No." Horst didn't know what else to say. He had been raised by loving parents who never told him he was adopted.

Hitler looked at the documents again. He put them down and stared at the table for a moment. "I hope to God it was not the will of my father that caused you this pain."

The hush at the table was eerie. Hitler was showing emotion he had not expressed very often around his senior leaders. They were shocked.

Hitler's face stiffened. He looked at Horst and said, "Can you be the brother I always longed for?" His eyes broadened. "How could my father be so inhumane? Is it possible he left you to the will of God at some monastery out in the wilderness?" His lips trembled a bit. "How could it be that you look so much like the leader of the Third Reich?" The Führer picked up the papers and shook them in the air. "I want answers!"

Everyone at the table took a deep breath. They didn't know how to respond.

Hitler looked over at Horst and began to smile. "Have they treated you well here in Berlin? Do you have a reasonable place to stay? If not, I will have you transported down to Bergof on the Obersalzburg. There you can relax and no one will know you are there."

Horst looked to Glossen to provide the answers, but Glossen figured the Führer only wanted them from his brother.

Horst answered, "I will do what you think is best."

Hitler asked for one of his security guards to come in the office. He instructed him to have his driver take Horst to Bergof immediately following the meeting. He said he would join him there in several weeks. With that, Hitler dismissed everyone but Horst.

Glossen slowly walked back to his office. He could not contain his emotion any longer—tears welled up in his eyes. He had finally succeeded in convincing Hitler that he had a brother. Now he had to devise a calculated plan to encourage the Führer to allow his brother to lessen his everyday stress by occasionally impersonating him. It was a long shot, but Glossen was fairly confident he could pull it off, especially after the meeting he had just attended. He quickly headed for a small bar near the Reich Chancellery where he could get his favorite beer.

chapter 14
Munich—1972

WITH THE OLYMPIC CLOSING ceremony a day away, Brian was spending more time finishing an initial draft of his article while still interviewing athletes and watching final events. The schedule was so intense that he really didn't have time to think about his ongoing dilemma. His gut reaction was that if he wanted to keep his job, he probably would have to go back to New York with a story good enough to please Binneker—then he would get on a plane, come back to Munich, and take care of unfinished business.

Laura was relieved to hear Brian say that. She had been getting restless and wanted to leave the country. Somehow, the idea of finding out about the twin didn't seem important anymore. Ronny had convinced her by saying they wouldn't be able to prove their theory and therefore would look like fools trying to tell it to the American public—especially with anti-Nazi sentiment still remaining high after twenty-seven years.

"I think I can figure it out. I just need time," Brian said.

"All the time in the world won't help." Laura sat down on a small wooden bench in the Olympic Village.

Brian hated a pessimist, especially when she was the woman he loved. He learned a good long time ago that being negative was always counterproductive. "Why can't you go along with what I say? I know there has to be a way to find out what's going on."

Laura stopped short of laughing. "You are so completely obsessed with Hitler and his supposed twin that you have lost all sense of reason."

Brian fired back. "What's wrong with you? You know they're trying to hide something. We have a duty to find out what that is."

"You have a duty. Not I," she replied, shaking her leg up and down. "I'm sick and tired of being scared. I just want to go back to the States."

"Okay. If that's what you want to do. I'll get you on a plane right after the closing ceremony."

"You need to go with me. Ronny too. We all need to get out of here."

"I don't think so, but I'll make a final decision by the time the Olympic torch is extinguished."

They waited for Ronny to show up. After confining himself to his room and the immediate area of the hotel just to be safe, he finally decided to make an appearance at the games. The day before, Laura had talked him into going to several of the finals and the closing ceremony.

"Thought I wouldn't come," Ronny said. "Didn't you?"

They moved through the crowds to the basketball semifinals. The American team was strong and had been favored over the Russians, who most felt would play against the Americans in the final game. Before the first game, Brian had interviewed several players on Team America. They were confident about going all the way. Brian's plan was to interview them again after their presumed win against the Soviet Union.

Later in the day, after the finalists were decided and bets were put down on either the American or Soviet team to take the gold medal, Brian wanted to find a few of the prominent athletes to get their reactions to the outcome of the Olympics so far. Each time, Laura and Ronny would stand on the sidelines, allowing Brian to do his job.

In the darkness directly following a hazy sunset, the three of them decided to take a walk along a side street adjacent to the main Olympic stadium to get some exercise. Brian told them he had made up his mind to finish his story back in New York since he also needed to take a rest from anything having to do with Hitler or the Third Reich.

"Good," Ronny said. "You are well advised to forget about it."

Laura seemed relieved. The nightmare would soon be over and they could get on with their lives.

As they crossed the street, Brian noticed several suspicious looking men standing on the corner who appeared to be watching their every move. This made him a little nervous, so he suggested they go back to the Olympic venue where they could be safe.

Before they could react, men appearing out of nowhere were running toward them. Brian motioned for Laura and Ronny to run in the opposite direction toward the Olympic Park so they could get away easier. He ran down the street trying to find a crowded building to go into or a back alley in which to hide. But within a matter of minutes, Brian was surrounded. He had no choices left.

*   *   *

He woke up slowly. He had that taste in his mouth that one gets after taking sleeping pills or sleeping with one's mouth open. The room was mostly dark. A bit of light shone from underneath a closed door. As much as he tried, he couldn't move. He attempted to focus his eyes, but found it to be difficult. Frustrated and angry, he couldn't remember how he had gotten there. He began to think about Laura and Ronny—if they were all right. His head pounded. It was the worst headache he had had in years. When he tried to move, his body still felt numb.

The door opened. He could hear someone enter. The stranger

pulled up a chair. "How are you feeling, Herr Bennett?" The German accent was very strong.

He had a hard time responding but managed to get the words out. "I've felt better."

"You are our guest. We want you to feel at home." The stranger had a very peculiar voice that was both loud and annoying. "I merely want to talk to you about a few things. That is all. Nothing to get upset about."

"Where am I?"

"That is not important. You need to get some rest." With that, the stranger put the chair back where he had gotten it and immediately left the room.

Brian was beginning to feel he could be at the point of no return, and he knew he was possibly facing a tough interrogation. What worried him the most was whether he would make it out alive. All he could do was hope for the best.

He must have been sleeping when the sound of a door opening startled him. He could feel the presence of someone. He heard a voice. "Are you willing to talk now? I can come back later." The face hung over him. It had a horrid little grin. The hair looked like it belonged to Einstein. The glasses were small, round, and hung down on the nose. He was a ghastly little man.

Brian tried to gain his composure. "Who are you? What do you want?" He could see an outline of someone else in the background. Perhaps a woman.

The old man sat down in the chair. "I want to talk to you about why you have come all the way to Munich. I want to know what you hope to gain."

"I'm a reporter. I came to cover the Olympics."

"Is that so? Is that why you have been traveling around the countryside—to Austria, to Italy? The Olympics are here in Munich. Or were you not aware of that?"

"Yes. I know." Brian wasn't sure what to say. "You're not interested in the Olympics, are you?"

"Oh, but I am, Herr Bennett. I only wish you shared the same enthusiasm."

Brian was starting to feel sick to his stomach. He asked for some water. He must have been drugged. He couldn't focus on anything for too long. He began to think about his fiancée. Was she all right? Did they have her in another room somewhere? Did they finally get the Bible?

The old man brought him a glass of water. Brian was reluctant to drink at first—thinking it could be poisoned or laced with drugs, but thirst overrode his common sense.

"So, Herr Bennett. What do you have to say for yourself? Why are you snooping around monasteries?"

"You know perfectly well why. I'm a reporter who's trying to get to the truth."

A reply came from the figure in the background—a woman's voice. "I think you should go back to New York where you came from."

Brian couldn't stop himself. "Hell no. I'm not going back until I find out what's going on."

The obnoxious little man stood right over Brian. "You must not get so worked up, Herr Bennett. It is not good for your health. The Third Reich did not die in 1945 as most people think. The death of the Führer did not change the sentiments of many loyal citizens. They made a pact that they would never let the image of the Third Reich die, regardless of what political party prevailed. They also decreed that Hitler's soul would be protected—his image, his private life and, most importantly, his political philosophies."

"You can't be serious!"

"You must not interfere with this sacred trust. You are not welcome here, Herr Bennett."

Brian wanted to tell the old man to go to hell, but he refrained. "Why are you so interested in me? What do you think I know that you don't want me to tell the world?"

"You have been warned already. You did not listen, did you, Herr Bennett?"

Before Brian could answer, the old man was gone—slamming the door behind him. Brian gradually sat up and teetered for a few seconds before he fell back onto his pillow. He felt faint.

When he woke up, he was sweating. The room seemed to be going around and around, but after a minute or so it stopped. The room was still dark. He sensed someone was there. He could just feel it.

"I think perhaps you would like to talk now," the old man said.

Brian tried to sit up but couldn't. "I have nothing to say."

"Really? I know you would like to see your fiancée. Is that not correct?"

"What have you done with her?"

"She is in no danger. She is safe and sound."

"What do you want from me?"

The old man's voice became a little more defined. "You have the undivided attention of the *Freundenreich*, and we are not at all pleased with what you are trying to do. We consider you an outsider who is sticking his nose where it does not belong. We are incensed that you are making up stories about the Führer—saying that he had a twin. All we really want is for you to stop this fruitless investigation."

Brian lifted his head off the pillow. "You just don't want to tell me the truth!"

"There is nothing to tell. You must stop this nonsense. If you do not, you and your friends will certainly pay the consequences."

Brian thought for a minute. He had found the documents that were at least a start to his investigation. He had seen a picture of a monk who more than resembled Hitler, and he had been told by several people to forget what he knew. There had to be a cover-up and this was an attempt by the *Freundenreich* to scare the hell out of him. "What are you people trying to hide?"

"Nothing! Why would we do such a thing? Now, I want you to listen carefully to me. You have a lot to live for, Herr Bennett. We already have what we want. We have the Bible and the documents. Now, do not let your obsessions ruin your life. I suggest you go home. If you do, you will never hear from us again."

* * *

The rain was cold for September. Brian aimlessly walked around the streets of Munich trying to get his bearings. He vaguely remembered where he had been—in a dark room somewhere being interrogated by a pitiful little man. He wanted to get back to Laura, but his mind went blank. He couldn't remember the name of the hotel or the location. Street names didn't mean anything, landmarks were no help; the more he wandered around the more he got lost. He worried about the safety of his fiancée and Ronny. What if they had met the same fate? What if it were worse?

He sat on a bench near the river, which was soaked after the rain had stopped. He didn't even know what day it was. He knew he had to cover the closing ceremony, but he wasn't quite sure how to get to the Olympic venue. Lost in thought, he felt a hand gripping his arm. Looking up, he saw that it was Ronny.

"Are you all right?" Ronny asked.

"Where's Laura?" Brian asked, looking around.

"She's fine. I'll take you back to the hotel."

Brian sat on the bed shaking from the chills. His head still hurt—more at the base of the neck than in his forehead. Laura had given him towels to wipe himself down. She suggested he take a hot bath to warm his body up. He declined. It took several minutes for him to get acclimated to his surroundings.

"I thought I would never see you again," Laura said. "They drugged you, didn't they?"

"I don't know. It feels like it. I can only remember a few things that happened to me."

"Maybe it will all come back to you if you just relax," Laura said.

"It was Wormser's doing," Ronny said. "The *Freundenreich* wanted to send us all a message."

"All I remember is an old man who looked like a mad scientist. He wanted me to go back to New York. I told him I knew they were hiding something." He looked around the room. "They have the Bible and documents, don't they?"

Laura looked over at Ronny. "Yes. They're gone."

"What happened?" Brian asked.

Ronny sat down on the bed. "Two men chased after us. They grabbed Laura's handbag and emptied it on the street. They took off with everything; we were defenseless to stop it."

"Damn it! What are we going to do without them?" Brian finally stood up and walked to the window.

Laura didn't know what to say. Ronny figured they should take a few deep breaths.

Brian turned around quickly. "What day is it? When's the closing ceremony?"

"The Olympics ended three days ago."

"Jesus! What the hell am I going to tell Binneker?"

"That should be the least of your worries," Laura said. "We need to figure out what to do about the *Freundenreich*."

Ronny said, "I managed to track down someone who knows where Heinrich Glossen lives near Chiemsee, roughly 85 kilometers southeast of here. We went to the location, found the house, and asked neighbors about him."

"What did they say?" Brian asked.

"Several said they hadn't seen him in some time. That would make sense if he was dead, but one neighbor in particular said he was just there a few weeks ago."

"We looked inside the house," Laura said. "It appears not to have been lived in for some time."

"So where does that put us?" Brian asked. "I think it's all over. They have the Bible, the documents. We have nothing."

Laura agreed. "Our investigation has more than ended. It was time to go home."

Ronny, who had played devil's advocate for so long, now actually believed they were on to something. "I'm willing to stick it out even though it appears we could be in for quite a ride."

Brian smiled at his friend. "Leave it to you to always be on the other side of an issue. I just don't know any more. The old man said that Hitler's soul would be protected—his image, his private life and, most importantly, his political philosophies. They will never let anyone try to prove Hitler had a twin. The old man more than said that."

"It's a losing battle, as they say," Laura said. "We don't need the aggravation. I'll make the travel arrangements."

*   *   *

Later that night, while Laura was taking a shower, the phone rang. The voice was sultry, soft—so much so that Brian thought the caller had the wrong number at first. The person on the other end wanted to meet with Brian as soon as possible. She suggested they meet in the early morning at dawn along the river several blocks east of his hotel. Brian desperately tried to find out who she was. She would only say her name was Marta and hung up.

Laura walked into the room. "Who was that?" She was suspicious right away. After Brian told her what he knew, she said, "Why would this woman want to talk to you? It doesn't sound right. It's a lure, dangled like a carrot in front of you by the Friends of the Third Reich."

"I'm not so sure," Brian said. "What bothers me is, I know I've heard that voice before. I'm going to meet with her."

"I'll go with you."

"No. You need to stay here. I can take care of myself."

"You can? Is that why you were kidnapped, drugged, and put through an interrogation?"

"Well, okay. You've made your point. But from the way she was talking, I think she has something to tell me. Something I need to know."

"I'll call Ronny and tell him not to pack," Laura suggested. They were scheduled to leave the next morning on a twelve-o'clock flight.

"No. Leave him out of it. Keep the plans the way they are."

*   *   *

The morning mist lingered across the water. Brian made his way east along the banks of the Isar River. He patiently waited near a lamppost. The streets were nearly empty—only a few people out for morning strolls. The figure approached in the glare of the sun as it peeked through the clouds. Brian couldn't make out who it was at first. Whoever it was wore a long coat and had their head covered. As the person finally walked up to him, she took off her hood. "Hello. My name is Marta."

Brian didn't respond for a moment. He just stared at her beautiful face. "I thought your name was Gerta."

"No. That is just what I wanted you to think. May we sit down?"

Brian glanced around, making sure they were alone. "What is this all about?"

"You were approached by a monk—a reluctant messenger. He gave you a name. It is very important." Marta stepped closer to Brian. "It is a long story, but I am obliged to tell it to you if you are willing to listen.

"The Friends of the Third Reich have a long and arduous history. It is a legacy passed down through decades, and it is now the responsibility of the children to keep the fires burning—much like I have done for years. Perhaps the first thoughts of it were in 1945 in London—far away from the burning cinders of Berlin or Munich. Heinrich Glossen had escaped the gallows by being smuggled outside of the country only days before Hitler shot himself in his bunker. Within a few months, he was safe and sound in London. He had left his wife and three children behind, knowing they would be spared.

"Glossen had stayed in London for five years. When he returned, he went directly to Freiburg, then Munich, finally settling near Chiemsee. By then, he had established the foundation for the *Freundenreich*. He held his first rally away from prying eyes in 1950 in Munich at an old beer hall. It was surprising to note that close to a thousand people attended. The idea of a new and innovative Reich appealed to many."

Brian didn't want to interrupt, but he felt compelled. "Hadn't the Germans learned their lesson?"

"They were more energized than ever. Many wanted to avenge the demise of the Third Reich. Many are angry that Hitler had been placed in a position where he saw no way out other than to take his own life. There was madness. I was a young girl then, and my parents went to every rally."

"This Glossen seemed to have a lot of influence. Much like Goebbels did," Brian said. "What did he really want?"

"I cannot be sure, but I think he wanted total power and to rule Germany as his Führer had. Glossen was obsessed with the greatness of Deutschland and had spent a lot of time talking with Hitler about how to make the Third Reich eternal."

"I thought Hitler wasn't accessible to many people—only the inner circle like Goebbels or Göring."

"That is not necessarily true. Yes, he was not fond of socializing, but he made himself available to certain individuals. It is well documented that Glossen had actually gone to Bergof on several occasions. He was very well respected by the Führer. Some say he had free access—at least from Goebbels' perspective."

"So, you said your parents belonged to the *Freundenreich*."

"Yes. They were taken in by it all. When I got older, probably nine or ten, my father tried to explain what the *Freundenreich* was all about by giving me lessons. I was required to read *Mein Kampf* by the time I was a teenager. My parents kept it in the house and cherished it like it was a Bible."

"So it was sacred to them. It's hard for me to understand how they would have felt."

"They were totally consumed with passion for the principles of the Third Reich. They were devastated by the death of the Führer. I do not think anyone like you could really understand."

"Why are you still involved with them?" Brian studied Marta.

"It was ingrained in my brain from the time I was a little girl. My father had convinced me that Hitler was a political genius who had made Germany into a great nation—one that that world had to reckon with. I always felt like it was my duty to honor and protect the Führer's legacy."

"But why are you so interested in me?"

"The *Freundenreich* has thrived as a secret society since it was formed, and is still in existence due to the dedication of its members. Their sole objective is to gain total power over Germany once again, as the Third Reich had done years earlier. Within the last several years, the *Freundenreich* has splintered into two factions. One still holds onto the old Nazi principles and wants to revive them. The other group is beginning to realize that Fascism can never be embraced again and would rather tell Hitler's story than keep it a secret."

"What secret?"

"I think you know what I mean."

"No. I really don't."

"You have knowledge of something most Germans would never believe. I will tell you what you want to know, but you must never tell anyone who told you."

Brian's mouth was dry. He barely managed to get the words out. "What is it?"

Marta went over and leaned against the railing, staring at the water. "I will tell you a story about Hitler's brother—his twin brother. You must listen to me. The twins were born in the late afternoon of April 20th in 1889."

"How do you know?"

"It is all based on a conversation Hitler's father had with a relative. He said that a midwife delivered the children. Adolf was healthy enough, but his brother was very sick—scrawny and not breathing very well. The father, who had repeatedly informed his wife he did not want any more children, decided that the weak baby had to be taken to a priest to be blessed. He made the long trek through the night to a monastery close to Linz. But he was confronted by a monk at Lambach and told to leave. He then went to Hagenmünster, a short distance to the east. Afraid they would simply bless the child and he would then be turned away again, he left his son on the doorstep, hoping he would be saved. A kind monk named Dimitrius found the baby in the early morning hours."

"I know the rest. A monk at the monastery told me."

"Brother Flavius!"

"You know him?"

"Yes. He belongs to the *Freundenreich*—at least the faction that wants the truth to be told."

"He gave me a picture of Brother Matthias. So he knew who I was, didn't he?"

"Yes. He was expecting you. The organization is so tight-knit, it is virtually impossible for members to be unaware of what is going on. He wanted you to have the picture so you would believe what you had doubted for so long."

Brian started to become agitated. "They took the picture when they killed Herr Schäffer. Now the Bible and documents are gone."

"I am so sorry. It is the work of the other faction that wants nothing to do with sharing Hitler's past. They will kill anyone who gets in their way. The next time they will not just kidnap you; it will be much worse. You must be careful."

"I figured they just wanted to scare the hell out of me."

"You must understand that if they had not thought you would comply with their wishes, they would have killed you. Without a doubt."

"Why are you telling me all this?" Brian asked. "If they find out, won't they come after you?"

"The group has threatened me in the past for saying too much. They take themselves far too seriously. I will take my chances."

"So tell me. Who's in this *Freundenreich*?"

"Many of the people you have already talked to are members. Anna, Dr. Heisler, Joseph Schäffer, and Brother Flavius want the truth to be known as I do. It is Manfred Wormser and his men you have to worry about. There is a network of loyal followers of Wormser that even includes the Abbot of Hagenmünster."

"But he said Hitler wasn't worthy of being alive. Why would a priest support Hitler?"

"All part of the disguise," Marta replied. "Hitler undoubtedly protected the Catholic Church and its clergy."

"What about the messenger?"

"The monk is very conflicted. He was a Hitler Youth Volunteer before he had found God, and he believes that Hitler was not an evil person. He supported Wormser's faction, but recently he seems to have had a change of heart and therefore had tipped you off about Glossen."

Brian had a disquieted look on his face. "Why in the hell did they kill Schäffer?"

"I am almost certain that Wormser found out that Schäffer was sympathetic to you and that he gave away something the *Freundenreich* considers sacred."

"The notebook."

"Yes. I believe it gave them the opportunity to get the picture of Brother Matthias back as well."

"So what do you think of Wormser?" Brian asked rather sarcastically.

Marta shook her head. "I hate him. He is a bastard and would think nothing of taking another person's life for the sake of the cause. He has always been ruthless, but within the last several years he has become unbearable."

Brian was beginning to feel like he was finally really getting somewhere. "If what you are saying about Hitler's brother is true, where is he now?"

"I do not know. To be honest with you, I have never known. I believe in my heart that he is alive, but I cannot prove it."

"Who would know?"

Marta carefully reached into her coat pocket and pulled out a piece of paper and a pen. She wrote down a name and address. "Here. You must talk to Fräulein Hildabrand."

"Who is she?"

"She was Heinrich Glossen's mistress."

Brian looked at the address. "She lives in Garmisch-Partenkirchen?"

"After Glossen left the country, his mistress went there to live because that is where she was born. And even though she was a very attractive woman, she never married."

"What happened to his wife and children?"

"You must ask her. I do not know."

Brian wasn't sure whether this was just another runaround. Fräulein Hildabrand might not even talk to him. But somehow, now more than before, he was convinced that Hitler did have a twin. If he could locate him, it would be an unbelievable story. Of course the *Freundenreich* would never allow that. So why should he even bother? "I'll need your help."

Marta smiled and touched Brian's face. "I have helped already, but I will never be far away." She started to leave, but then turned around. "You must consider the possibilities. If Glossen did find the Führer's twin brother, what would that have meant to the Third Reich?" Smiling, she walked quickly away, pulling her hood up over her head.

Brian stood and watched as she faded into the scenery. What the hell was he going to tell Laura and Ronny? He knew he had to find Fräulein Hildabrand and talk to her. He took the long way back to the hotel so he could think it over.

"Cancel the flight?" Laura slammed the top of her suitcase down. "Are you out of your mind?"

Brian tried to explain, but Laura gave the impression she didn't want to listen. He told her Marta's story and the fact that they knew her as Gerta Honiker. And she had given him the name of Glossen's mistress.

"But you said Marta—or Gerta, or whatever her name is—belongs to this neo-Nazi group. Why would you believe her or even want to associate with her? A little dangerous, don't you think?"

Brian ignored Laura's common sense. "I believe if I can locate this mistress, I can find out more about Hitler's relationship with his brother."

"Why? How would she know?"

"Glossen may have told her. Remember, she was his mistress. Pillow talk. Stuff like that."

"Did she say whether Brother Matthias was still alive?"

"She didn't know. But it's conceivable that Fräulein Hildabrand would be privy to that information."

"Is this really necessary?" Laura asked.

"It's more than important that I talk to the mistress. You can leave if you want. I'll understand."

Irritated, Laura looked out the window and then at the clock.

"Okay. I'll go with you. But Ronny will probably want to get back to New York. I'll give him a call."

The next morning they sat at an outside café. The sun was beginning to burn off the cool air. Brian sipped his coffee while Ronny demolished a sweet roll. Laura looked at a map.

"You know," Brian said, "I've been thinking about this ever since Marta told me to consider the possibilities for the Third Reich if Hitler's twin existed. What if their plan was to use the twin to their advantage?"

"What do you mean?" Laura asked.

"It's entirely possible that Glossen's plan all along was to have the twin take over as the Führer if he somehow became incapacitated. More than that, he could certainly have been a pawn if the Führer was ever threatened or captured by the enemy."

"That possibly could be true," Ronny said, with a slight grin on his face. "I've decided to stay in Munich while you go down to Garmisch. I'll try to find out what I can about the organization of the *Freundenreich*."

Laura wasn't happy. "You must be careful. It looks like they are always one step in front of us."

Brian looked over at Ronny. "I thought you were afraid they would find out about your Jewish ancestry. You should go back to New York."

"No. I'll stay here."

"We should leave today," Laura said. "It won't take us that long to get down there—probably only about four hours or so. We can get a hotel right in the city, eat dinner, and look for Glossen's former mistress tomorrow."

Brian pulled out the piece of paper with Fräulein Hildabrand's address on it: 80 St. Martin Strasse. He wasn't sure where that was, but he was confident they wouldn't have any problem finding it.

"You need to get as much information from the mistress as you can," Ronny suggested. "If nothing else, she could tell you things about Hitler that would be beneficial to know. It is entirely possible that the mistress will not want to talk about the supposed twin, or even Glossen. She could even be part of the *Freundenreich* and therefore should not be trusted." He didn't say anything else for a few seconds.

"What's the matter?" Laura asked.

"I can't figure what Marta's motives are. I don't understand why she lied to us in New York. She seems to be keeping a close eye on us, and that bothers me."

Laura was grateful for the warning. Brian remained silent and smiled, as he looked past everyone. He was one step closer.

chapter 15
Berlin—1945

THE SNOW-COVERED STREETS LACKED a certain beauty in the war-torn city ravaged by Allied bombing. Glossen walked slowly toward the Reich Chancellery. It had taken a number of direct hits from heavy bombs and many of the broken windows were now boarded up. He was planning to attend a meeting between Goebbels and the Führer. But before that he had to take care of some last minute paperwork in his office.

When he walked in, Eva handed him a memo. In his office, he read it carefully. It was from Horst. The note was nothing short of preposterous. In it, the twin concluded that Adolf was no longer competent to run the Third Reich. He wanted Glossen to subdue him so he could make the decisions that would ultimately win the war. Glossen called for Eva to make an appointment for him to see the Führer. But before he could finish his sentence, Manfred Wormser walked in.

"You seem to always come at the wrong time," Glossen said, sitting down.

"Indeed. I understand you are dangerously close to treason."

Glossen slammed the note on his desk. "What do you mean?"

Wormser smiled. "You do not think I know what you are up to?"

Glossen tried not to reach across the desk and strangle his deputy. "Of course you must assume I am plotting something terrible against our Führer. Is that it?"

"You do not think I know how Horst is impersonating our Führer more than he should be? I think you are taking advantage of a sick man."

"I am doing no such thing. It is all by decree of Hitler himself. I am merely complying with orders."

"So what do you have in your hands?" Wormser asked.

"It is none of your concern. I must ask you to leave as I have a lot of work to do."

"I asked you what you have in your hands." Wormser stood up.

"You are out of line. Leave now or I will call the guards."

Wormser snickered and quickly responded, "You will do no such thing, Herr Glossen. I will tell you this: I do not trust you, and if I think you are undermining the Führer, I will have you arrested." He stormed out the door.

That afternoon, Glossen cornered Hitler's brother before his meeting with the Führer. Horst was staying in the garden shelter, an underground bunker adjacent to the Chancellery garden. The Führer had been splitting his time between his office and the bunker because of the air raid threats, and he thought Horst should stay there as well. They sat down and Glossen brought out the memo. "What is the meaning of this?" He held the note high in the air.

"I have a reasonable explanation. I feel compassion for the Führer. I can see the terrible condition he is in. It does not take a medical degree. After thinking about it for a good long time, I have decided it is probably better for me to make the command decisions since I have become the embodiment of my brother. I know his thoughts, his feelings, and, more importantly, his visions for the future."

"But you are not the Führer! Surely you must understand that."

"Yes. Of course. But he is a sick man and I am the only one that can help."

Glossen really couldn't dispute that. Horst was absolutely correct, but it was the ego Glossen thought he had to contain. It was completely up to Hitler whether he would relinquish his control—something Glossen doubted very much. "You cannot just assume you are in command. It is not that simple."

"I know I am somewhat belligerent, but I believe that what I desire to do is for the good of the Reich. My brother must come to his senses. We must win the war at any cost."

Realizing he was close to being late to his meeting, Glossen told Horst that they would talk at a later time.

Goebbels escorted Glossen into the map room where Hitler was sitting in a small chair. The air raid shelter had two stories. The top level was being used for administrative personnel and distinguished visitors. The Führer and his immediate staff had designated the lower story, which had 18 rooms, for use. The ambiance was somewhat nicer than Wolfsschanze, Hitler's bunker complex and headquarters in East Prussia, but brute concrete walls still loomed throughout the facility. The setting was dismal, to say the least.

By then, Hitler was relying almost exclusively on the advice and consent of Joseph Goebbels. One of the first things he had done after returning from East Prussia was to visit Goebbels and his family at their home. Over the years, Hitler had become suspicious of other members of the Reich leadership. He continually questioned their loyalty to him and the Nazi regime. But Goebbels was different. Hitler had affection for him that knew no bounds. Glossen could sense the closeness between them.

They sat down next to the Führer. Hitler began, "Because of the impending Allied advance, I want to start preparations for the government to be moved out of Berlin to an area near Berchtesgarden. All ministries and commands will be relocated there. I want the preparations to begin immediately. At some point all Nazi offices, including mine, will be moved to that location." He looked at Goebbels. "I expect you to take care of it."

Goebbels replied, "It might be better to hold our ground in Berlin."

Hitler put up his finger and said he would not hear of it.

Goebbels straightened his posture. "Yes, mein Führer. I will make the necessary arrangements."

"We have some time," Hitler said. "We have not lost this war yet. The outcome of the war will certainly be in our favor. The German armament production and the willingness of the soldiers to make the ultimate sacrifice for their country are unparalleled."

"We should begin to plan earnestly for our own protection, in the unlikely event we lose the war," Goebbels suggested. "I recommend we have escape routes planned, even if we are in Berchtesgarden."

Hitler thought about it for a minute or so. His reaction was anticipated. "I will not abandon the German people by running into the woods. It is up to others to do what they want."

"Mein Führer," Glossen said. "I want to talk about how you view your brother's contribution to the Reich and his possible future. I am concerned about the fate of the former monk."

Hitler sneered. "I know about the letter."

Glossen didn't know what to say.

"I want to know why my brother thinks he has become the Führer. Can you tell me that?"

Glossen replied, "Horst really did not mean to suggest that he wanted to push you aside—only that he wanted to help if it was necessary."

"I want to see him personally. The sooner the better."

"Yes, mein Führer," Glossen replied.

Hitler addressed Goebbels. "And I would muzzle that barbarian Wormser if you know what is good for you. I really could never stand him." Glossen looked over at Goebbels, whose eyes were fixated on Hitler's face.

Immediately following the meeting, Glossen went back to his

office, where he asked Eva to summon Wormser. Within a half hour the Jew Killer walked into his office.

"What have you done?" Glossen asked.

"You seem out of sorts, Herr Glossen. What is the matter?"

"What did you tell the Führer?"

Wormser sported an evil smile. "Only the truth: that you have prompted Hitler's brother to take over the Reich so you can really be in charge. A plot you will not get away with."

Glossen couldn't believe his ears. "You told the Führer I was plotting to take over the Third Reich?"

"Of course. Why are you so surprised?" Wormser's face began to twitch.

"You bastard! I ought to have you shot on the spot." He reached for the phone.

Wormser laughed and said, "I would not be so quick to act. Goebbels will not allow it and we both know that."

After Wormser left, Glossen sat back in his chair and thought about what was going to happen next.

*   *   *

Several weeks later, Glossen sat with Horst in what looked like a gloomy cell—a room void of the most common of things. The bed was little more than a cot. The dresser was a converted ammunition case. A single painting hung on the wall: the Führer in his dress uniform. Horst was depressed and saddened, much like his brother, but he felt he had a higher purpose. He could still remember the things he had been taught at the monastery: to be worthy of God's earthly plan, to love his brother. He believed in his heart that Germany was destined to be a great nation. His brother was only trying to make that happen. "I have been thinking. The Führer must go to Berchtesgarden as soon as possible."

"And what will you do?" Glossen asked.

"Remain here. That way the German people will not think their Führer abandoned them."

"He will not allow such a thing. He would rather have you go to the new headquarters."

"No. I have already talked to him."

"When? This is simply not possible." Glossen had never envisioned this course of events in his plan. He couldn't let Horst stay behind and be captured by the enemy, or worse, while Hitler escaped. "You will leave with us all if and when the Führer gives the order."

"You do not understand. It has been blessed at the highest level. We must take immediate steps to protect the Führer."

Glossen left the room and went to find Hitler. When he did, he asked if they could talk for a few minutes. Goebbels had just departed and Glossen thought it was a good opportunity to get to the bottom of Horst's story.

"I have given my expressed consent to my brother that he can remain here, but only on a temporary basis." Hitler stared at Glossen. "I have made provisions for him to exit the city when he believes he is threatened."

"But, mein Führer, what if he cannot get out of the city?"

"I have every confidence that he will. Otherwise, I would not agree to such a thing. Do you understand my wishes?"

Glossen had no choice but to agree. He was concerned that Hitler had lost his mind. Their world was coming down on top of them and he was too blind to see it. Glossen knew Horst would be a sitting duck if he were left in Berlin.

*   *   *

Later, in the first week of April, Glossen was summoned to Goebbels' office. It was a brief but poignant meeting. The Propaganda Minister began by ordering Glossen to take the Führer to Berghof. The plan was for him to remain there temporarily. Within a week's time, Goebbels would instruct Glossen where to take Hitler.

"What will become of Horst? He must be evacuated as well."

"He will not go until later. We have taken care of those plans. You are responsible just for the Führer."

Glossen began to feel a bit agitated knowing they were taking advantage of him. After all, he was the one who had found Horst, brought him to Berlin, and made this all happen. Now he was being pushed out of the picture. But what could he do? Refuse to accompany the Führer to Berchtesgarden? Disobey Goebbels—his mentor? The truth was that he didn't trust them. They would sooner let Horst take the fall for his brother than try to ensure his safety. "When do we leave?"

"In the morning. Eva Braun has just arrived unexpectedly and we need to accelerate the schedule." Goebbels brought out an envelope and handed it to Glossen. "Do not open this until I give you the word."

"What does it contain?" Glossen asked.

"I will only say that it is important. Do not misplace it," Goebbels said. "I fear the worst for the Reich and I will do everything in my power to ensure that we surrender with dignity—something I know the Führer would never condone, wanting instead to fight to the end."

*   *   *

The phone call woke Glossen up out of a sound sleep.

"The Führer has decided to stay in Berlin," Goebbels said. "At least for the time being. You must report to my office in the morning."

Glossen looked at his watch. It was three in the morning. He thought briefly what Goebbels had said and then he turned over and went back to sleep.

chapter 16
Bavaria—1972

LAURA HELD THE MAP in her lap. They headed south through the beautiful hamlet of Obermammergau, site of the *Passion Play*, and stopped and looked around briefly. Stopping at Ettall, they walked around to get some exercise. Laura wanted to take a tour of the Abbey, which sat on a hill overlooking the town. For centuries, monks had been making beers and liqueurs and selling them to make money for the cloister. They decided not to go in, but rather walked around the periphery of the huge and magnificent courtyard. Staying slightly more than an hour, they then continued on their way, negotiating the difficult mountain pass into the Garmisch area.

Laura read the travel book out loud. Garmish-Partenkirchen, located in southernmost state of Bavaria, was actually two separate cities prior to the 1936 Winter Olympics. Partenkirchen was first documented in the year 257 A.D. as a Roman way station called

The Caretaker's Bible

Parthanum on the road from Rome to Augsburg. During the Middle Ages, it flourished as part of the Oriental trade route.

The city was famous for other things as well; the composer Richard Strauss had lived and was now buried there, and mad King Ludwig II had built many castles in the surrounding area, such as Neuschwanstein and Lindenhof. Now, Garmish-Partenkirchen was a winter sports capital. It had over 40 ski lifts, 11 cable cars, and a cogwheel train that provided service to more than 68 miles of ski slopes. The Olympic ski and ice stadiums from 1936 still remained.

They parked their car near the Hauptstrasse and walked around looking for a small Gästhaus. Their plan was to stay two nights so they could adequately discuss matters with Fräulein Hildabrand. Within no time, they had found a small, charming place to stay. Brian suggested they go to dinner and attempt to see the Fräulein in the morning.

*   *   *

Brian was dressed when Laura returned from a morning stroll around the Hauptstrasse. She told him she was smitten with the beauty of the German border town. Her first observation was that there were many American tourists visiting the area. She also noticed how active the town was at seven-thirty in the morning. She could see why: the mountains towering over the city chalets painted a breathless panorama—especially beneath the cloudless and serene morning sky.

"Can we talk," Laura said. "I'm concerned about why we're here: to talk to the former mistress of a prominent Nazi. It's extremely unlikely we'll get much out of her unless she's bitter about being deserted in the end. I can't fathom what she knows about Hitler or his twin. To me, it's unlikely that the Fräulein would know very much, if anything, about Brother Matthias."

Brian didn't say much other than that he wanted to go directly to 80 St. Martin Strasse.

It didn't take long to find the house. Brian knocked on the door.

After a minute or so, an older lady answered. Laura stepped forward and asked if she spoke English. When she nodded yes, Laura asked, "Are you Fräulein Hildabrand?"

She immediately said that she was not; she was the housekeeper. Laura asked if the Fräulein was at home. The housekeeper said she would have to go get her as the Fräulein was eating breakfast. She asked for them to come in and wait in the foyer.

"I am Fräulein Hildabrand," said the lady as she greeted them. She was incredibly beautiful for her age, Brian thought to himself, as she had to be in her late 70s or early 80s. "How may I help you?"

Very pleased that she spoke English, Brian explained that they were in Garmisch for only a short time and wanted to ask her a few questions about her life during the Nazi regime. She immediately wanted to know how they had learned her name and what exactly they wanted to know.

"We understand you were the mistress of Heinrich Glossen," Laura said nonchalantly.

She had a cold stare on her face. Brian thought Laura had obviously said the wrong thing.

"Why have you really come here?" the Fräulein asked.

Laura tried to explain. "We are researching several key individuals who had supported Hitler in order to carry out the objectives of the Third Reich."

"How dare you come here and ask me these questions."

"We are interested in Herr Glossen," Brian said. "If we could just have a few minutes of your time?"

"I am not sure I should say anything." The Fräulein looked away and said, "And what do I have to gain by that?"

"Knowing you told the truth," Brian replied. "That's all we can ask."

She thought for a moment. "They will know."

"Who?" Laura asked.

"The *Freundenreich*." She appeared nervous. "I must ask you to leave."

The Caretaker's Bible

Brian said, "I want to know everything you know about the Friends of the Third Reich, but we will leave if you really feel uneasy."

After a few moments of what appeared to be indecisiveness, she escorted them into her living room and introduced herself as Helga. "I have tried to forget my past. That way, I will not have to be placed in a position where I will be forced to reveal things I am forbidden to tell."

Brian explained that he was certain they had not been followed on their way down from Munich. He told her how he had gotten her name.

"I met Marta a number of years ago at a restaurant in town. Marta warned me about individuals in the *Freundenreich* who wanted to take total control and who would stop at nothing to silence everyone who defied them. But I already knew that. I have dealt with them before, but I have no reason to believe they will ever harm me, because of my relationship with Heinrich Glossen."

"You don't have to tell us," Laura said. "We understand."

Brian was anxious to get what he came for and gave his fiancée a dirty look. "I assure you, we would never divulge you as a source of information."

"I have never revealed my story to anyone," Helga replied. "It has been so many years."

"Please!" Brian said. "We really need to know."

"In 1939 I was working as a secretary at the Reichsbank Directorate in Berlin. I worked for an economist and banker named Otto Hammer. I actually had started working there three years earlier and had worked my way up to become the secretary to one of the top influential finance experts of the Third Reich. Because of my duties, I had contacts with several key members of Hitler's staff. It was not uncommon for Göring or Goebbels to visit us on a bimonthly basis. In August of 1939, I met Heinrich Glossen. He had been appointed by Goebbels to ensure that the Reichsbank was complying with the Nazi grand scheme of propaganda that was beginning to become more important in keeping Hitler's master plan intact.

"When we first met, I did not like him very much because he was arrogant. It would be an understatement to say he was a good-looking man. He never let his guard down. The third time we met, Glossen asked me out to dinner. I wanted to refuse, but he was not one to take no for an answer. Immediately I knew that he was very intelligent and savvy. I figured he would be well liked by Hitler, as the Führer was drawn to smart and crafty individuals who could help him promote the Third Reich."

"Did he say what he actually did for the Führer?" Brian asked.

"You must understand that Heinrich worked for Goebbels. Everything he did was under the direct orders of the Propaganda Minister. I know, however, that Heinrich's ideas were quickly made known to Hitler—not necessarily by Goebbels, but by others. I also know the Propaganda Minister was as egotistical as Heinrich, if not more so. He would surely have let the Führer think Heinrich's ideas were his own. Heinrich was assigned to oversee the development of propaganda within several departments—finance, politics, and military. This actually gave him more power than perhaps Goebbels had initially foreseen. He worked hard—never less than twelve hours a day—and he had his own department of more than twenty people to manage."

"Was he married at the time?" Laura asked.

"Yes. He had two small children. I remember seeing them at several gala events. He always insisted I attend, even though he would be there with his wife. He said it made him feel important. I did not want to upset him, so I went. But by our third date, Heinrich and I had become intimate. I was taken with his sense of romance. He showered me with flowers and a beautiful diamond necklace for Christmas that year. In the beginning of 1940, Heinrich expressed his concern that I was working while I was being seen with him. He asked me to resign. I refused."

"You must have been flattered that a man of Glossen's stature was so interested in you," Brian suggested.

"That is not true. I dated other men with more—much more—influence in the government. I simply had fallen in love with

The Caretaker's Bible

Heinrich. There was no denying it. By the summer of 1940, I asked Heinrich to divorce his wife and marry me. He said it could never be. He had an obligation to his wife, and besides, the Führer did not like scandals of any kind and would have been furious with him for doing so. At first, I considered breaking off the relationship, but Heinrich begged me not to. He told me he would make it up to me. In fact, he put me up at a downtown hotel in Berlin in a suite on the top floor. I decided at the end of 1940 to quit my job and become his mistress full time."

"He was good to you?" Laura asked.

"I had everything I ever wanted: jewelry, furs, expensive clothes—everything, except, of course, his hand in marriage. On many occasions when his wife could not attend a gala, I would go in her place. He would always tell me not to be as foolish as to think that his wife did not know about our relationship. He was a romantic man, and I fell hopelessly in love with him."

"Were you privy to his routine relationship with Hitler?" Brian asked.

"We only talked about it briefly. Heinrich claimed he was sworn to secrecy and could not under any circumstances reveal the intimate inner dealings of the Third Reich. I recall on one particular occasion that Heinrich seemed annoyed at Goebbels. After some prodding on my part, he told me that Göring, who had dressed him down in front of the Führer, had embarrassed him. The exchange had to do with military matters that Göring insisted Heinrich knew nothing about, therefore Göring said his opinion was useless. Heinrich became furious with Goebbels because he never once said a word in his defense. It was well known by everyone in the inner circle that Hitler was very malleable and could be easily persuaded by others to form opinions about people without thinking them through.

"Over time, Heinrich became more and more open with me. I could not get over how he would come to my suite and just explode like he had been keeping something inside of him forever. He had such a temper. I believe he took his job so seriously that it affected his health. One time, he was so upset at Goebbels that he spent the entire evening throwing up in my bathroom. I concluded early on in our relationship that the tensions of being a key and trusted figure in the Third Reich were practically suicidal. On numerous occasions I asked Heinrich to take a vacation in order to get some rest. He would refuse—always."

"Did he ever talk about his family?" Laura asked.

"Of course. Heinrich loved his children and would talk of them often. On many occasions he actually brought his children to my suite for brief visits. They would always be very polite and well mannered. But I always felt awkward when his children were around. He was so stern with them."

"What happened to his family after the war?" Laura asked.

Helga shook her head. "I am not completely sure. I have been told the wife had committed suicide and that the children had left the country, but I never knew where they had gone."

"What about Goebbels? Did you ever meet him?" Brian asked.

Helga got a funny look on her face as if she didn't want to talk about it. Laura could tell she wasn't comfortable with the question and told her it wasn't important.

Helga sat up straight and said, "I met with Goebbels more than I would have liked. In my opinion he was a nasty human being who only had one goal in life: to plant a big kiss on Hitler's rear end. It gave him ultimate pleasure to at least try. He tended to use people for his own gain. In 1941, he put Heinrich in charge of coordinating with the SS to further alienate the Jews. It was a simple decree. Jews who had completed their sixth year were forbidden to be in public without wearing the Jewish star, which consisted of a six-pointed star, outlined with black wording that said "Jew." It had to be permanently sewn to the left breast of clothing. In a series of talks with the Führer himself, Goebbels had Heinrich explain the rationale behind what they were doing. Of course, as was the case with the Propaganda Minister, he took all the credit when Hitler approved the plan. Heinrich started to become more involved in other matters such as Foreign Affairs, specifically to provide direct assistance to Joachim von Ribbentrop, the Foreign Minister.

"In 1941, Hitler had made a decision to invade Russia. He

The Caretaker's Bible

actually believed Russia was preparing to attack Germany that summer—something he had long held would not happen. It fell upon Heinrich's shoulders to energize German citizens by painting a picture that the German army could defeat the Russians quickly because of the political weakness of the Russian regime and the fact that Germany was technically superior to the Russians in every way. Winning support from his countrymen mattered to Hitler. In reality, he would ultimately do what he wanted, but he demanded concurrence from the masses."

"So what you're saying is that Glossen really ran the propaganda machine for Goebbels," Brian said.

"Yes. But don't misunderstand me; Goebbels was in charge—at least in Hitler's eyes."

"I can imagine," Laura said.

Helga continued, "Heinrich would constantly tell me how he received orders from his boss to defend the military incursion into Russia to the public as being noble and important for the survival of Germany. It was not uncommon for Heinrich to work directly with the military commanders as well. The tension of his job had to be monumental. I could see it was taking its toll by 1945."

"Why didn't he just tell Goebbels he was up to his neck?" Laura asked.

Helga laughed. "That is easy to say, but in reality Goebbels would have thrown him to the lions. Heinrich would have been ostracized and probably sooner or later executed for treason. Because he knew so much about the inner workings of the Third Reich, it would have been a matter of state security to eliminate him. I recall an incident in which Heinrich had a falling out with Goebbels. In the summer of 1943, Heinrich accompanied Goebbels to Wolfsschanze, as he had done on numerous occasions. By then the Führer had isolated himself in the massive underground bunker complex under the main headquarters. Sparse, it was nothing but bare concrete walls and old wooden furniture.

"Goebbels made a speech that Hitler actually listened to, but he dismissed the basic premise, which was to consider a compromise in the war that would be more inclined toward a peaceful solution.

Heinrich quickly sided with Hitler, saying that the Führer's efforts toward expansionism had already gone too far and that the war had to be finalized in Germany's favor. Goebbels was severely embarrassed by Heinrich's comments, and when they departed Wolfsschanze, the Propaganda Minister threatened to fire him or have him confined to his office in the Reich Chancellery permanently. Heinrich apparently apologized for his indiscretion. But it took several months for Goebbels to feel comfortable enough again to have confidence in him. Heinrich told me later that he was only trying to gain the Führer's confidence and testing Goebbels' patience at the same time."

Brian stood up and stretched. Helga offered them some tea. While they waited for her to return, they walked around the rather large living room. The furniture was elegant; it looked like it had a French design with dark, rich, stripped colors. It was very well decorated. What Brian noticed almost right away were three oil paintings that looked similar to the ones he had seen in Herr Schäffer's house.

Helga returned and put the tray on the coffee table. Pouring the tea, she asked if what she was saying was of any importance.

Brian replied, "I thank you for taking the time to answer our questions. I think everything you told us so far is exactly what we needed to know. You mentioned the *Freundenreich* earlier. What do you know about them?"

"All I know is that they are evil. They will kill anyone that they feel threatened by. Members of the group have visited me many times over the years. They always say that as far as they are concerned, Nazi Germany is still alive and that I am advised not to talk about my past."

"What do you know that is so important that the *Freundenreich* would take your life if you told someone?" Brian asked.

Helga appeared confused by the question. "I do not know what you mean."

Brian put his teacup down and stood up, walking over to the fireplace. "We have reason to believe Adolf Hitler had a twin. What do you know about that?"

The Caretaker's Bible

Helga's manner changed quickly. "I must now ask you to leave." She started to gather the teacups on the tray.

"Please," Laura said. "We must know. We have come so far."

"We know you are taking a chance even talking to us," Brian said, "let alone sharing secrets of the Reich. We really need to know whether Hitler had a twin or not. If so, I want to know what became of him."

She trembled while sitting in her chair. "I must not say anything. I simply cannot."

Laura tried to console her. "Yes. It's all right."

She began staring at the fireplace as she talked. "Only a few people knew the truth. Many in the *Freundenreich* consider it a myth—one that solidifies loyalty among the members. It is a closely guarded secret. My life has always been in danger, and now, whether I tell you or not, the *Freundenreich* will know you have been here.

"At the end of 1941, I attended a small Third Reich get-together for the senior members, their families, secretaries, and office workers. It was a magnificent affair, just as they all were. The Nazis spared no expense when having a good time. I wore a beautiful blue gown with sparkling diamond earrings. Heinrich had asked me to go since his wife was ill at the time. During the course of the night, Hitler joined the party and made a point of walking around to each table and exchanging niceties. Everyone was thrilled at the chance to talk to him and shake his hand. When we left for the night, Heinrich laughed and asked how I enjoyed socializing with the Führer. I replied that it was certainly an honor. What he said next shocked me. He told me that the Führer had come down with a very bad cold and was confined to bed. When I asked how that could be since I had just talked to him, Heinrich said it was not Hitler I had addressed. It was an impostor."

"An impostor!" Laura looked over at Brian.

"Heinrich told me that they had found the perfect double for the Führer who could be used for special occasions if it were necessary."

"Why would they do that?" Laura asked.

"Glossen never really explained why then. He only said that I would find out in due time. It was not necessarily a secret that Hitler was not in the best of health, and in fact had been taking medicine prescribed by his doctor for several years."

"But an impostor?" Laura said.

Helga replied, "I think the Nazi leadership was afraid that their Führer could die at any time and they had to be prepared."

Brian remembered reading somewhere that Hitler's health had degraded after he reached the age of 50. It was possible that the senior leadership was concerned. "So what did Glossen tell you later?"

"A few months after the party I received a call from Heinrich. He said he had someone he wanted me to meet. I thought it would be nice to have the person come to my apartment. Heinrich readily agreed as long as it was under the cover of darkness. I had a friend prepare a wealth of hors d'oeuvres, and I bought the best wine I could find for the evening. I planned it for a Saturday night and paid special attention to ensuring everything was in its proper place. When they arrived and I opened the door, I was absolutely shocked. There with Heinrich stood a man who was the spitting image of Hitler."

"What did you do?" Laura asked.

"I must have looked awkward. I gasped for breath. Glossen immediately told me not to worry since it was only a friend—not the Führer."

Laura shook her head. "Did you believe him?"

"Not at first. He looked and sounded just like Hitler. But after a few moments, Heinrich formally introduced his friend as Horst and said that he was the twin brother of Adolf Hitler."

Brian practically choked when he heard the name. "Horst!"

"That is what Glossen called him. I cannot be sure of his real name. We spent the entire evening talking about Horst's love for his brother and the reasons why he even attempted to impersonate him. He loved him dearly and knew his brother's frail health could keep him from ruling the Third Reich. He was humbled by the fact that he could pass himself off as the Führer. The only thing I never found out was whether Hitler felt the same way about Horst."

The Caretaker's Bible

"Did he say anything about his past?" Brian was adamant that a twin couldn't just materialize out of thin air.

"We never discussed it. Even later when I prodded Heinrich about Horst's past, he declined to talk about it. What was strange is that after that evening at my apartment, I never saw Horst again—except of course if he had been impersonating his brother."

"Do you believe he routinely stood in for the Führer?" Brian asked.

"I have no idea. I am not even sure Heinrich was telling the truth about the impersonation. All I know is that Horst had to be Hitler's twin. I saw it with my own eyes."

Brian was now convinced. But there were still many unanswered questions. *How did they find the twin? Was it Brother Matthias? Did he really become a double for the Führer?* "Is there anyone else you might know that could substantiate your story?"

"I believe you will want to talk to Heinrich's former secretary." She went over to her bookcase and wrote down a name and address. Brian looked at the small piece of paper. It read Eva Dofmünster, 501 Marlybone Drive, South Kensington, London, England.

"Do you know if she's still alive?" Brian asked.

"His former secretary is now retired after having worked for a British investment firm for many years. She had left Germany several years after the war ended. She was privy to what went on at the Chancellery. If Horst was impersonating his brother, she would probably know."

"Does she belong to the *Freundenreich*?" Laura asked.

"I cannot even speculate. I am positive, however, that she is the only person that will be able to talk intelligently about the twin. In my opinion, it is worth a try."

The housekeeper interrupted them. "Excuse me. Several men in dark suits are standing at the door. What should I do?"

Brian quickly motioned for them to leave out the back door. It had to be the *Freundenreich*. He grabbed Helga by the arm and told her to come with them. She immediately declined; it was her house and she would not leave. Laura tried to change her mind, but Helga insisted they leave, saying she feared for their lives.

They made their way down a back alley to an adjoining street. Angry that Helga had refused to come, Brian decided he wanted to go back. "Her life is in danger. We should have stayed and protected her."

"I know how you feel, but I have to disagree. We all could have been killed or taken away. Helga's fate is in the hands of God."

"But if we had never gone there, this wouldn't have happened."

"I'm not so sure. She has been visited before. Perhaps this is just a chance occurrence—a routine stop just to ensure Helga is complying with their wishes."

"They know we're on to their secret and they can't let us get away with it," Brian said. "We should wait awhile before we go to our car since it's parked on Helga's street. I have an idea. Let's take a cab over to the Zugspitze, take the cable car up to the summit, and spend the afternoon there. Then later we can come back and get our car."

* * *

The temperature at the very top of the Zugspitze was freezing. It was snowing and the flakes glistened in the outside lights of the massive tourist lodge. They sat inside drinking hot chocolate. Laura spent a lot of time looking around for suspicious patrons. It had never been her personality to be paranoid, but ever since she had met Manfred Wormser, she was sure they couldn't take any chances.

"What do you make of Helga's story about meeting Hitler's twin?" Brian asked.

"It's all was very interesting. I believe Helga actually met someone who looked like Hitler, but I can't be positive it was his twin. What bothers me is that the high command of the Third Reich would even think of substituting an impostor for Hitler. It's hard to believe."

"I wouldn't put it past Goebbels to do such a thing. Remember, he was the Propaganda Minister. The Third Reich had to be protected at all costs—even if they had to use a double to be the Führer. I strongly suspect that it would have been natural for them to pursue a twin brother if they found out that he existed."

"But how would they have known?" Laura asked.

"That's what we have to find out." Brian took a sip of his hot chocolate. "Don't you think it's strange that the brother's name was Horst?"

"I don't know. Why?"

"The caretaker. His name was Horst."

Laura hadn't made the connection. "So what are you saying? That the caretaker could be Hitler's twin?"

Even Brian had to laugh. "I don't think so. Why would he be a caretaker? Why would he be there, and why would he have befriended me?" The look on Laura's face showed she wasn't convinced.

The afternoon wore on. They took a walk on the deck overlooking the gold cross and orb that sat on the very top of the mountain. It was bitter cold now. The fog was so intense that they could no longer see the mountains around the summit, so they departed.

When they finally made it back to their car, Brian wanted to see if Helga was all right. Laura thought they should just go. After all, the perpetrators could still be there in the house.

He knocked on the door, but there was no answer. Brian decided to go around to the back door. He knocked and yelled out Helga's name several times. Again, there was no answer. Everything looked dark. Against Laura's better judgment that they leave, Brian tried to jimmy the lock to get in. It almost seemed too easy. They walked around the entire house. No one was there. There was no sign of a struggle. Perhaps she had gone out for the evening. Laura finally convinced Brian to leave. She said she felt uneasy and believed they could be walking into a trap.

Brian could not think of anything else but the evil of the *Freundenreich*. He made up his mind to drive straight through to Munich even if it took all night—continuing to look out his rear view mirror.

chapter 17
Freiburg, Germany— 1950

It had been raining most of August while the university had been welcoming students for the new semester. The sentiment in Germany, even after five years of freedom from Nazi tyranny, was mixed, but most Germans were trying to forget the horrible legacy of the Third Reich. Chancellor Adenauer and the newly formed government promised to protect its citizens from further threats of dictatorship, even though the Soviets had very recently annexed Berlin as a communist state.

Heinrich Glossen sat in a small café in the heart of the city drinking black forest wine. He had only recently returned from London and wanted desperately to keep his presence a secret. Not knowing exactly what he would do, he contemplated his future with every sip.

While in London, Glossen had managed to find several other

The Caretaker's Bible

former Nazis who had fled before the Soviets captured Berlin. They had agreed to change their identities, trying to blend in as best as they could with other immigrants living in the city.

Glossen remembered that during the first several months he was there he had been approached by British Intelligence wanting to know who he was and what he was doing in London. Lucky for him, they had no documentation on him and they took his word that he had escaped the terrible Nazi rule since he had Jewish grandparents. He honestly believed the five years he spent there were enough to give Germans time to forget who he was or what he had stood for under Hitler.

Now he was back where he had so effortlessly taught years before. He wanted to start a new life in a city he loved, but was still fearful of retaliation. The Nuremberg trials had just ended the year before. It was certainly possible that the American and German governments were still looking for devout Nazis. But he didn't look the same. He had dyed his hair brown and wore a heavy beard.

Glossen pulled out a letter and stared at it. It was from one of his old colleagues. He had replied to the former Nazi that he would meet him in Freiburg in August at the café. So he waited.

As he was about to depart after a lengthy wait, the old colleague came in and without much difficulty they found one another.

"I thought perhaps you would not come," Glossen said.

"Yes, I am sure you would dismiss my curiosity in what you have been doing the last five years," Wormser replied. He sat down.

Glossen smiled a bit. His old colleague didn't look much different and that bothered him considering the fact that Nazis were still fair game. "I have been fine. And you?"

"I think we should take a walk."

They went to a secluded park only minutes from the café.

"The Germany we once knew is forever gone," Wormser said. "We must consider what that means for us."

"We are still soldiers, but we will be hunted down and killed for our past lives."

"The Nazi heritage must be preserved."

Glossen laughed. "You must be mad. How can that be?"

"Do you now still swear allegiance to the Führer?"

Glossen paused. "To the Third Reich? To what the Führer stood for? I do not know. Does it matter now?"

"Yes. Of course. What about Hitler's legacy? What about the twin?"

Glossen stared at Wormser. "What about him? No one will believe he ever existed."

Wormser explained his irrational philosophy about what he thought they should do. "Even with the dangers we face, we should continue to foster the creed and mantle of the Third Reich. It is not out of the question that at some point in the future, the Third Reich could re-emerge as a formidable form of government that would be accepted by the citizens."

"That is nonsense and you know it. How can you be so naive? The best we can do is to protect the secrets of the Reich."

"What do you mean?" Wormser asked.

"It is possible to form a secret society of Nazi sympathizers. We cannot be so arrogant as to think it will ever amount to anything, but we could try and protect the image of the Führer and his twin."

"I understand there are a number of former Nazis still in Munich. Perhaps we could find them and begin to form an alliance."

Glossen laughed. "Of course, but we must be careful. If we expose our hand now, we will be caught. We must do it in secret."

"We can meet in private. What is important is that we find as many sympathizers as possible. We can form a network of eyes and ears that can keep us informed of what the government is doing."

"I am not convinced. I am not sure I trust you, since you were the only one that tried to ruin what I set out to do. I do not know what else to say."

"Someone had to keep you from making mistakes. Surely you never took any of that seriously. I was simply doing my job."

Glossen stared at his old colleague before letting out a horrendous laugh. "Doing your job? You were trying to get me fired. Why should I now begin a lifelong association with a madman?"

"Come now. I think you should thank me for my attempts

at leadership, especially in matters of the twin. That was a very difficult time for everyone concerned."

"Yes, I suppose it was," Glossen replied, remembering Horst well.

"We must go to Munich. I believe we should make every effort to contact fellow Nazis as soon as possible."

"What if they do not want anything to do with this?"

"I think you will be surprised." Wormser sat thinking for a moment. "You must promise me that you will never change your mind, you will never abandon your allegiance to the Third Reich. No one must know about Hitler's association with his twin. Is that understood?"

"I can only say what I feel today. I will pledge allegiance. We will go to Munich, solicit followers, and hold a rally to begin what I believe will be a new German Reich—one that will be strong and never ending. We will nurture these new friends of the Third Reich."

They shook hands rather reluctantly and went back to the café to share a drink.

chapter 18
Munich—1972

BRIAN NOTICED RONNY LOOKING out his hotel room window when they walked in. Ronny explained he had done a bit of research during the time they were away. He learned that Manfred Wormser had actually worked under Heinrich Glossen as a deputy in his division between 1940 and the end of the war. They had created a strange kind of bond and Wormser was partly instrumental in helping Glossen form the *Freundenreich*.

"Where did you get that information?" Brian asked.

"I have my sources. I think that between the two of them, they had created one of the most feared and despicable groups since the Nazi Party existed. The way I see it, Wormser has always been the bad guy countering Glossen's often good nature about the future of the German people."

"So you think Wormser is the one behind all this terror?" Laura asked. "He scared the hell out of me at the restaurant."

"I'm positive," Ronny said, "that Wormser and Glossen really hadn't agreed on the purpose of the *Freundenreich*—perhaps from the very beginning. It evolved over time. Wormser may have been a dyed-in-the-wool Nazi that nothing could change, and Glossen may have mellowed out over the years."

Laura explained what had happened on their trip. "Even though there are a lot of loose ends, I now believe without a doubt that Hitler had a twin and that the *Freundenreich* is desperately trying to keep it a secret. I'm worried that Fräulein Hildabrand has been kidnapped—or even worse: killed because of our visit."

Brian pulled out the piece of paper Helga had given him and showed it to Ronny. "We need to talk to this woman." Before he could finish, Ronny said he knew that Eva Dofmünster had been Glossen's private secretary.

"How did you know?" Laura asked.

Ronny stared at Laura with a smirk on his face. "She may well know a lot more than Glossen's mistress told you or was willing to reveal. I assume that as a secretary, Eva was cognizant of most of what went on in the Chancellery. If Hitler had a twin, she will be able to confirm it. She may even know if he is still alive."

"That's if she'll talk to us. She might tell us to go straight to hell." Brian was honest with himself. This was the last chance he had to figure this all out. If she didn't know or wouldn't tell them anything, it was all over.

"I have to draw the line," Laura said. "I'm not going to England. In fact, I'm planning on going back to New York within a few days. I've had it. We should all go home."

"Why? What if Eva can tell us what we want to know?"

"It doesn't matter. You're just going to get yourself killed. What for? A story that no one will believe."

Ronny chimed in, "Perhaps if we keep digging, we'll find out something really important."

Brian patted Ronny on the back. "Agreed."

Laura picked up the receiver. "I'm calling the airport to make reservations. Anyone else going?" No one replied.

Brian walked over to where Ronny was standing. "What else did you find out about Manfred Wormser?"

"He has an interesting past. He was hired by Goebbels to be a henchman for his organization—to do things he didn't want to do. He was a thoroughly despicable human being. There were even rumors that he had killed his brother because he wouldn't pledge allegiance to the Nazis. In 1936, Wormser's name became known to the senior Nazi leadership when Himmler uncovered a covert plot by several Gestapo members to assassinate Jesse Owens at the Olympic games in Berlin. Wormser was the mastermind. With nothing more than a slap on the wrist, Wormser continued on with his duties as a squad leader for the Gestapo. In 1938, Wormser ingratiated himself by his efforts during the *Kristallnacht*—a night instigated by the murder of Ernst von Rath in Paris by a teenage Polish Jew. Wormser was credited with orchestrating and killing many of the Jews during the blood bath in Berlin. Because of his heroic efforts during the night, he impressed many of the leaders, including Goebbels, who had been the real perpetrator of the violence."

"From everything you're telling me, this guy doesn't have a single thread of conscience," Brian said.

"Goebbels approached Glossen in the late summer of 1939 about the Jew Killer. The Propaganda Minister believed that Wormser could be of great benefit to enhancing the propaganda machine and steering it along the right path. After meeting with Wormser, Glossen asked him to join the ranks. Because of who he was and what he had done, Wormser was indispensable and held the respect of Himmler, Göring, and Ribbentrop, to name a few. By 1940, Wormser had become a prominent member of Glossen's staff. Even though the two of them didn't always agree on every issue, it appeared they seemed to at least tolerate each other."

"Do you think Wormser was out for Glossen's job?" Brian asked.

"It's very possible, but it never occurred," Ronny replied. "There was an incident that occurred sometime in 1943 in which Wormser tried to set Glossen up. But the attempt failed miserably and Goebbels himself chastised Wormser terribly."

Brian sat down on the bed. "What happened?"

"I just read it in a German history book and I'm not sure of

The Caretaker's Bible

the entire story, but supposedly Wormser had concocted a plan to discredit Glossen. In many private discussions, the Jew Killer had found out that Glossen didn't personally condone the extermination of innocent people regardless of race, but he closed his eyes to appease Goebbels. Wormser wrote a report about what he suspected and submitted it to Hitler's personal secretary—bypassing Goebbels. It backfired when the personal secretary called Goebbels to a meeting to explain the paper before he showed it to the Führer. Goebbels became incensed when he read the report. There were several accounts that Wormser had been banished for a time—not heard from or seen for several months."

"So that's why you feel Glossen and Wormser are at odds in the *Freundenreich*," Brian said.

"No. They formed the *Freundenreich* much later, obviously ignoring personal prejudices. It is apparent that Glossen seemed to be more attuned to preserving the grandeur of Nazi politics and the greatness of the state while Wormser was still looking to establish a totally Aryan race while at the same time immortalizing Hitler's persona."

"Can we talk about something else?" Laura suggested. "I can't get a flight until the day after next and I'm not very happy about it."

Brian looked at his watch and realized they needed to get going. He thought they should meet for dinner that night, which would give Laura the next day to get packed and well rested for the flight back to New York.

They decided to eat at a restaurant directly behind their hotel on Steinsdorf Strasse. Getting there early, Laura and Brian asked to sit closer to the front so Ronny could readily see them when he arrived. Brian was trying to be understanding of Laura's wish to go home, but he thought he needed her help in uncovering the Nazi secret that could shock the world.

"You really need to get back to New York yourself," Laura said. "What about your story? Did your editor get it?"

"I sent a copy of the story back to the publisher by mail and I know it's been received. I told Binneker several weeks ago I'm on to a story and want to pursue it to the very end."

"What did he say?"

Brian laughed. "He wanted to know what was so important. I told him to be patient."

"Have you talked to him since?"

"No. But he'll understand. I'm planning to go to London to interview Eva Dofmünster. If I'm lucky, she'll be able to provide substantive clues about Hitler's twin and, more importantly, information about what had happened to him."

"I can't imagine she'll want to share what she knows," Laura said.

"I'm fairly confident. I believe, because of who she was, Eva will have knowledge of much of what went on in the back rooms of the Chancellery."

Ronny joined them, took his coat off, and sat down. They ordered wine to celebrate their last meal together in Munich.

"So are you really planning on staying here?" Laura asked, touching Ronny's arm.

"Sure. I think I can really be of some assistance to Brian. I have some new information that could be helpful. I talked to a man this afternoon that claims to know quite a bit about the Glossen family history. He confirmed that the wife had indeed killed herself."

"Where? When?" Brian asked. "Was it before or after the war ended?"

"According to the source, it was several months after—in June of 1945 in Berlin. She had been despondent after Glossen left for London."

"Why didn't he take his family to England with him in the first place?" Laura asked.

"It's not clear. I guess he didn't think they would be in danger staying in Germany."

Brian sipped his wine. "What happened to his children?"

"Supposedly, they ended up in New York City, but only the daughter stayed in the States. The son came back to Germany sometime between 1965 and 1970."

The Caretaker's Bible

"Where?" Brian asked.

"Here. In Munich. My source swears he doesn't know where he lives and admits he hasn't seen him in a while, but says he exists. His name is Rudolf."

"We need to track him down," Brian suggested.

"Do you really think he'll want to be bothered?" Laura asked. "He probably belongs to the *Freundenreich*."

"Finding him could be of some value," Ronny said. "In my opinion, the more people we talk to the better. I'll try to get some leads on where Rudolf lives, or at least the addresses of others who know who he is. I'll also go back to the library and do more research on other members of the Third Reich who could have possibly escaped the hands of death."

By now Laura was astonished by Ronny's enthusiasm over something he had once said was ludicrous. Even he had to laugh.

Brian had been staring at the front of the restaurant—specifically at two men dressed in long black coats who looked suspicious. They were making him nervous. Then, quickly, they entered the establishment and, with no warning, pulled long-nosed pistols out from under their coats and yelled for everyone to get down. They pointed the guns at Brian's table. There was total commotion—patrons running to get out of the way. Brian pushed Laura down off her chair and shielded her. Ronny tried to jump under the table. It only lasted a few moments, but it seemed like an eternity.

*   *   *

The bright lights on the ceiling of the hospital made the impression in Brian's mind that he was dead. This daunting vision had been preceded in the ambulance by seeing swirls of red against a white background. He began to hear voices. That was good, he thought. Of course it could have been his guardian angel. Something blocked the light. It was a dark figure that very slowly came into focus. He could see the face of what he believed was his fiancée. It looked like her, but how could that be if he were dead?

The revelation that he was still alive came when Laura touched his lips with her finger and said she loved him. He began to look around. He couldn't understand how he had ended up in a hospital. He had no recollection of what had happened in the restaurant. His head felt like it was going to explode. His whole body ached and he just wanted to sleep.

The next morning, the doctor let Laura take Brian for a short walk. They went down the hallway to talk to the doctor about Ronny. She explained what had happened. Brian seemed confused at first, but as she talked it all started to come back to him.

Laura thought that was a good sign. "We should have known that sooner or later they would try to stop us. I think they are getting desperate. Ronny's wounds are much more severe than the ones you sustained. In fact, the doctor warned me he could very possibly die; it is that critical. I feel such a sense of guilt. I was virtually unscathed in the attack—but only because you wanted to be a hero; I'm grateful for that. I've already cancelled my flight. I know I'm needed here."

Sitting down, they waited to be allowed to see Ronny, and Laura couldn't stop the tears from streaming down her face. Brian held her as she said this was turning into an unbelievable nightmare. If only they had just gone home after being approached by Wormser, none of this would have happened.

The doctor called for them. They followed him into a small dark room. There Ronny lay hooked up to IV bags and looking as close to death as anyone could. His breathing was very erratic. The doctor stood right next to Laura and explained the nature of his wounds. He had been shot in the upper stomach area and the upper chest. He had lost a great deal of blood and was now coming in and out of consciousness. If they were lucky, he could stabilize within a few days and probably recover, but if infection set in, he could easily die very quickly.

Laura went over and placed her hand on his face. His eyes were closed, but he seemed to respond by smiling slightly. She said she was feeling a bit ill so a nurse placed a chair beside the bed so she could continue to be by his side. A nurse escorted Brian back down the hall.

*   *   *

The next day, Laura walked into Brian's room and pulled up a chair. He was awake and sitting up in bed. She told him that she had completely lost her sense of time. After talking to one of the nurses, she realized she had been there for two days.

Brian said he was recovering fairly well. But his shoulder was extremely sore where the bullet had penetrated.

"You look a little better."

"How is Ronny? They won't let me see him."

"He's still in critical condition."

Brian asked her to come closer. "Are you all right?"

"Yes. At least physically." She sat down and held his hand. "Why didn't we just go home a long time ago? I know how much the story means to you, but I can't see an end to the madness. We could have all been killed. Since Ronny is still in a very serious condition, I've made my mind up to stay in Munich at least until he starts to get better. Then, I want you both to come home. This story is not worth it."

Brian stared straight ahead. "I wish I could, but—"

"But what? You will never get what you're after. You must believe me!" Laura had never been so adamant about anything in her life. "I know in my heart if you stay here, you will surely be killed. There's no doubt in my mind."

Brian looked away. "I'm tired and want to get some rest."

Laura's nerves getting the best of her, she stormed out of the room and went to get something to eat.

*   *   *

A difficult week had passed but Brian had been informed he would be released within a day or so. He again accompanied Laura down the hall to see their friend. Now conscious and lucid, Ronny held court. He was infuriated that this had happened to them. Unfortunately, he had been told that he might be staying in the hospital another two or three weeks. His prognosis was good, but he needed more time to recover. He had no intention of going home when he was finally released. He wanted to prove to those bastards that he would not cower in the corner.

"You need to rest and not worry about that," Laura said. "They've proved their point. We get the hint. I say we all go back to New York."

Ronny looked over at Brian. "So what are you going to do?"

He shrugged his shoulders. "I don't know." Remembering the piece of paper with Eva Dofmünster's address on it, Brian panicked. Looking at Laura, he asked, "Where is it?"

Reluctantly, she reached in her handbag and handed it to him. "Is this what you're looking for?"

He grabbed the note and looked at it like it was Holy Scripture. "What if she has all the answers? She could be the key to this whole story."

Laura's cynical laugh was loud. "You don't get it, do you? Even if Brother Matthias is still alive, the *Freundenreich* will never let you get near him. It's a waste of time."

Ronny raised both hands. "Stop it. We're all supposed to be dead now. But we're not. I'm not going to let these Nazis get away with this. I say we break the story." Brian was taken aback by Ronny's attitude since he had always been nothing short of a pessimist since he arrived in Munich.

Laura felt exhausted. But she knew one thing—she had had enough. With or without Brian or Ronny, she was going home. Brian agreed to take her to the airport to see if she could get on standby. Then he had to decide whether he wanted to wait for Ronny to get better or go to London himself.

"I don't know if I'll be up to going anytime soon. It may be better I stay here and try to get more information."

"I won't be long," Brian said. "I'll probably only be a few days."

"You're making a mistake." Laura paced the floor. "I can't believe you're so foolish as to want to stick around for the next Nazi attack."

Brian countered quickly. "It's not a matter of hanging around so the Nazis can execute us. It is matter of telling the truth. We have to expose their lies."

The next morning, Brian and his fiancée were standing at a check-in counter at Munich airport. There apparently was room on a TWA flight that left at eleven o'clock. After checking her luggage in, they went to find the gate. Sitting down, they didn't talk for the longest time. Finally, Laura pleaded with Brian to change his mind. He knew she couldn't really understand his obsession—something that gripped his soul so completely that it was virtually impossible for him to break free. He assured Laura that he would be all right. She needed to go home and get her life back in order.

They kissed and he watched her walk to the plane—not sure he would ever see her again. On the way back to the hospital, he began to plan ahead. He would go to London within the next day or so. With any luck, he would get what he was looking for from Glossen's former secretary. Once he came back to Munich, he would meet up with Ronny and they could compare notes.

Ronny was sitting up in bed when Brian walked in. "Is she gone?"

"On her way home. I hated to let her go, but I believe she will be safer in the States than staying with us." He told Ronny his plan and asked him what he thought.

Still sore and tired from the exercises the physical therapist was making him do, Ronny didn't have a problem with staying behind. His doctor had just informed him that he could be released in two days to a week.

Brian's confidence may have clouded his judgment, but he was convinced Eva knew not only the identity of Brother Matthias—or Horst, if they were one in the same—but also what happened to him. "I guess Eva saw quite a bit from where she sat as Glossen's secretary. Her observations could be very interesting indeed."

"What are you going to do if she refuses to talk?"

"I don't know. I'll figure it out when the time comes. But I'll tell you one thing, I'll do my best to convince her to tell me what she knows. That's all I can do."

"Just tell her she'll go down in history if she levels with you."

"My only concern is that the *Freundenreich* will get to her first—pay her a nasty visit before I get there or worse get to her after I leave."

"I guess you have to consider that a distinct possibility. If they did kidnap Glossen's former mistress, they could have found out she gave you Eva's address."

"I know, but I'll have to take the chance. I really believe I'm destined to write this story."

*   *   *

Back in the hotel room, Brian lay on the bed. He felt exhausted and wanted to get some sleep. He had started to doze off when the phone rang. The voice on the other end was almost indistinguishable, but the individual asked if Brian could please come to Olympic Park within the hour. Looking at his watch, he agreed. He knew he could be taking a terrible risk, but he had a gut feeling it was something important.

After getting out of the cab, he walked slowly to the Olympic Stadium. The darkness was only illuminated by a few building lights. He heard a voice coming from a side entrance to the stadium. As the figure walked closer, her face was revealed. It was Marta, and she asked Brian to take a walk around the track. It would be safer there.

"I'm glad you called," Brian said. "I need to talk to you."

"You're short of breath."

"My fiancée, my friend and I were almost killed. Since it had to be the work of the *Freundenreich*, I want to know if you know anything about it."

"They don't want you to succeed."

"We talked to Fräulein Hildabrand."

"I know."

"I think they kidnapped her. Several men came to the door while we were there. We got out the back."

Marta put a hand on Brian's arm. "She's fine."

"How do you know?"

"She's in a safe house in Füssen. Those men at the door belong to us. They are protecting her."

"Good. She gave me a name," Brian said.

"Yes. Eva Dofmünster."

"Helga said she would know more than anyone else about Hitler's twin."

"It is possible, certainly. Eva had daily contact with Glossen and knew his schedule and everyone he associated with."

"Why did you really call me?" Brian stopped, grabbed Marta by the shoulders, and shook her. "Tell me. Am I in danger? What?"

"I am just concerned about your well-being. I know about the shooting at the restaurant. Initially, I was led to believe all three of you had been killed. Then later, I found out just the opposite."

"They're crazy," Brian fumed. "What in the hell do they want?"

"You were lucky, you know. They are brutal. Those men were either incompetent or didn't have a clear shot. They wanted you dead."

"Who?"

"The other faction. Wormser's men."

"So you answer to Glossen? Why do you care?"

"It is very hard to explain, but you must be careful. We can only do so much. They will stop you if you get too close."

"So tell me."

"In 1965 Glossen and Wormser had a terrible falling out—finally becoming disenchanted with each other. Glossen wanted to banish Wormser from the group, but Wormser decided to try to split the *Freundenreich* in two. He decreed at the time that he would eventually take over as its leader. In 1970, Glossen concocted a plan to make Hitler's brother's identity known. Wormser, of course, opposed such action. I must confess, I want the world to know about Hitler's brother—that he had been a Benedictine monk."

"You know, I'm not so sure anyone will believe it."

"If you think that would be the case, then why are you so desperately trying to prove it?" Marta asked.

Brian was having a hard time coming up with a credible answer.

"The only thing I can think of is that finding and revealing the truth have simply become an obsession."

"A very dangerous one," Marta remarked. "The *Freundenreich* very seldom loses when it comes to playing games—especially cat and mouse. There is no doubt your obsessions could get you killed."

"Please. You don't have to tell me that."

"If Brother Matthias is still alive and you somehow find him, Wormser will become enraged and track you down to the ends of the earth. So you see, finding him would be just the beginning."

"I'm going to see Eva Dofmünster as soon as I can get a flight into Heathrow. I can only hope the *Freundenreich* doesn't suspect I know about her. I'm fairly optimistic she will be able to help me."

"You must be careful. Are you really prepared?"

"I have no choice." Out of a sense of anticipation, Brian began to reflect. He actually wished someone else had found the documents in the Bible. It was a very strange destiny that had befallen him. He didn't know why, but somehow he had become preoccupied with cracking the story—more so than with any other he had ever covered as an investigative reporter. He was angry with himself because not only was he jeopardizing his job by chasing the illusive story, his fiancée and a friend had almost been killed because of it. But then he began to think what it would mean if he could actually find Hitler's twin.

"If you must go, time is of the essence. You must leave right away. There is no telling whether the *Freundenreich* knows or suspects you are here. I believe Eva will talk to you. But you must hurry."

Brian began to feel like Marta was somehow trying valiantly to protect him. It didn't make sense to him why, but he was grateful he was getting the help.

They had walked the full circle of the track and were back at the entrance. Marta leaned over and gave Brian a kiss on the cheek while squeezing his arm. He watched her disappear into the shadows.

*   *   *

Brian sat on the bed. He stared at the piece of paper with Eva's address on it. This was his last chance, he figured. If he came away empty, he would have to pack it in. He wanted to call Laura, but he knew she would be in some sort of meeting, so why even brother. His plan was to go to the airport in the morning and try to get a flight out to London as soon as he could. He would call Ronny and tell him what he was doing—assuring him he would be back in a few days.

The night was long and Brian tossed and turned. He was filled with anticipation over his meeting with Eva. Unintended consequences were not far from his mind.

chapter 19
London, England— 1972

BRIAN REGISTERED IN A small hotel on Kings Road in Chelsea. As he took a cab to South Kensington to find Eva, he couldn't believe the number of hippies standing around the street corners with spiked hair, combat boots, and chains hanging from their belts. The smell of marijuana seemed to hang in the air.

The cab crossed over Old Brompton Road and almost immediately turned right. Brian asked to be left off at the corner of Eva's street. He stood there for several minutes and observed the neighborhood. He noticed an older woman walking slowly with the aid of a cane down the street from the other end. From what he could see, she was slender, had dark gray hair, and was well dressed. He watched as she gradually walked up the stairs to Eva's address. Waiting five minutes, he knocked on the door.

After a minute or so, Eva answered. Brian was taken completely

The Caretaker's Bible

by surprise when Eva said she knew who he was and had been expecting him for some time. "Please come in and make yourself at home." Eva spoke fairly good English, but still had a very strong German accent.

Her face showed signs of age. Wrinkles masked her attractiveness, but she had beautifully radiant blue eyes.

Brian explained his reason for being there and told Eva he believed she was possibly the only person left he could talk to who would know anything about Hitler's supposed twin.

Eva took Brian into her small sitting room and asked him to have a seat. "Would you like something to drink? You are fortunate to know the truth. Not many do."

Brian couldn't believe how undaunted she seemed.

Setting the tray down on the small coffee table, Eva poured their tea and began talking about the past. "I starting working for Heinrich Glossen almost immediately when he arrived from the university. Prior to that I had been an assistant secretary to Goebbels. When Heinrich entered the scene, Goebbels asked me to act as a secretary for him so he could put his department in order."

"What was Glossen like?"

"He was a wonderful man. I remember his sincerity and his incredible intelligence. It was a change for me. I never considered Goebbels as an especially bright man—only crafty and calculating. When Heinrich showed up, the propaganda mechanism seemed to take on a new dimension. If nothing else, his sanity was unequalled."

"What intrigued Glossen the most?"

"Heinrich was completely submersed in trying to revamp the Ministry of Propaganda from the very beginning. He objected to a great deal of Goebbels' proclamations and they would often argue about them well into the night. But on a personal level, they got along very well. Heinrich knew that the Führer respected Goebbels immensely, and he wanted to take advantage of that. I especially remember Heinrich being angry at the speed with which the Führer carried out his everyday affairs. It seemed to lack organization and Heinrich was clever enough to devise a scheme to allow the Führer to manage his time better. Goebbels was leery of the tenacity of such a robust plan. He was more concerned about what Hitler would think of it. But in the end, after Goebbels finally came around and explained the plan to the Führer, Hitler just ignored it anyway."

Brian understood historical perspectives were interesting, but they were not why he had come. "How did they find out about Hitler's twin?"

"It was Glossen's idea. One day late in September 1939, Heinrich showed me a picture of an individual I thought was Adolf Hitler. He laughed and said it was a monk who lived in Austria. Glossen's sister lived in Linz at the time, and her friend's brother was a monk associated with the monastery at Hagenmünster. According to Heinrich, the monk's brother gave the photo to his sister, who thought it was uncanny because it resembled Hitler and forwarded the picture to him."

"What did he do next?"

"Heinrich did not show it to anyone but me at first. I am positive he had concocted a callous motive immediately upon seeing the picture. Hitler's physicians believed his health was declining due to stress from all he had taken on. Heinrich became so obsessed with the photo that he planned a trip to the monastery to meet with the middle-aged monk. He spent endless hours trying to find a picture of the Führer that he could take with him that appeared similar to the one he had of Brother Matthias. In late October of 1939, Heinrich and several associates went to Hagenmünster. I remember his haunting explanation as if it were yesterday."

Eva poured another round of tea and presented the cup to Brian, who seemed mesmerized by the story.

"So they came and got Brother Matthias. Just like that."

"Yes. He never returned to the monastery, as far as I know."

"What happened when he got to Berlin?"

"It was complicated. Apparently they had shielded him from just about everyone when he first got there. They had placed him in a hotel room in the city and posted SS guards so he would be protected and could not escape. He was not allowed to leave. All luxuries were provided for him. Heinrich spent many hours with the monk, trying to prepare him for his eventual meeting with his brother. The only other individuals that knew about Brother Matthias were Goebbels, Himmler, Göring, Ribbentrop, and a handful of security guards who were sworn to complete secrecy."

"They had to be brainwashing him," Brian said. "Weren't they?"

"I am not sure, but I do know that Brother Matthias had been severely depressed ever since he had arrived. He missed Hagenmünster terribly. Heinrich would sometimes vent in my office about not being able to get through to the monk. I think it was interesting that only a handful of people even knew about the existence of Hitler's brother. It was a well-executed plan—one Heinrich called Operation Sibling. Heinrich's goal was to introduce Horst to Hitler in the early part of 1940. Not sure how it would go, he agonized over it so much that he nearly reached the point of madness. But he became more confident because Goebbels was thrilled the first time he had met Horst. It was like seeing a real life replica of the Führer standing right in front of him. He took an instant liking to the monk, even though it was obvious Horst did not want to be there. Goebbels realized they had to allow some time for Horst to acclimate to his surroundings and get used to who he really was. It would be difficult, but it had to happen.

"But there was a fly in the ointment. Heinrich introduced Horst to Manfred Wormser, who had no patience for pampering the monk or anyone else. He wanted results rather than idle preparation, as he called it. I can remember Wormser's remarks in my office about how Horst was being treated like a king when in fact he was a common man not worthy of the luxurious treatment. I know it must have been hard for the shy monk to deal with the total arrogance of Wormser. Heinrich would argue with Wormser, saying that they had to take their time and let Horst realize his fate."

Brian was beginning to believe that Wormser was nothing more than the embodiment of evil. It was obvious the Jew Killer didn't value any life, except, perhaps, his own. "How did you cope with a madman like Manfred Wormser?"

Eva's face stiffened—her eyes practically squinting. "I hated him. He thought he was in charge—conveniently forgetting he worked for Heinrich. There were many times when Wormser tried to tell me what to do. I learned very quickly not to interrupt or disagree with him. In every case I would tell my boss what Wormser had said to me. I can remember the two of them arguing in one of the back offices over something Wormser had asked me to do. Heinrich would tell his underling he was out of line and Wormser would always come up with a reason why he was in the right. The consequences were extremely difficult. Wormser would constantly take out his anger on others, including me. I decided to quit before Christmas 1939, but Heinrich refused to hear of it, and, as I found out later, he had threatened to fire Wormser if he did not apologize to me."

"Did he?"

"Yes. But he was not sincere in anything he ever did."

Brian stood up and walked around. "How did you meet Horst?"

"I think it was very strange. It was in January of 1940, I believe, when Heinrich asked me to come into his office. He had his cook prepare a small breakfast for us. Although it was not uncommon for us to eat breakfast together, this time it somehow seemed different, and then I knew why. He asked me if I wanted to meet the Führer's brother. I had been informed earlier of the monk's existence, but I remember feeling numb because I did not think I was qualified as someone who would be allowed to meet such a distinguished person. Heinrich assured me that he considered me worthy of being introduced to the man he was now routinely calling Horst. The meeting would take place in the monk's hotel room.

"The excitement I felt was unparalleled. It was on a Saturday evening in the middle of January when I finally met Horst. Heinrich escorted me to the hotel, which was only minutes from the Chancellery. The tight security seemed to be unprecedented. We went directly to the third floor and walked to an end room. Guards were posted outside. Once inside the suite, Heinrich asked me to have a seat for a few minutes in the living quarters while he went to get Horst, who was in another room. I was very nervous, which did not seem to make sense. After all, I was just meeting a monk who possessed a slight resemblance to the Führer.

"They came out of nowhere. Horst was standing there looking at me. I could feel my heart pumping like never before. As I stood to greet the monk, I marveled at his appearance. Even though he was dressed in plain clothes, he looked and acted like Hitler. His hair was somewhat shorter and his mustache bushier, but he had a charisma much like his brother. It was uncanny. Even when he talked, it almost sounded like the Führer. But it was his eyes that made the difference. They were mesmerizing like Hitler's eyes—dark, rich, and able to convey a sense that he was staring through the person to whom he was talking."

"What did he say? Did he seem unhappy to you?"

"No. I must admit he acted like he wanted to be there. Perhaps they had started to brainwash him to get him ready to meet his brother. Heinrich even told me that a series of medical doctors had seen Horst routinely since he had arrived."

Brian was having a hard time believing that someone like a monk, who had given his life to God, could be persuaded to deny his past and become loyal to a mere mortal he had never met, even if he did think that man could be his brother.

"The Nazis had their ways. Heinrich assembled a group of doctors who specialized in altering the psyche. They were undoubtedly the best in the world. No one had a chance when confronted with these doctors' unbelievable knowledge."

"What did Horst say to you that night to make you believe he might have been brainwashed?"

"I can only remember some of what he said, but it was odd to me. He was especially looking forward to meeting the Führer. He would not necessarily denounce his upbringing in the church, but said he thought the Third Reich was not as bad as some made it out to be. I can still see the smile on his face when he talked about knowing he had a twin brother."

"When did he meet Hitler?"

"Not for a long time after that. Horst endured a very calculated transition period. It was lengthy and Glossen kept me informed of how they planned to transform Horst into Hitler's brother and protégée. Heinrich needed my help."

"What kind of help?" Brian asked.

Stiff from sitting so long, Eva stood up for a minute. "He asked me to come into his office and take a seat. That usually meant he had something to tell me of great importance. Glossen was happier that day, happier than I had seen him in weeks, even months. He said that now they were very close to bringing Horst to the Chancellery to meet the Führer."

"What did he want you to do?"

"He asked me to entertain Horst in one of the anterooms prior to the meeting taking place. He thought if I talked to him and gained his trust, I could calm him down."

"Because you had already met him, and he knew who you were."

"Yes. I am convinced that Heinrich had introduced us for just that purpose because he was an incredibly thorough individual. He always thought of everything. I waited almost an entire month before he brought up the subject of Horst again. He had selected the twentieth of February for the day of the meeting. By then Hitler was involved in a number of initiatives that were taking up a lot of his time. Looking haggard and often maniacal, Hitler was desperately trying to understand day-to-day events—wanting to know infinitesimal details, and at the same time weighing the consequences of his actions concerning war. But things were not going well. Besides having to postpone his attack on the West in January due to what he considered incompetence, he was informed of a British destroyer intercepting a German prison ship somewhere in Norwegian waters in February. A number of British prisoners had been rescued, and this infuriated Hitler beyond reason.

"I recall Heinrich reacting day to day as he monitored Hitler's work schedule and, more importantly, his mood. This demanding activity placed great stress on Heinrich and it showed in his everyday dealings with his immediate staff. He most certainly was also under a great deal of pressure from Goebbels, who wanted Hitler to meet his brother no later than the spring of 1940. The problem Heinrich faced was dealing with the mounting problems that plagued the Führer's efforts to achieve his goals. There never seemed to be a right time to drop the bombshell. Heinrich continuously agonized over it as if it were the only thing that mattered. What did not help was Manfred Wormser's interference on inopportune occasions. Heinrich's patience dwindled as Wormser constantly accused him of gross incompetence in the handling of Horst's situation, which he called an incredible failure, and the whole affair seemed to go on forever."

"I guess at that point Glossen was ready to throw his hands up and quit," Brian said before excusing himself to go to the bathroom.

When he returned, Eva had tears in her eyes. She apologized and said that telling the story made it seem like everything had just happened the week before. "I believe Heinrich persevered because he was totally dedicated to the idea that Hitler had to be protected unequivocally—which meant giving him the opportunity to rest in order to decrease the amount of stress he was feeling, which was affecting his health. The days leading up to the anticipated meeting between Horst and the Führer are etched in my memory."

The story she told gripped Brian's attention so much that he was speechless. Eva was patient and sipped her tea.

"Glossen must have been devastated after he met with Hitler." Brian sat back in his chair.

"I was worried about him because he initially became very depressed. He had been so positive he could convince the Führer he had a brother that it was hard to accept defeat. And it got worse. Only a day after Hitler dismissed Glossen, Goebbels called a meeting with Heinrich to discover what had gone wrong. Goebbels was infuriated and took Glossen to task saying that Horst should be taken back to Hagenmünster."

"What did Wormser say?" Brian asked. "I imagine he took the opportunity to gloat."

"It was a week later when Wormser showed up at Glossen's office uninvited and unannounced. He burst in against my wishes and cornered my boss. I could easily hear the exchange. It was very confrontational. Wormser accused Heinrich of alienating the Führer, while Heinrich laughed and replied he had done no such thing. Wormser suggested that devastating consequences had been prompted by Heinrich's actions. Naturally Heinrich disagreed and was adamant that it was not easy for anyone to find out they had a brother they knew nothing about. Wormser accused him of twisting the truth. He said that Horst was no more Hitler's brother than he was. Heinrich replied that Wormser was perceptive, as they looked nothing alike. Wormser yelled back, saying Heinrich's callousness had put a black mark against the Ministry of Propaganda and asked him to step down. Heinrich laughed wildly. He said he would not succumb to Wormser's fantasies and planned to accept what happened to him as fate and nothing else. Life and the Ministry of Propaganda would go on."

Brian smiled. "I can't believe how ignorant Wormser was."

"I remember Wormser storming out of the office. In the weeks following the meeting, Heinrich began to agonize over what he was going to do with Horst. What he thought would be a feather in his cap became a thorn in his side. It was a difficult decision, but he was sure he would have to take him back to Hagenmünster."

"It must have been difficult to know that after all he had done, he couldn't get Hitler's attention."

"It was difficult. Hitler's schedule was filled with war planning. He had decided to execute *Exercise Weser* against Norway first before initiating *Case Yellow*—the attack against the West. The attack against Norway would begin on the ninth of April in 1940. The Norwegians had not noticed German troops and naval forces along the Baltic coast in March and early April. Hitler's generals had found that British Naval forces were converging on Norway at the same time that they were, and they had enough of an advantage to surprise them. It was a gamble that worked. After six weeks of fierce fighting, the Allied forces were driven out, thus giving an unbelievable victory to Germany. The Führer was in his glory and now was prepared to attack the West. Unfortunately, many of his generals complained that as Commander in Chief of the military he was extremely ill equipped to be in charge—far too excitable, prone to blame others for his mistakes, and possessed of a sense of the theatrical instead of precise methodical reasoning."

Brian got up to walk around and stretch his legs.

Eva continued. "A week before his birthday, which was normally celebrated with a party attended by his immediate staff and selected guests, Hitler summoned Goebbels to his office unexpectedly late in the day. The meeting lasted only fifteen minutes. I will never forget the look on Heinrich's face when he came to my office. He asked me to join him, as he had something wonderful to tell me. I wanted to know what was so important. Heinrich smiled, saying he had received a call from the Minister and was informed the Führer wanted to meet Horst and that he had already told the monk of his good fortune. I wanted to know what had changed Hitler's mind. Heinrich said he was not sure, but according to Goebbels, Hitler wanted the opportunity to at least meet Horst and talk to him. Heinrich called it a victory. He said that the Führer wanted to see Horst within the next two days. Heinrich thought that Hitler must have begun to think what it would be like to have a twin brother. That could be the only explanation for wanting to meet him.

"I suspected that even if Hitler acknowledged Horst as his brother, he would never want the fact made public. Heinrich said he had no way of knowing that but told me it was worth thinking about. He knew if he could convince Hitler to allow Horst to pose as the Führer in appropriate situations, he would have succeeded in what he was trying to do. I told him I was concerned that they not could possibly keep the twin's existence a total secret. I was positive the newspapers would find out. Heinrich seemed to be oblivious. I concluded that day that perhaps I was the one who was more concerned about Horst's welfare. But it was what happened next that, even to this day, puzzles me more than anything else."

"That was when Horst was introduced to Hitler?"

"Yes, the Führer accepted his brother without reservation, but it was the meeting afterward between the Führer and his brother that I am referring to."

"What went on at that meeting?" Brian asked.

"I never found out. No one would say. Horst never revealed what the Führer had said to him."

Brian could tell Eva was getting tired. He wanted to ask her more questions, but he knew she probably had told him enough for now.

"I need some rest," she said. "Can you come back tomorrow?"

"Of course. But whatever happened to Horst? Is he still alive?"

"I am not sure. I have heard two different stories: one that he died years ago and another that he is alive and well, living in Austria."

"What about Glossen? I was told he died."

Eva hesitated for a moment. She got up and retrieved a small address book from the kitchen. "Here is his address." Brian expected it to say Chiemsee, but it read Florence, Italy.

"Where?"

"He usually stays at the Hotel Dorian by the Duomo. That is where you will find him."

"How do you know he is still alive?"

"I know. You must trust me."

"Thank you for your time. I must confess. I have already met Manfred Wormser."

Her face went pale. "Where? When?"

"It's not important, but I have to say you're right. He is a terrible human being."

Focused, Eva's look burrowed straight through Brian's eyes. "If you have already met Wormser, it could be too late. You may never get to see Glossen. You must go now. There is not much time left."

Brian knew she was right. Instead of meeting her again the next day, he decided to check out of his hotel and take a cab directly to Heathrow. He would go to Munich first and check on Ronny. Then he would go find Heinrich Glossen. With that visit, he hoped all his questions would be answered.

chapter 20
Munich—1972

BRIAN WAS SURPRISED TO find out that Ronny had been discharged. The nurses claimed they didn't have a record of where he had gone, but Brian assumed he had gone back to the hotel where he had been staying before the attack. He was right.

When he got there, Ronny closed the door and offered Brian a glass of wine. He said he had been out of the hospital for a day or so and now felt much better.

"Glossen's alive! I think Hitler's twin could be alive too."

"You're certain?"

"No, but I think we need to check it out."

"I have news of my own. I tracked down Glossen's son. It wasn't easy, but I found out where he was living and paid him a visit."

"You talked to him?"

"He was antagonistic at first, but he offered to talk for a short while. As the conversation went on, Rudolf became more forthcoming with information about his father. In 1945, after his father had gone to London and his mother had committed suicide, he said that he and his sister were raised by his mother's sister in Frankfurt. In late 1950, his father settled in Munich and then Chiemsee. He didn't remarry but began living with a woman who didn't like children. Consequently, they stayed with the aunt. On rare occasions they visited their father. He had become bitter over the German defeat and would lecture them constantly about how Hitler's legacy would never die. By then he had formed the *Freundenreich*. He was actively engaged in chairing meetings, spouting propaganda, and holding rallies."

"Did he talk about anyone else?"

"I asked Rudolf pointedly about his father's relationship with Manfred Wormser. He said that Wormser had contacted his father when he returned to Germany. Wormser had managed to escape to Italy initially, then he went to Switzerland. Rudolf remembered his father saying he had not heard from Wormser the entire time he had been in London. Then one day Wormser showed up, wanting to be of any assistance he could to Glossen. As Rudolf had put it, it was a strange marriage. They really didn't get along well, but he felt his father needed someone like Wormser to keep recruits in line. Rudolf was amazed at the number of Germans who joined the cause. He became worried that his father was trying to stage a Nazi comeback, and at the age of seventeen he convinced his sister to immigrate to the United States. They had distant relatives living in New York City, so they went there. He worked for a time on the docks until he got a break when he met an editor at the *New York Times*. She got him a job first setting type, then doing odd jobs around the office.

"In just a few years he was writing articles on his own that garnered the attention of a few of the senior managers. Eventually, he was elevated to a staff writing position. By then he had married the editor and they had had two children. His sister worked as a maid for the longest time. Then she met an electrician, got married, and moved to northern New York state. In 1970, Rudolf decided he wanted to return to Germany. His explanation was peculiar. He said that even though he had grown to love America, he always longed for his native country. Both of his children had been accepted at colleges in New England and his wife had become the senior editor for the newspaper. She didn't want to leave and so he returned to Germany by himself. Apparently, he wouldn't divorce his wife and was living in Munich alone."

"Has he seen his father since he's been here?" Brian asked.

"He claims they're estranged. Rudolf admitted that he has seen him once since coming back to Germany."

"Does that sound reasonable?"

"Sure. Rudolf made no bones about the fact that he didn't like his father—saying he could live without him."

Brian explained some of what he had found out when he visited Eva, especially about Hitler's twin.

Ronny thought for a moment. "I think it's possible that Horst may still be alive. After the war, Horst probably faded into the countryside. With good health, he could still be living somewhere in Europe."

"According to Eva, he could have been living in Austria. But at this point, I'm more interested in finding Glossen. I'm convinced the former hero of German propaganda will know exactly what has happened to Horst. But I'm not sure what to do." He smiled at Ronny. "Perhaps we should find Rudolf and talk to him again."

"I'll try to contact him. However, it is entirely possible that he won't want to be subjected to another interrogation."

Brian figured it was practical to stay at the same hotel, so he got a room on Ronny's floor at the opposite end of the hallway. Immediately lying down, he faded in and out of sleep—tired from the trip to London.

When he awoke, the room was completely dark. When he looked out the window, he could see an endless stream of headlights coming past the hotel. His eyes finally focused enough to see the time on the clock. It was nine o'clock at night. He had a woozy feeling; it was almost like a sense of inebriation, even though he had only had one glass of wine earlier. As he was sitting on the bed and trying to wake up, the phone rang. Thinking it was probably Ronny, he quickly picked it up.

The masculine voice was somewhat muddled, but the words were in English. "Meet me at the *Englischer Garten* at midnight—at the entrance closest to the Palace. Bring Herr Whitaker with you."

"Who is this?" he asked. But the person hung up. Brian slammed the receiver down. He slowly paced the floor. It probably was a trap and he didn't think he wanted to be responsible for something happening to Ronny. Agonizing over it, he decided to go to talk it over with his friend.

"Who in the hell could it be?" Ronny asked, half asleep.

"I can't be certain."

"Why should we go at all?"

"You should stay here. I'll go. That way if something happens to me, you can inform the authorities and continue on with our investigation."

"I think you're being foolish. We should just ignore the call."

"What if it is someone trying to give us some important information?"

Ronny started to get dressed. "I can't let you do this alone."

It was cold and the wind was bitter. They walked cautiously along a large pathway into the park best known as a beerfest pavilion. Not many people were there. They could hear footsteps behind them. Ronny waited for the worst.

"You must not fear for your lives," the interloper said. They both turned around. Brian didn't recognize the gentleman, but Ronny did. It was Rudolf Glossen. He asked them to follow him to a secluded spot. There he would explain everything.

They sat down at a table. It was getting colder and both Brian and Ronny were pulling their collars up over their ears.

"What the hell is going on?" Ronny asked.

Rudolf replied, "I do not mean to alarm you, but I must warn you of the dangers you are facing."

"Who told you how you could reach me?" Brian asked.

"We've been watching you. I talked to Eva Dofmünster yesterday. She said she thought you would come back to Munich to touch base with Ronny."

"What is this really about?" Brian asked. "Why would Eva call you?"

"It was very complicated. Unless you are German, it is hard to understand. The first thing you have to realize is that both Eva and I belong to the *Freundenreich*. Because there are now two distinct factions of the group—one headed up by my father and the other one headed up by Wormser, we are at war over how to preserve the glory of the Führer."

"But you went to America to start a new life," Brian said. "Why would you come back here? And why get involved in the *Freundenreich*?"

Rudolf inhaled sharply. "Because Wormser killed my wife. That bastard murdered her out of vengeance against my father. I could never change the fact that I was the son of Heinrich Glossen. No matter what I did, it followed me like the plague. Over the years, Wormser's goons, who were always trying to make life rough for the Glossen family, had visited me often. I even sent my children away to live in New England so they could be protected."

"What about your sister?" Brian asked.

"She was not spared the abuse of those bastards. They hounded her so much and for so long that she had to leave her husband and go underground."

"Where is she now?" Brian asked.

Rudolf half smiled. "You have met her." He cupped his hands over his mouth, blowing warm air into them to get warm.

Brian looked over at Ronny. "Where?"

"Her name is Marta."

The stunning revelation left both men speechless.

"She has been designated by my faction of the *Freundenreich* to be a guardian angel to you both in our quest to tell the truth."

"Why didn't you just tell me this the other day?" Ronny asked.

"I was taken by surprise I guess. I never thought anyone would find me."

Brian's intrigue was turning into frustration. "So do you know where your father is?"

"Yes. In Italy, as Eva told you."

"You're positive."

"You must go and talk with him. He can help you."

"Do you know if Horst is still alive?" Brian asked.

Rudolf shook his head. "My father is the only one that can tell you that."

Brian wanted to reach out and grab Rudolf and shake him. "But you know, don't you?"

"No. I don't have any idea if he is still alive. I—"

Brian interrupted. "But you know he existed."

"Of course. It is true; Hitler had a twin. It is hard to believe, but he did. But if Horst is still alive, it will be virtually impossible to prove it."

Somehow Brian didn't believe Rudolf. If he lied about why he was back in Munich, he would lie about Horst. But it was immaterial. He would go to Florence and get what he wanted from the one man who could put it all into perspective.

Rudolf wished them luck and disappeared into the night. Brian and Ronny looked at each other. Things were becoming more bizarre.

"I know we're getting closer to the truth," Brian said. "But I don't know what to make out of Rudolf's story about Marta."

"Do you believe him?" Ronny asked.

"Not totally. But I think he was trying to tell us something. I believe what a friend once told me: that as climbers approach the summit of a mountain, the more difficult it becomes to get to the top because of unknown forces working against them. It's amazing we have gotten this far. To finally reach the summit means we have to get past Wormser's men."

Ronny didn't like the odds. He knew he could easily walk away. "What are you going to do now?"

"I'm not absolutely sure, but I think I should book an airline ticket to Florence. It's obvious that the only person who can lead me to Horst is Heinrich Glossen."

"What if everything you've been told was a lie?" Ronny asked. "What then?"

"I'll have to take my chances."

*   *   *

Back in the hotel room, Brian booked a flight for the day after next. That way he would have a day to think about things and prepare for what he was getting himself into. He called Laura. She expressed concern that he had not called for a while, and he apologized. He wanted to tell her as much as he could, but he only had time to summarize most of it. She became angry when he said he was going to Italy to find Glossen. Knowing the possible consequences, she tried to persuade him not to go. But he couldn't think of reason not to meet with Glossen. He told Laura he would call her again as soon as he could.

Lying on his bed, he began to think about Marta—how she had first appeared in New York without warning and with a story about being a budding novelist. Perhaps Rudolf was right; she was a guardian angel. But what bothered Brian was how she knew that he had possession of the Bible and, more importantly, the documents. He was beginning to think it was a setup—he was supposed to have gotten the Bible. For some reason he had been chosen as the one to tell the story to the world. *So was the caretaker he met at the villa really a caretaker? Could it have been Hitler's twin?* Brian tried to think back and visualize the man's appearance. The more he thought about it, the more he believed it could have been. But it didn't make any sense to him. The *Freundenreich* was an enigma that couldn't be explained in any reasonable fashion. He just hoped he could find Glossen. And, with luck, he might be able to see Marta again. Tired, he fell asleep.

*   *   *

The next evening Brian and Ronny went to a small restaurant near Olympic Park. Ronny ordered two Pilsners and made a toast to their friendship.

Ronny smiled. "I've made a decision to go to Italy with you—if for no other reason than to give you moral support. I won't be able to live with myself if something happens to you."

"I appreciate your concern, Ronny. But I don't want you in

harm's way. You should go back to the States, or at least stay here in Munich. This is getting serious."

"I wanted to go home a long time ago, but after going through all of this, I'm not going anywhere now."

"You must understand," Brian said. "For some unknown reason, I believe I'm the chosen one. It sounds crazy, but I know I alone have to solve the mystery."

"That doesn't make any sense," Ronny replied.

"I know." Brian had to laugh. "It's essentially unexplainable."

It was the weight of a hand he felt first—on his shoulder pressing down. Slowly turning his head he saw the black onyx ring.

"Herr Bennett. How nice to see you this evening. You must introduce me to your friend." Wormser sat down and extended his hand to Ronny while looking at Brian. "I would have thought you would have gone back to America weeks ago. You must like Munich this time of year."

"What do you want?" Brian asked. "We're trying to have a private meal."

"Are you really? We must talk." Wormser took off his coat and asked the waiter to hang it up. "You don't mind if I smoke, do you?"

Brian ignored him. Wormser methodically took a cigarette out of his case and slowly lit it. "Now tell me, Herr Bennett. Are you still trying to find out if the Führer had a twin brother? Of course, it is utter nonsense and you know it. But I believe you are very stubborn."

"I know all about you, Wormser. For some reason I can't explain, you are hell-bent on making sure I don't find out."

The smoke he exhaled was directed at both of them. "I do not know why you are so persistent. There is nothing to tell. My conscious is clear."

"You told me Heinrich Glossen was dead. I believe he is alive," Brian said.

Wormser smiled. "Is that so? You really believe he is alive? I think you have been misinformed."

Brian knew that no matter what he said, Wormser would

disagree, so he tried to change the subject. "We're leaving. Going back to the United States tomorrow. I'm sure you're glad to hear that."

"Tomorrow. I must say that is very convenient. Why would you abandon your story, Herr Bennett? You are such an inquisitive reporter. I am very disappointed."

"I know when I'm defeated. You win. Is that what you want to hear?"

"Yes, if I thought you were serious. Come now, Herr Bennett. Do you expect me to believe for a moment that you are giving up? That would not be like you. I am not an amateur at these things, Herr Bennett. I have been around for a while and definitely do not like to be lied to."

"You can think what you want, but my stay in Munich is over." Brian looked over at Ronny.

"And what about you?" Wormser stared at Ronny with intensity.

"I'm returning as well."

Wormser took another puff of his cigarette. "Your mother is Jewish, I understand."

Ronny's throat clamped shut for a second. "Yes. But how in the hell did you know that? It has nothing to do with me."

"Of course not. But perhaps it is time to go home and visit with her." Wormser started taping his foot—his eyes vibrating back and forth. He directed his attention toward Brian. "And I would suggest you go back to New York and see your beautiful fiancée. Forget about all this. You must leave for everyone's sake."

"What the hell does that mean?" Brian asked.

"Only that you owe it to yourselves to protect the ones you love. That is all I am saying."

Brian pointed his finger directly at the Nazi. "If you ever think about hurting my fiancée or Ronny's mother, I will track you down and kill you. Do you understand me?"

Wormser calmly put out his cigarette and gripped the table. "I warn you, Herr Bennett. You would already be dead if it were not for the absolute incompetence of my men. If you carry on with this nonsense, I personally will ensure that your death will be carried out. I will be watching your every move." Sneering at the both of them, he stood up and asked the waiter for his coat.

They watched as the Jew Killer stormed out of the restaurant.

Ronny didn't say much on the way back to the hotel. Brian was deep in thought—planning his next move.

chapter 21
Florence, Italy—1972

BRIAN WALKED OUT OF his hotel near the Palazzo Davanzati, which had been built in the fourteenth century, and walked toward the Piazza della Republica on his way to the Duomo—the large cathedral that can be seen for miles from outside of the city. According to his map, the Hotel Dorian was located on Via de Pucci, just beyond the church.

The beauty of Florence hadn't faded in Brian's memory—he felt like he had never left since his June visit. All around, as far as one could see, orange roofs and iron balconies complemented dark tan-colored stucco facades. The endless flow of sightseers even in the early November chill confirmed for Brian the city's tremendous lure. He thought there was no other place on earth like this beloved city. As he wandered through the Piazza della Republica, dozens of pigeons flew in and out of groups of people as they walked, and children ran and played in the enormous open plaza.

When he finally reached the Hotel Dorian, he stood in the

shadows across the street. He wasn't quite convinced what he was going to do. Even though he had a vague description from Rudolf, he really didn't know what Heinrich Glossen looked like. He thought he would have to take a chance and go ask the concierge if Glossen was staying at the hotel. First he just wanted to observe what was going on.

As far as he was concerned, he had reached the final hurdle. If he could just talk with Glossen for several minutes, he believed he could find out everything he needed to know. The risk he was taking, though, couldn't have been any greater. He knew Wormser hadn't believed for one moment that he was going back to the States. He looked around, realizing he was probably being watched as he stood there. It was a scary feeling. The only thing he could feel positive about was the fact that Ronny had gone back to States to check up on his mother and Laura to make sure they were all right.

In the lobby of the Dorian, he politely asked if Glossen was staying there and said that, if so, he needed the room number. The concierge fumbled through his register and said he had no such name listed. Brian expected as much, but it still didn't disarm his angst. In a contemptuous voice, he attempted to describe Glossen, but the young man shook his head and waited on someone else.

Brian wasn't sure whether to hang around in the lobby or walk around outside, hoping to get a glimpse of Glossen. As he began to meander down the sidewalk, he happened to notice several men standing on the corner across the street. They looked suspicious to him. He looked behind him. Two men had just come out of the hotel and were talking and pointing in his direction. He decided to keep walking toward San Lorenzo. If they gave chase, he would have to try to outsmart them somehow. His best bet would be to get into the church. He would have to figure the rest out later.

The marathon started right on cue. Brian found himself running wildly in and out of people that were walking along looking at the sights. His assailants pursued him relentlessly. He could see a yellow Peugeot coming down the street. Worried he was about to be kidnapped, he ran faster. The car bypassed him at first and then abruptly stopped. The driver yelled for him to get in. She didn't waste any time putting the car in gear.

"What are you doing here?" Brian asked.

"Getting you to safety," Marta replied. "What does it look like I'm doing?"

She raced along a few back streets until they were far enough away, then slowed down and headed for her hotel. "You must remain with me. They know where you are staying."

That was everything he needed to know. The former Nazis were getting closer and he knew he would have to remain one step ahead of Wormser. Normally being confident in most situations, he didn't like the feeling that came with being a marked man.

They quickly walked up a flight of stairs to Marta's hotel room.

Once inside, Brian walked over to the window after hearing a noise that sounded like a diesel engine. From his vantage point he could see the Stazione Centrale—the Central Train Station. Looking around, he could tell Marta had elected to stay in what he figured was a one-star establishment. It was more of an apartment than a hotel. It was probably somewhere the other faction wouldn't think she would be. He immediately noticed that there was just one bedroom, but there was a fairly large sofa in the living area.

"Make yourself at home." Marta went over to the closet and hung her coat up and signaled for his. She locked the door and joined him on the sofa.

He sat down, crossed his legs, and adjusted his collar. "How did you find this place?"

"It belongs to a friend. I know quite a few people in Florence, as I had lived here off and on for a number of years. I am positive Wormser's men won't be able to find it. You look nervous."

Brian wanted to laugh it off, but was now very concerned that the bar had been finally raised to such a level that he wouldn't be able to get over it. It was like being so close, but so far away.

"So you want to talk to my father."

"Yes. I saw your brother the other day in Munich. He told me that your father was here."

"He is alive and well. Right here in Florence."

"Why have you repeatedly lied to me? What is your role in all of this?"

Marta asked if he wanted a glass of wine since it was going to be a long night. "Being the daughter of Heinrich Glossen is not something I am necessarily proud of. He was always a good father to my brother and me, but the fact that he was such an influential member of the Third Reich has always bothered me—that he could have been even partially responsible for the deaths of millions of Jewish people. Over the years, he convinced me that he never sanctioned such violence himself, but rather sought to come up with other solutions."

"He was involved in propaganda," Brian said. "How could he ever rationalize Hitler's actions without compromising his principles?"

"Apparently he felt that as long as he personally did not condone it, he would be spared in the afterlife. I know how it sounds, but I believe my father never wavered from that position. I can remember times as a young girl when he would come home and sit down and bang his head against the table, cursing about how things had gone at the Chancellery. I cannot think of a time when he was really happy and carefree. Hitler had everyone so stressed out because of his obsession with war that they could never relax, even at home."

"Did your father ever drink?"

"Yes. He may have even been an alcoholic." Brian could tell Marta didn't like to talk about it. "There were many times when I would see my father sitting in his big chair with a bottle of wine or whiskey and a glass in his lap. He would still be in his uniform, but it would be disheveled and his hair would be a mess."

Brian thought how terrible it must have been for a young girl to see her father that way. "Was he ever abusive?"

"He had a mean streak—shouting a lot—but never struck my mother, my brother, or me. He was a hunter and probably took his aggression out on defenseless animals."

"Did he ever talk about his relationship with the Führer?"

"On many occasions I overheard my mother and father discussing

The Caretaker's Bible

details of the Third Reich and how he was trusted by Hitler to help bolster Germany's quest for power. My father believed that Hitler was the only person that could make that happen. It was not uncommon for the Führer to ask Goebbels for my father's input on a matter of grave importance. I cannot be sure of the influence my father had on Hitler, but I have to presume it was considerable. The only example I can think of right now is my father's molding of the relationship between Hitler and Benito Mussolini. The Führer had long had a problem dealing with the Italian dictator. It was well understood that Mussolini had ambitions to extend Italian authority into the Balkans and along the Danube. This conflicted with the Führer's plan to expand southeast and solidify the *Anschluss* within his home country of Austria.

"My father had been instrumental in developing a plan to deal with the extent of Mussolini's aspirations. He convinced Hitler to seemingly take Mussolini into his confidence and create an Axis partnership that could be exercised to the benefit of both countries. This would serve to give the Italian a false sense of security. My father believed that it was a much better tactic than directly alienating Mussolini, thus creating an adversarial relationship."

Marta got up, going over to get another bottle of wine. "That is when my father first fell in love with Florence."

Brian went over to the window, pushed the curtains out of the way, and peered out, looking for anyone suspicious. "During the war?"

"He came here with Hitler in 1940 to meet with Mussolini. I am not sure of all the details, but I know that my father, along with others like Goebbels, had accompanied the Führer. They met with the Italian dictator concerning Mussolini's pending attack on Greece. Unfortunately, Hitler found out two hours before he arrived for the meeting that Italy had launched the attack that morning. Apparently Hitler never lost his temper during the entire meeting—rather he showed tolerance toward Mussolini in order to mislead him. Even though my father did not stay here long, he was taken with the beauty of Florence. He once told me that Florence is where his heart resides."

"But your father has lived in Germany most of his life."

Marta smiled. "He lived in both Berlin and Munich for a number of years, but from 1945 on he has spent a fair amount of time in Italy."

As Brian sat back down, there was a knock at the door. His heart pounded a bit faster. If it was Wormser's men, he was finished. Not wanting Marta to open it, he motioned for her to keep quiet. She insisted he go into the other room while she answered the door.

"Who was that?" Brian asked when they had left.

"A friend." Marta opened the container and took out the pizza. Not having much food in the apartment, she had asked the owner of a small *trattatoria* to bring them some food in the late afternoon. It was safer than going out to eat where they could easily be spotted.

Brian had only eaten a small continental breakfast and was starving. Marta hadn't eaten all day. They devoured the pizza within minutes.

"Why have I been chosen?"

"I am not sure." Marta took a drink of her wine.

"And why you? Why were you selected? I mean to watch over me."

She hesitated at first. "Over a year ago my father asked me to meet him in Munich about a matter he considered very important. When I arrived, Rudolf was already there. According to my father, he needed to take care of something and wanted our help. He would not elaborate, but he said it concerned finally telling the truth about the Führer's twin brother. My brother and I had first been told about Horst many years earlier and sworn to secrecy. Now my father was asking us to help make the story public."

"Why?" Brian asked.

"Because the time is right. At least that is what my father told me. For the sake of history, if nothing else, he believes the German people need to know about Horst."

"Is he still alive?"

"As I told you before, I believe he is, but I cannot prove it. My father will not admit it, but he will not deny it either."

Brian explained to her what Eva had said about Horst—that he had gained the confidence of Hitler, who had apparently accepted him as his brother.

"My father said that once the Führer met Horst, he became an integral part of his life. Hitler immediately sent his brother to Berghof, where he stayed for the longest time. During those days, Eva Braun and many of her friends frequented the retreat. Servants and housekeepers were working there much of the time. Many of the leaders, including Goebbels, Göring, and Himmler, were concerned that Horst had been sent to the Obersalzberg. In their minds the closely guarded secret was in jeopardy of compromise from the prospect of loose-lipped individuals saying more than they should. Horst had been given several rooms to use for his own to ensure his privacy. Hitler, on his first visit to his lair since his brother's arrival, made it absolutely clear that no one was to bother Horst and that they were under strict orders not to reveal Horst's existence. It was during that visit that Hitler got to know his brother. They would spend time together well into the night talking about many issues of the day."

"How did Horst become so absorbed in Nazi principles?" Brian asked. "He was brought up in the church and, as far as I can tell, he was a man of God."

"It is a mystery to me as well. Perhaps the only answer is that he had been made to think he was special and that his lot in life was to love and support his brother. The Nazis were very good at mind manipulation, you know. They had been doing experiments for years on altering the psyche. Because of his supposed identity, Horst had become a major victim in their psychological operations. Late in 1941, my father had a meeting with Goebbels behind closed doors. It was then that he began to solidify his vision for Operation Sibling. The idea was to substitute Horst as the Führer in what was perceived as a series of initial experiments to see if staff members could be taken in. If so, they could expand the operation to include meetings with foreign dignitaries. Goebbels seemed to reject the idea at first because he did not think Hitler would agree to such foolishness, but he thought it would not hurt to bring it to his attention, as he had been ill at the time and could use the rest. In a meeting at Berghof between Goebbels and the Führer, Hitler uncharacteristically agreed to allow his brother to stand in for him, but only for occasions when it was absolutely necessary. It was obvious to my father that Hitler was weary. Somehow his brazen ego had faded. He was vulnerable."

The early evening had now turned dark. Marta lit a few candles and they both sat on the sofa sipping their wine. Brian couldn't help notice how beautiful Marta was in the light of the candles' glow. From the first time he had met her, he had been taken by her attractiveness. Being alone with her now was hard for him to endure, but staring at her face, his heart was racing.

"Are you all right?" Marta asked. "You look upset."

"Just anxious. That's all."

Marta continued. "The hardest part of my father's plan was to perfect Adolf's mannerisms. Another challenge was to insure the inflection of voice was correct, as Adolf frequently changed tones and octaves. Horst was made to practice for weeks before my father considered him ready. The first time they tried it was just around his immediate staff. Through a number of interactions over several days, it was obvious to my father it was going to work. No one appeared to question Horst's performance. The second time it occurred was at a staff meeting with several of the Führer's top generals and military aides. Goebbels and my father were in attendance. They met at the Chancellery to discuss the attack on the Soviet regime. Hitler was ill but, in the interest of time, did not want to have the meeting cancelled. The discussion centered on the Führer's plan to capture Leningrad and then Moscow. Horst was specifically instructed not to make crucial decisions at the meeting, but rather to impart the Führer's objectives. In a meeting that lasted well over an hour, Horst performed admirably—laying out intensions and confidently answering questions. My father would later comment that no one could have recognized that their Führer was not addressing them. The initial success of this important meeting was promising to my father. He knew he could use Horst as often as was necessary to protect Hitler's health. Near the end of 1941, Horst was asked to again fill in for his brother."

Brian was now more than intrigued. "What happened?"

"It was on 14 December at Berghof, just seven days after the Japanese attacked Pearl Harbor and three days after Hitler made his historic speech declaring war on the United States. Hitler had come down with what his physicians called a mild flu. He had been scheduled for several weeks to meet with an emissary from Italy personally selected by Mussolini to gain insight into current German operations, especially in Russia. My father had spent two days preparing Horst for the meeting. As usual, the concern was that they did not want Horst to say something off-the-cuff that could be construed as a new direction or a possible rejection of standing policy in regard to the war effort.

"The day of the meeting, the Italian emissary, an aide, and a translator were in attendance. My father sat in, along with a staff translator from the Chancellery. It was well known that Hitler could not speak any language but German—or at least refused to even try. Horst, on the other hand, had an extensive background in Latin and could easily converse in Italian, but of course he was forbidden to do so as it would be out of character for the Führer. The meeting lasted well past one hour. While Hitler slept no more than several rooms away from the meeting, Horst assured the emissary that as the Führer he would ensure that Mussolini would be informed of any crucial modification to his war plans. After Horst said that he was tired, the meeting was terminated and the Italians were escorted to a waiting car."

"It seems like your father had an infallible plan." Brian had to stretch his legs and began to walk around the room. Marta said she was going to change into something a little more comfortable.

Brian looked out the window. He began to realize how unbelievable all of this really sounded. But somehow he knew it was true. Looking ahead, he started to think about the story he would write once all was said and done. It would undoubtedly be the most explosive story to ever hit the streets. If he could just get to Glossen, he knew he would have it made. *What if Horst was still* alive? *What if he could talk to him?* All of these questions surged in his brain like a roller coaster.

"Sorry I cannot offer you something more to eat," Marta said.

Brian didn't care. He stared at her as she sat down in her blue satin nightgown. Resisting temptation was not something Brian was really good at, and her seductive apparel didn't help. "I really don't have to stay, if this is going to be awkward."

Marta laughed. "I think you have no choice." She wanted to continue her story. Brian listened—fixated on her profile in the candlelight. "My father made an indelible impression on the Führer because of his profound effort to find his brother and his ingenious plan of impersonation, even though Hitler had always been against delegating his powers to anyone. After all these years, my father still cannot explain it. In April of 1942, Hitler was supposed to make the last of several key speeches to the German masses to restore confidence in his leadership. It was going to be an important speech because Hitler planned to admit the seriousness of the situation on the Eastern Front but that he had personally mastered the solution for victory. At the last minute, two days before the speech was to be given, he became ill once again; the symptoms led to a diagnosis of mental strain. By now these spells were common occurrences. His doctors dispensed so much medicine to him that even if he had started to get better he would have had difficulty making the speech. My father asked Horst to stand in. This time the twin was petrified. The fact that he would be addressing the entire German nation terrified him. My father had his hands full. The Führer often did not stick to his script, so they had to write a speech because it was imperative that Horst say only the right things. After the April speech, Hitler was briefed on how successful it had been. Even my father could not believe how well Horst had done."

Thinking about the brainwashing started to bother Brian. "How could a monk faithful to his church and his God ever be persuaded to turn his back on that?"

"Horst, for whatever reason, had decided he had to honor his fate. He must have convinced himself that he was doing God's will by helping his brother. As an example, I tell you the story of how a simple blunder almost exposed the secret to the world."

Brian watched as she opened yet another bottle of wine. He wasn't sure how much more he could drink without passing out. He was making an effort to stay awake. He listened as he walked a straight line back and forth between the sofa and the window.

"In February 1942, Hitler made a young architect the Minister for Armaments and Munitions. His name was Albert Speer. He soon showed himself to be a dynamic organizer with the ability to perform any job he was given, regardless of the difficulty. Within no time Speer became the czar of German war production. Hitler soon trusted him unlike anyone else had ever been, except Goebbels. This started to concern my father, who thought he had gained the unprecedented confidence of the Führer. In several meetings between the two, staffers became alarmed at the antagonistic manner in which they regarded one other. Over time my father began to feel as if Speer was trying to usurp his authority to wage propaganda. On many occasions Speer had consulted with Goebbels concerning his ideas on how to better describe war production issues to the German people. It was obvious that my father had met his match and wasn't happy about it.

"In the early summer of 1942, Horst was making one of his numerous visits to Wolfsschanze. My father was with him and they had planned to stay only a few days before they would go back to Berghof. The Führer was used to constant visits from his lieutenants. There he could gather them around in his conference room—find out what was going on, and ensure they understood his unwavering objectives to win the war. When his top advisors were there with their adjutants, they would meet at noon and each one would cover their respective areas. Once Hitler heard each one, he would make a command decision about how to proceed. It appeared to be an organized way to command the war effort and it suited Hitler's personality perfectly."

"It's obvious Hitler had such a controlling personality that it's no surprise that he got as far as he did," Brian said. "Although, it's still hard to fathom. Can we take a break?"

"I am not finished. On a particular day in June, Adolf and Horst were having a get-together, having been encouraged by my father to break up the monotony of the Führer's dismal existence in the bunker. Unbeknownst to Hitler, Speer and a reporter for a German newspaper were en route to Wolfsschanze. In what could only be described as a total breakdown in communications, Speer and the reporter were allowed to enter the bunker unannounced. The result of that security breach was potentially damaging. When they walked into the conference room, Hitler was talking to Horst at the table and my father was sitting on the side. The Führer became enraged. Before Speer could say anything, he summoned his security force to the room and demanded an explanation as to why he had not been told of the Minister's arrival. The young architect apologized. After several minutes of confusion, Hitler introduced Speer and the reporter to his brother. My father asked to see Speer privately. In a separate room, he explained to Albert that if this secret ever got out, it would destroy everything they had ever worked for. But he was really concerned about the reporter. He had to assume Speer would not leak such a thing for fear that the Führer would suspect him. But the reporter was different."

"What did your father do?" Brian asked.

"He had the reporter shot. It gave him the upper hand." She smiled. "It was his way of putting Speer on notice. That way Hitler would know without question the identity of the culprit if a leak occurred." Marta gave him a subtle wink.

Brian plopped down on the sofa. He was getting tired, but he was afraid he was going to miss something. Marta's suggestive posture was alluring. "You know you are a beautiful woman."

"You are very flattering." She moved a little closer.

"No, I mean it."

"I have wanted to tell you for so long that I find you attractive."

Brian smiled. "I think I knew it all along."

"I was hoping you would say that. We have nowhere to go and the night will be long."

He was quickly loosing his inhibitions. Her soft smile made his heart melt. He found himself edging closer and closer to her, and he couldn't deny that he wanted her more than anyone else at that moment. Her lips were supple as they kissed—still sticking to his as they separated with their eyes fixated on one another.

They slowly made love on the sofa.

Afterward, they retreated to her bedroom. Brian already felt a tinge of guilt, but he certainly didn't want it to show. Lying there in her arms, he at least knew he was safe from harm, even if only for the night.

Marta made herself more comfortable by propping her up against the pillow. "You still cannot figure this all out, can you?"

"Never in my wildest dreams did I ever think I'd be trying to find the twin brother of Adolf Hitler. If someone had come to me a year ago and asked me to follow the lead on this story, I would have said they were crazy. Sometimes I still feel like none of this is real."

"It must be hard for you," Marta said. "I cannot understand how you convinced yourself to pursue the story, especially after knowing what the dangers are."

"It's like being swept up by a force I really can't explain. But let's face it, it's an unbelievable story." He just shook his head. "I don't even know what I would do if I ever met Hitler's twin—what questions to ask, or how to begin."

"You must be careful, you know." Marta touched his face.

"If I can just stay out of Wormser's way, I should be all right."

"The Jew Killer will do everything in his power to make sure you do not succeed. He does not value life as you or I. He will not allow you to find out the truth." Marta looked away for a moment. "Wormser is the epitome of Nazism. He lives and breathes it. It is in his blood. He is more fanatical than Hitler ever was, and perhaps even more dangerous. Over the years he has killed numerous people who had supposedly found out about Horst. He never asked questions, never tried to pacify any of them or even find out what they knew. He just killed them."

"Why does he hate your father so much?" Brian asked.

"Because they do not agree on what the *Freundenreich* stands for. The organization has been torn in half and is now at each other's throats. Wormser cannot tolerate that, and has declared war against my father. He wants the spoils. All of it for himself."

"Why don't you just go back to the States? You'd be safer there."

"I wish it were that easy. If I go back and they want to kill me, they will find me. But Wormser knows the stakes if that happens. My father will track him and his men down and have them eliminated on the spot. So for the time being, I stay here."

"So you're protected, so to speak." Brian put his arms behind his neck.

"Nothing of the sort. I cannot rest for a minute. Letting down my guard would be a serious error that could never be erased. One should never trust the obvious. Do you agree?"

Brian had no reason to disagree. He was captive to his own emotions and wayward compulsions. That's the real reason he was in this mess and he knew it.

Marta said, "Living in the moment is the only way I can deal with the stress. I am positive that Wormser will not hurt me for fear of retaliation."

"Has he ever tried to kill your father?"

"I think so. Several times. But my father refuses to acknowledge it. In the last two years he has had two close calls. I am sure it is the work of Wormser's men. He wants to be in charge. It is that simple."

"When can I meet your father?"

"I have already taken care of it. I will drop you off near the Piazza della Signoria tomorrow morning. Early. He will be waiting by the Palazzo Vecchio."

"How do you know he'll be there?" Brian asked.

Marta laughed. "He will probably be standing in the shadows, but I assure you, he will be there."

Brian couldn't believe his good fortune after everything he had gone through.

"You are the chosen one, you know," Marta said.

Brian rose up off the pillow. "Why?"

The Caretaker's Bible

"I do not know all the details, but spending two weeks at Villa Pontevechio was not just a coincidence."

"How do you know about the villa?"

"My father owns it. Has for years." She looked over at him. "I have been there. It is very nice."

"So I was somehow chosen to go to the villa and become the bearer of Hitler's Bible? Then who the hell is the caretaker?"

"I do not know anything about a caretaker," Marta replied.

"His name is Horst. Sound familiar?"

"I told you. I know nothing about the caretaker."

Brian figured she had to be lying. But it didn't appear like she was going to give in even if she did know more. He was positive she was trying to drive him crazy. It was absolutely bizarre that everyone he had ever talked to only knew so much about the story. Then he started to think. Maybe that's the way it was supposed to be—a ploy to ensure that no one knew the whole truth. "Why does your father want me to tell the brother's story?"

"He never told me, but I am sure he has a good reason."

"If your father wants to tell the world about Hitler's brother, then he must be dead. I can't think of any other reason why he would do it."

Marta stayed silent for a moment, looking at her nails. "You might have a point."

Brian really didn't believe that. He was convinced that Horst the caretaker had to be the brother of Adolf Hitler. It made sense to him now. "It's as if Horst wanted to tell his story and summoned me to the villa to ensure I got the Bible. But why?"

"You must ask my father all your questions. Only he can tell you the truth." Marta put her nightgown back on. She went to get the bottle of wine they had left in the living room.

"I feel like I've been on a scavenger hunt—a damn merry-go-round for the last six months. I hope to hell your father will tell me what I want to know."

"There is an old saying: You must not look back at the road that took you there after you have crossed the bridge. I think you are on the other side now," she said. "I am sure your mystery will be solved and life will go on."

"I certainly hope so." He laid there in restless thought after Marta blew out the candles, knowing that he would soon meet the illusive and legendary Heinrich Glossen—falling asleep somewhere between his feelings of doubt and certainty.

chapter 22
Florence—1972

THE YELLOW PEUGEOT HUGGED the back streets, slowing down—the lights cutting off. The fog was heavy and it seemed to hang especially low, almost touching the pavement. Brian agreed to meet Marta back at the same spot within two hours. He got out of the car, got his bearings, and walked to the Piazza della Signoria. It was cold and he was glad he had worn a coat. As he approached the piazza, he could see the shadows of the statutes in front of the Palazzo Vecchio cast across the square from lights on several of the buildings.

Brian began to wonder if he was walking into a trap. It hadn't crossed his mind when he was lying in a warm bed with a beautiful woman, but now he couldn't think of anything else. As he neared the Palazzo Vecchio, he could see a faint outline of a figure off to the side by the Loggia dei Lanzi. The fog obstructed his view. As he got closer, he could clearly see a man standing there. What if it were Manfred Wormser?

"You must be Brian Bennett." The figure came closer. "I am Heinrich Glossen." He reached out his hand.

Brian noticed how tall and thin he appeared. He had a closely cropped gray beard, squared jaw, a long Romanesque nose, and a tan face that held his age well. He was wearing a long dark coat and fedora. They began walking toward the River Arno. Brian was in awe of the man he thought he would never meet.

"Has my daughter been taking care of you?"

"Yes. I'm sure I would have been killed if it weren't for your daughter's quick thinking."

"She has always been a caring person. I say you are very lucky."

"I appreciate you taking the time to talk to me."

Glossen grinned. "You have come a long way to find the truth. I do not want to disappoint you."

They continued walking toward the Arno. Brian looked at every alley, every corner, and every shadow as they talked—convinced they would be ambushed at any time.

Glossen started talking about his life as a Nazi. "I lived on the fringes of the Third Reich as a professor of economics at Freiburg University. I grew up in a fairly liberal family; my father was a concert musician and my mother a thespian and a writer. After graduating from the university with honors and a Ph.D., I worked in a bank for several years before receiving the opportunity to teach. It took me two years to become a full professor.

"In January 1939, I was paid a first visit from a Nazi recruiter—a young man who said he was there at the behest of the Minister of Propaganda. According to the young Nazi, they had been watching me and believed I would be an asset to the ministry. The recruiter handed me a card and said he was there on the direct orders of Joseph Goebbels. I remember feeling elated that someone as high up as Goebbels would even be interested in me. It was hard to believe. I asked him to give me time to think about it, and later sat down and talked it over with my wife. I never totally believed in what Hitler was doing. I thought that the Nazi treatment of Jews was wrong and the ideology of German expansion was misguided. However,

I thought that perhaps I could help shape the destiny of the Third Reich if I could gain the trust of the leaders.

"By the next visit, which was three months later, I was ready to join the cause. I was asked to come to Berlin and have an audience with Goebbels. The meeting occurred on a chilly day in April. I was whisked into the Chancellery and taken to the office of the Ministry of Propaganda. I patiently passed the time in a waiting room. When I finally met Goebbels, it seemed like instant gratification for both of us. We took a liking to each other immediately—so much so that I was given an office that same morning."

"It must have been a shock to be a professor in a university one day and a servant of the Third Reich the next," Brian commented.

"I still wonder why I gave up my freedom so easily. I was astounded at the pace at which the Nazi regime operated. The tension was tremendous, and I was caught up in it the first day I walked into the Chancellery. One of the first things I was asked to do was to develop an economic plan for the Pact of Steel treaty between Germany and Italy that would tie the two countries economically, politically, and militarily. I drafted a rather hasty economic agreement that would suffice for what the Führer wanted to accomplish. On the 23rd of May, the day after the treaty was signed, Goebbels and I sat in a meeting during which Hitler addressed his Army, Navy, and Air Force officers concerning his plans to expand eastward. He expressed his desire to invade Poland as soon as it was possible. I remember thinking then that this was something Mussolini would not have expected and certainly would not have condoned had he heard about it.

"In the next several months after that, I was asked to help draft paperwork aimed at justifying Hitler's expansion to the east—something I had always detested. But I did it with flair, and it was well received by the Führer."

Brian said, "I can't understand what it must have been like to give up one's principles for the sake of power."

"No one can understand unless they were there. I had agonized over many of my decisions, but I realized I had made a commitment that was irreversible. There is no other way to explain it. But it was what occurred on the second of September, the day after Germany invaded Poland, that changed my life forever. I received a letter from my sister. In it she had included a picture of a monk from the monastery at Hagenmünster and she jokingly wrote that he reminded her of the Führer."

"What did you do when you saw the picture?"

"I had to sit down. It was the most amazing thing I had ever seen. I did not show it to anyone at first, but I took my secretary into my confidence later that month. I had to show it to somebody. It was the Führer. There was no denying it."

"Yes, I can imagine. It must have been incredible."

"When I showed it to the Minister of Propaganda, he just stared at the photo for the longest time. He wanted to meet the man in the photo personally. I made plans to go to the monastery after a meeting with Goebbels. I decided that the monk would have to be brought to Berlin at the earliest possible date."

"Eva Dofmünster explained it all to me," Brian said.

Glossen's smile looked sincere. "You are fortunate to have met her. She is a wonderful lady. Now she is a loyal member of my *Freundenreich*."

"That must make you feel proud," Brian said.

Glossen grinned. "I can recall the many days she spent in my office assuring me with her wonderful smile and gentle personality."

They crossed over the street toward the Ponte Vecchio. The river had a dark greenish color to it in the streetlights. The weather seemed a little colder now.

"I want you to understand the fervor that existed in the Third Reich," Glossen said. "I suppose no one can really comprehend the full sense of it, but I hope I can make you appreciate what I went through."

"Did you ever think when you brought Brother Matthias to Berlin that it would end up the way it did?"

"I had no such expectations. Why Hitler eventually accepted his brother is still a mystery to me. I had always hoped that the Führer would do so, but I believed the odds were against it. There were many obstacles to making it all work—the least of which was convincing Brother Matthias to adopt a more German-sounding name. But over a period of time, Horst started to become familiar with his destiny. There was no doubt in anyone's mind that he was the twin brother of the Führer. The idea of having Horst impersonate his brother is something I had concocted early on. I thought it would allow Hitler to take a break from time to time. It was after the speech Horst gave in April 1942 that the plan became invaluable. Not only did Goebbels and the others believe he was effective, Hitler thought his brother was magnificent, although he called me into his sparse office at the bunker in East Prussia and told me he would not stand for Horst taking over. He would always remain in control. But the logistics had become very difficult since Hitler had moved his operation to Reagensberg. The bunker complex was in the middle of a forest, and in my opinion it was eerie. Walking to the complex from the small airfield, one could only see a bright light emanating from the trees. Barking dogs would always give me the chills.

"We were forced to move Horst around constantly to accommodate any situation. He spent a considerable amount of time at Berghof, and divvied up the rest of his time at the complex or at the Chancellery. This actually gave me an idea. I often had Horst impersonate Hitler at the Chancellery for meetings, otherwise Hitler would have had to travel there from East Prussia. Conveniently, the meetings were always inconsequential and never required a command decision on the spot. But in January 1942, unfortunately my plan had a gapping hole torn out of the middle of it. Horst was forced to make a decision that affected millions of people. While at the Chancellery for a temporary visit, Horst was approached by Reinhard Heydrich, the head of the Gestapo, and asked for permission to move a rather large number of Jews from Buckenwald to Auschwitz. Horst agreed. When the Führer found out, he exploded—wanting to get rid of not only me, but Goebbels as well. After calling us into a room, he yelled at us for hours."

"Heydrich was never informed about Hitler's brother?"

"Goebbels refused to tell him, and for good reason. I cannot even begin to explain the heinous personality of Heydrich. He was more sadistic than any other man I have ever known—including Manfred Wormser. Had Heydrich found out he had been addressing an impostor, he would have shot him on the spot. To this day I cannot understand how Heydrich could have been taken in. He was suspicious of everyone and everything."

They stopped at the middle of the Ponte Vecchio and gazed at the water. "I know Horst was an identical twin, but it seems to me that he couldn't have had all of Hitler's traits," Brian said.

"You would be surprised. There were times when I even thought I was talking to Hitler himself. The transformation from monk to dictator was amazing. It was all the work of highly trained psychologists. They worked day and night for months to get the shy monk ready for his future calling."

"What did you do to ensure that the doctors and attending staffs were kept quiet?" Brian asked.

"Why would you want to know that? It is not important."

Brian insisted.

Glossen laughed. "I had every intention of paying them money for their services. But the Propaganda Minister became concerned once the monk became more proficient at his role. Goebbels was convinced that the men and women who had helped transform Brother Matthias into Horst would reveal the secret in the end."

"So what happened?"

"He had them eliminated," Glossen replied. "I tried to intervene but I was informed I had no influence over the matter."

"They were killed?"

"Yes. Shot by a firing squad. In early 1943 Goebbels summoned them all to a private party at a Nazi-owned house outside of Berlin. After they ate and drank the night away, Goebbels had them herded outside where they were executed. They were then buried on the property. Goebbels told me if Horst could fool Heydrich, then there was no further need for any of them."

"I can't believe he just had them shot."

"Yes. It is hard to believe."

"So you were kept busy catering to Hitler's every whim?"

The Caretaker's Bible

"Yes. Besides worrying about Horst, which was a full time job, I was fully engaged in other matters of the Reich. Goebbels expected a lot from me. Since May of 1942, when the Negroes had been placed in a fully segregated unit of the U.S. Army to fight Fascism, I had been drafting propaganda in the form of newspaper articles to dismiss the importance of America's intervention. Since 1941, I had been involved in war planning by helping Goebbels to take advantage of opportunities that could be beneficial to the Führer. I played a crucial role in drafting a memorandum on political plans for the Russian people. I was instrumental in writing a proclamation that would give the Russians greater freedom from the oppressions of the Soviet government."

"You were obviously a very influential part of the Third Reich," Brian said.

"It was all very deceiving. Nothing was as it appeared in the Third Reich. Nothing was as important as supporting the Führer from the moment a person woke up in the morning until he closed his eyes at night. But it all was a means to an end. That's the way the leadership looked at it."

"How did you ever tolerate Wormser?"

"I regret the day I first met him. Because Goebbels had been introduced to Wormser several months prior to our meeting, it was a foregone conclusion that he would hire the young antagonist. Even in the initial interview, I could tell Wormser was going to be trouble. To say the young SS soldier was maniacal, I would consider an understatement. The one thing that stood out in the interview was Wormser's hatred of Jews. My impression was that Manfred believed he could single-handedly effect the complete elimination of Jewish people. After the meeting, I went to the Propaganda Minister and complained that it would unwise to bring Wormser into the fold. Goebbels refused to listen and forced my hand.

"An already tepid relationship between Wormser and myself became worse when he found out about Horst. Goebbels had informed him after Horst had already been in Berlin for a month. As far as I was concerned, Wormser did not have a need to know. The timing could not have been worse when one day Wormser burst into a back office where Horst and I were talking. He demanded to know why he had not been told. I immediately whisked Wormser into another room and tried to calm him down. The last thing I needed was for Hitler's brother to become so scared it would virtually be impossible to gain his trust. Wormser was a thorn in my side from that moment on."

"Was Goebbels so dense he couldn't see through Wormser?" Brian asked as they began walking toward the end of the bridge.

"The Propaganda Minister was simply trying to create a balance in his directorate. He needed someone who had the will to comply with the Führer's plan to eliminate the Jews—someone who could not only craft a good story, but who could help make it happen. I admitted early on to Goebbels that I did not have the passion that the Führer had in that regard. In the fall of 1940, Wormser directly supported the Propaganda Minister by drafting a plan to segregate the Jewish population in Warsaw within an enclosed ghetto surrounded by an eight-foot wall. This was submitted to Hitler, who approved it on the spot. This was just the beginning to Wormser's own reign of terror. He repeatedly looked for possibilities and drafted many proposals that he tried to get in front of the Führer.

"Over the next two years, Wormser worked in conjunction with people like Reinhard Heydrich to solidify what they called the Final Solution. He was involved in helping define the rules and regulations of the Third Reich's proclamation to eliminate all European Jews. It was what he wanted to do. More than that, he felt he was good at it. I remember trying to persuade him on numerous occasions to stop the nonsense and to concentrate on more important issues—only to be told to mind my own business."

After crossing over the Ponte Vecchio, they headed toward the Pitti Palace.

"I must admit, I am tired of talking about Wormser," Glossen said.

"But I want to know why you ever got involved with Wormser after the war, when you created the *Freundenreich*."

"It was only because I realized at the time I needed someone like Wormser to bring a strong, disciplined, and ultraconservative aspect to the group. I certainly had not changed my personal feelings for Wormser, but I considered the arrangement to be nothing more than business. But even that bond degraded quickly over time, and our group split in two. Looking back, I am glad it had happened that way. The only problem is that Wormser is not content with the arrangement. He wants to be completely in charge like the Führer was. Unfortunately, his quest for power has grown more maniacal over the last few years."

"He wants to kill you and your family."

"It appears that way. But I did not agree to come here to talk about him. I thought you came to Florence to find out the truth about Horst."

Brian apologized. "I do want to talk about the twin."

Glossen continued. "It was in mid 1943 when things began to heat up concerning Hitler's brother. In April of that year, Hitler had met with Mussolini in Salzburg to discuss the war in Russia. In his typical unwavering style, Hitler dismissed Mussolini's plea for peace with Russia. After being completely humiliated by the inflammatory rhetoric, Mussolini went back to Italy a defeated man. Shortly after that meeting, the Allies invaded Tunis and Bizerta in Tunisia, capturing over 250,000 men with all their equipment. Hitler waited for the inevitable—the Allied invasion of Italy.

"It occurred on the tenth of July in Sicily. After a hasty meeting with his top advisors, Hitler immediately had a memo sent to Mussolini requesting his presence at Feltre in northern Italy for a conference. The evening before Hitler was to leave for Feltre, he began complaining of terrible stomach pain. Goebbels thought the meeting should not be cancelled, and he solicited Horst to go instead of the Führer. What was different about this meeting was that Horst seemed to have taken on his brother's character as if he were possessed.

"In the morning before lunch, Horst talked nonstop about the possible consequences of the Allied invasion, and after lunch he continued where he had left off. He had no script nor had he been coached about what to say. Although Goebbels, Göring, and I were present at the meeting to intervene if needed, it was not necessary. It was absolutely astounding to witness Horst in action; his performance was unsurpassed. When Hitler was briefed on his brother's handling of the meeting, he asked to see Horst privately. I asked Horst what had transpired in that meeting without receiving a reply. To this day no one knows what Hitler and his brother discussed. But it became apparent after their meeting that the Führer was more than willing to allow Horst to impersonate him.

"It was true that by mid 1943 Hitler's health had become an issue that could have affected the Third Reich. He had been relegated to taking many different types of painkillers virtually every day. Many of his top advisors were concerned that the Führer was possibly not fit to lead Germany to victory. Another critical problem that Goebbels and Himmler had discovered was that many high-ranking officials, mostly military men, were plotting to kill Hitler. In the summer and fall of 1943, they had uncovered no less than six plots to eliminate the Führer. Goebbels and Himmler differed on whether they should inform Hitler about the incidents. Himmler believed it was counterproductive, while Goebbels thought it was absolutely necessary that they make the Führer aware."

As they reached the Pitti Palace, Brian was beginning to get nervous. Dawn was breaking and he worried they would be seen. He wanted to head back to the Piazza della Signoria. He cautioned Glossen to remain alert to anything suspicious.

Glossen laughed. "I know the dangers well enough. It does not matter. Meeting with you is a kind of catharsis for my soul. It gives me the chance to relive the past—something I do not do very often. I have made up my mind to make the most out of every day, as each one could be my last. There can be no other way to live."

Brian thought how depressing it must have been for Glossen now that he had become a man who had to constantly look over his shoulder because he did what he thought was right. "Was there ever a time when you regretted finding Hitler's brother?"

"In the initial stages of preparing Horst to meet the Führer, I had some reservations. I felt some pangs of conscience about subjecting a naïve monk to such an incredible undertaking. I actually convinced myself that it was God's will that Hitler meet his brother. My feeling was that, if nothing else, the ordeal was for the good of the Reich. What happened in the last two years of the Nazi regime proved my prophecy beyond any doubt.

"In September 1943, Horst asked to have a private meeting with me in Berghof. It was immediately obvious that something was bothering him. I was shocked when Hitler's brother told me he did not think he was doing enough to support the Reich. He wanted more duties. Had I created a monster? Horst's demeanor was crass. He believed he had more to offer. It was then that I had an idea. What if I permanently replaced Hitler with his brother, even if for only for long periods at a time to give the Führer a rest? Would Goebbels go along with it? Could we pull it off? After the meeting, I went back to Berlin and discussed his idea with the Propaganda Minister. But Goebbels was reluctant. He did not feel it was such a good idea since the war effort was so critical. However, he said he would think it over, and that was exactly what I wanted to hear."

They stopped for a minute. Brian thought he could almost finish the story. Horst was given enough to keep him occupied, but he never got the opportunity to act as the Führer on a continual basis. It wouldn't have made sense. Horst would have been well protected and surely hidden after Hitler's death. Brian was getting anxious. He could visualize himself standing in front of the twin asking him dozens of questions. His compulsions were taking over. "When can I meet Horst?" He glanced around for anything out of the ordinary.

Glossen appeared perplexed. "I thought you wanted to know the whole story?"

"Of course."

"It is not possible to meet him."

"Why not?" Brian asked, impatiently.

"Because he died in 1945."

chapter 23
Florence—1972

BRIAN'S AMBITIONS DIED WITH Glossen's stark revelation. He repeated what he said to ensure that Glossen had heard him correctly. Glossen immediately confirmed it. He said he understood Brian's disappointment, but nevertheless there was more to the story.

Brian couldn't even begin to describe the emotions he felt over Glossen's disclosure. He had somehow convinced himself that Horst was still alive. Now it was all gone—everything he had hoped for. He wondered what had gone so terribly wrong. Walking back over the Ponte Vecchio, he decided he had nothing to lose, so he asked Glossen to continue.

"By December 1943, Hitler had been suffering from trembling of his left arm and leg, and it was thought to be a nerve disorder. His condition was steadily getting worse. Horst believed his brother needed a rest. He volunteered to take his place at his bunker complex in Reagensberg. At first I dismissed it as a bad idea, but after talking to Goebbels I changed my mind. The plan entailed Hitler going to spend time at Berchesgarten while Horst essentially became the titular Führer. Hitler agreed to the arrangement as long as he could always remain in control. With this in mind, I made the switch in the first week of December at the bunker in East Prussia.

"It was during this time that I discovered something unusual and quite amusing. A chambermaid at Berghof told me that Eva Braun had confided in her that she could not tell Hitler from his brother. I immediately thought this was very strange. But as I was reminded by several of his staff, Hitler apparently refrained from sexual relations with Eva. Of course that could never be verified, but I realized it could have been possible. As the story goes, Adolf showed up at the chalet and Eva assumed it was Horst—thinking the Führer was war planning in East Prussia. She was ambivalent for much of the time he was there—so much so that Hitler at one point demanded an explanation. When she broke down and said she thought he was Horst, he laughed so hard he started choking, scaring the hell out of everyone. Even after it was all over, Eva wanted to call for the doctor, but Adolf would not have it. If nothing else, this incident confirmed for the Führer that Eva was faithful. It consoled him in a great time of stress."

Brian stopped and looked at the view of houses along the river while Glossen kept talking.

"Horst had a few causes for laughter himself. In the second week he was at the bunker, he had an unexpected visitor. Albert Speer swore he called ahead first, but none of the security personnel knew anything about it. Horst, playing the part impeccably, berated Speer, saying that he was not anyone special and that if he showed up again unannounced he would be fired. I remember the look on Speer's face. It was unforgettable. The wonder boy had been taken to task, and he did not like it. Horst reveled in his phantomlike power. After an hour of listening to Speer discussing war production, V-1 flying bombs, V-2 rockets, and U-Boats, Horst wanted to know what Germany was going to have to show in the end for having built these incredible weapons. Speer sat silent—obviously not expecting the question."

"So Horst actually did take on his brother's personality," Brian said.

"Yes. It was a marvelous sight to behold. I witnessed a transformation right in front of my eyes. Hitler himself could not have done a better job of putting Speer in his place."

"I thought the Führer liked Albert Speer. Wasn't this really uncharacteristic of him—something the Führer wouldn't have done? I mean didn't Speer suspect something?"

"The Armaments Minister's sinister stare was chilling. He never challenged Horst, but must have had suspicions. Apparently Speer decided to cut his visit short, staying only a few hours. In my opinion, he would have not done so if he thought he was in the presence of Adolf Hitler."

Brian grinned. "It sounds like Horst was becoming very proficient at being the Führer."

"In the evening, I sat down with Horst and tried to understand what had come over him. As we talked, I could see the fiery look in Horst's eyes. It was disconcerting. In no uncertain terms, Horst proceeded to inform me that he no longer considered himself a novice. He was the Führer. I became enraged. I reminded him of who he was and where he had come from not so long ago. It was absolute heresy for him to believe that he could cast his brother out of the way. For over an hour, I relentlessly lectured Horst on the consequences of such an ego. Horst fought back, saying he was just doing what I and all the other Nazis wanted: being an impersonator. But now, because he had become so adept at it, he was being punished. I found it hard to argue with him.

"A week later, I flew to Berlin to meet with one of Hitler's physicians. We met behind closed doors. According to the doctor, the Führer's health was questionable at best. He made references to the fact that Hitler was not at all a well man and that several other doctors had verified this diagnosis. They were not at all sure what was wrong with him, but they unanimously agreed that stress affected his health greatly. I was unsure what the doctor was really trying to tell me, but I offered to talk to Hitler at length about his daily schedules and his tremendous workload. The doctor believed that the Führer had to rest as much as possible for the sake of the regime and the preservation of Germany as a world power. They were prepared to give him as many drugs as it took to eradicate the pain. However, they did not want to administer medicine to the detriment of the welfare of the Reich."

Brian began to wonder what would have happened if Hitler had suddenly died. He figured the Third Reich would have been in absolute turmoil. "Goebbels had to realize Horst was his savior if anything happened to Hitler."

"When I returned to East Prussia, I began to think about what the doctor had said. It was then that I sketched out a plan. The war effort was taking a toll on Hitler. That was a given. It made perfect sense for me to make a permanent switch. The idea would be that Hitler could run the Third Reich as he had always done, and his brother would simply be the mouthpiece. In my mind, it would even be better for the Reich in the long run because Hitler would perhaps be in a position to make more calculating decisions while out of the public eye. I believed all along that Germany would prevail in the war but I wanted to give the Reich as many advantages as possible. After reviewing the plan several times, I believed it was worthy to be brought to the forefront. Of course there were still two obstacles—one being Goebbels and the other being the Führer himself. On the recommendation from the Propaganda Minister, we would wait until Hitler's health seemed to affect his leadership to make the replacement. In July 1944, that became a reality.

"In the first week of July, Goebbels had arranged for Hitler and his brother to meet at Berghof. The Propaganda Minister had been informed that Hitler had been secretly taking pills to relieve his pain, pills administered by his personal physician, Dr. Morrell. Unfortunately, it had been determined by an independent doctor that the pills contained large quantities of strychnine and belladonna, and thus it was assumed that Hitler was slowly being poisoned. Even the Führer's skin was beginning to turn a yellowish color. In Goebbels' opinion, it was affecting his overall thinking process. But there was a bitter exchange between the two of us and Hitler when we broached the subject of having Horst permanently intercede on his behalf. The Führer's response was typical. He questioned our mental capacity to be in leadership positions, our loyalty and, most of all, our apparent utter disrespect for our leader. Hitler reminded us that he had a series of conferences planned for that month that focused on the state of the war effort. He maintained that he was in perfect health and did not need Horst's help at that time. When it was necessary, he would inform us of his plans."

"It's obvious Hitler was so caught up in being the Führer that he was beginning to change his mind."

"It was the third conference, held on the twentieth of July, that changed everything. Goebbels demanded that Horst be at the bunker complex in case they needed him. It was a rather hot day and the bunker was stifling from the heat. Even the small fans dispersed throughout the complex did not really help. Horst was, as usual, relegated to one of the back rooms. By now, he was more than used to the routine—constantly being whisked from one place to another under cover, keeping abreast of the war effort, and waiting in the wings to perform, which was probably the most difficult part. Hitler appeared to be in great spirits that day and was eager to host the conference. He had risen early, taken breakfast, and spent an hour or so preparing for the meeting. The attendees began arriving in the late morning, including General Claus von Stauffenberg, who had been at the other two conferences with a briefcase practically strapped to his lap. He was scheduled to discuss the creation of the new Volksgrenadier divisions. Promptly at twelve-thirty in the afternoon, Hitler commenced with a few opening remarks. Himmler and Göring had been invited to attend, but had not shown up. Goebbels, still in Berlin for a meeting, was available by phone if needed.

"I stood near the Führer in the corner of the room observing. Twelve minutes into the proceedings, an explosion ripped through the conference room, sending debris everywhere and men to the ground. Immediately, one of Hitler's adjutants grabbed him and took him outside. Although horribly shaken, the Führer was not seriously injured. I feel as if I was spared that day; I had been knocked against the far wall. After removing rubble that dropped from the ceiling, I knew I had to escape the fire that was burning steadily. With dust and debris in my lungs, I started to make my way outside. But I realized Horst was still in the back room. I ran back there to find the twin lying on the floor coughing, but otherwise unharmed. I helped him outside. I knew that Mussolini was arriving that afternoon to see the Führer. This presented me with a dilemma. Should I summarily replace Hitler with his brother, or let Hitler muddle through the meeting? After several minutes of reflective thought, I decided the twin would remain behind closed doors. It was at that moment that I realized Horst would now have a much bigger role to play."

"Hitler's confidence had to have been shaken after that assassination attempt," Brian said.

Glossen laughed. "Hitler was furious. He became more paranoid than anyone had ever seen him. I wanted to transport him back to Berlin while the complex was being cleaned up and reconstructed, but he declined. His afternoon with the Italian dictator went well; he even joked about the ill-fated assassination attempt. After midnight, he addressed the German people, assuring them that he was alive and well. Within days of the incident, he was informed of von Shauffenberg's treachery. He was infuriated.

"It was then that Hitler asked to meet with Goebbels, Horst, and myself on the last day of July. We convened in one of the back rooms of the complex. The musty smell seemed to be worse now with the lingering remnants of dust particles from the explosion. The Führer was emphatic that he be protected from any future attempts on his life. He appeared fragile that day. For over an hour Hitler ranted and raved about how he could not concentrate on winning the war if he had to be constantly looking over his shoulder. Hitler shocked all of us when he announced that he wanted his brother to be in the forefront while he led the country to victory in the shadows. I can never forget the look on Horst's face. He appeared dazed. But for me, the request was something that was bothersome. Even though it was what I had previously proposed, I could not get over the fact that the Führer was asking his brother to risk his own life to save his."

Brian just stared at Glossen.

"I must admit that even though it fit neatly into my plan, it seemed to me to be callous at the time."

Brian believed he was beginning to detect a sense of remorse from a man whom he hadn't expected to reveal such emotion. "It's obvious. Hitler was a desperate man."

"He refused to have Horst leave his side. And that is the way it was for the next four months. Hitler stayed in the background while his brother interacted with the world. The Führer was confined to his bed most of the time during that period—constant headaches, stomach cramps, and a perpetual sore throat. Horst met with cabinet members, military advisors, and a host of ancillary workers while Hitler lay in pain locked behind the door of a back room. But there was no mistake who was in charge. Every morning, Hitler would instruct his brother how to carry on. The Führer would bark out orders and ask Horst to repeat what he had said. At the end, he would always expect his brother to stand at attention and salute him. It became a very strange ritual.

"In October, Albert Speer again made a surprise visit to the bunker complex. His sole purpose was to brief the Führer on the current status of armament production for the Reich. He immediately demanded to know whom he was addressing. He said he would not talk to an impostor, and attempted to trick both Horst and me into making a mistake. When he did not get anywhere, he boasted that he would assuredly increase the rate of production for the weapons they needed, despite all the Allied bombing. In short, Speer intimated that he had done his part. He wanted to know how the Führer was proceeding so he could adjust the timetable for weapons to be shipped to the appropriate front. Horst sidestepped the issue by saying he needed some time to finalize his plan. Speer, apparently not believing for one moment he was talking to Hitler, laughed and said that they would surely lose the war if the Führer had that kind of attitude. Horst immediately had the guards forcefully remove Speer."

"Didn't Horst start to realize that he was being used?" Brian asked, as they now moved past jewelry and clothing stores on the Ponte Vecchio bridge.

"Horst never looked at it that way. He believed it was an honor to serve the Führer. It was hard to understand how Brother Matthias had turned into the Horst that I knew in 1944. It was perhaps unexplainable. At times I thought I was talking to a zombie—as if Horst had taken over Adolf Hitler's brain. I did not realize how serious it was until January of 1945, right after Hitler had moved back to Berlin to take up residency in the Chancellery. Apparently Wormser had tried to tell the Führer that I was plotting against him by manipulating Horst to take his place."

Brian watched birds swooping down over the Arno. "If Wormser had been successful, you would have been shot yourself."

"It is very likely. After that incident I developed a hatred for Wormser—even greater than I could explain."

"But you joined forces with him again. I still don't understand."

"As I said before, it was business."

"So after January, did you stay in Berlin?"

"Yes, for a while. Hitler began using the shelter almost exclusively in February. Along with Goebbels, he had moved his office to the first story of the bunker. They also had segregated a room on the lower level for Horst. Their everyday existence was anything but a routine matter. Hitler was convinced they were winning the war, and he had them develop propaganda campaigns against the Allied forces. By the middle of March, Hitler had finalized the scorched earth policy that would be executed if he believed there was no hope for victory. It included destroying most—if not all—of his major infrastructure. At one point,

Albert Speer visited the shelter and presented Hitler with a memorandum that clearly countered the Führer's wishes. Speer believed that even in the face of defeat they should not destroy their remaining assets, as that action would not affect the outcome. In a short note, Speer predicted the end of the Third Reich in four to six weeks. When Hitler read those words, he promptly crumpled the note up, shoved it in his pocket, and dismissed everyone in the room.

"By this time, many of the leaders, such as Göring, Himmler, Ribbentrop, and others, were frequently visiting Hitler. I believe they were vying for position. Hitler never had delineated a plan of succession should he be eliminated—only because he swore he would fight until the end. All of them seemed to have the impression that naming a successor was necessary. Hitler was publicly opposed to such action. But in a personal conversation I had with the Führer, I learned something quite different. Hitler had never believed in suicide, but for some reason, he had changed his mind. Citing Schopenhauer's view that life was not worth living if it brought only disillusionment, the Führer stressed that his own poor health was reason enough to end his life. He was distressed that Germany was on the brink of being taken by the Allies—something he did not think he could bear to witness. I still remember the look on Hitler's face. The sincerity of that moment was astounding."

"It must have seemed strange to hear the Führer say those things," Brian said. "What did you do?"

"What could I do? I tried to reassure Hitler that he was the one and only Führer. I recommended he talk to his brother, which I knew would give him solace. By then, Hitler had decided to go to Berchtesgarden and temporarily leave his brother in Berlin."

"Did you see Horst before you left?" Brian asked.

"Only briefly, the morning we departed. He was as proud as he could be that he was going to carry on as the Führer while his brother was taken out of harm's way."

"It does sound unbelievable," Brian said.

"The metamorphosis I witnessed over the four-and-a-half years Horst had lived in Berlin was incredible. I find it hard even to begin to describe it. The trip to Berchtesgarden was difficult for all concerned. Hitler especially found it unsettling, even though he believed he would be safe there. He spent most of the drive reminiscing about his life, personal feelings, and his goals and objectives for a unified Nazi Germany.

"Two days after arriving at Berghof in preparation for setting up a new Chancellery in an old office building in the city, I received a coded message from Goebbels that signified the time to open the envelope I had been given earlier. In it was an address and explicit instructions how to get there."

"What did it say?" Brian asked.

"The Minister of Propaganda ordered me to take the Führer to an abandoned chalet near Lucerne, Switzerland. The chalet was owned by a family friend of Goebbels. We were to stay there for an extended period of time—indefinitely, if necessary. The owner would ensure sustenance for as long as we needed."

"What did Hitler do when you informed him about the letter?"

Glossen laughed. "Well, he didn't seem at all angry. In fact, he gave me the impression he already knew about it."

"But what about Horst?"

Glossen stopped walking and faced Brian. "I think you know what happened next. In late April, Berlin was under siege from the Russians. The Americans were not far away. The entire city was doomed. The war was as good as over."

Brian could tell Glossen was upset by the wretched look on his face. He had to assume that Glossen regretted leaving Horst in the bunker on that April day. "I can't believe Hitler left his own brother there to suffer the consequences."

"If reports are accurate, Horst took his own life and that of Eva Braun on the thirtieth of April. Nazi soldiers burned them in the garden and the Russians found their scorched bodies."

"That can't be true. But what happened to Hitler?"

"That, I believe, Herr Bennett, is why you have come all this way."

Brian's pulse beat faster. "What do you mean?"

"The Führer lives!" Glossen exclaimed. "He wants to see you. I can arrange everything."

"He's still alive?"

"Yes. Of course. But you have already met him. The caretaker at the villa. He remembers you well."

"What! How can that be?" Brian said in a barely audible whisper.

"I believe the Führer has quite a story to tell you. He is dying of cancer and doesn't have much longer."

"Where does he live?"

"On Lake Garda." Glossen smiled. "On the eastern shore by Bardolino. They all know him there as Horst the caretaker. I will escort you there myself in the morning if you wish."

Brian looked at the beauty of the Palazzo Vecchio in the light of dawn. When he turned around to say goodbye to Glossen, the former Nazi wasn't there.

Without hesitation, he made his way to find Marta on the side street—still looking over his shoulder for Glossen.

chapter 24
Florence—1972

To Brian, it seemed inconceivable that Adolf Hitler could still be alive. The very idea that his twin brother committed suicide inside the Führerbunker instead of him was difficult to imagine. It didn't make sense. But why would Glossen lie? Why would he make up such an outrageous story if it weren't true? He knew one thing for sure: he was going to find out the truth the next day.

Standing on the corner, he waited. After ten minutes of trying to look invisible, Brian realized Marta had either already come and gone, or was not coming at all. Being as cautious as he could, he slipped through back alleys and along smaller streets until he got to her apartment complex. The yellow Peugeot was parked out front. When he reached her floor, he knocked on the door, but no one answered. He asked a tenant leaving her apartment if she had seen Marta. She claimed she had not and kept walking down the stairs.

When he tried the doorknob, the door opened. Letting himself inside, he looked around. Nothing seemed disturbed. But Marta wasn't there. She had agreed to pick him up, so Brian had to assume something went wrong. He scoured the rooms for any sign of a hasty departure. He looked for notes that could give him a clue where she might have gone.

The only conclusion was that Marta must have sensed trouble, known she was being followed. He wasn't sure how to proceed. His options were few: stay there and wait for her to come back or go and try to make contact with Glossen again. Either one had its risks. If he stayed in the apartment, Wormser's men could be staking it out. If he left and went to the Hotel Dorian, he would be in plain sight. However, he had a gut feeling he shouldn't stay there. Looking at his watch, he noted that it was only seven o'clock in the morning. He didn't want to be weighed down with luggage, so he decided to leave it where it was.

He moved slowly and inconspicuously through the morning crowd on their way to work, trying not to stand out. It was obvious to Brian that he was probably being followed, but he hadn't seen any signs of Wormser's men. As he entered the Piazza del Mercato Centrate, he could see the church of San Lorenzo in front of him. He walked along the storefronts staying out of the open.

At the end of a long promenade, he saw a woman with a hat and long coat standing still—looking like she was going to cross the street. When he turned his head for a second and turned back, she was gone. Passing a small alley, he heard a voice calling his name. Thinking it was a trap, he hesitated for a moment, and then he realized it was Marta.

"We must go. Quickly. They are on to us. They will kill you if they find us." She pointed across the street and said they had to act without delay.

"I know Hitler's alive."

Marta couldn't resist. "Of course. Why else would Wormser want you dead?"

They had walked only a few steps before all hell broke loose. Men seemed to swarm toward them from all directions. Brian and Marta began to run as fast as they could toward the church. He hoped he could fool them by appearing to bypass the church, then suddenly going inside. It worked; they hid in the shadows and watched the assailants pass by. Then they entered the church.

"I went to your apartment. I knew something had to be wrong," Brian said.

"A friend warned me that strange men were hanging around the building. So I left. I knew it had to be them. I am afraid they are going to kill my father."

"They've tried to kill him before. He can take care of himself."

"I do not think so. He is getting frail and it will not take much for him to give in. He has told me many times that he has lived his life and does not fear dying."

"Wormser won't kill your father. It's me he's after. Right? I'm convinced if I were out of the way, it wouldn't make sense to kill your father or anyone else."

"What are we going to do?" Marta asked.

"Let me think." They walked quietly to one side of chapel and sat down. "We eventually have to get to the Hotel Dorian. If we can make contact with your father without being noticed, we can perhaps slip away and travel to Lake Garda."

"But they will know we are going there. They will be waiting for us."

"I know it isn't going to be easy, but I'm willing to try. So tell me, how did you know I wouldn't stay in the apartment? And how did you know where I would be?"

"Intuition. You are pretty predictable. I knew you would try to find my father again."

Brian began to gauge their chances of making contact with Glossen and safely traveling to Lake Garda together. Success seemed unlikely. "Wormser's men will probably be guarding the Hotel Dorian so that your father can't leave without being noticed. We have to think of a way to distract them, even if only for a few minutes."

"We should perhaps stay here as long as necessary," Marta suggested.

Brian slumped in the pew. "You knew Hitler was alive all along, didn't you?"

"Yes. But my father ordered me not to tell you."

Brian wanted to feel betrayed, but he perfectly understood why Marta would want to obey her father's wishes. "Have you ever met him?"

"Only once. My father took me to Lake Garda for Hitler's eightieth birthday. It was very strange. Besides his entourage of security guards, some of his neighbors were there who knew him as Horst, and he celebrated his birthday as a retired caretaker—not as the former Führer of the Third Reich. I brought a homemade cake and he ate several big pieces because he loved sweets so much."

"Don't the neighbors think there's something wrong with a retired caretaker having armed guards around the house?"

"That is what was so weird. It did not seem to faze them. But I guess everyone knows Hitler died in 1945. Why would they suspect anything? I will never forget the party. Even Manfred Wormser and his men showed up at the end. By then the neighbors had gone."

"What did your father say?" Brian asked.

"I saw the angered look on my father's face. But he never said anything negative to Wormser. After a small exchange, he just ignored him."

Brian was still having a hard time believing all of this. Why was it that when he was so close, he still felt like he had when he first went to Hagenmünster—unsure of himself and confused?

"What are you going to ask the Führer when you see him?"

"I'm not positive." He thought back to his days at the villa and his conversations with Horst—trying to remember everything the caretaker had said. Brian's impression of Horst was that he was a lonely old German who had come to resent the war after years of reliving it. He believed the discussions revealed a great deal about the caretaker's life, and Brian had grown fond of him. It seemed odd now. But this time he would have another opportunity to make it right, knowing, as he did, the caretaker's real identity.

Marta was getting anxious. "We must find my father and get out of Florence."

"We're taking our lives into our own hands," Brian said. "You do understand that?" She nodded her head. They huddled in the pew for another few minutes trying to calm themselves before they departed the church.

As they walked toward the Hotel Dorian, Brian could tell that Marta was scared, but he also knew she was determined. Approaching the hotel from the other side of the street, they saw an ambulance arrive at the entrance. Marta said her heart was in her throat. She didn't have a good feeling about it. Against her better judgment, she decided to go into the lobby of the hotel. Brian had reservations but agreed to accompany her.

A terrible scene greeted them. Women were screaming, and several men were trying to calm people down. Blood covered the foyer furniture, and a large vase of flowers lay broken on top of a bloodstained body. Marta rushed to the aide of the victim. Brian could already tell by the clothes the gentleman was wearing that it was Heinrich Glossen. He couldn't have envisioned a worse nightmare.

Marta tried desperately to revive her father, ignoring the fact that he obviously had been shot in the head at pointblank range. There was nothing she could do. Brian grabbed her and pulled her away as the medics covered the body. He consoled her while he looked around. It was entirely possible that the killer was still there. Frantically, he tried to decide what to do next. He assumed Marta would want to stay with her father, but the more he thought about it, the more he believed that was not a good idea. If they killed Glossen, she would definitely be on their list too.

"We need to get out of here. We need to head for the Stazione Centrale. I wonder how often trains go to Milan?"

"I cannot leave my father."

"Marta, there's nothing you can do for him now. I know you love him, but they'll kill you next."

They carried Glossen out to the ambulance. Brian knew that she would want a proper burial for her father. She would have to make a quick decision. "We must leave now."

She looked into Brian's eyes. "I cannot leave. I do not know what they will do with him."

"Once we're safe, you will be able to come back and pay your respects. We can't waste any more time."

"Please, I love him very much."

"I know, but your life's in danger. You have to trust me."

Minutes later they were in a cab racing for the train station.

"We will have to take a cab from Milan to Lake Garda," Marta said. "Do you remember where Horst lives?"

Brian pulled out a note he had written with the name of the town on it. "No. But when we can get to this town, we should be able to find him." Brian began to think about the implications of Glossen's death. The *Freundenreich* now belonged completely to Manfred Wormser. Worse, Wormser now had the sole power to pick and choose who should live and who should die while he protected his precious Führer.

No matter what Brian thought about the *Freundenreich*, he believed Glossen's ideas for its existence were much more honorable than his former colleague's. Even though he knew Glossen was a diehard Nazi, he had found him to be a sincere and forthright human being. It was his passion and determination not to give in to Wormser's kind that was impressive. However, Brian couldn't excuse how he had abandoned Hitler's twin in the end. Now, Brian couldn't help but feel a little guilty. If he hadn't been so damn compulsive about running down this story, Glossen would probably still be alive.

"What are we going to do when we get to the station?" Marta asked. "I cannot begin to imagine that Wormser's men will not figure us out."

"I'm positive we're not being followed. With any luck at all, we can get a train to Milan soon after we arrive. If not, we will have to lay low and avoid drawing attention to ourselves."

They immediately went to the counter to inquire about the schedule. The earliest train to Milan was in thirty minutes. They bought tickets and walked to the platform. Glancing around, Brian

The Caretaker's Bible

saw no one suspicious. Marta was still in shock from finding her father dead.

"Maybe I should stay in Florence. I wish things could have been different. My life has been nothing but a lie. I had spent all those years in the States trying to deny who I am—only to come back to Germany to protect my father, even after all he had done for the Nazis. Now I am more confused than ever. Even though I have never shared the ideals or philosophy of my father, I have always felt a bond with him."

Brian was trying to visualize how it all was going to play out. Given that Horst the caretaker really was Hitler, Brian was certain he wanted to find out what any journalist would want to know from such a historic figure: what made him tick. *Why did he believe the things he did? What drove him to be a dictator? Why did he kill innocent people?* When he thought about it, the idea of interviewing a man who by all accounts had died in April 1945 seemed preposterous and almost paranormal. But if Glossen were telling the truth, meeting with the Führer would be the most incredible thing any journalist could ever achieve.

"I do not think we should go. I have a bad feeling about this," Marta said.

Brian smiled. "You're just nervous. We'll get through it." He looked at his watch. They were close to leaving.

The announcement came over the loudspeaker. The train to Milan was ready for boarding. Brian thought it would be better to wait to board until the very end, in case Wormser's men spotted them. That way they could get on board quickly as the train was departing, perhaps leaving the assailants behind. He had already concocted a plan if they were pursued. They moved closer to the front of the platform from where they were standing on the side. Marta's palms were sweaty. She feared the worst.

As they started to move toward the train, Brian saw two dubious looking men approaching from the front of the building. Out of the corner of his eye, he saw a steward with a large baggage cart passing to the side of them heading for another train. This was their opportunity, he thought. As the men got closer, he grabbed Marta's arm and darted around the cart, knocking it over and spilling the luggage all over the platform. The train was already in motion. They had to hurry. With a bit of good fortune the assailants would be out of luck, and they would be on the train.

Everything was going as planned, but without warning Marta broke away and said she couldn't go. She ran across to the opposite side of the platform. As Brian jumped on the train, he witnessed her being taken away at gunpoint by the two men. The only explanation he could think of was that she had panicked at the last minute, not wanting to leave her father for fear she would never see him again.

He wanted to save her. He knew it wasn't possible for her to survive the madness of the *Freundenreich*. He was angry with himself for not staying and protecting her, but he knew she was the master of her own fate. Now she was at the mercy of Wormser and nothing good could come out of that.

Sitting down, he tried to blend in. He was not looking forward to the four-hour trip to Milan. He surveyed the passengers, possessed with a paranoia he had never felt before. In the corner reading a newspaper was a man with a dark suit and a funny looking mustache. Others he noticed looked sinister as well. Brian assumed they had to be part of the Friends of the Third Reich. He figured they were probably everywhere throughout the train.

After a couple of hours of trying to stay awake, he sensed someone standing next to him. Looking up, he saw an attractive brunette, probably his age or slightly older, dressed in a light tan poncho with a paisley scarf wrapped around her neck. He stared at her eyes, her face; he knew he had seen her before somewhere. At least she looked vaguely familiar.

"Mind if I join you? I am traveling alone."

"No. Please have a seat." He stood up to let her pass. Her accent? It sounded familiar. There was no doubt she was pretty— beauty pageant face, stunning white teeth. "Are you by any chance Italian?"

"German, actually. But I live now in Milan. You are an American."

"Yes. I'm going to Milan to see friends."

"Where do they live?"

"Outside the city," Brian replied. "Do you take this ride often?"

"Frequently. Yes. My name is Bridget." She reached out her hand.

Brian introduced himself. He decided he needed to be somewhat guarded. At this point no one could be trusted. "This is my first time riding the train."

"I am a fashion designer and I spend a great deal of time in Florence and Rome selling my creations. On occasion, I visit New York as well. What do you do for a living, Herr Bennett?"

Brian explained what he did as succinctly as possible.

"So, you are a writer. Are you here for a story?"

He began to suspect something. He was positive he had seen this woman before somewhere. It was driving him crazy. She seemed to be leading the conversation. "No. Just here to see a friend."

"Are you married?" she asked.

"No. Engaged."

"That is a shame. You are a very handsome man."

Brian didn't know quite what to say, so he just thanked her. "Have you been in Germany lately?"

"Yes. Of course. Why?"

"You look familiar. I can't place where I've seen you, but it most definitely was in Munich."

She sat there for a moment—her eyes shifting back and forth. "Herr Bennett, we must talk. You have no idea what you are getting yourself into."

Slowly the vision came back to him. It was something he didn't want to think about. She had been one of his abductors. While lying on the bed in Munich, he could only partially see her face, but he remembered her voice. "What do you want?"

"I must warn you. You are in grave danger."

"Tell me something I don't already know." He wanted to lash out at her, but he didn't want to create a scene.

She reached into her purse and handed him a small piece of

paper and excused herself. Brian read the note. *Meet me in the next car in the rear by the toilets in five minutes.*

Brian's adrenaline surged. His first reaction was that this had to be an ambush. Looking at his watch, he knew they had roughly an hour until they reached Milan.

The five minutes seemed like an eternity. He was tormented over whether to meet with Bridget. What if she had something of value to tell him? What if she were trying to help him?

Brian wandered back to the toilets. He saw no one and silently stood by the men's room, getting butterflies in his stomach. He heard someone approach, but it was not Bridget. The passenger smiled and went directly into the ladies restroom. The scream was deafening. She ran out the door, yelling for help. Brian quickly went in to see why the passenger was so upset. There on the floor lay Bridget—dead—strangled with a leather rope. Her eyes were wide open and she had a frozen look of terror on her face.

By then, several other passengers had come back to help after hearing the screams. In the confusion, Brian decided to nonchalantly go back to his seat. Foremost on his mind was the fact that Bridget had something to tell him and was murdered because of it. He was beginning to feel boxed in.

Brian's temples throbbed. He could feel the sweat on his forehead. Marta was right; they weren't going to let him see the Führer and would do anything to ensure that he didn't. He felt like a sacrificial lamb waiting for the slaughter. He tried not to panic, knowing he had to keep a level head.

The train was slowing down, coming into the Stazione Centrale. He could see three men enter his car from an adjacent one. It was obvious who they were. Brian decided he would wait until the passengers started to file out before he made his move. The exit was right behind him. As he started to move, the men gave chase. Brian leaped forward, knocking over several passengers as if they were bowling pins. Descending the steps, he looked for a way out. The assailants were not far behind—guns drawn. The crowded platform worked in Brian's favor. Wormser's goons couldn't fire without endangering other people.

Running as fast as he could, Brian noticed an unmarked door and went in. It looked like some kind of work area, but there were stairs leading up to the ground level. Skipping every other step, he rushed up—hearing German voices in the background. Once upstairs, he ran down several corridors until he found an exit leading outside. On the street without time to stop and get his bearings, Brian went into a pastry delicatessen and sat down in the rear. Completely out of breath and with no options left, he waited for Wormser's men, but they never came.

After forty-five minutes, Brian went back out on the street. It was now late afternoon. He looked for a cab.

Chapter 25
Bardolino, Italy—1972

Nighttime had settled in by the time Brian arrived. The cab driver dropped him off at the middle of the small town square. The cold wind cascading off the lake stung him in the face like a slap from a jealous woman. He stood on the side of the street looking at the boat masts in the dim light of the street lamps and tried to contemplate what to do next.

Seeing lights at the far end of the square, he walked briskly, practically running to get there. It was a *tratatoria*—not fancy, probably for the locals, he thought. There were only several old men sitting at a table in the back playing cards. Smoke hung high in the rafters. Brian went inside and asked to be seated. He wanted to get warm and collect his thoughts, so he asked the waiter for some coffee.

Sitting there, Brian began to think what he would do if confronted

The Caretaker's Bible

by Wormser's men. The simple truth was that he was defenseless. But if his luck held, he could get to Horst's house before they caught him. Then it was anybody's guess what would happen once he got inside the fortress.

"Excuse me," Brian said, talking slowly and using a kind of sign language. "I'm looking for a gentleman who lives in this town. He goes by the name of Horst the caretaker."

The waiter smiled. "You are an American."

"Yes. Do you know who I'm talking about?"

He gave Brian a refill. "Horst. Yes. He lives several kilometers away from here. Are you a friend of his?"

"I'm trying to find him. He is an old acquaintance." Brian held the cup in his hands to get warm.

"If you wait until I close up, I will take you there myself."

"How long?"

"Perhaps an hour. Would you like anything for an evening meal?"

Brian couldn't eat. He was too nervous. He just waved his hand and said he could use more coffee. It was at times like this that Brian hated to get melancholy. But the man he had waited months to meet was dead and the fate of his daughter was unknown. His fiancée and good friend had almost been killed. He was now a hunted man—and all because of a story. All because he couldn't let it go. Now he was faced with meeting one of the most feared and hated dictators the world had ever known. Brian had to be honest. He didn't hold a lot of hope that this incredible story would ever make the printed page. Even if he did interview the Führer, he was positive Hitler would somehow disappear from the face of the earth and he would be left with nothing more than a perceived hoax.

The waiter startled Brian while he was deep in thought. "Are you ready? We are closing."

They made their way along several back roads in the waiter's beat-up '50s BMW. Finally slowing down, the waiter pointed in front of him. "Horst lives up there."

Brian looked up and saw a house way up on a hill overlooking the town. "Are you sure?"

"Yes. That is where he lives."

Brian thanked the waiter, got out of the car, and waited until it was out of sight. Stealing across the street, he found a small dirt road that looked like a driveway. Halfway up, he could hear voices outside of the house—several men speaking German. They were obviously the guards he had to get past. He moved off the road onto the grass and hid behind some trees. He couldn't see much except a light coming from a fixture in front of the house. His only chance, he thought, was to get around to the back. There he could get a good view of the rear of the mansion and the surrounding area.

Moving quietly to the side, he could see several of the guards through a break in the trees. Brian waited for a few seconds to catch his breath and then continued.

At the back of the house, he noticed that there were no guards—at least outside the back door. That seemed peculiar to him. Scanning the immediate area, he saw no one, but he could still hear voices around the front.

He took a deep breath. It was a now-or-never kind of impulse. He couldn't back down now and he knew it. He put his hand on the doorknob. To his surprise, the back door was open. Brian's first inclination was that this was too easy. It had to be a trick. Turning a corner, he could see a light emanating from a room down the corridor. As he got closer, he could see French doors. Peeking in, he saw a man sitting in a chair reading a book. As far as he could tell, it was Horst the caretaker, appearing old and frail. Brian looked both ways to see if anyone was coming before he gently opened the door to go in.

The voice took Brian by surprise. "I have been waiting for you, Herr Bennett," the old man said. "What has taken you so long?" He put his book down on his lap and smiled.

Brian walked closer to the old man, still not believing for one moment he was talking to Adolf Hitler. "I've had some help, I admit. But others didn't want me to ever get to meet with you again."

"Yes. I suspect you are correct." Hitler offered Brian a chair. "Please, make yourself comfortable."

Brian looked around the room. Large and L-shaped, it was

magnificent and had a massive picture window overlooking the town. It was elaborately decorated with paintings and watercolors. An easel with an unfinished oil painting sat in the far corner. The furniture was covered in rich German tapestry. Brian gazed at the man he knew as Horst. His skin looked whitish—absent of the richer tan tones that he had sported in June. He appeared sickly. Brian felt a little nervous—not sure how to continue, what to say. He was also worried that he would be shot dead by the guards at any moment.

"You managed to avoid security. I say you are very determined, Herr Bennett."

"It wasn't easy. I will tell you that."

Hitler laughed. "You know, I liked you the first day we met. There is something about you, but I cannot figure out what it is. Perhaps your sense of modesty." Brian stared at the old man. "I did my research before you ever set foot on the grounds of Villa Pontevechio. I knew who you were." Pointing to several *Time* magazines on a bookshelf, he said, "I have read some of your articles. Heinrich Glossen gave them to me. I decided you would be the one who could best tell the story, because I was told you are the best investigative reporter in the business. You were my only choice."

"Why didn't you just tell me who you were when we were at the villa?" Brian asked.

Hitler looked up at the ceiling for a moment. "Do you really think you would have believed me if I had just told you who I was?"

Brian began to smirk. "No. Of course not."

"I think, Herr Bennett, you have answered your own question." Hitler smiled. "I truly believed that your compulsion to investigate the documents in the Bible would lead you to one conclusion: that I had a twin brother."

"So you placed the documents in the Bible knowing I would find them."

"I was not so sure. It was a chance I had to take," Hitler replied.

"I asked Glossen to send his daughter to New York to try to find out what was going on."

"Like a spy."

"If you insist. She was merely my eyes and ears, but she never could verify if you had found the documents. But when you first showed up at Hagenmünster, I knew all was well. The quest to find the truth had taken over your soul. You could not resist."

"Glossen is dead." Brian sat back in his chair.

Hitler's smile seemed to degrade. "How do you know this?"

"I saw him. Shot in the head in the lobby of the Hotel Dorian."

"Are you positive?"

"Yes. I also think Wormser's men have Marta."

"It is all caused by the sins of the *Freundenreich*. They are errant men wanting to relive a world that has passed us by. They have neither the will nor the sheer brawn and intelligence to rekindle the Third Reich."

"But they are trying to protect you. Do they really think they can revive the Nazi Party like it was in the 1940s?"

"They all are desperate men. Glossen has always been the reasonable one. He is smart enough to understand that any idea of a future Reich is impossible. I remember a conversation we had years ago, just after I had met my twin. Glossen had insisted that I write down my goals and objectives for the future so they could be used for posterity in case the Reich faltered. I thought then that Glossen either was a traitor or that he knew something I could not possibly have envisioned. Perhaps he was right. But now I have told him there was only one time in Germany's rich history that required Nazi rule. It has come and gone. Glossen understood that."

"But what about Wormser?"

Hitler smiled. "That is a different matter. Wormser is a criminal—someone who would rather watch an execution than a play or an opera, one who would rather see blood staining the streets than patients recovering in the hospital. I have no respect for that kind of individual. In my opinion, Wormser firmly holds the belief that he is destined to resurrect the Reich any way he can. And that he will be the new Führer."

"Doesn't that somehow bother you?" Brian asked.

"On the contrary. Manfred Wormser could not lead a group of young girls at a summer camp, let alone the Nazi Party. He is incompetent. Wormser is only good at one thing: murder. It is madness to think that Wormser can put two clear thoughts together in succession in order to run a government. As far as I can tell, Herr Wormser fancies himself more of a statesman than he really is. He thinks it his sworn duty to protect me. From what? I have asked him that many times."

"He's determined. I will give you that," Brian said. "How long have you lived here?"

"Close to twenty-two years. Before that, in Switzerland after the war. I missed the comfort of Austria, my homeland, but I never looked back and was just glad to be alive. You must understand I am not referring to the Austrian state that I have considered since I was a young man to be decaying from within and politically bankrupt. I mean the beauty and inspiration of the wonderful countryside. I must say, my experiences while living in Vienna really formed the basis for what I had become at the time—leading to my rise as a political leader. Even though I learned valuable lessons from the utter deprivation of living as a poor man in Vienna during those early years, it was Munich and the experiences of World War I that had shaped my convictions about the future of my adopted country. Defeat in 1918 didn't settle well with me. The consequences of war were devastating for the German people. In reality, it set the stage for an unrest that eventually erupted into fervor, thus allowing the Nazi Party to prevail. The early years in Munich after the war became my classroom where I could teach other disgruntled patriots the errors of the Weimar Republic. I benefited greatly from my military service, which was where I realized the power I had as an orator. I could not believe how quickly I could convince the confused patrons of a beer hall to join the German Workers' Party.

"There was one an incident in 1920. While in Berlin researching the nationalist movement there, several members of the Party decided they wanted to lead rather than follow. Back in Munich, I initially offered my resignation, but because of my propaganda skills and ability to excite the masses, they retracted their position. I demanded that I have overall power and that the committee be disbanded. More importantly, I disagreed with the committee's idea that the German National Socialist Workers' Party, as it was being called, was exclusively reserved for the lower middle class that were nationalist, radical, and anti-capitalist. In my opinion, membership in the Party should not have been limited to any particular class. To prove it, I solicited the assistance of ex-military officers and intellectuals alike. It was then that the Party began to take shape."

"But there had to be so much resistance then," Brian remarked. "How did you think you could really get away with overthrowing the government?"

"Many Germans were insecure at the time and there was considerable disorder in the country. I believed in my heart that Nazism was the answer to Germany's prayers. It was what would make us a strong nation. Even when I was imprisoned in Landsberg in 1924 with other National Socialists, I became convinced more than ever in the nine months I was there that the languishing German Republic needed a savior. I appointed myself to that position and swore that I would lead the Nazi Party to victory. In the tenuous years after my imprisonment, I weathered many trials and tribulations, the worst of which was my struggle with Otto and Gregor Strasser, who were Berlin publishers. The brothers had conspired to take over the National Socialist Party and expel me from the organization. Even Goebbels, who had long sided with the Strasser brothers, politicked at the time for my resignation. But in 1926 he changed his mind abruptly and began supporting my future. In time, the Strassers abandoned their quest to take over the leadership and I saw creative skills in Goebbels and made him the propaganda chief of the Party."

Brian leaned forward for a moment. "From what I understand, Joseph Goebbels was certainly very influential and you relied on his talent as a propaganda monger."

The Caretaker's Bible

"Goebbels was not as ideal as you might think. He was obstinate, foul mouthed, and certainly a womanizer."

"But then why did you keep him as one of your closest confidants?"

"Do you like everyone you work with, Herr Bennett? Even with all his inadequacies, Goebbels was perhaps the most loyal individual ever to serve me."

Brian stood and admired a painting that looked like it could be any small square in a German village. "You very much liked Heinrich Glossen as well."

"Yes. There is a man of integrity. A source of light in an otherwise dismal and dark forest. Heinrich's contributions from 1939 until the end of the war were unparalleled. Above all, he was a needed contrast to Goebbels' often-devious side."

"Glossen gave you great strength."

"Yes, I suppose. But I remember one of my happiest hours was in 1933 when I became Chancellor of the Reich, well before I ever met Heinrich Glossen. Those were the years that excited me more than any others. There was everything to gain with not much to lose. I recall the feelings of exoneration when I became what many said I never would: the head of the German state. It gave me the ultimate power to do what I needed to do. In the beginning, my goal was to rid Germany of the communist scourge, as Marxism was a disease that had to be stopped."

"So you saw it as a threat?"

"When I saw the Reichstag building burn right in front of my eyes, hate swelled up in my soul. I decided at that moment I would never allow the menace of foul-minded communism to ever, ever corrupt the German way of life. Germany had to be protected at any cost and I swore that I would keep it strong until the day I died."

"Some historians say you had the Reichstag burned down on purpose to cast blame on the communists."

"That is nonsense. I would have never have done such a thing." Hitler paused. "The early days of power were difficult. On many occasions I had to defend my steadfast principles to consummate political naysayers that wanted either to gain favor with President von Hindenburg or to make me look incompetent as the Chancellor. I had ways of dealing with these opportunists. Some of them disappeared and others were given options that if not taken resulted in something terrible happening to a family member. I took solace knowing I had the SA and SS at my disposal."

"Is that how you took care of your problems?"

"Please understand me, Herr Bennett. I never had someone eliminated unless there was a very good reason."

"I certainly hope not."

Hitler continued. "I believe the sweat and toil of the early years made me a better dictator by giving me a sense of humility. Establishing a power base was not as easy as some would believe. Being elected as the Chancellor did not mean I had total control. I made laws for the Reichstag, yes, but did not consider that real power. In August 1934, President von Hindenburg died, and this presented me with the opportunity I needed. Then and only then did I declare myself to be both Chancellor and President, which essentially made me the dictator of the German State, the Third Reich. I had long seen a weakness in other European countries. It was this that made me want to take advantage of their shortcomings. I honestly believed the Nazi Reich was the solution to a united Europe. To me, it was a foregone conclusion that none of my neighbors knew anything about the greatness of Nazi rule. Therefore, I knew I had to wage a campaign against them to get their attention."

It was hard for Brian to imagine that the Führer really believed that he could conquer Europe. "You must have known it would never work."

"No, not at all. Germany certainly had the biggest and best Army compared to the rest of Europe. Perhaps Russia could have been comparable, but they were disorganized and undernourished."

"If that's the case, why didn't the Russians lose the war?"

Hitler scoffed. "It was my generals and their staff. We would have won if it were not for their insolence and treachery. I distinctly recall an incident in 1941 when I gave the order to attack Russia. I had heard from a reliable source that several of my generals were seen laughing in the war room, saying that I had taken on more than

I could possibly handle and that the Reich was almost assuredly doomed. My reaction was one of bitterness and disgust. I should have had them shot on the spot rather than suffer the humiliating loss to Stalin. We should have prevailed."

Hitler walked over to his bookcase, neatly placed the book he had been reading on a shelf, and then sat back down. Sighing, he said, "I assure you, Herr Bennett, the one and only reason we lost the war was because of incompetence. There is no other way to describe it."

Brian liked that he had struck a chord. His questions were arousing emotion, giving Hitler the opportunity to say what he really felt. And the more the Führer talked, the more Brian felt like he was actually talking to Adolf Hitler. He was experiencing the culmination of feelings he had been repressing since he had talked to Glossen. Brian had resigned himself from the very beginning to tracking down and talking to Hitler's twin brother, and now he faced a man who was supposed to have died in 1945. The world will not believe it, he thought. Who in their right mind would think that Adolf Hitler could still be alive? He asked an obvious question: "What about your immediate staff—your cabinet? Were they incompetent?"

"Many were loyal. Some were not. I never really trusted them. They were for the most part ambitious, egotistical, and anxious to stab me in the back. Of course, there were assassination attempts. They were obviously unsuccessful and I assure you the people responsible paid dearly. They were jealous of my insight, my vision for Germany's future. They would rather have had me dead while they pursued their ill-fated objectives."

Brian thought about that for a moment. It had to have been a strange stroke of luck that Hitler was never even hurt in any of these attempts. It was like he had been foreordained or destined to remain the leader of the Third Reich.

A thunderous sound startled the both of them. Brian looked to the side and saw Wormser and two guards busting through the French doors. The guards stood in the background with their guns drawn while Wormser approached them. Standing at attention and rigidly raising his right arm, he yelled out, *"Heil Hitler,"* and then looked over at Brian. "You must have known I would find you. It was only a matter of time."

"I never doubted that. But you appear to be a little late." Brian shifted his eyes over to see Hitler's reaction. The Führer seemed to be in disbelief—staring at Wormser.

"It is never too late to protect the Führer. But I give you credit, Herr Bennett. You never gave up your quest to find him. This is commendable." Wormser's overall composure was one of frustration. His face showed his agitation—his eyes began to twitch, his nostrils flaring.

"I'm just a reporter trying to get a story. One that you didn't want told. I now understand why you were so adamant about stopping me. What you didn't realize, perhaps, is that I thought right up until the end that I had been looking for Hitler's twin—not Hitler himself. This is more than I could have asked for."

"I must be clear, Herr Bennett. The world is not ready to learn that the Führer is still alive. His privacy is what is at stake. Surely you can understand that."

Brian pointed to the Führer. "I didn't do this on my own. I uncovered the documents in a Bible I received from Horst the caretaker—the Führer—in June at a villa in Tuscany. I was set up to find the truth, and I did."

"The *Freundenreich* lives to protect the Führer. We know the truth that no one else should ever know. It was that traitor Glossen who betrayed us and gave you the chance to find the truth. That is why he had to die." Wormser shouted that he had even gotten the Bible and the documents back and given them to Hitler. It was his responsibility to do so. Lips quivering, he said he answered to no other power than his Führer.

Brian watched as Hitler got out of his chair. He stood in front of his old colleague. Wormser almost seemed to cower in his presence. Hitler spoke slowly. "You are misguided, uninformed and, above all, incompetent. Only a fool would not know that I was the one who asked for Herr Bennett's help. I want the world to know that I survived the Allied onslaught—that I did not succumb to the terrible devastation of my beloved Berlin. The Führer lives and I want the world to be informed of such good news."

"But, mein Führer," Wormser pleaded, "they will kill you."

"It no longer matters. I do not have much longer to live anyway."

Forgetting himself, Wormser yelled out at the top of his lungs. "It does matter, mein Führer. I have sworn to protect you. I will not let this man ruin what I have given my life to." Wormser drew his pistol and pointed it at Brian. "They are all dead. Marta, Eva, Helga, and Rudolf. Is that what you want to know, Herr Bennett? None of them can give credibility to your story."

Hitler moved and stood between Wormser and Brian. "You will put your gun away, and when you do, you will leave."

Shaking, Wormser asked his Führer to please stand aside so he could complete his mission. Hitler asked for the gun. Wormser pleaded that he was simply doing his duty. Hitler again asked for the gun. Brian stood motionless. His lips were dry and he could hardly breathe.

Brian watched as a humbled and humiliated apostle relinquished his weapon to his Führer. Hitler stared at Wormser for the longest time. Then, nonchalantly, he said, "I should have done this years ago." He pointed the gun at Wormser and, to Brian's surprise, fired. The Jew Killer violently fell back against the wall—his face showing signs of disbelief. Blood saturated his chest. The two guards rushed to Wormser's side and soon confirmed that he was dead. Hitler asked them to remove the body and leave them alone.

Brian was at a loss as to what to say. Hitler sat down and asked Brian to join him—the moment was surreal. They didn't say much at first. Brian was left to wonder if Wormser had been bluffing about the fate of those who could corroborate his story. Given Wormser's history, however, he had to assume they probably were dead.

"I am indebted to you for wanting to always tell the truth. Most reporters are not so inclined to work so hard," Hitler said. Brian could tell that Hitler was still upset by the incident: his voice was trembling. "I will tell you anything you want to know if you think the world might be interested in it."

Brian, still shaking from the episode, stood up and walked around the room. "I want to talk about your brother. What did you really think when you first met him?"

"I was suspicious but I remember feeling butterflies when we first met. I am not sure what he felt. Perhaps the same. It is unacceptable to me that my father would have left my brother to die on the steps of a monastery, one similar to the abbey I had attended when I took singing lessons as a small boy."

"Where?" Brian asked.

"Lambach monastery. It was there when I saw a work of art that touched my soul. I remembered it much later when I was trying to create a symbol that would readily be identified with German Nationalism. Ironically, placing the ancient symbol being used as the monastery coat of arms on a flag of the Third Reich was perhaps the best thing I ever did to promote the cause of Nazism."

"Do you realize that your brother lived only 50 kilometers away from Lambach? He grew up in the small town of Freistadt and attended classes full time at Hagenmünster when he was fifteen."

"We talked about it many times. I am sorry I never knew my brother when we were young. That is the time to make a bond. It is much harder when you are older and set in your ways. In 1935 Goebbels came to me and said he had an individual that very much resembled me and that I should meet him. It was an episode I will never forget. The Minister of Propaganda actually believed he could bring to me an impostor and that I would be impressed. It was the one and only time I thought to dismiss Goebbels for such impertinence. Much later, when I was first told about Horst and the fact that he had been born on the same day in the same province of Austria, I began to wonder. However, my first reaction was to ignore it, and I made my feelings known to Glossen. But the more I thought about it, the more I decided it would not hurt to simply meet the man." Hitler seemed distant now. "When he stood in front of me, the heavens opened up. I could see his soul when I looked into his eyes. He was the brother I had always wanted."

"So you accepted Horst as your flesh and blood from the very beginning."

The Caretaker's Bible

"When Glossen introduced me to him, I wanted to make my own mind up about Horst. I asked for everyone to leave us alone. It was then I studied my brother. Peering at the probable impostor, I could almost feel his emotions; I almost knew what Horst was thinking. It was very odd. Part of me didn't want to believe it. I looked for a reason to reject Horst. After all, I was the one and only Führer. There could be no other. But as I began to talk to the man standing before me, I realized there was no other explanation than that Horst and I were related. Later, at our first meeting at Bergof, I began to really know my brother. Not being able to get over the initial shock I felt about the revelation that Horst had been a Benedictine monk, I began to relish the idea. I realized there could not have been a bigger difference between the two of us in terms of our upbringing. The idea that he had dedicated his heart to God and I was the leader of a nation somehow intrigued me. I believed we were essentially the same—guiding the souls of men to a higher destiny."

"But you must have felt threatened when Goebbels proposed he impersonate you," Brian said.

Hitler's face showed his frustration. "It was arrogance on their part. They really believed I could be replaced. I wanted nothing to do with their scheme. Then one day I had a very poignant discussion with my brother. It was at the Berghof, several days before I conferred with Goebbels about the subject. Horst had expressed his concern over my health. He said he could see the wear and tear everyday events were having on my overall well-being. He wanted to help by doing the only thing he could think of: giving me a rest by standing in for me. It was not what I wanted to hear, but when I thought about it, I came to the conclusion that it was in my best interest and that my brother would be up to the task.

"After the first several impersonations, I became more convinced I had been blessed by being introduced to my brother and gave all the credit to Heinrich Glossen—a man I admired more than any of my deputies, except, perhaps, Goebbels. Horst seemed to have captured all of my traits: he was a gifted speaker with animated mannerisms and the ability to charm even the most suspicious of individuals. It was perfect. No one would ever conclude they were being confronted by a fraud. Horst and I became closer over the years."

Hitler stood up and walked over to the bookcase in the corner. Bending over he picked up a book and handed it to Brian as he sat down. Brian stared at the Bible he hadn't seen since right before Wormser's men had abducted him. Hitler smiled. "You seem to have lost this and I thought you would want it back."

"Yes. I would."

Hitler pointed at the Bible. "This is what brought you all this way to Bordolino. I knew you would figure it out. It was just a matter of time. I did not want to die without the world knowing of my plight and my incredible life after the war ended. But do you think America will believe any of this?"

Brian shook his head. "I don't know. It sounds way too far-fetched to be credible. Most people I know will just think it's a terrible bastardization of reality. It will be inconceivable to Americans that a man as despised as you were could have really survived the war. And that you could have had a twin. I guess most people will dismiss it all as being pure fiction."

"But you are well respected as a journalist. You must make them believe it. People will listen to you." Hitler shook his finger at Brian. "This is why you were chosen. I trust you to tell my story. What you think of me, it does not matter. There is not anything I will not tell you. I have waited my whole life for this."

"I know everything I need to know about you. Besides, I wanted to interview your brother. I only just learned that he died in your place in 1945."

"Do not change the subject," Hitler yelled out. "I am proud of being the Führer. I especially remember a day in 1936 when I stood tall in front of the German people and told them of my vision for the future of the glorious Third Reich. It was all I could do to contain myself. I was infused with a higher power that somehow manifested itself in my soul. The years I had spent in Munich had sharpened my desire to make Germany the model and inspiration for a better Europe. It was my right as a visionary to ensure Germany's place

The Caretaker's Bible

in history. I was her savior. No one else but I could have made it so. Do you think I was a savage? Look at the good I did!"

"You were a dictator." Brian sat up in his chair.

"Yes, of course. People do not know what they want. They have to be told and then they must be convinced. Only then can they realize their destiny." Hitler's eyes widened. They looked almost darker. "I never wanted anything more than a nation of blue-blooded citizens working together to create a new world order."

"The best I can tell, you wanted to create a Europe full of Germans."

Hitler raised his fist. "What do you know? Only what you have been told. You cannot possibly understand what I have been through—what made me want to change Germany for the better. I recall a night when I was a young man in Vienna and I saw a philosopher-statesman give a speech. The entire audience was in his grasp. I was mesmerized. His voice was at a high pitch and his wild gestures seemed to entrance everyone. Looking around the crowd in the concert hall, I could not believe what I saw—men and women with their mouths agape, standing frozen in place. It brought tears to my eyes—that a man could control the masses as he did. It was then that I knew I had the same gift. Every time I have told a story since I was a child, I have been able to hold people's attention.

"In the 1920s in Munich, I realized that to be a leader, you had to be able to move the masses. It was then that I first started to understand propaganda. People could not be subjected to complicated rhetoric. It had to be simple and most definitely arousing. It was obvious to me that human emotions perpetually controlled human behavior. If I could gain someone's attention initially, by speaking in a highly demonstrative manner, I could evoke passion in most observers. I learned early on to make every word count; every gesture was for a reason. I would never finish a speech until I knew I had touched every single person in the audience. Later in my reign as dictator, I brought all my talents to bear to keep the citizens of Germany loyal to the cause. I learned during World War I that wearing a uniform, marching, and saluting created a sense of loyalty and cohesiveness. I also realized that constant mass meetings and rallies spawned a certain kind of enthusiasm that was certainly needed to bolster the Nazi regime. Over the years leading up to 1933, I increasingly became confident that I could lead Germany to greater heights. And even with the horrible defeat by the Allies in 1945, I still believed I had reached my goal."

Brian scratched his head. "But didn't you realize that being a dictator would fail in the end?"

"It was not my own people who hated me. They understood what was at stake. It was the Allied hatred of the Third Reich that destroyed what I had spent years creating." Hitler was livid as he talked. "I am bitter that my generals could not complete what we set out to do—that they faltered when it really counted. I am convinced that Germany could have won the war if they had listened to what I had said. They were insolent. Always thinking they knew better than their Führer. I knew what was best for Germany. Not one of them had a vision for the future."

"Back at the villa, you said that you thought Germany had made mistakes in the war. Weren't you giving the orders?"

"Of course," Hitler said. "But no one was listening."

"I don't understand. You gave the order to attack Russia, for instance. And as history bears out, it was a tactical error that ended in the Russians taking control of the front and pushing you back into Berlin where it all ended." Brian shrugged his shoulders. "You alluded to that at the villa."

"I did not bring you here to judge my actions during the war—or me, for that matter. You must forget your preconceived notions about the Third Reich and pay attention to what I have to say. It was not easy being the Führer. It was not glamorous, and often times not rewarding. It was a monumental effort trying to be the savior of millions of people. When the Nazi Party began to take root, I immediately met with Goebbels, Göring, and Himmler, three men I considered key to the survival of the Third Reich, and I empathically told them that they were the eyes and ears of the Führer. But more than that, I told them that to ensure the survival of the Nazi Party, they had to promote a sense of total and unmitigated loyalty among not only the SA and SS but also the average German citizen. I believe leaders cannot go wrong with good men around them. I believe the men I selected were like pillars holding up a magnificent building. I trusted them with my life."

"But in the end none of them could help you," Brian commented.

"Yes. I suppose you are correct." Hitler's demeanor appeared sullen. "Leaving Berlin when I did in 1945 was the worst mistake of my life. I succumbed to pressure from Goebbels and Glossen, who said that I would be better off going into exile. The plan seemed simple and well thought out at the time, but it backfired. Provisions had been made to ensure that Horst and my deputies would be evacuated at a pre-designated time in mid-April. It was still a mystery to me why they never got out of Berlin in time. I regret that it did not happen."

"But you were still giving the orders, right?"

"Of course, but it did not matter. I realize now I should not have abandoned my responsibilities. I should have stayed in Berlin. I sacrificed my brother to save my own life. I had no reason to believe my brother would perish there in such terrible circumstances. I should have insisted Horst be taken away instead of me."

By now Brian was pacing the floor. He kept thinking to himself that he had no pen or paper—no camera. It was frustrating. "It is my understanding that it was your brother's idea that he stay in Berlin, while you were silently taken away."

"Nonsense! It was Glossen's idea. He convinced me. Horst knew nothing about it."

"I think it was your brother's idea," Brian said. "He told Glossen he had already talked it over with you. But that conversation never occurred, did it? Maybe you wanted to save your own soul."

Hitler's voice seemed to fade and he began taking long breaths. "Glossen told me that Horst was more than competent to give the orders and make decisions until they could get him to safety. I trusted Heinrich's judgment, but he failed in the end. I was as surprised as everyone else when later I read historical accounts of what transpired in the last days at the bunker."

"From what I know, he took on your persona—made decisions

you would have made, presented the Führer as a man willing to fight to the end, even married Eva Braun," Brian said. "What made him want to take his own life?"

"Duty. Honor. You cannot imagine how committed he was to our cause. Eva wanted immortality. She was the most loyal person I ever met. It never surprised me that she married Horst in the end. She played along like a trooper. It is obvious that she knew she would never leave Berlin or see me again. She was acting out a part that would help promote the image of a noble dictator carrying out a lifelong ambition in the face of defeat. As sad as it is that they took their own lives, I am convinced that it gave me a second life—as anonymous as it has been."

"I know you must have loved your brother. It had to be difficult to know he died for you."

Hitler smiled. "It was fate. He was an incredible man."

Brian thought back to something the caretaker had said at the villa about the Allies bombing the monastery at Mount Cassino in Italy. It made sense to him now. Hitler's respect for his brother's beliefs made him angry that an army would purposely try to destroy a holy and sacred place. Though Brian kept thinking about it, he couldn't understand how a man that was so passionate about his brother, another human being, could have willfully wanted to destroy millions of lives. He recalled what the caretaker had said at the villa about the Holocaust. Brian knew that if nothing else, readers would want to know what possessed a man to attempt the virtual extermination of an entire race. Staring directly into Hitler's eyes, he simply asked.

Hitler didn't answer at first—his face contorting, his breathing labored. Brian went over to the unfinished painting propped up on the easel. It looked like it was supposed to be Berschtsgarden in the summer—perhaps Berghof surrounded by beautiful countryside. "It was never what anyone thought." The voice was faint and Brian glanced around at the Führer. He looked like a feeble grandfather sitting hunched over in his chair—aged, meek, sad.

Wanting to figure out the painting, Brian explored it. "There is no reasonable explanation for what you and your henchmen did.

It defies the very essence of humanity to think that human beings who didn't measure up to your standards would just be summarily executed. I think the world deserves an answer."

He waited for a response. When he still didn't get one, he turned around. There, he saw an old man slumped in his chair—his pulse gone, his dark eyes still open. Feeling both frustration and relief, Brian just stood and looked at the body for what seemed a lifetime.

Suddenly, two guards entered the room. One of them checked Hitler for any sign of life before disappearing briefly. Moments later they came back accompanying a man who said he was the Führer's physician. Once the death was confirmed, the doctor had the guards carry Hitler out of the room. Before he departed, the doctor told Brian he was welcome to stay for a short while as they now planned on vacating the house. Brian knew he had no choice but to accept what the doctor said. Still standing there, entranced in the moment, he couldn't get the image of the Führer's tortured face out of his mind.

"Where are you taking him?" Brian asked.

"Somewhere no one will ever suspect," the doctor replied.

chapter 26
New York City—1972

SNOW LIGHTLY FELL, ACCENTING the Christmas decorations in Rockefeller Center and Times Square. Brian and Laura walked arm and arm toward the landmark ice-skating rink made ready every holiday season. Having returned to New York only days earlier, Brian was still suffering from jet lag, not to mention shock from meeting and talking to an aged Adolf Hitler, but he knew the intentions of the *Freundenreich* had died when he did and that was consolation enough.

Even though Brian felt good about what he had accomplished, he had just spent the entire morning cleaning out his office after informing Binneker that he no longer worked for *Time* magazine. He'd rather drive a cab—it would be less stressful.

"I can certainly understand why," Laura replied.

"I never thought it would turn out this way. When I was growing up, I never imagined standing face to face with one of the most feared dictators of the twentieth century—especially when that dictator was supposed to be dead. I know it was my passion that drove me over the edge. And now I don't have a job or anything to show for six months of investigating."

"There still could be a story. Both Ronny and I were witnesses."

Brian started smiling. "And what am I going to say? That I found out that Hitler had a twin, that he was a monk, that he impersonated the Führer and eventually died in the Führerbunker? And that I tracked down the real Hitler, had a conversation with him, and watched him die right in front of my eyes?"

Laura couldn't help but laugh. It did sound absolutely preposterous. "You thought you had a story. You went where your heart took you."

"And now look at me." He looked over at a man standing on the corner with a tin cup. "See that guy over there? That's what I'm going to be doing next."

Donnatello's was crowded, but they managed to get a table for three in the back. Before they ordered drinks, Ronny showed up and apologized for being late.

"I understand you're out of a job," Ronny said, looking over at Brian. "I'm sorry. I've taken a teaching position at Harvard and will be leaving within the month."

"That's wonderful," Laura said. "But I'm sorry to see you leave. I think Brian should write a book about what happened to us."

"He should at least write an article about it," Ronny replied. "That way the last six months wouldn't have been a waste of time."

Brian smiled. "I don't know. Perhaps I'll think it over."

Out of the corner of his eye, he saw a tall brunette standing in the front of the restaurant with her back facing him. He got up and walked up to her. "Excuse me," he said. She turned around, but when he realized it wasn't Marta, he apologized, saying he thought she was someone else.

They tried to ignore the obvious while they ate dinner—each one wanting to discuss something else. But they couldn't. They needed to gain closure. They needed to get the story off their chests.

In the end, they all realized that even though it was an astounding tale, it was best left a collection of cherished memories and nothing else.

Later in the evening after dessert, Laura took Hitler's Bible out of her handbag and put it on the table. "See? This is what started it all." She thumbed through it while Brian paid the bill.

Standing up, Brian put his arm around Laura. "You know, on second thought, maybe I could write this story. It'll just have to be a work of fiction."

"You always did say you wanted to write a novel. You could call it *The Caretaker's Bible*," Laura suggested with her natural smile. She picked it up, fumbling a bit, and stuck it back in her handbag. She laughed out loud, saying something her grandfather used to tell when she was a young girl—that bad habits are hard to break, so just live with the consequences.

They stood for several minutes and watched carolers sing their hearts out on the corner—then called it a night. Ronny hailed a cab. Brian slowly walked Laura home.

"When should we get married," Laura asked.

"I don't know. How bout next April."

"That would be wonderful. I have to be honest with you, I never want to talk about Hitler again."

"You know what I think?"

"What?"

"I think Adolf Hitler finally got what he deserved many years ago."

"What's that?"

He smiled. "A chance to stand before the Alter of God and explain the unexplainable before being cast into the bowls of hell."

"I think you're right," Laura replied, as she put her arm around Brian.

Printed in the United States
142498LV00004B/26/P